# Dead Flowers

# Books by Deborah Grabien

## The JP Kinkaid Chronicles

Rock and Roll Never Forgets
While My Guitar Gently Weeps
London Calling
Graceland
Book of Days
Uncle John's Band
Dead Flowers
Comfortably Numb *
Gimme Shelter *

## The Haunted Ballads

The Weaver and the Factory Maid
The Famous Flower of Serving Men
Matty Groves
Cruel Sister
New-Slain Knight
Geordie *

## Other Novels

Woman of Fire
Fire Queen
Plainsong
And Then Put Out the Light
Still Life With Devils
Dark's Tale

*\* forthcoming*

# Dead Flowers

Book #7 of the JP Kinkaid Chronicles

## Deborah Grabien

**Plus One Press**

*San Francisco*

Plus One Press

DEAD FLOWERS. Copyright © 2012 by Deborah Grabien. All rights reserved. Printed in the United States of America. For information, address Plus One Press, 2885 Golden Gate Avenue, San Francisco, California, 94118.

www.plusonepress.com

Book Design by Plus One Press

Front cover photo by Denise Dunne, copyright ©2012, used with permission and our deepest thanks!

Publisher's Cataloging-in-Publication Data

Grabien, Deborah.
Dead flowers : book #7 of the jp kinkaid chronicles / Deborah Grabien.—1st. Plus One Press ed.
p. cm.
ISBN: 0-9844362-9-4
ISBN: 978-0-9844362-9-3
1. Rock Musicians—Fiction. 2. Musical Fiction. 3. Murder—Fiction.
I. Title. II. Title: Dead Flowers
PS3557.R1145 D43 2012
813'.54—dc22
2012910370

First Edition: September, 2012

10 9 8 7 6 5 4 3 2 1

*For patient women everywhere*

# *Acknowledgements*

WIP-readers, all of them, get my thanks, as usual. As does Nic, who listened to me cackling like a deranged hen as I wrote the earlier part of this one, and then watched me change moods entirely as the book went on. Writing books is like that.

A special tip of the hat to Henry Wimmer, for driving the bus, and Marjorie Kamby, for helping run Carla's office.

# Dead Flowers

# Chapter One

*"Good evening, Chico!"*

Opening nights are something special. I've done hundreds of them with Blacklight, more than I want to count, and they're always a trip: walking out onstage, picking up your axe, and giving it the best of whatever it is you've got to put out there. And no one knows what's going to happen next.

If you didn't know how this worked, you'd probably think there's a huge difference between opening night in front of ninety thousand people at Wembley and opening night in front of thirteen hundred people. You'd be right, but only in the details. If you get nervous on first nights, you're going to be twitchy no matter what. The size of the crowd doesn't matter.

*"The Laxson Auditorium is proud to present..."*

"Wow, it's really loud out there." Tony Mancuso had come up

next to me. "Hope we don't fuck it up."

I lifted an eyebrow. I may not get nervous, usually, but for whatever reason, Tony was edgy as hell. That seemed weird to me—after all, he did the Book of Days tour with Blacklight, as our keyboard player, and we ended that tour playing soccer stadiums in front of a hundred thousand people. Besides, he's a pro. He's been playing for audiences larger than this one with his own band, the Bombardiers, for forty years.

"Yeah, sounds like a good crowd. Not to worry, mate, we'll rock the house." I had one eye on the backstage door. We were going on in about one minute. Where in hell was my wife? She'd said she'd be back in a minute, but...

"Hey, John." She'd come up behind me. "Miss me?"

I let my breath out. "Oi, love. Queue for the loo?"

Bree's got a particular way of sending me out onstage, first night or any other: reaching between my legs, a good hard squeeze, and *do a good gig, baby* whispered in one ear. She'd got into doing that back in 2005, and if I said I didn't dig it, I'd be lying. Besides, like most musicians, I'm superstitious. These days, I don't fancy heading onstage without it.

This was a night of firsts, though: the first full tour of my local band, the Fog City Geezers, and first time Bree and I had ever travelled together on a tour bus. This was also the first time she'd been the only band wife along for the ride on any kind of tour at all. It used to be she avoided even being seen with me in public, never mind touring.

That had eased up over the years since we'd got married, at least. I just hoped that, with all those firsts, she didn't decide, *right, everything's new, might as well dump the old traditional way.* I was going to be very cross if she did that.

"...Tony Mancuso, Kris Corcoran, Billy DuMont and JP Kinkaid..."

Not to worry; apparently, we were not only not losing old hab-

2

its, we were adding to the one we've already got. She slipped in close behind, and did her ritual thing, which is sending me out with a pocketful of sex to use in the music. She got one hand between my thighs, cupped, and gave a good hard squeeze.

Right round that point, I'd have expected her to do her whisper thing, wishing me a good gig, and then give me my nuts back. Not tonight, though. Instead, she added a nice new twist: she bit the side of my neck, a good solid nip. She still hadn't let go of the family jewels, either.

"Do a good gig, baby," she whispered, and finally let go.

*"Put your hands together and give it up…"*

"Gordon *Bennett*, Bree!" I'd been expecting the squeeze, but not the nip on the neck. That was having a sort of doubling effect on the first half of the ritual: I could barely walk. It's a good thing I always wear loose trousers.

*"…The Fog City Geezers!"*

Yeah, first nights are special. It's a particular sort of energy, where you put it all out there and see how it works, where it doesn't work, what needs fixing and what needs feeding. If anyone in the band's going to have issues down the road, that first gig is where you take notice.

One other thing that was new about this tour: we were recording it, every show, every song. The idea was to cherry-pick the best versions of individual songs and put them together as the Geezers' first CD release on Fluorescent Records. I'm not sure how many bands go for live performance as their first release, but that's what we'd done.

We'd brought the Bombardiers' long-time soundman, Damon Gelb, along with us. He's been mixing Geezer shows since the beginning. Damon's brilliant at what he does, and what with his fee for the tour being picked up by Fluorescent, he knew his wages were guaranteed. That meant he could concentrate entirely on doing his job, instead of worrying about getting paid

3

beyond the usual per diem. Soundboard people can get the short end of the stick when money's tight; over the years, there'd been times I'd suspected the Bombardiers had had to keep him waiting for his wages. That wasn't going to be a problem with this tour. Fluorescent is Blacklight's own label. We own it. No worries for Damon on that score.

It also meant we hadn't skimped when it came to hiring the tour bus. Not that I would have, especially not with Bree along, but having Fluorescent pick up the cost meant we didn't have to listen to Kris Corcoran and Billy Dumont making money jokes about Tony, calling him Bankcuso, and all that rubbish. They don't get on me about having a lot of money, because I've had it since they've known me. But Tony getting rich by touring with Blacklight, that was different. The rest of the Bombardiers never let him forget it. The teasing gets really old really fast, so I was just as glad the label was paying for the bus, and not me or Tony.

Nerves or no nerves, we played a good solid first set, kicking it off with a favourite cover of ours, Bill Monroe's "Rocky Road Blues." It's a kickass thing, very unusual for Monroe. We've been known to close a set with it, but we'd decided to open with it this tour, just let the gig burn from the first eight bars. It worked really well. By the time we'd got to the second verse, Tony's keyboard sounded like a hungry tiger looking for flesh to rip, and I'd locked up with Kris Corcoran's bass in the kind of musical slap-and-tickle that sounded like groins in "go" mode. What the hell, might as well, you know? It would have been a shame to waste that little extra kick Bree'd sent me onstage with.

So the band was blazing from the first note, and we ramped it up from there. Doug Hewlett, our roadie, had set up my stool; I've got multiple sclerosis, and being able to sit down and play when the disease kicks up is probably responsible for me being able to play live gigs as often as I do. I've got a heart condition as well, something the doctor calls monomorphic ventricular tachycardia, which is a fancy way of saying I've got some scarring on my heart. I wear a little tickybox regulator implanted in my chest, to keep the ventricles moving in the proper rhythm.

The heart thing's not really an issue when it comes to playing. The multiple sclerosis, though, that doesn't negotiate: it just nails me. It's a miserable unpredictable fucking bitch of a disease. Even when it's laying back, I can't let myself forget about it. You never know when it's going to hit, or how hard. Tonight it wasn't too bad, and thank God for it, because kicking off a tour with an exacerbation or a relapse is no fun at all. Hard on me, hard on the band, and really hard on Bree.

Musically, we'd worked out the set lists and settled on a basic rollercoaster deal: start out hot, let things cool down, and then rip up it hot again to close the set. That particular blueprint went straight out the window early on, though; the whole musical vibe of the evening was edgy and bitchy. The audience wanted to go hot and stay there, and when you play live, you go with the audience vibe. You try pushing your agenda, you'll end up playing a crap gig.

The nearest thing to a quiet song we bothered with that first set was a cover of the Stones' "Sweet Virginia," and that didn't turn out quite the way we'd planned, either. The song was a new one for us; Tony had suggested it, and once we'd heard what he was doing with Ian Stewart's original piano part, we caught that edge and ran with it like a stable full of racehorses who'd just heard the starting bell go. The way the audience reacted to it, it was clear this particular cover was going to be Tony's showcase number for the rest of the tour.

Good job, too, because Tony needed some kind of outlet; his wife, Katia, hadn't come along for the ride. Katia wanting to stay home surprised me. It worried me as well, because it was the first time I could remember her not wanting to hit the road with him in over thirty years.

5

That old saw, about some bloke's wife being his "other half"? That's Katia. She handles Tony's money and handled what there was even before he'd toured with Blacklight and stuffed the family coffers. She makes sure he eats properly. She also does the less fun side of the job, which is calling him on his shit. She'd got used to touring in style during Book of Days, but even though this one wasn't private jets and suites at the Four Seasons, it was the sort of deal I'd have picked her to go for, every time. I'd been tearing my hair out, trying to work out the logistics of how to fit two couples into a tour bus with one bedroom, when Bree let me know Katia wasn't coming along.

I know I'm not the world's most observant bloke, but Tony is one of my oldest friends. Something was off, not right. He was edgy and snapping at people, and that's just not like him. He likes to joke that he's so mellow he must be adopted, because no one can be that calm and Italian at the same time. Besides, he's got forty years of smoking pot behind him. Nothing like being an old stoner to keep the inner peace, yeah? But things weren't right.

Of course, I'd leaned on Bree about it, and that nearly led to a row, because Bree wasn't telling. She went close-mouthed on me instead, and that, by itself, was pretty unnerving. Bree's so loyal, it's ridiculous. If Katia had told her what was going on and asked her to keep it to herself, Bree wasn't going to break that confidence, not even to me. And of course, that meant there was a confidence to break.

The set break in the middle of first night wasn't the place to worry about it, though, and even if I'd been inclined to do that, Tony seemed to have relaxed. I've always thought that making really good music's got a lot in common with having really good sex: either it leaves you energised, wanting hours more of it, or it leaves you mellow. It's an orgasmic thing, you know? Maybe he was reacting to how hot we'd run on "Sweet Virginia," but whatever it was, Tony was definitely doing the mellow.

Bree was already in the band room by the time we got offstage. The break was twenty minutes, plenty of time to get a plate of food down, and she'd made sure my dinner was waiting for me. Food is Bree's thing—she's a professional cook. With me having had two heart attacks on top of the MS, she's got a vested interest in what I eat. Besides, she'd put together a cookbook, for people with special food needs. I had the feeling she was going to spend every meal on the tour mentally comparing her own recipes with everything anyone put in front of me, just so that she could roll her eyes at it.

She'd got herself a plate, as well. I was pleased to see it, because that kept me from having to nag at her. She's got diabetes, the less serious kind, and she copes by taking pills and eating a particular way. With all the attention she puts into making sure I get fed properly, sometimes she forgets to get her own dinner. Not tonight, though; she got an asparagus spear on the end of her fork, bit the tip off, chewed a moment, and made a face.

"Overcooked. I wish people would realise there are better ways to cook these things than steaming the crap out of them. Oh well. Where's Henry? Doug and Damon both got some food. Doesn't the bus driver get a dinner break? What are you grinning about?"

This was our first day on the tour bus, we'd been on the road a grand total of three hours, and damned if she hadn't already decided that Henry Wimmer, our driver, wasn't being properly looked after. He was a skinny bloke, yeah, but I had the feeling he was skinny the same way I was: genetics, not starvation. No matter, though: if Bree'd got it into her head that Henry needed feeding, there was fuck-all I could do about it. Whether the poor sod knew it or not, he was going to get fed. My wife's got a nurturing streak so wide, we could have parked the tour bus on it and still had room for a couple of roadcases.

"Not to worry," I told her. "Henry may be skinny, but he eats. When we get back on the bus for the night, have a butchers at that little basket next to the driver's seat. He keeps it full of sweets."

She shook her head, sending her hair swinging. She'd got it cut to shoulder length recently, for the first time since I've known her, and the shorter look swung beautifully. More bounce, yeah? "I saw that. But that's *candy*, John. That's not food. How can he possibly do all that driving if all he eats is sugar?"

Crikey, she was turning me on. Bree getting focussed and fierce always has that effect on me. I found myself wondering just how up for a nice slap-and-tickle she was likely to be, with the rest of the band, the crew, and the skinny kid with the sweet tooth snoring away in bunks just the other side of a thin dividing door.

The bus was a luxury Prevost model, top of the line: six bunks stacked up three to a side, and right behind them, all the way at the back, an actual bedroom with a queen-sized bed. Since I was the only one who'd brought his old lady along, I got the actual bedroom, but there was no getting away from the fact that it was a bus, with no real walls and not much in the way of sound buffering. Since I was planning to nibble on my favourite bits of my wife with the rest of the band sharing the space, it could get iffy. She was already having to cope with being the only significant other on the bus.

The lights flickered twice, and I grabbed a bottle of Volvic. That's my water of choice, and even though the Geezers' contract rider is nice and short, and deals mostly with the tech side of things, I do ask that they have plenty of Volvic for me. It's not just pampered rockstar whim bullshit, either. I've noticed over the years that Volvic does good stuff for my digestion, and at my age, with my health being as messed up as it is, I'll take every advantage I can get.

The lights in the band room flickered again. This time, the noise level from the crowd went up; that meant the houselights had gone down. The promoter stuck his head round the door.

"Hey, guys. You ready? Got everything you need?"

He sounded so nervous, I couldn't help suspecting he'd had to deal with some divas playing here. It was a college gig, not really the sort of venue you'd expect to bring out the pampered prats, but, well, there you go: I've seen some of those contract riders. I've known a lot of musicians, as well, and there are plenty of blokes who'll make a promoter's life miserable, if hot and cold running groupies aren't provided.

That's not us. We're not divas, any of us. We don't piss and moan about the band room having a stack of paper plates instead of china. We don't stomp our feet and whinge and demand scented candles, or particular vintages of champagne, or whatever. I'm not dissing that, mind you—touring is hard work, and whatever it takes to get you through, I get that. It just doesn't happen to be our thing.

"Yeah, we're good. Cheers, mate." I got to my feet, snatched a quick kiss off Bree, and nodded my head at the rest of the crew.

The Fog City Geezers is my band. I put the band together, I front it, and I lead us onstage. It was time for the second set. I headed for the door.

"Here we go." The houselights had gone down, and if the noise level out there was anything to go by, the crowd was ready for some serious tunes. "Showtime. Let's go give the people what they want."

I've been a working musician since I was fifteen years old. Back in the early days, when I was still living at home with my parents in London, I did one tour as a hired hand with Bergen Sandoval's band. I was one of six blokes, all touring virgins, packed like tinned kippers into Bergen's rickety old van. We did fourteen gigs in twenty miserable days, and we went from Southampton to Glasgow to do it.

Bergen didn't pay us. He didn't have tuppence to rub together, or at least that was his line of bullshit at the time, and we were so young and so chuffed at being asked to gig with him that we didn't think to question the "no per diem" policy. No per diem meant we either slept in the van, or used whatever we'd managed to pry out of Bergen for the previous night's gig to pay for our own accommodations. It was as miserable a touring experience as I've ever been saddled with.

I'd actually ended that tour on my nineteenth birthday, stuck in a B&B in Leeds in a midwinter sleet storm with the drummer and trumpet player. We had no way to pay the woman who owned the place, because Bergen had slipped off and left us there with no explanation and no pay. I'd had to ring my dad in London, and get him to wire me up some dosh, because the woman had our gear and wasn't letting it go until she saw something to cover two nights accommodations.

Yeah, I know, young and thick as a half-stack of bricks. It's like my dad said to me, after that little clusterfuck: *you live and learn, John my lad, or you won't live long.*

After coping with that sort of rubbish, Blacklight was a revelation. Joining a band nearly at the top meant going from being thankful I was short and thin so I could stretch out in the back seat of a van, to hired private jets and suites at the Four Seasons. Quite a change, that was. But before we'd got to the private jets, the band had toured the Continent using rented tour buses. I'd done one of those tours with them, before they actually asked me to come on as a member of the band.

So I wasn't a complete tour bus virgin. But the bus Blacklight hired to get them from Hamburg to Rotterdam to Paris and back out again in the seventies, nice as it had been, was nothing like as sophisticated as the one Carla Fanucci, Blacklight's American ops and PR manager, had rented for the Geezers to use. This was in a class by itself.

I know sod-all about cars. I've never even learned to drive. But

I'd had Carla send me all the gen on the bus, well ahead of hitting the road. There was no way I was heading out on tour without knowing what to expect.

Of course, there was no need for me to have worried. Carla's been running things for Blacklight for a long time, and she's never let us down. She doesn't skimp on anything or cut corners, either; as I found out, the bus she'd got us was luxurious enough to have got its own write-up in a few industry rags. Hardwood floors, full kitchen, satellite uplink, the lot.

Still, luxury doesn't always mean comfort, you know? I've stayed in five-star hotels and come out with a stiff neck and a sore back the morning after a gig, thanks to down pillows and extra-soft mattresses. Besides, you've got to deal with reality, and the reality is that you can have all the hardwood floors and leather sofas on earth, but you're still stuck on a bus.

So, yeah, I'd been worried about cramped quarters and one loo for eight people and no fridge for my interferon, right up to the point where the town car and liveried driver Carla'd sent to pick us up pulled into the parking lot next door to the Bombardiers' rehearsal studio on Freelon Street, right up alongside of the tour bus. That was when I realised the glossy brochures Carla'd sent didn't do that bus any justice at all.

We were the last ones to arrive. We weren't late, but the rest of the band happens to live closer to the South of Market area than we do. I was already out of the car, waiting for the driver to get the door for Bree, when the entire band came through the door of the Starbucks at the far end of the parking lot and headed for me at a fast trot. Billy Dumont, our drummer, was leading the charge. He got close enough for me to see the look on his face; not good. *Shit, problem, bad way to begin a tour, right, it's your band Johnny, deal with it...*

"Hi, Bree, JP. Hey. Wow." He sounded stoned. That was ridiculous, though—Billy stopped smoking pot back when Reagan was president. "JP, dude, about this bus?"

"What about the bus?" I was tipping the driver, watching the rest of the band catch up with Billy. Whatever it was, it had to be major. "Do I need to ring Carla? What's wrong? Talk to me—oi, Kris, Tony. What's the problem?"

"Problem? Who said anything about a problem?" Billy was damned near bouncing in place, and it hit me suddenly: they weren't worried, they were blissed. "It's fucking amazing! Two bathrooms! Oak floors! It's got a cooktop and a freezer-fridge and a little media center dropdown screen deal for DVDs and stuff, suspended in every bunk! Oh, Bree, whoa, sorry, let me get that for you..."

"No, let me. You guys save it for the stage."

We all jumped a mile. None of us had noticed the driver come up, but out of nowhere, there he was: a tall bloke, damned near as skinny as me, with a big friendly grin and a completely shaved head, of all things. Before I could say a word, he'd hoisted Bree's suitcase in his left hand; you'd have thought it weighed ten pounds, instead of fifty. Obviously, a born roadie.

"Hey, JP Kinkaid, for real and for sure!" He stuck his right hand out, and I shook it. "Henry Wimmer, known around the industry as the Hankster. I'll be behind the wheel of this sucker for you—this will be the eleventh time I've taken her out. You've got the gold standard for tour buses, here. She's even got her own nickname—we call this one Magic. No, no, really, I'll carry the luggage. That's part of my job."

I'd got my hand back, which was a good thing, since he was apparently going to want his own free to carry my suitcase. He had a good grip, nice and firm, but he wasn't one of those blokes who prove how strong they are by bruising your knuckles. Next to me, Bree was giving him a good long scoping-out; I had the feeling she was making a mental list of what she'd have to shovel down his throat to get some meat on his bones.

12

I watched him get my luggage in his right hand. "Hankster? Interesting nickname."

He'd turned toward the bus, balancing our suitcases, but he shot me a friendly grin over his shoulder. "Hankster, as in rhymes with prankster, as in merry. It's a Neil Cassady thing. Let me show you and your lady the Magic Bus—the rest of the guys have already had the Grand Tour. My manifest says you get the stateroom. That's right, isn't it?"

We followed him up the steps. Outside, Damon and Doug were stashing guitars and road cases in the storage compartment under the main body of Henry Wimmer's half million-dollar version of whatever it was Jack Kerouac had been writing about, probably well before Henry was born. And yeah, I knew what Henry'd been on about, with the "Hankster the Prankster" riff. I'd got the reference. I've never actually read the book myself, but I've been in San Francisco long enough to not be totally lost when someone mentions Neil Cassady. Even if the only thing I'd ever got at City Lights was eyestrain from squinting at the titles as Bree looked for books full of obscure South American poetry, I know about "On The Road" and "Howl."

Henry'd gone up the steps already, and was waiting for us. Just beyond him, I saw what looked to be a big leather driver's seat. I was wondering why he didn't at least put the bags down when I caught Bree's eye, and we had one of those nice little marital mind-reading moments we get, sometimes: *Henry's not going to stash our luggage yet because he wants to show off the bus, so let's not keep him waiting.* I saw her mouth twitch up into a grin. Yeah, definitely thinking the same thing.

I nodded at Henry. "Right. Off we go." We headed up the steps into the Magic Bus.

I'd been right about the big leather driver's chair. The thing was enormous, big enough to easily fit Henry—there was no way in hell I was calling a grown man Hankster—twice over.

13

"Nice. Is that a built-in cup holder in the arm rest? And a Bluetooth hook-up?" Bree was behind me, one step down, but she's taller than I am and wasn't having any trouble seeing over my shoulder. She sounded amused. "And they gave you a door to the rest of the bus that actually closes? Pretty clever of the designers, to make sure you can keep the passengers from distracting you from the road."

"You haven't seen anything yet." Billy was one step down, right behind Bree. He was still bouncing, and still sounding stoned. "Just wait. It'll blow your mind. Yo, Hankster! Lead the way, man."

Henry pushed the door leading to the rest of the bus aside, and headed in. I took a look over his shoulder down the length of the bus, at the rolling hotel we were going to have to live in for the next month, and made a mental note to send Carla a shitload of roses, and of course a nice little bonus cheque. The bus was fantastic.

The thing about buses is, they aren't particularly wide. They're made to roll down the highway, and that means they legally can't be any wider than will fit between the white lines, at least while they're moving. It was something I'd worried about, looking over the specs Carla'd sent along: one hundred two inches wide isn't much room, not when you're talking about eight people. Neither is forty-five feet long, especially since some of that has to be given over to the driver. Our front hallway is longer than that.

Speaking just for myself, I don't mind either way about the elbow room. The band are all old friends. We've got reasonably good at reading each other's signals over the years: *right, back off, breathing room please.* Bree was a different story, though. Yeah, she's known these blokes almost as long as I have. But she's very private, and she was looking at being the only woman in tight quarters with six blokes who aren't me for a month. I honestly couldn't suss out how she was going to cope.

Henry had paused inside the first compartment. They'd done everything, cabinets and floors, in pale light wood, and the chairs were very light leather. The room was cheerful and bright. And it was wide, quite a lot wider than the one hundred two inches the spec had mentioned, in fact...

"First up, the Great Lounge and the galley. The bump-out's open right now, since we're parked. We've got two of them, and obviously, they both stay shut while we're on the road, but when we're parked, we get a lot of room. Nice, isn't it? Hard to say no to three extra feet of space, right? The bedroom has the other bump-out. The switches are right here on the wall. Hit that, and we slide back to road width."

Henry was looking back toward me, but not actually at me. It took me a moment to realise he wasn't talking to me, he was talking over my shoulder, to Bree. "I'm supposed to check with you about the galley. There's a pantry behind the driver's compartment, across from the TV. Fridge and freezer, convection and microwave oven, flat two-burner cooktop. I have instructions to ask if you have a preference for cookware and equipment to stock it with—right now, it's pretty basic stuff. But Carla said anything we add in here is totally your call, and anything you want, I go get it and it gets added to the rental cost. Just let me know."

"I will, thanks. But I'm sure it's fine the way it is."

Her voice was cool, almost chilly. That surprised me. After all, a kitchen is a kitchen, and she's a cook. But she sounded so unenthusiastic, you'd have thought he'd been offering her a leaky toilet or something, rather than a kitchen stocked with anything she wanted. I made a mental note to ask her about that later.

I stopped long enough to stash my four doses of interferon in the fridge—it has to be refrigerated, and it's very tricky stuff. Everyone waited for me to finish up.

"Carry on," I told them, and Henry moved along. He was digging playing MC; this bloke really loved driving the bus.

"Next up, we've got the front head. Magic has two heads and a shower—there's also a washer-dryer combo down in the lower level. When we're parked, we do laundry and stuff."

He gave the pale wood doorframe a fond little pat. You'd have thought he was some house-proud homeowner, showing off his two up and two down bungalow, with its mod cons and extra guest loo. "This is such a cool bus. Gotta love Magic."

"Show him the bunks." Billy was bouncing again. His fingers kept wanting to tap, I could tell. Billy's pure drummer: his hands want to beat a rhythm even when he's got no sticks to beat with. "I mean, he won't be sleeping in one, but he's gotta see them. Man, they've all got Playstations! And DVD players!"

I grinned at Bree. She smiled back, but it was gone a moment later. *Damn.* No idea what was bugging her, but hopefully it wasn't the realisation that she'd be sharing a tight space with a collection of rowdy rockers, all male. If that was the problem, she was in for a long month. Either that, or I was, because she might just bolt screaming back to 2828 Clay Street.

"Here's the bunks." Henry pulled back a curtain. I honestly couldn't see what Billy was so chuffed about. Lying on your back on a single-width mattress isn't my cuppa, especially since I don't do stuff like Playstations. "Magic's configured to sleep six in these, so that's the band, crew and yours truly. Mr. and Mrs. Kinkaid have the stateroom, at the back—here, let me show you. There's a nice big closet in there, and one out here, for the rest of us. When you're unpacked, I'll put your suitcases down below. Just let me know."

"Yeah, I will." I was watching Bree, trying to get a read on her reactions. No luck there; she was completely impassive. Definitely a marital conversation coming up later. "This looks nice and comfy. How long have we got before we hit the road and head for Chico?"

"About half an hour." Damon had come up, and was lounging

in the doorway. "New venue for us, so I want an extra hour for set-up and soundcheck. Does that work for you, JP?"

"Your call, mate. You're doing the soundboard. But yeah, sounds good. Plenty of time to unpack." I caught Bree's eye, finally, and she gave me a tiny nod and an even tinier smile: *it's going to be fine.* "Give us ten minutes to stash our gear, and another minute to hit the Starbucks. After that, let's get this show on the road."

# Chapter Two

That old saw, the one about not being able to teach an old dog new tricks? Turns out that's wrong. That first night on the road, between pinning my wife to the bed on a moving bus and having to mind the decibel levels on the conversation that followed, we managed to pull off a couple of new tricks.

On the whole "sex on a bus" thing, I'd expected pushback from Bree. What with her being as private as she is, I'd braced for a flat no: *are you out of your mind, there are six guys playing video games about four feet away, no way!* I'd have gone along with that; I don't ever need to make Bree uncomfortable and anyway, she doesn't owe me sex, on a tour bus or anywhere else.

So, of course, she surprised me. We'd got back to Magic, hit our nice private head—the rest of the crew were sharing the front head, and leaving the back one for us—and said goodnight. I'd taken my night meds, the antispasmodics and muscle relaxants that let me sleep. The bus was already rolling, heading north, overnighting somewhere in Oregon on the way to Eugene and then Seattle. I turned to Bree, trying to work out the best way to talk her into a nice cuddle, and got my first major surprise of the Geezers tour. Her eyes were bright green, her sexual *go* signal.

"Shhh." Her voice was barely a whisper. She reached out and got one hand on me, and jerked her head toward the front of the bus. "I wonder who's still awake? Besides Henry, I mean?"

"Don't really care, do I?" I kept my own voice down, which wasn't easy, not with what she was doing. The girl meant business. It was pretty obvious I wasn't going to have to put any work into seducing my wife, not that night.

I got both hands on her, and pulled her up tight. She bit back a giggle. That surprised the hell out of me, because Bree's not a giggler. But she was right at the edge of giggling just then. You couldn't miss it. She sounded about fourteen.

"Shhh!" She kissed me, good and hard, tongue tip to tongue tip. You'd have thought we were a couple of randy kids, about to get down to it with her parents in the next room, or something. For a moment, the vibe took me all the way back, thirty years and more, and she was a teenager again, with one difference: she'd never been this relaxed as a teenager.

She snaked one hand between my thighs and hung on, her pre-show ritual thing. This time, I returned the favour; I had the other arm hard around her waist, listening to her suck in her breath, holding back noise. On the other side of the door, I could hear a loo being flushed, a quiet murmur of someone talking to someone else, being considerate, keeping their own voices down: *wouldn't want to disturb them back there, JP's probably asleep already, first day on the road and a hell of a show, long tour coming up...*

"Right," I told my wife, just above a whisper. "Come *here*."

Half an hour later, I was trying to catch my breath and being really thankful for the tickybox doing what it does best, which is regulating my heartbeat. I had no clue whether the bed had squeaked or not, and I didn't give a rat's arse either way. I'd have laid odds that the motor would drown out the small noises, anyway. Next to me, Bree—salty and sweet, her skin damp with sweat—was practically purring. On the other side of the thin bedroom door, the bus was silent and probably dark for the night, except for Henry at the wheel. Just for a moment, I found myself wondering if he was scarfing down some of the candy bars he kept stashed in the basket...

"Hello, darling." I turned over on my side, and got one arm over her. My voice couldn't have been heard more than three feet away—okay, maybe it could, but only as a kind of murmur, no words. "Wow. Bree, I don't know what got into you—right, okay, not the best choice of words. Whatever it was, not what I was expecting, you know? Wow."

"Really?" She leaned into me, and ran her tongue down the side of my neck, and her hands were busy. Crikey. Not only was she apparently a fan of serious slap and tickle on a bus, but it was beginning to look as if she was up for at least one encore. She was keeping her voice modulated nice and low. No point in waking the rest of the bus, yeah? "What were you expecting? Me telling you to keep your hands to yourself? Slapping your face and demanding that you stop?"

I managed to catch both of her hands in mine. She might have been ready for another go, but my legs were twitchy and my breath had gone walkabout. "Yeah, pretty much. Oi! Hang on a minute, will you? Let me come back down before you get me back up, all right?"

"Spoilsport. No, I'm kidding—whenever you're ready." She rearranged herself, but kept us skin to skin. She was keeping her own voice modulated, even and low. "You really thought I wouldn't be up for it? Why?"

I had one hand resting on her cheek. The room was much darker than our bedroom at home. There, we have light-filtering shades, but we weren't at home, we were in an oversized luxury bus, rolling down a state highway. Since I didn't much fancy giving someone in the cab of an 18-wheeler one lane over the chance to play peeping tom, we'd kept the blinds drawn. The room was damned near pitch-dark, even after my eyes had got adjusted to it.

"That's a weird question, coming from the woman who refused to tour with me for twenty years," I told her. "I'd have thought having to bite back noise with the band four feet away would have hit all your privacy buttons."

"It did. Just—a different set of privacy buttons."

My heart had settled down nicely. One thing the tickybox does is, it takes away all the worry about what my heart's up to. Bree'd been terrified about sex after my heart attack—she thought every time I got short of breath, that was the inhale that was going to kill me. But a few months after the surgery in London, she'd finally realised that the ICD was going to make damned sure my heart wouldn't spark out on me. She could depend on it; she didn't have to worry about it. And as soon as that got through to her, we'd got our sex life back. Maybe it wasn't the same level of heat it had been before the heart attack, but it was pretty bloody hot.

"John?" Soft, quiet murmur in the dark. There was something really intimate about it; yeah, so, there were five other people a few feet away. Didn't matter. We might as well have been on our own planet. "Thanks for bringing me along."

There wasn't really any need to answer that. She knew, we both knew, that the thank-you was as much an apology as it was anything else.

The kicker was, it was really me who ought to have apologised. All those years of wanting her along, being shirty about her refusing to come with me? That was my own damned fault. I'd been too lazy to bother divorcing my first wife and Bree had lived in a state of terror that, one day, Cilla would come back and take everything that mattered away from her. In Bree's head, Cilla would have had that right. And knowing now how manipulative Cilla had really been, understanding how passive I'd been about it, Bree'd been right to worry.

I pulled her up close, just holding on. The movement of the bus was really soothing; I had the feeling that, if she really wanted an encore tonight, she might be out of luck. "Glad you're here, lady. But you didn't look too pleased when Henry asked you about stocking the galley. What was that about, then?"

She sighed. I could feel her heartbeat, up against me. She'd sorted out how to cuddle without hitting the tickybox within hours of them putting the damned thing in.

"Bree...?"

"Oh, I'm just being silly." Her voice went up a couple of decibels; outside, we both heard a faint squeak as someone turned over in his bunk. She hushed herself back down. "Whoa. Sorry. I just—John, they're not going to expect me to cook for everyone every night, are they? Because now that the cookbook's going to be published, I'm going to have to talk about it and talk about it and *talk* about it, and I really don't want to have to be Chef in Residence on the bus. I mean, I'm happy to cook for them sometimes, and of course I'll cook you anything you want, but I don't –"

"Oi!" I sat up, staring down at her. I could just make out her shape in the dark. "Bree, love, of course no one's going to saddle you with that. You can't seriously think Carla was trying to guilt you into wearing an apron. She wouldn't do that."

She reached up, and laid a hand on my lips. "Shhh! No, I knew she wasn't doing that. But it would be a natural thing for the guys in the band to think, John. Wouldn't it? After all, I've been feeding

22

most of them for years. They all know I'm a cook. And I just want a break from being Bree Kinkaid, head of Noshing But The Best Catering Services. I'm going to have to play SuperChef at some point, I know that. But right now, I just don't want to be the unholy love child of Julia Child and James Beard. I don't want to be anything except Bree Kinkaid, the woman on your arm."

I grinned down at her. She couldn't see it, of course, but that didn't matter. I slid back down and pulled her hard up against me, wrapping us together in the blackness. The bed had a nice soft blanket, Vellux I think they call it—we've got one of those on our bed at home, taking the place of a top sheet against our skin. The blanket was soft, but it wasn't nearly as velvety as the dark room around us.

"Works for me." I found her neck, and nuzzled it at the nape. Funny thing about that—there's something about the back of Bree from the waist up, her spine and neck, that just turns me on, and always has. I didn't have to see it; touching it did the trick just as well. "You got it. One minor change, though. How about the woman *in* my arms...?"

So yeah, old dogs, new tricks. I don't know whether it was the sex, or the absolute blackness of the room, or the motion of the wheels moving us north up Highway 99, but whatever it was, I slept long and deep, and so did Bree. We were both only just getting our eyes unglued when Henry rapped on the door at about ten the next morning.

"Half a mo, all right?" I was watching Bree, sliding out of bed and scrabbling for something to throw on. We hadn't thought about that last night—she sleeps nude at home, but that wasn't going to fly, not on the bus. The bus wasn't moving; sometime during the night, he'd got us somewhere and parked Magic, and us along with it. "Right, okay, we're decent. You can come in."

He stayed outside. "Just wanted to let you know you can open the bump-out if you like. And showers are fine. We're parked for the next little while. There's a pot of good strong coffee already made, and I stocked the fridge yesterday, so there's—oh, whoa, hey, hi."

Bree'd opened the door. "Sorry, but I can't talk to people through a closed door. It's just—wrong, somehow. Henry, can I ask you something? Two things?"

"Sure. Answering questions is part of the gig." She wasn't as tall as he was, not in bare feet, but she was still imposing, wrapped up in my funky old paisley robe. He looked wary. "What do you need?"

"Wait a minute, okay? John needs his morning meds." She was gathering my pills, and the water she'd left on her bedside table. "Here you go, babe. Okay, question one: where are we?"

I blinked at her, Henry didn't. "In a trucker's rest stop on Highway 99, in Medford, Oregon. I was planning on having us parked here for about another hour and a half. After that, we can either spend the rest of the day up in town, or we can hit the road and go straight for Eugene, if anyone wants an early look at tomorrow's venue. Personally, I'd vote for Eugene—it's a college town, so there a lot more to do there. Restaurants and stuff. Did you say you had two questions for me? What's the second question?"

She'd slipped out into the hallway and past him, obviously heading for the coffee. Bree doesn't really like having her morning routine mucked with, and caffeine was always the second thing she hit, after she got me my meds. I wondered if I ought to remind her that she hadn't brushed her hair—it was wild and messy, all over the place.

"Yes, I did." She stopped, looking him up and down, scoping him out top to bottom. Both his eyebrows were where his hairline would have been, if he hadn't shaved his head. "When was the last time you had a decent healthy meal...?"

24

*"Good evening, Seattle!"*

Even before we left San Francisco for that first gig in Chino, we'd known the Seattle gig was going to be intense.

One of the lead songs from the CD we were recording was a thing called "Americaland." I'd written the music for it, and Curt Lind, frontman for Mad At Our Dads, had written the lyrics in about eight minutes. He'd blown my mind in the process, picking up the edge I'd found in the music, and knowing straight off that the song lyric had to be political, angry, regretful, passionate. He'd known, bone-deep, just what was wanted, and he'd done it. The result was, he'd written a brilliant song about interstices, about the way America's become a place where you can't take a breath anymore, because if you sit and rest, the cops move you along.

We were all hot on having that one, live and kicking, on the CD. It was the obvious choice for the first single release, as well: timely lyrics, vicious music, and it covered both ends of the generation spectrum. Definitely a Geezer number, and not one Curt's band would likely cover. They're far more emo.

Problem was, Mad At Our Dads had hit the road themselves a few weeks back, and that made getting the Geezers and MAOD in the same place at the same time tricky. Carla'd pulled out the two tour schedules, looked them over, reached into her magic hat, and come up with the Geezers' Seattle gig as the ideal place for our one shot at recording "Americaland" live.

It was a brilliant choice, and a bit of serendipity, as well. While the Geezers were booked into a trendy 1500+ seat converted warehouse a stone's throw from the local sports stadium, MAOD were in the middle of the only four-day break they'd get in their own tour schedule. And the gig they were due to play, two days after ours, was also Seattle, at SoDo's sister venue.

*"Welcome to the Showbox SoDo! You're going to be glad you came out tonight, because the show we have for you is going to kick the jams right through the ceiling…"*

25

"Uncle John?" Solange Lind had come up next to me. "Is Aunt Bree around anywhere?"

"Hello, love. Yeah, she's just gone to get a glass of bubbly. She'll be back in a minute." I lifted one eyebrow. "You and Curt having a nice reunion, then? Catching up on things?"

She turned bright pink, which answered that question without a word spoken. I'd seen her once or twice since she and Curt had got married in our front room at 2828 Clay Street, but only for a few minutes at a time. They'd had to put off the honeymoon; the groom was on tour and the bride was a brand-new student at the San Francisco Chef's Academy. Neither schedule had any breathing room, never mind actual wiggle room.

Plus, Solange was contributing to my wife's mystery project, which turned out to be a cookbook specifically for people who have special food issues that no one else can be arsed to provide for. Luke's daughter, Blacklight's only band baby, is the nearest thing I have to a niece, but even with her living ten minutes away instead of on another continent, I'd only seen her in five-minute chunks since we'd hosted her wedding, and even those five minutes had been devoted to her doing something else.

"...with a very special surprise guest..."

"Hey. Hi, Solange." Bree'd come back, just in time for the pre-show ritual. She'd stopped being shy about it, which was fine with me. Of course, if I'm being honest about it, I don't mind about her being shy, or not shy. I don't really give a rat's arse, so long as does it.

She did it now, a solid squeeze. "Do a good gig, babe."

"Oooh!" Curt had come up and slipped an arm round his wife, just in time to see Bree do her thing. I had a moment of envy, missing my lost youth: here he was, fronting his band, on tour for the past month nearly non-stop, and he was fresh and bouncing and full of the kind of energy I can barely remember having. On the other hand, Bree was doing what she was doing, and Solange wasn't, so maybe young Curtis was doing a little envying of his own. "Is that a musical tradition? Maybe a rock and roll version of 'break a leg'? I like it. Solange, I don't suppose...?"

"You shut your gob, you." She was bright pink again, but she was laughing, too, and she leaned up to kiss him. "Don't even go there."

"...*ladies and gents, boys and girls...*"

"Damn, they're adorable." Bree breathed it into my ear. She still had me in a solid grip. "Curt's a charmer, isn't he?"

I twisted my head to whisper back at her. The grip was having a major effect, below decks: I was looking forward to getting her back to Magic after the show. "Yeah, and he knows it. Girl's going to have her hands full, over the years. Um—Bree? Speaking of having your hands full, can I have my nuts back, please? We're about to go on, assuming I can walk."

"...*put your hands together for Billy Dumont, Kris Corcoran, Tony Mancuso and JP Kinkaid...*"

She bit my ear, but she let go. "Well, if you insist. See you in the band room at the break. I already arranged for them to have some food ready for you. Do a good gig, baby."

"*The Fog City Geezers!*"

It was one hell of a first set. This was the fourth gig of the tour, and I'd been noticing a trend: we'd started out every show really hot. That's unusual, just on general principles; most shows, you kick it off hot for a song or two, then take it down a notch. That's pretty much a necessity, because if you run too hot too early and for too long, you burn out before the second set. And the second set, the closer, is the one the audience really remembers.

But we'd stayed hot all the way through the first three shows, and Seattle was no different. I had no idea if we could keep that up for the whole tour—after all, we're none of us twenty anymore, and touring is hard work. But that night at the Showbox

SoDo was something special, and we all knew it. While it was happening, we were all stoked, and riding that wave.

I keep the set lists and song selections for the Geezers completely separate from Blacklight. That's commonsense, really; I don't have anything like Mac's vocal chops, and Blacklight's reached the level of icon status a band only gets with longevity. The Geezers are more about the funky stuff: blues, country, classic rock and roll, the Fats Domino era. I love playing all that, and I don't get to do it with Blacklight.

So I'm not sure why, or when, the idea to cover a very old Blacklight tune, "Heart Attack," had come into my head. But when I let it slip during rehearsals that I'd been earwormed with it and wondering if it might not work as a Geezers number, the band was so enthusiastic that we just took it from there. It wasn't going to be done at every show—Tony and I were going to have to do a lead and harmony trade-off on the vocals, in a style very different from Mac's version. Mac's was very much an *I'm a horny tomcat and I'm going to sink my teeth into the back of your neck so come see me right now, lady* thing. Tricky, yeah?

The rehearsals made it clear the song was going to work for us. It's a funky twelve-bar thing, edging on dirty. Between the wailing slide guitar and barrelhouse piano the Geezers added to it, and the difference between the way Mac sings it and we sing it, the versions felt far enough apart so that we weren't simply recycling old Blacklight material. We'd actually taken the song and made it our own.

We opened the Seattle show with it, and it brought the house down. The average age out there was a mix of young and old, anywhere from twenty to sixty-plus. Still, at least half the faces treating the front rows like a mosh pit didn't look old enough to remember Blacklight's original version; it was off the *Partly Possible* album, back in the early eighties. But there were shrieks of recognition at the first notes, and everyone out there was singing along, or at least mouthing along. They all knew the words. Amazing energy.

So yeah, we were cooking from the first note. There was a mass of bodies up close to the stage, dancing, moving. With that much going on directly front of house, I didn't spend much time checking out the area behind the backstage rope, especially for the first few numbers. I did see Bree dancing; I always check to see where she is, because that's how I set and keep my comfort level. Usually, at Geezer gigs, she's sharing a table with Katia Mancuso and Sandra Corcoran, and they'll all be up and dancing halfway through the second song. But of course, she was on her own this tour, and anyway, the venue was new to me. I had no idea which table she'd parked herself at.

Five songs, six. We headed into the set closer, a cover of the Rufus Thomas song, "Walkin' the Dog." Over the years, that's become my personal shout-out when I'm onstage with the Geezers, a secret little in-joke between me and Bree, all about her fondness for wearing things with lots of buttons, and about my fondness for undoing them. As we were finishing up, I looked for her, wanting eye contact.

She wasn't dancing. She was staring, and not at me. She was looking back toward the band room, and there was something odd about the way she was holding herself. When something gets to her, she tenses up. You can always tell, because her shoulders turtle up and turn into boulders. The harder the hunch, the closer she is to flipping her shit.

Right that moment, she wasn't tensed up. But she was concentrated—you couldn't miss it. Whatever or whoever she was looking at was getting her full attention. That wasn't sitting well with me, because I happen to think her attention belongs on me, at least when I'm playing her a tune.

We jammed hard into the finish, gave it the usual flourishes that signal the audience there's a break coming up, and let the crowd go nuts for a minute. Nice loud audience they were, too, but just that moment, I wanted to get offstage and see what in hell was going on.

I slipped Little Queenie off my shoulder and into her stand, and stepped up to the mic. Bree had already disappeared.

"Right. We're going to take a break, but we'll back shortly, with a very special guest. Stick around, people, you won't want to miss this. See you in a bit."

I was actually the last one offstage. While I'd been doing my thing, talking to the audience, the rest of the band had already headed backstage for some food. I got off myself, and made the hard right down the corridor toward the band room. There was no sign of Bree; she was probably already inside, standing guard over my supper.

There was a woman partially blocking the doorway, standing just inside, with her back to the house: a redhead, but not Bree. There was something familiar about that back...

"Hello, JP." The voice came from just behind me. "Decent set. You've got better over the years. More subtle."

Oh, bloody *hell*.

I had it, now. The redhead blocking the door, that was Suzanne McElroy, Solange's stepsister. Last I'd heard, she was on the road, being backup singer for the miserable snivelling mingy self-important hulking shit drawling away behind me.

I turned around, nice and slow. I wasn't trying to match his drama-queen thing—it was just that, after forty years, even the sound of his voice still made me want to bash him in the face with something heavy and possibly studded with nails or knobs. The strength of the reaction, not to mention how immediate it was, was disturbing.

The tickybox had ramped up. I was meeting Bergen Sandoval's eye and keeping my voice even and cool, but I was giving my inside hardware a good talking-to: *right, no rubbish from you, I don't want one stray heartbeat, we clear?* This was my gig, my audience, and my turf, and I was damned if I was going to let him push me into bloodying his nose or having him escorted out the back by way of the venue security bloke's Doc Marten. Letting even a hint of weakness show with Bergen Sandoval was a huge sodding mistake. He was mean enough to screw you straight through your trousers, and mingy enough to charge you for the lube he hadn't bothered using, while he was doing up his own buttons and strolling away afterwards.

"Hello, Bergen. Haven't seen you in forever." *Yeah, and what a pity we couldn't have left it that way.* He still had the famous dye job—he'd always bleached his hair to nearly white, and put this stupid theatrical red streak off to one side, just over his right ear. It had always made him look a right ponce, and it didn't look any better with thirty years' worth of wrinkles, either. "What brings you to Seattle?"

"Chicks." He was rocking gently, back and forth, heel to ball of foot. Anyone who'd ever seen him onstage would know that motion—he practises it, and no, I'm not joking. I'd watched him do it in the band room mirror, back in the day. "Two of them, actually. Oh, and anyway, a reasonable way to kill some time."

The fucker was trying to piss me off, you know? He'd played this sort of game back when I was a green kid, paying for the privilege of touring with the great Bergen Sandoval: his little tricks, designed to make you feel he was important and you were nothing. This time, though, it wasn't going to fly. For one thing, we were stablemates for the same record label, and for another, I owned a chunk of the label, and he didn't.

"Glad we could ease your boredom, Bergen. So, which two women? Anyone I know?"

Back and forth, ball to heel. He had his hands in pockets. He was a big bloke, well over six feet. It was weird, because I remembered him as hulking, but he wasn't, not anymore. He was

31

nearly as skinny as me, but I noticed a soft little roll of extra flesh, right round the middle. I had a sudden feeling that under the sleeves of the pricey leather jacket, he probably had the kind of stringy muscle a middle-aged man gets from working out to avoid looking his age. We're much more conceited than the birds are, you know? Sad but true.

"Well, yes, of course you know them. Both of them." He really did sound bored. "Suzanne wanted to see her sister and her sister's bright shiny new husband. That was one. And the hot bird who runs your shit for you—Carla? Right, Carla."

"Carla?" Damn. Of course Carla must have had a hand in it— he couldn't have got on the guest list, otherwise. If anyone had run it past me first, he'd have been out on the sidewalk, arguing with the security staff about how important he was. "What about her?"

"Well, there's the Fluorescent bash, of course." He lifted both eyebrows; I must have looked as fuddled as I felt, because he sounded as if he thought I was completely dim. "Next month? In LA? At the Plus Minus, Silver Streak's new club? And oh, since I'm mixing down my new CD at ALS, Carla thought I ought to come along and check out your piano player. If he's halfway decent, I'll probably use him."

I had my own hands jammed into my pockets, now. It seemed the best way to keep them from smashing Bergen's face in. They were clenched into tight hard fists. "Yeah, well, I'm afraid that's not on, at least for a month or so. But if you ask him really nicely—instead of assuming he wants to dance for his per diem— he might be up for it when the tour's over, and – "

I stopped in mid-sentence. Bergen's face had changed, in a way I recognised all too well. He was about as conceited a bag of ego as I've ever come across, but he has an eye for women, even if he doesn't have a clue what they're about, beyond breasts and arses. The woman he was looking at right then, just over my shoulder, was giving him all sorts of ideas...

"John? Your dinner's getting cold."

"Right." I hadn't even noticed getting my arm round Bree's waist, but I must have done, because there it was. I turned both of us toward the band room, hard and fast. "Ta, love. I need some dinner. Almost time for the second set."

# Chapter Three

On a good long list of things I don't see myself forgiving Bergen Sandoval for any time soon, ruining my memories of the Seattle show is right up there in the top ten.

What really narks me is that the second set was everything we'd wanted, everything we'd hoped for, one of the best sets we're ever likely to play. We premiered "Americaland" and recorded a monster version of it, and Curt damned near torched the place, he was so hot. The entire band was stoned-happy over it, and the audience was through the roof.

From the first crunch of me and Kris locking up, the crowd went quiet, surprised, almost tense. Then Curt opened his mouth—*Boy's got his shoes off, eyes closed, feet crossed, lying in a public park, pretending it's a beach/Boy's just a dreamer, no job, no home, can't even count the things that are out of his reach*—and the noise levels out in the house started up, right along with the in-tensity. There was a feeling in the air, an expectation; you couldn't miss it, and it was building with every line, every snarl-ing wolf howl guitar riff, every jerk of the mic in Curt's hand.

By the time we'd hit the first hard punch of the lyric—*no place to go, nowhere to be, the gutter or the morgue or the Arabian Sea*—we knew we had them. And by the time we all hit the mics, backing up Curt on the vocal hook—*'cause it's Americaland, this is Americaland* —they were chanting along with us, the entire house: *Americaland! Americaland!* It was bone-chilling, in its own way, really primal, but we were all grinning like maniacs. We'd written ourselves an anthem.

So "Americaland" should have pushed that second set in Seat-tle well up into my list of favourite Geezers gigs. After all, it's on the CD, the proof of just how amazing that version was. But be-tween keeping an eye on my wife to make sure Bergen didn't try something, and wondering how to keep my keyboard player from getting suckered into deserting the Geezers in favour of getting shafted by an expert in the art of fucking people over, my atten-tion got hijacked. Even the four bites of supper I managed to get down went sour in my stomach.

I wasn't really worried about Bree, not beyond not wanting her being bothered. If Bergen was dim enough to grab her, she'd probably have had his bollocks dangling from her ears by the end of the night, and I'm damned if I'd have done anything more than make sure no one interrupted her while she was getting them. Bree doesn't do well with stray touches from anyone but me, even from people she knows; a stranger trying to grope her was in for serious hurt. She'd proved that with the Bombardiers' late lead singer, a few years back.

The problem was, she knew how important this gig was for the Geezers as a band, and for me personally. It would have been just like her to grit her teeth and put up with Bergen's shite, if she thought reacting to it would make my life harder. I was damned if I wanted her to have to cope. Besides, if he did try anything, I wanted the pleasure of doing some nuclear-level reacting myself. I'd seen the way the grooves around his mouth got deeper when she'd come up next to me. He'd always had a thing for redheads.

The thing with Tony, though, that was going to be tricky. He didn't know what Bergen was, and I couldn't think how to get that across without sounding like a mean prat myself. Katia wasn't here to cover his arse, not this time. This was on me.

I knew Bergen Sandoval. I knew how he worked, his tricks, his technique, what he got up to, to get what he wanted. And Tony was vulnerable, for the worst possible reason: it had taken him far too long to get the industry respect he's deserved all along. Inferiority complex thing, you know? Maybe not bad, but it was there, little hints of it.

Bergen had always been a mean sod, but he's not stupid. He's as sharp as Bree's best chef's knife, especially when it comes to reading someone else's weak spots. So I already knew, heading onstage for the second set, that Bergen had seen just how to get Tony to come get shit on at Bergen's sessions in LA. What I didn't know was how to prevent it.

The way things turned out, it wouldn't have mattered what I'd come up with. It was a lost cause before the set break was even over.

The arm I'd dropped round Bree, when I saw the effect she was having on Bergen, had been shaking. That was rage, but once she felt the tremor, she got it into her head that my MS was acting up, and of course after that, there was fuck-all I could say or do to convince her that no, really, I was just shaking because I wanted to bash Bergen in the face with a roadcase and couldn't unless I wanted the Geezers to finish the tour without me, since I'd be in jail.

Once she decided it was the MS, she had me backstage, sitting down, and trying to eat before I could blink. She was so damned fierce about it, she actually planted herself in front of me to make sure I didn't get up unless I'd eaten first. I didn't get a vote—hell, I didn't get a word in. My wife simply wasn't taking no.

What I did get was a nice clear view of Bergen, swanning over to Tony and opening his usual vial of snake oil, the fucking wanker. He pulled out every trick in his personal kit bag: handshake that went on a fraction longer than it needed to, admiring, *been wanting to meet you forever*, his usual line of bullshit. I recognised every damned move. I'd have been dim not to, since he'd used them on me, that first time. The pissy little sod could have written a book on how to get people who didn't know him to bend over for him…

"John?" Bree was fixated on the plate of food that I wasn't emptying nearly fast enough. "You've only got about ten minutes. Is something wrong with your dinner? I can get them to bring you something else if this isn't –"

"No, it's fine. Just not very hungry right now."

She wasn't looking convinced. I managed another mouthful of what might as well have been cardboard, and kept my eyes on Bergen and Tony. Not as easy as it sounds, not with Bree planted in front of me, and the band room packed out with people. I caught a glimpse of Bergen's dye job, bending over. He was probably telling Tony how much he'd dug the piano solo on some obscure Bombardiers tune from thirty years ago, which of course he'd never listened to until he decided to get Tony playing for him. I could picture that smarmy miserable little grin.

"JP? Hi, how are you? Isn't this fun? Oh hello, Bree."

The last time I'd seen Suzanne McElroy, she'd been sitting on the sofa in our front room, listening as her stepdad read Mac's old chum Almanzor al-Wahid—who had daughters who were twin terrors and oh, yeah, also happened to have his own emirate—the riot act, for being a shitty parent. She'd been pretty quiet just then,

37

but nothing I knew about the girl left me thinking she'd stay quiet for long. The first time I'd met her, she'd been not quite legal age, at school with Solange, and she'd tried to get me to take her home and do her. The second time I'd met her, she'd acted as if I'd done what she'd wanted the first time I'd met her, and Bree hadn't talked to me for the better part of two miserable days.

So, okay, she's not in my top ten favourite people. But she's Luke's stepdaughter, and Solange's stepsister. That makes her Blacklight family. And just because she was one of Bergen's backup singers, that didn't give me any reason to not treat her the same way I would Solange.

"Oi, Suzanne. How's the tour going? Bergen treating you all right, then?"

Yeah, I know. I probably should have sussed it before then; Bergen had made it pretty clear what was going on. But until I saw her face change, watched her mouth tighten up and her shoulders stiffen and the look of possessive anxiety she threw over her shoulder at Bergen, it hadn't even occurred to me.

"Yes, thanks. Um—excuse me, okay? I'll see you later."

She was gone, edging away, back towards Bergen. This time, I got a clear view, and was left wishing I hadn't: Suzanne reached Bergen where he was still talking to Tony. I saw the way she moved, the way she hovered over him, the look on her face when he said whatever he said to her. If I thought I'd wanted to smash Bergen's face in before, I hadn't known the half of it. He looked like a damned satyr.

"Son of a *bitch*! Are you fucking kidding me!"

I jumped. I'd been so busy watching what was going on, I hadn't noticed my wife turning to watch, as well. She's got even less reason to like Suzanne than I do, but right then, she looked to be in full outraged Valkyrie mama bear mode. Her hands were balled up into solid fists.

"John? Please tell me that isn't what I think it is?"

"I wish I could, love. But yeah, I know Bergen. They're having it off, no question."

Bree swung back around, staring down at me. "But—dear God, that can't be right. It can't be what's going on. She's Solange's age! How old is he, anyway?"

"Sixty-plus. He's at least five years older than me—he'd been established for years when I came along."

"Jesus." She looked disgusted. "John, I don't want to be judgmental about any friend of yours, and I hate to say this, but that guy is a pervert. She's a third his age, and she works for him. And what is she thinking!"

I glanced across the room. *Shit.* Bergen was rubbing Suzanne's bottom. He wasn't paying her any attention beyond that, because he was still shmoozing all over Tony. Even though he wasn't actually bothering to look at Suzanne, she was doing enough looking for both of them, and it was the sort of look that would have had her stepdad peeling long bloody strips off Bergen's wrinkled hide, had Luke been there to see it: possessive, anxious, and completely pathetic. She looked like a dog who was afraid of a good hard kick, and with what I remembered about the way Bergen treated women, she had a good chance of that fear being validated.

Bree was staring at me, and I met her eye. "Yeah, well, no worries about offending me, Bree. He's no friend of mine. No love lost between us—he ripped me off and fucked me over, back when you were about eight years old and I was a teenager. I think he's a mean shit. No, I've had enough supper, ta. Truth is, I've lost my appetite."

So yeah, Bergen managed to thoroughly fuck up my memories of the second set at the Showbox SoDo. It's not that I played badly, or phoned it in; I don't let anything get between me and playing. But I should have been digging it, not just playing well, and I got robbed of that. I don't know if Bergen has that effect on everyone, or if it's just me, but speaking just for myself, I find he manages to cock it up on multiple levels just by opening his mouth, and he always has.

It didn't get any better in the band room after the show, either. Tony had played even above his usual brilliance for the entire second set. I was pretty sure I knew what that little extra tiara sparkle was in aid of, and I wasn't wrong. We'd barely got offstage between the set closer and the encore when he pulled me aside.

"JP, listen. We get a couple of days off between the Universal City gig and the Fluorescent party, right?"

Oh, bloody hell. Bergen had got to him, all right; the look on Tony's face, you'd have thought Paul McCartney had yanked him out of the crowd and asked him to sit in and jam on "I've Just Seen A Face," or something.

"Yeah, we do." I don't know how I managed to keep my voice normal, but I did. "Three days, I think. Might be four—but we may be adding a second show. Carla would know."

He couldn't seem to hold my eye. "Cool. Fucking awesome! Bergen asked if I had the time to maybe lay down some keyboard on his new CD, and well, I told him yes of course, as long as it doesn't mess with our own schedule."

I stayed quiet—not easy, under the circs. He gave a little laugh, self-conscious and completely un-Tony. "He actually mentioned the piano solo I did on 'Sugar Baby Blues', do you believe that? Off our second album? I mean, what did that album sell, like, fifty copies?"

He looked blissed. The crowd was making a lot of noise; we were still front of house, just beside the stage, no walls between us and the wave of voices. Not exactly the moment or the setting to sit Tony down and warn him not to expect anything except being treated like something the cat dragged in.

I nodded back at him, and managed a smile. It felt more like I was dying of tetanus or something, it was that forced. But that was the best I could do, since there was no way I could manage a real smile for him just then.

We gave the crowd a couple of minutes, let it build, and headed back onstage for the encore. I'd arranged it with Curt beforehand, so we had two guitarists, me and him, and we shared the vocals on "Walkin' the Dog." Looking out in the crowd behind the velvet rope, I spotted Bree dancing. She gets deep into it, lost in the music, but she looked up and met my eye, and I nodded. Solange was a few feet away, off her left shoulder.

Looking at the stage, Bree completely missed a weird little tableau a few feet off to her right. Bergen was staring at her, and if I thought he'd looked like a satyr while he was fondling Suzanne, this was much worse. He was looking at my wife as if he wanted to pour chocolate sauce and whipped cream all over her.

Just off to his right, Suzanne was staring at him. She was turned too far toward him for me to see her face properly, but I could see her hands, clenching and unclenching. Her entire body looked as tight as an overstretched guitar string.

Right. Time to break this rubbish up.

I moved sideways, toward the edge of the stage. Curt was nailing the vocal; he's a born frontman, and he had the crowd's full attention. The PRS he'd bought to replace Slim, the PRS he'd lost in the 707 Club fire, was handling the lead work.

I got to the far edge, and looked down at my wife. She was looking up at me—not at Curt, not at the rest of the band, and not at Bergen Sandoval, either.

I jerked my head, and she headed straight for me. I'd confused the hell out of her; last time I'd jerked my head at her quite that way from onstage, she'd been sixteen, standing in the wings at Blacklight's Hurricane Felina benefit at the Cow Palace, as a volunteer for the local free clinic. Quite a long time ago, now.

She was right below me, looking bewildered. She lifted her shoulders—*what?*

41

I grinned at her, and blew her a kiss. Nice and visible, for the whole crowd to see; not just your basic lip pucker but the whole nine yards, kissing the palm of my hand, blowing the invisible kiss off the palm in her direction, the lot. Pure teenage boy letting his best girl know about it, yeah?

I watched her jaw drop. She ducked her head, just for a moment, red hair swinging. When she looked back up at me, she lifted a hand to her mouth and blew my kiss straight back at me.

There were people watching from the audience, now, and Bree was getting fist-pumps and grins from the crowd. Bergen and Suzanne were watching, as well; Bergen looked annoyed, but I couldn't quite tell what Suzanne was thinking, because all I got was her profile.

The song was almost over, and I edged back towards the rest of the band. I hit my effects rig and dragged the last few bars of the song into a flat-out, balls to the wall hard rock thing that Rufus Thomas probably hadn't had in mind when he wrote it: screaming wailing guitars, Kris using his funky old P Bass like a club or a thunder machine, Billy nailing it, Tony just riding the strings with the top end of the keyboard...

*"Thank you, Seattle, and goodnight!"*

Bowing to the crowd, Blacklight style, with our arms around each other's waists. House lights up. Offstage, chugging a bottle of cold water. Towelling down, cooling off, nattering with the local media and the rest of the band. I kept my arm around my wife and one eye on Bergen, until Henry stuck his head around the door.

"Guys? Ready to head out? The bus is out back. Doug and Damon say the load-out should be done in about half an hour."

"Right." I got to my feet, and pulled Bree up with me. "Our posh ride's outside, and it's Portland tomorrow night. Curt, that was brilliant work. Cheers, mate. Solange, we'll see you soon, I hope. You coming down to LA for the Fluorescent bash? Ought to be quite the party."

42

"Oh, do come." Bergen was rocking, heel to toe, back and forth. He sounded completely bored. "My annoying producers will be there, and anyway, the crumpet here wants to see more of her ornamental big sister."

Quite a knack for insulting people, Bergen had. The annoying producers he'd just dissed happened to be the Bunker Brothers, Cal Wilson and Stu Corrigan, Blacklight's rhythm section. He was really something, was Bergen: he'd managed to nail the band, insult Suzanne, and offend the entire Hedley-Lind contingent, *bang bang bang*, without ever stopping to reload.

Next to me, I felt Bree go stiff. She hadn't gone nearly as stiff as Solange had, though—for one amazing moment, I saw Luke peering out of his daughter's eyes, the day he'd shoved a tabloid reporter who was hassling him with rude questions about Solange up against a wall and threatened to beat the shit out of him. The tickybox in my chest ramped up, and then came down again. I was breathing more heavily than usual.

"John?" Bree had got hold of my arm. She and Solange had exchanged one fast look; she wasn't looking at Bergen Sandoval. "Can we go? I really want to get out of these shoes. Solange, sweetie, I'll call you about book stuff next week."

Out the door, up the ramp, and safely up the stairs onto Magic. Underneath, I could feel the engines warming up, and the bus rumbling as the crew loaded in equipment. I wasn't really letting my breath out until we'd left Seattle behind. And I wasn't even going to think about how to clue Tony in to the truth about Bergen until I got a good night's sleep.

*"Good evening, San Francisco, and welcome to the Fillmore!"*

"JP? Are you okay?" Carla'd come up next to me; two minutes earlier, she'd been off huddling in the band room with her assistant, an annoying kid named Andy Valdon. "You look worried. Is there a problem?"

*"We've got an incredible show for you tonight, pure San Francisco high energy for all you hometown peeps…"*

"No, no problem. I'm fine."

I wasn't sure if that was true, but Carla'd flown up for this, and she had enough on her plate without me piling on. Besides, just before your new opening act hits the stage, on what happens to be both bands' home turf, is no time to throw angst or attitude.

Carla's not dim, though, and she was right. I was edgy. Some tours, everything goes perfectly, other times everything seems hexed. I've been on both kinds—crikey, after touring for forty years, I'd have thought there were no surprises left. But this was the first time I'd done a tour where everything mechanical was flawless, and every undercurrent that could possibly grow teeth not only did, but used them to bite the band in the arse.

*"…our own Fog City Geezers, joined for the first time on the bill by one of the Bay Area's most kickass players…"*

"I'm kind of curious about these guys." Tony nodded in the general direction of the stage. "I've never seen them live before. You?"

"First for me, as well." I was looking for Bree. She'd been in a peculiar mood since we'd got here. "Where's Katia?"

There was no answer. I turned, just in time to catch what looked like a shrug. *Shit.* I don't want to go all daytime telly over it, but if Tony and Katia were losing it after thirty years, it was going to suck, and not just for me. Bree and Katia are best friends; for a long time, Katia was the nearest thing to a close friend Bree had or even wanted, outside of me.

*"…San Francisco's own Elaine Wilde…"*

Tony must have seen something in my face. "I think she and Bree went to order dinner. They'll be back. Hey, whose kid was that, backstage? Do you know?"

"That's Martina Wilde, Elaine's daughter." Trust Carla to have the gen. "She told me to call her Maret. Interesting nickname, isn't it? Apparently, she's a classical guitarist in training. She's a

44

student at the Horizons Academy—second year. I gather she's a prodigy."

"Poor brat. But that's a good school." Carla'd pronounced the kid's name weirdly: Ma-RAY. "Can't say she doesn't come by it honestly, what with being a guitar player's kid."

"...opening tonight for the Fog City Geezers, give it up for the Bay Area's own..."

"I think you may have just acquired a fan, or maybe a junior groupie." Bree was back, with Katia in tow. "I don't know about her mother, but that child was watching you like you were the Holy Grail or something, backstage. I ordered you a burger and salad. Is that okay?"

Katia moved up next to Tony, and handed him a beer; if there were problems or storms, they weren't front of house just then. Good. I got one arm round my wife, and pulled her close; the house lights were down and the noise levels were up. I had to lean up to reach her ear.

"Yeah, a burger's fine. Elaine Wilde's daughter was watching me? I can't imagine why she'd bother with me, can you? If she wants a guitar player to worship, her mum's a damned good one, from everything I've heard."

"Well, we're about to find out."

Bree's voice was neutral enough, but she felt tense. Not tense enough for me to push her about it, but still, not really relaxed. Unless she was stressing over Tony and Katia, I couldn't imagine where the tension was coming from.

"...WildeChild!"

We watched the first few numbers from just inside the backstage ropes. I'd heard them before, of course. I keep up with local talent and, anyway, Carla had sent me a CD, a three-tune demo sampler, when Fluorescent was first negotiating to sign them to the label. Typical four-piece combo: bass, drums, keyboard and guitar, with Elaine fronting the band. From what I'd heard so far,

45

they leaned toward hard rock, with more edge to it than the Geezers, and a lot less blues and alt-country in the mix.

The first thing I noticed was that Elaine Wilde was a fan of beating the shit out of a tricked-out Paul. She definitely knew her way around a guitar. She was a solid singer as well, in the Chrissie Hynde mould, but with more smoke and a lot more grit in her voice. If the sampling of tunes Carla'd sent was anything to go by, Elaine was a better than average songwriter, as well.

All things considered, WildeChild looked to be a nice addition to the label. I'd already had an enthusiastic email from Cal Wilson; the Bunker Brothers were quite hot to produce her first CD for Fluorescent. I'd found myself hoping that working with WildeChild might be enough of a diversion to keep Cal and Stu from strangling Bergen.

Their being asked to open tonight was about whether the band would work as an opening act for the Geezers as a touring combo. Carla'd come up with the idea, with some backup from Andy Valdon. It was the obvious move: new to the label, both bands with solid local followings in the same venue market. Why not let the newcomers open for the bigger name and get them joint exposure on a regional tour, especially since we'd have CDs coming out less than a two weeks apart?

If their style had been too far off from the Geezers, I'd have had to talk to Carla about it. So far, though, that didn't look to be an issue, even if their fan base was different. I'd noticed a higher percentage of blokes than the Geezers usually see—we get a pretty even balance between men and women. The extra males out there looked to be younger than our audience, as well. Instead of the older, mellower crowd the Geezers draw, the crowd up near the stage for WildeChild looked to be thinking about turning the first twenty or so rows of the Fillmore's dance floor into a replay from the old punk days. There were a lot of tats and piercings.

I watched Elaine Wilde slamming about onstage for their first two songs. We'd been introduced backstage, but Carla'd got her by the elbow and was making the rounds, so all I'd got was the usual exchange of nods and smiles and *nice to meet you, welcome to the label* noises.

First impression was of a dark-eyed brunette, just Bree's age, in leather gear so tight it looked painted on. She had a nice clear speaking voice, different from her singing; that had some serious growl in it. I didn't get much more than that, not in ten seconds of small talk in a crowded band room. One thing I had noticed was, she'd been in high heels and we'd been eye level, so she was actually shorter than me. Interesting, because onstage she was an Amazon. It was all in the vibe, the presentation. She had major stage presence up there.

"...*think you're getting some of this, honey not so much—you can look, but you better not touch...*"

Elaine had planted herself at the edge of the stage. She used an old-fashioned mic stand, good and phallic, and "use" was the word, all right. I found myself grinning; she'd taken more than a few notes from the Malcolm Sharpe playbook. She had his "mic stand between the knees, deep crouch" thing happening...

"They're a good band. She's—really good. Isn't she? A really good guitar player?"

I turned, and looked at Bree. I couldn't be sure, but there seemed to be something peculiar going on in her voice, an odd little hitch. I just couldn't quite sort out what it was.

"Yeah, damned good, actually. Perfect frontwoman for that lot, as well—gives them direction. I suspect they'd be a lot less interesting without her." I felt a sudden tremor, going down my right leg, and swore under my breath; last thing I need just before a live gig is for the MS to nail me. "Damn, I've gone shaky. Too much standing about. Bree, love, I need to sit for a minute, all right?"

Of course, that redirected her attention, straight back onto me. She led the way back to the band room, muscling people out of our way, got me settled in a chair, and went off in search of some water for me.

I sat back and closed my eyes. Right. *You've got a set to play. Sort out what's tingling, and try for some Zen.* Right leg shaking. Right foot tingling. *Fuck.* What about the hands...?

"Um—hi. You're—aren't you JP Kinkaid?"

I opened my eyes. It was the kid I'd seen in the band room before the show, Elaine Wilde's daughter. She looked a lot like her mum, maybe even darker around the eyes and hair. What had Carla said the kid's name was? Mary, Mara, something like that?

I held out a hand, and she shook it: no nervousness, a nice easy grip. She had calluses on all the appropriate fingers, and I noticed the nails on her right hand were longer than the ones on her left hand. Definitely a guitar player.

"Yeah, I'm John Kinkaid. You're Elaine Wilde's daughter, right? I'm sorry, I don't think I got your name...?"

"I'm Martina Wilde. Everyone calls me Maret." She had a light clear voice, and I wondered how old she was. She didn't look much over eleven or twelve. "Can I ask you something? About music, I mean?"

There was something intense about her. I remembered what Bree'd said, about the kid looking at me as if I were the Holy Grail. I smiled at her. "Can't imagine why not. Ask away."

I don't know anything about kids. I've never had any, and never really hung out with any, either. I've got no clue about whether the whole quicksilver lightning-fast change, between being confident and being shy, is how they all get at that age, or what. But that kid went from not being bothered to going pink round the edges, and not wanting to meet my eyes anymore, in about two seconds. I lifted an eyebrow, and waited.

"Um." I could practically hear her convincing herself it was okay to ask. "Were you—did you always play what you play now?

48

Or did you have to learn to play other kinds of music first? Before they let you play rock and roll, I mean?"

"What, standards or classical, you mean?" Over the kid's shoulder, I saw Bree edging her way through the crowd, with a bottle of Volvic in each hand. "No, none of that. I started playing because I heard an old song called 'Daisy Chain Blues', a record with a bloke called Bulldog Moody on it. He was a session player back in the forties and fifties: rhythm, mostly blues. That's what I played first. Still do."

"Oh. Okay." She looked down at her shoes; still on the shy thing, apparently. "I just wondered."

"You're at school, yeah? Music school?"

She jerked her head back up. "Well, of course. I'm second year at Horizons Academy. Where did *you* go to school?"

I bit back a grin. She already had a touch of the unconscious snobbery kids at specialised art schools get, especially music schools. "I didn't. Had a few lessons, that's all, but really, I learned on my own. I was a few years younger than you are now when I started playing. I picked up some jazz guitar chops after I'd started playing sessions—I was playing professionally at fifteen. Classical guitar, I leave that to people like Segovia and Bream. I'm a blues player. But I learned from listening and playing, mostly. That's just the way it went down, you know? Oi, love, one of those water bottles for me? Bree, did you meet Martina Wilde? This is my wife, Bree Godwin Kinkaid."

"Hello, Martina. It's nice to meet you." There it was again, something weird going on in Bree's voice. And this time, her shoulders were tight, at the edge of hunching. What in hell was all this?

"No one calls me Martina, except my professor, when he thinks I'm not working hard enough. I'm Maret." She was still staring at me; she hadn't even glanced at Bree. "You never went to school? Really?"

I almost laughed. Yeah, I know, that would have been well past tactless and into cruel, she was that young. Hard not to, though—she looked so shocked. "Of course I did school. You can't not, can you? They get just as shirty about that in London as they do here. Not music school, though, just the regular comprehensive school. That what you meant?"

The kid was looking at me as if I'd just fallen out of the sky and started speaking in tongues, or something. "Wow. Did you—well—study? Practice, I mean? If no one was making you, did you practice anyway?"

I had one eye on Bree. There was a conversation coming up later, once we got home. The big thing about being in San Francisco is that we were home. We could desert Magic for a couple of nights and head off to 2828 Clay Street, to our cats and our own bed. Bree calls that home court advantage, it's where she says she feels safest.

Yeah, well, 2828's my home court, as well. And I wanted to know why a kid asking me questions about guitar practice was causing that stony look on Bree's face, or why she wouldn't meet my eye.

"I'm sorry. Maybe I shouldn't have asked that?"

I jerked my head back toward the kid. She'd gone bright pink, chewing her lower lip and looking flustered. It took me a moment, but I finally sussed it: I'd taken too long to answer her, and she thought she'd dropped a brick.

"Nothing to be sorry for. I've got multiple sclerosis and it's playing me up tonight. Not a good time for it. Hang on a minute, I need to take a pill."

Outside, WildeChild was winding down; as the opening act, they got a shorter set than the Geezers did as the headliners. I knocked back my pills, and turned my attention back to Maret Wilde and her questions.

"Hell yeah, I practiced," I told her. "I practiced until my fingers bled. I had an old Washburn acoustic, and the day I figured out why a diminished chord was called that, I actually left a bloodstain on the fretboard. That axe had a mahogany neck, rosewood fretboard with a nice dark finish, but you could see the stain if you looked. So yeah, I practiced."

Something happened to Bree's face when I said that, just for a moment; it went softer somehow, twisting up as if she was in pain. Maret Wilde looked as if she thought I was some sort of fantastic weird storyteller Hans Christian Andersen bloke, or something: fascinated. The kid's eyes were blazing at me.

"Really? You practiced so hard you left a bloodstain? Truly?"

"Yeah, under the sixth fret, the A and D strings, between the fret markers. Freaked my dad out, that bloodstain did. The idea of them making me practice, what a joke. They were too busy telling me to step away from the axe for five minutes and go out of doors, and hang out with my friends. You couldn't get the guitar out of my hands, most days. Ah, I think your mum's set's about done, yeah? Bree, do we know when food's supposed to be—never mind, here it comes. Good, plenty of time to eat before we go on."

I still couldn't sort out what was getting up Bree's nose. She'd planted herself next to me, making sure I ate, and of course, I returned the favour; a hungry diabetic is a pissy cross diabetic. All that was normal. What wasn't normal was how hard she was trying to keep me from seeing she was losing it. I'm not exaggerating: she was in a battle royal with her own shoulders, trying to keep them down where they belonged, trying to stop me noticing. And her shoulders were winning.

They didn't ease up any when WildeChild finished their encore and the band room suddenly got very full of Elaine Wilde. Not her band, so much—the three blokes were actually pretty low-key and laid back. Elaine was a different story. For a small bird, she took up a lot of space, and just as much air. She looked around, got corralled by Andy Valdon and a couple of hangers-on, spotted me, and shook them off.

"Hey, finally! JP Kinkaid!"

She waved at me across the room, and started over. And out of nowhere, Bree's shoulders were hard tight mauls of muscle on bone. What the fuck...?

I didn't get an answer, not then. Shaking Andy off is easy, but if Carla decides she wants you there, you're there, mate. Even Mac Sharpe has never managed the trick of doing something if Carla wants him doing something else. Carla apparently wanted Elaine and her entire band, for some sort of interview thing with the bloke from the San Francisco *Chronicle*, because she'd got herself and the newspaper bloke between Elaine and me.

So I didn't get to do more than smile and wave at the new kids that night. The Geezers took the stage and showed all the not-quite-rowdies left over from WildeChild's set a few things about high octane rock and roll. By the time we'd done our encore and were ready to head out ourselves, the only member of WildeChild still in the building was the bassist. Turned out Maret didn't usually come to her mum's gigs, at least not on school nights, and Elaine had taken the kid home. Bree seemed to have relaxed by then, at least a bit.

We left the equipment for Henry and the roadies to deal with. I gathered up Little Queenie in one hand, got Bree's hand with the other, and headed off to 2828 Clay Street, where we keep our cats, our bed, and our home court advantage. Whether she knew it or not, my wife had a few questions coming her way.

# Chapter Four

One thing about Bree: she never uses sex as a tool, or a weapon, or anything other than her own personal favourite tour bus to multiple orgasms. But I wonder, now, if she knew I was going to want the truth about why she was having trouble coping with the two Wildes. If the workout she gave me that night back at Clay Street was anything to go by, she really was hoping to knock the memory out of my circuitry by basically blowing the top of my skull straight off. It didn't work—her bad luck—but the attempt was brilliant.

I rolled over and draped an arm over her. She'd done a better job relaxing all the knots out of my muscles than an hour with a masseuse and a soak in a hot tub could have done; the MS tingles had backed down, as well. Bree has a talent for kicking the world all the way to the curb when it's just her and me and a nice rowdy belly-bump. That doesn't always work for coping with the MS, but tonight, the disease had eased off. Maybe she'd shocked it into behaving itself.

"Hello, darling." I stroked her hair. It's much shorter than it used to be, but still one of my favourite things in the world to touch, along with her naked back and her neck and the rest of her. "Lovely to be home for a night or two, isn't it?"

"Mmmm." Relaxed as I was, I had nothing on Bree. She was as limp as leftover spaghetti. "Sleepy."

"Yeah, there's a shock." I was still stroking her hair. "What was that about, tonight? With Elaine Wilde and her kid?"

She went rigid.

I don't like surprising Bree, and she doesn't like surprises from me. She's got good reasons for not liking surprises; we've got major history, there. But on this one, much as I didn't like doing it, I wasn't letting her off the hook without her clueing me in. Because this wasn't just about the two of us, you know? This was band business. And I tell you what, I don't like surprises, either.

I slid my hand down from her hair to her shoulder, and any inclination to let the conversation wait went west. She was rock-hard, every bit as taut as she'd been earlier.

I sat up and looked down at her. Lying there, looking to be made out of marble, she had her eyes locked on mine. Even in the dimness, she looked absolutely miserable. She seemed to be holding her breath.

"Bree, look. I don't know what the story is, or what's going on with you about this woman and her kid, but I can't just ignore it, can I? This is the Geezers we're talking about. WildeChild's opening for us, they've signed with our label, and that means I've got to work with them. So just dish, love, will you please? Get it over. What's the story? What happened with you two? I didn't even know you knew her."

54

"I don't." I could hear the ragged edge of tears in her voice. "I've never met the woman before in my life."

I blinked down at her. "Oh, *shit*," she said, and let her breath out. There were tears on her face now, not just in her voice, and her shoulders were shaking.

I pulled her up, and gathered her in.

Yeah, I know. I can be dim, but this was as bizarre as it gets. I had just enough sense to shut up and wait. When she'd had enough of crying—Bree's not much for tears—she'd tell me what in hell was going on.

"I'm sorry." She was sniffling against my shoulder, her chin just about an inch off where the edge of the tickybox lives, under my left collarbone. "I'm an idiot. I'm a petty mean stupid little dumbass. I'm sorry. I just wish—it's just –"

She stopped. I kissed each cheek, getting a taste of salt on each side. There was no point in pushing; she was going to tell me, I could see that.

"Why does she have to be a guitar player!"

I was so startled that, if I'd been carrying her instead of just letting her lean against me, I'd have dropped her. The question came out like someone had just suctioned a plug of hair out of a blocked drain, and let the water out: full force.

"Bree, what –"

"Why does she have to be hot, and cute?" If I'd worried about her belting up and not telling me, I'd missed all the cues; the words were pouring out and they weren't stopping. The penny had dropped, all right, with a sodding huge thump. "Why does she have to play a goddamned Les Paul? Why does she have to wear leather and fucking look *good* in it?"

"Bree, baby, I don't –"

"Why does she have to be younger than me and why does she have to not give a rat's ass what anyone thinks of her and why does she have to be able to do what you do and be able to talk to

55

you about it and know exactly what you mean when you talk about humbuckers or string gauges or 1969 Deluxes –"

"Gordon *Bennett!*" I'd pulled back, just blinking at her in the darkness. "Bree, for fuck's sake, you're having me on, yeah? You're not jealous of Elaine Wilde. You can't be. That's nuts."

"Nuts?" Her hands had balled into fists, and all of a sudden, the tension in those shoulders was different. For one insane moment, I honestly thought my wife was going to take a swing at me. It was as if we'd gone down Alice in Wonderland's rabbit hole, into a land with caterpillars smoking hookahs on magic mushrooms, or something. "Nuts to be scared because you've got some hot shit cross between Mick Jagger and Tina Turner hooking up with you? Nuts to be freaked out because she can share the joy you get from playing, from writing music, in a way I can't ever share?"

"I didn't say freaked out, did I? I didn't say scared, either." We were eye to eye again, just enough moonlight to see what was happening in her face, and this time, I was keeping my voice even. "I said jealous. And yeah, I said nuts. Crikey, Bree, you'd have to be, to not trust me after all this time. So she plays a Les Paul, so what? You didn't lose it like this when we played with Heart, back on the Book of Days tour. Nancy Wilson didn't flip your switches, and if we're talking about a hot chick who knows her way around a Les Paul, she's the gold standard. So what the hell is the real story here? Because I don't buy that this is about Elaine Wilde being a musician, you know? Not unless you're jealous of that kid, as well."

She said something, a noise, all the way back in her throat—not words at all, not really. And then she reared back, and slapped me.

I just sat there, jaw half-cocked, gawking at her. It wasn't a hard slap, she hadn't put any serious intent behind the arm, but Bree's not a little thing and I'd felt it, you know? Besides, I was gobsmacked. In thirty years together, nothing like this had ever happened before. I didn't have any desire to belt her back, but I didn't know how to cope, either. Just as well, because she was out of bed before I could move or react or do much of anything at all, running out of the bedroom and down the hall, toward our four unused guestrooms. A moment later, I heard a door slam.

I waited a few minutes, letting the tickybox kick in and do its thing. My heart was slamming away like a race car engine, and I wanted to calm down before I went after her.

All four of our guestrooms have perfectly good locks on the inside. So she could have locked herself in for the night, if she really wanted to keep me out. Apparently she wasn't really going for that, because the door to the second bedroom opened with no problem when I pushed at it.

She was curled on top of the covers, eyes wide open, staring off into the darkness. There was something about that pose, knees drawn up as if she were trying not to shiver, that got to me, just twisted my heart up. Shit, I'd put her through enough grief in the early days to have justified a hundred nights when she'd curled up alone, in this same hunched foetal pose. For all I knew, she'd done just that, every night of those times I'd been in London, taking care of the sick woman I hadn't bothered divorcing all those years.

I came across the room, curled up next to her, and pulled her up against me. I wasn't thinking too hard—I just opened my mouth and let the words come. I'm not much for talking, not usually, but I find I do best when I don't put too much thought into it and go with instinct, when I do talk.

"This isn't about Elaine Wilde, is it?" I had no clue what was going to come out, but I had my arms draped over Bree and she wasn't acting as if she had any thoughts about taking another swing at me, or running off screaming, or anything like that. Might as well keep going, even if I had no real idea what I was going to say next. "Not really. It's about the prodigy at the posh

57

school. It's about her having a kid. Why, Bree?"

As soon as I asked it, I could have saved her the trouble of ever slapping me again, and slapped myself. It was so damned obvious, a bloke with half a brain could have seen it.

We've got some big dark patches in our history, me and Bree. There are these gaps, whole chunks of time early on, when I'd been gone and she'd been here and things had happened. One of the darkest patches happened the morning of her eighteenth birthday, when she'd miscarried a child I had no idea she was carrying, and lost the ability to ever carry another one at the same time. She'd never told me about it, not then and not later. I only knew because her mum had let it slip, decades after the whole mess had gone down.

"I'm sorry." It was a bare whisper, no emotion at all, just a statement of fact. "I'm really sorry, John."

I turned her around, and brought us face to face. Her eyes were dry, and her shoulders were relaxed again, but there was something in her face that got to me, in a way I can't properly describe—a blankness, almost an emptiness.

"You've got nothing to be sorry for, Bree. Nothing at all." I'd gone back to stroking her hair. My voice sounded nice and normal and steady. I wasn't feeling normal, or steady. "Not sure what you're apologising for, anyway. Slapping me? Crikey, love, you had reason to do that a million times over, back in the day. Hell, I ought to be thankful you didn't put your shoulder into it. Hard to gig with a broken jaw."

I leaned forward, and kissed her nose. And suddenly she was back, life in her face, that empty thing had moved off and she was Bree again, there with me.

But she wasn't talking, not yet. Right now, this seemed to be on me. It was time to deal with it.

"You don't need to feel threatened, love. Not now, not ever, not by anyone or anything. What did you call Elaine Wilde, a cross between Tina Turner and Mick Jagger? Good call, that was, since I haven't got the faintest desire to roger either of them. Wilde's a good guitar player. So are about three hundred other people you and I both know. Not an issue, Bree."

She still wasn't talking. I took a deep breath.

"And the whole thing about that kid? You still trying to blame yourself for what happened when you were eighteen? You didn't do me out of a damned thing, Bree. You didn't deprive me of anything. I'd have been on the first plane if I'd known, and you know that. That's the only thing I regret, that I didn't know. But under the circs, I don't know how much use I'd have been to you when it happened. Just—I won't have you thinking you failed at something, at being a mother or anything else. You never failed me, not at anything, not ever. All right?"

She'd begun to shake, long jerky tremors. In a bizarre way, they reminded of the way she ripples in the middle of something a lot more fun than this had to be for her. I didn't know if anything I'd said had got through the sense of failure, or made it easier. I hoped it had.

"John?"

I lifted one eyebrow. She held her hands out to me, and they were steady.

"It's getting chilly in here. Can we go back to our own bed?"

"Yeah, sounds like a plan."

I swung my legs to the floor, and pulled her to her feet. We stood there a moment, holding hands in the dark. Downstairs, one of the cats was talking, a sort of plaintive complaining noise.

"Bree—I meant what I said, every word of it. We all right, now?"

"Always on." She headed for the door, pulling me after. "Always burning. Let's get some sleep—we're back on the bus tomorrow night."

When it comes to getting things organised, Carla does it better than most anyone on the planet. She knows how to get it done, and she knows how to delegate. She keeps most of the gen she needs in some scary section of her brain that no one else on earth has. She's got this talent, an inner filing system thing: whatever she needs to know about anything is right there, waiting to be retrieved. The one time I could remember her slipping up on anything at all, Bree'd wondered if they were snowboarding in Hell.

So I really haven't got much to measure a cock-up on her part against. I'm not even sure if booking all three rooms at Another Line Studios in Los Angeles was her idea, or whether Andy came up with it. All I know is, whoever was responsible for putting the Geezers in Studio A, WildeChild in B, and Bergen Sandoval in C, with the Bunker Brothers running back and forth between Elaine Wilde and Bergen Sandoval, should get some kind of award for bad planning. It was a disaster looking for someone to happen to, and of course it happened.

We finished the tour with WildeChild opening. They turned out to be quite a good fit with the Geezers—Elaine had come out and jammed with us at the Vegas show, adding her guitar and a solid strong female vocal to our cover of the Stones' "Live With Me." I'd been worried about Bree's reaction, but there hadn't been any. Bree was cool with it, and I thought I knew why: for whatever reason, Elaine Wilde hadn't brought her kid on the road with her. I didn't know whether the late night meltdown had let Bree sort things out in her head, or whether not having to stare at the kid 24/7 made it possible for her to deal with Elaine, and I wasn't nearly dim enough to ask.

Whatever the story was, Bree was at least able to sit in the same band room as our opening act without her shoulders knotting. All things considered, I was ready to call that a win; close up and personal, Elaine Wilde turned out to be fearless, upfront, opinionated as hell, and ready to talk about anything except her daughter.

Considering Bree's initial reaction, I was pretty sure Elaine wasn't ever going to be number one with a bullet on my wife's list. She had the kind of vibe that would normally have Bree changing seats to get away from her. So far as I could tell, they never managed to get particularly matey—Bree doesn't usually make friends easily anyway. But if they weren't friends, there was no drama that I could see, either.

We finished up at the Gibson Amphitheatre, in Universal City. That was a big show, much bigger than the rest of the tour venues—the Amphitheatre seats six thousand people, and we'd been playing mostly house capacities maxing out at about a third of that. But the gig was brilliant. We sold the place out, and Elaine came out and jammed with us on the two encores. She slipped offstage just before we did our usual band of brothers thing, arms round each other, bowing, goodnight, all that. Then the house-lights went up, and the Fluorescent Records West Coast New Artists tour was officially in the bag.

While the place emptied out, I stretched out on the band room sofa, trying for a few minutes rest before I had to go out and be sociable with the local press. Right that moment, I was dizzy as the blonde in a bad joke. I hadn't told Bree, but the last three days of the tour, the MS had ramped up. It wasn't huge, not a full-scale relapse or exacerbation, but it was enough to make me worry that it was going to take my legs out from under me. The best way to prevent that happening is to not be a macho idiot: over the years, I've learned the hard way that when the body says *right, close your eyes and sit for the next hour* or whatever, I do it. Bree'd gone out front to hunt up some cold juice for herself. I just hoped I could get the room to stop doing the fandango around me before she got back...

"JP? Are you okay?" It was Carla's voice. "Sorry—can I bother you for a second?"

I opened my eyes, slow and careful. Good; the room had

stopped spinning. I focussed on Carla, who was standing there, with a bloke in tow. I swung my legs to the ground.

"I'm fine." I had a mean little jab behind one eye, the beginnings of a tension headache. *Shit.* It was going to be nice, getting into an actual hotel suite at the Beverly Wilshire tonight, curling up with my wife for a good long kip, with invisible staff to handle laundry, and room service, and a long hot luxurious shower in the morning and not having to share any of that with anyone but Bree.

Meanwhile, though, the bloke was holding out a hand, and beaming at me. I shook his hand, and managed a smile of my own. I knew who he was straight off—the mass of shiny grey hair was unique.

"Derek Silver, yeah? Silver Streak? You haven't changed at all. Good to see you."

He shook my hand, a nice easy grip. I hadn't been blowing smoke; he really did look the same as he had when the Geezers had done three nights at one of his clubs in West Hollywood. Not a type to change much, even with age: I'd told Bree once that Silver looked like a mop handle with a head of fantastic hair, and the description still held.

"JP Kinkaid! Holy shit, man, it's been years! When did you guys play the Latitude? Six years ago now, was it? Carla tells me I'm getting all of you at ALS. No worries—Fluorescent has the entire place booked to itself, all three rooms. Damn, I love working with labels who aren't afraid to blow a little cash on the talent. And I actually get the Bunker Brothers producing two different CDs in my place at the same time! How cool is that?"

I opened my mouth, and shut it again. I was going to have to find my stash of TyCos; the headache was really making itself felt. Actually, it seemed to be causing audio hallucinations, because there was no way he could have just said what I thought I'd heard him say.

62

"Cal and Stu aren't producing the Geezers CD." I was watching Carla out of the corner of my eye. She was looking nervous, for some reason, and Andy, who'd just come in with her, was avoiding us altogether. I wasn't sure if I was projecting or whatever, but he didn't seem to want to get too close. "Tony Mancuso and I are doing that together. The Bunker Brothers sound is much too polished for what I'm after for our CD—ours is live, and I want it good and gritty. Not sure where you got the idea –"

"Oh, no, sorry. I didn't mean that. I knew you were handling your own mixdown." He was rocking back and forth, heel to toe. Something about the movement was familiar, and it got on my last nerve. "I meant about them doing Bergen Sandoval's new one, and WildeChild's. Tony Mancuso is going to be one busy guy, between the Geezers CD and the keyboard overdubs for Bergen."

"What!"

I jerked my head, winced, and looked over Carla's shoulder. Elaine Wilde had come up behind them.

There was no doubt she'd heard at least the last part of the conversation. Her face had gone hard and cold, and her mouth—she has one of those full-lipped mobile mouths that never seem to hold still—was clamped so thin and tight, you could barely see it. Her shoulders just then could have given Bree at her tensest a run for her money. What I couldn't suss out was what had done all that.

Whatever it was, it didn't look as if Streak was aware of it. He turned around, got one look at her, and lit up like a Christmas tree.

"Hey, Elaine Wilde! I've wanted to meet you forever—well, at least since *The Wrong Side of Last Night* came out. For a first album, that was a monster. Great, great stuff. That's one of the few albums I wish I could have had a hand in producing."

"Thanks." She wasn't relaxing, not at all. "Did I just hear you say something about Bergen Sandoval?"

*Shit.*

She'd said Bergen's name as if she was putting a hex on someone. There was hate in those two words, hate she either couldn't or wasn't bothering to suppress or hide.

The only thing that ought to have surprised me was that I was surprised. Considering the way he was, both about other musicians and women, she'd probably got hit with a double dose of the patented Sandoval bullshit. I had no clue whether the hate was personal or professional or both. Whatever it was, it was ugly, and it was right there on the surface.

"Yes, the Bunker Brothers are producing Bergen Sandoval's new one, as soon as he gets in off the road. That's tomorrow morning. His ALS sessions start tomorrow afternoon. Stu Corrigan will be handling Bergen's, and Cal Wilson will be working with you." There was trouble in Carla's face. She doesn't like being blindsided, and it was pretty clear that this was something she hadn't been aware of. "You were told about this, Elaine. It's not news. Andy sent the email out a week ago, as part of the Fluorescent updates. If you had a problem with it, why didn't you let us know?"

"I didn't read it." Elaine turned toward Carla. She was so stiff, she looked as if she might break off at the neck, like a lily on a weak stem. "It was addressed to a blind list. I assume that if something affects me personally, the label's rep is going to have the courtesy to let me know directly. As far as I'm concerned, a blind list is spam. I don't read spam."

Elaine's tone was very much the star talking to the subordinate. I doubt that was deliberate—she was too focussed on being freaked about Bergen. But Carla had stiffened up. I saw Tony turn and stare at us. Andy was edging for the door.

"Then I suggest you start paying attention to what comes to you in email from my office, Elaine, no matter who else you think is getting it too." Carla's voice was black ice. "If I, or my assistant, send something out to the Fluorescent family, it's because we want them to know about something that affects them all. That holds whether it's you, or the Geezers, or anyone else. Every member of Blacklight knows that much."

"Hurray for Blacklight." Elaine was barely listening. She was fixed on Streak, who'd taken a step backward. I didn't blame him; if there was a row coming up, I wanted to be well out of it. Where in hell had Bree got off to, anyway...? "I want to make something clear right here and now: I will have nothing, nothing at all, to do with Bergen Sandoval. Nada, zip, zilch, squat, fucking diddly. Are we clear about that? You'd better keep that asshole out of my way, out of my sight, and out of my sessions."

I hadn't thought it was possible for her to get any more hate into her voice, but I was wrong. She silenced the entire band room with the force of it. Even Carla stayed quiet; there was too much raw venom in Elaine Wilde's voice to respond to it.

Elaine turned on her heel, and went. Everyone in the room moved back to let her through. I noticed that the three other members of her band were careful not to make eye contact. Whatever the deal was between her and Bergen, it was old news to the WildeChild crew.

She nearly collided with Bree in the doorway. I heard the murmur of polite noise, as my wife manoeuvred around Elaine and into the band room, balancing a glass of juice. My headache had hit the "brain being split apart by marlin spikes" stage of MS-induced migraine, and my jaw had numbed up, but I could see that Bree was looking wiped out; she was a bad colour, as well. Not good. If we were both sickening for something, it was going to completely fuck with the recording schedule. And of course, Bree took one look at me and knew what was up.

"Carla, we need a car and a driver, please, back to the hotel. John needs to get to bed." She was quiet a moment, and through the roaring headache, I heard her sigh. "So do I. I'm not feeling too good myself. John, want to lean on me...?"

65

We headed for the door. Whatever was up with Elaine Wilde, whatever had happened between her and Bergen Sandoval, no matter how curious Bree was about why Elaine had gone storming out, it was going to have to wait.

# Chapter Five

As an old session player, I've got a soft spot for a decent studio. For a sideman, the studio is a sort of natural home, and I'm actually a bit of a connoisseur when it comes to places to record. I've got a nice little basement setup at home in San Francisco, and the Bombardiers have their full studio over on Freelon Street. Luke Hedley's mobile, at his farm in Kent, is as tricked out as it gets; I always do good work there. We've done five or six Blacklight CDs at Luke's, including *Book of Days*. A good working environment makes brilliant music that much easier.

Another Line, Silver Streak's place in West Hollywood, was tucked into a side street off North Doheny, and I took a shine to it the minute I walked in the door. It had the feel of some of the old-time studios, places like Wally Heider and His Masters

Wheels back in San Francisco in the seventies and eighties. The equipment was state of the art.

Tony'd apparently got the same vibe off it that I'd got. "Wow. Yo, Streak? This place is kickass. Reminds me of the good old days, back when Kilgren was doing the Plant in Sausalito. Are all the studios the same size?"

"This one and room two are. Three is bigger—we've got WildeChild in there." I must have raised an eyebrow, because he hurried into explanation. "Carla said the Bunker Brothers laid out what they wanted. It makes sense, JP. The Geezers are doing mixdown and Bergen's doing mostly overdubs and mixdowns. But Elaine's got the whole band in there, full session."

"Yeah, I wasn't arguing. Works for me."

"Cool." We'd left the door open, and people were arriving. "Whoa, sounds like Bergen's here. I'll catch you later. Let me know if you need anything, okay…?"

"Yeah, I will. Not to worry—we're just waiting for our sound engineer to get here."

I got up and stretched. A good long sleep-in, with the *Do Not Disturb* sign hung over the door and instructions left with the desk staff at the Beverly Wilshire to hold our calls, had taken some of the edge off the relapse, but even doping myself all the way out of it hadn't kicked it completely. Everything ached, not badly, just enough to remind me to take breaks and not stay on my feet for too long without a rest. At least the trigeminal neuralgia had done its thing and gone. Not being able to communicate what I wanted in a mixing session would have been an issue. And of course, if this was flu kicking in…

Tony was watching me. "Hey, JP, you okay? And how's Bree doing? I thought she looked pretty funky last night. She coming down with something?"

"I'm all right, pretty much. Bree picked up a bug, though. Something's definitely making the rounds—Andy left early last night, Kris was saying his tum was dodgy, and I noticed Hank was laying off the sweets for a change. He looked a bit green. Just a typical tour bug. Bree's staying in bed today."

"Damn, I'm sorry. Katia was talking about shopping—hey, Damon. Good, we're here. We ready to roll? Someone want to get the door? What are we starting with…?"

We got quite a lot of work done that morning. As I say, it was a good soundproof work environment, once the door was closed. I had no clue how things were going in the two rooms next door; we were deep into balancing the sound I wanted and picking the best performances of ten songs from the tour. All my attention was on that.

The Bunker Brothers had flown in late the previous night. The way I understood it from Andy, Bergen's sessions had been scheduled for today and tomorrow, with the Bunkers splitting up the initial work between them: one would handle Bergen, the other would be working with Elaine's crew.

It was going to be a nice reunion. I hadn't seen Cal or Stu since my heart attack, back in London. I'd been pretty rocky, adjusting to the tickybox and getting over a massive infection that had nearly taken me out. Plus, Bree hadn't wanted visitors; I hadn't known it then, but she'd been unwelcoming, to say the least. Mac told me later they'd all been terrified to even offer help, because they were certain Bree would kill anyone who even looked like interfering with her taking care of me.

Damon had brought what he called his goodie bag with him, a roadcase full of hard drives. Carla had told him to give her a wish list, what he wanted for both the tour and the sessions. I doubt he thought he'd get much of it, but Fluorescent hadn't stinted, and he'd got it all. Carla had signed off on the small Digidesign re-cording console Damon had been lusting after, and the complete Pro Tools suite to make it work. We'd recorded every gig to hard drives, and here they were, ready to be uploaded to the ALS console. Damon was thoroughly blissed; he couldn't wait to get his hands into the new gear, and see what he could make it all do.

We got straight down to it. I remembered four standout performances, and playback proved my memory was working: they were killer versions. Between those and "Americaland," we had half the CD ready for mixdown. Tony said he wanted to use the Vegas version of "Sweet Virginia," so we played it back, and he'd nailed it; something about that one had a kind of movement to it that even the best of the other versions didn't have. Three hours in the mixing room, half the CD mapped out and ready for Damon to hit with Pro Tools. Not a bad morning's work.

After awhile, I remembered to get up and walk, and sort out what I wanted to do about lunch. I'd promised Bree I wouldn't get too involved to remember to take care of myself; I've got a habit of doing that, but with the MS, it just won't fly. Damon and Tony told me what they wanted, I left them discussing whether Curt's vocal on "Americaland" needed any special processing, and went off to see about food.

It turned out there were a half-dozen places on Melrose the studio used on a regular basis, and they all deliver. LA is cool that way—even the best restaurants will send someone over with your nosh. I'd just given the list to the ALS receptionist when the door to reception opened, and Stu Corrigan and Cal Wilson popped out. I headed over, ready for a few minutes of catching up, but the looks on their faces stopped me short.

Cal generally hasn't got much temperament, but he looked to be right at the edge of exasperation. Stu, Irish to his boot heels and with the temper to match, looked as if he wanted to throttle someone. *Shit.* Not good.

"Hey, JP." Cal was keeping his voice fairly even, but his face was tight. He's a very bony bloke, and when he gets tense, every muscle telegraphs it. "You finished already, or just taking a break?"

70

"Lunch break. I promised Bree I'd remember to eat. We're not finished, but we've got the list sorted out, and five of the songs ready for mixdown. Tony and Damon Gelb are back in One, handling it."

I looked from Cal to Stu, and back again. I'd been wondering whether they were going back and forth between Two and Three, or if they'd really split the duties to start. If they'd done that, going by the looks on both their faces, WildeChild and Bergen were both being tricky. "Crikey, you both look like someone stole your pony. I'm guessing yours aren't going as well as the Geezer session?"

When Stu Corrigan loses his temper—really loses it—he frightens roadies and small children. He's actually quite a nice bloke, but he's got no patience for bullshit, and he's got a very short fuse. Blacklight deals with that by making damned sure he doesn't have to cope; Ian Hendry, our manager, is brilliant at handling things, and what he doesn't do, Carla keeps in line. But this wasn't Blacklight, and on this one, the Bunker Brothers had no buffers.

"That bloody little shit is going to drive me out of my fucking mind!" Stu was seriously narked, and not in the mood to give a damn whether the receptionist heard him or not. If he was calling Bergen "little," he was about to flip his shit entirely; Bergen was easily six inches taller than he is. "I swore last time I worked with Bergen Sandoval that I'd never do it again, on anything at all. Cal, you want to tell me again why I shouldn't go back in there and peel long bleeding strips off his wrinkled conceited arse?"

"Because he's a Fluorescent recording artist." Cal sounded grim. The receptionist was keeping her face properly bored and blank, but she was listening, all right. Her head was tilted ever so slightly towards us. "Because his backup singer is Luke's daughter. Because you don't want to spend the next ten years in a California jail. You want to swap acts, Stu, just say the word and I'm there. I'm not finding Elaine Wilde any cup of tea to work with, either."

This wasn't the kind of conversation I want to have with anyone outside the family circle listening in. The last thing we needed was for any of this fetch up as meat for some snotty gossip columnist with breast enhancements. I jerked my head toward the receptionist.

"Look, mates, let's go sit, all right? Or walk, I don't mind which one. Standing in one place too long gets the legs shaking, and I promised Bree I'd be sensible. Besides, I'm just coming off a relapse, and I'm damned if I want to push it."

We headed off into the studio's kitchen. It served as the break room, and it was as well set up as the rest of Streak's place. That was no surprise—after all, when you've been in the top tier of club owners in a club town like LA for as long as Streak, you know how often a working session is going to end in crazed demands for carbs at one in the morning. There was a posh espresso maker and a machine dispensing salty snacks and protein bars. There was a basket of fresh fruit on the main table, as well, plus the usual soda and water, and cold beer.

I got myself settled, rotating both feet at the ankles, trying not to wince. I hadn't been joking, about standing in one place not being the best idea.

I looked at my mates, trying to gauge just what was going on in the other two studios. The Bunker Brothers had been producing other acts for thirty years. The first time, they'd done it as a favour for a friend's kid and ended up with a Eurovision contest winner. They knew every possible stupid stunt an act could pull, and they were prepared, every time.

But here they were, both of them ready to rip. Stu wanting to choke Bergen might not be a shock, but if nice even-tempered Cal was already up to the eyeballs with Elaine Wilde, things were going badly. "Okay," I told them. "Talk to me. What in hell's going on back there?"

Cal opened his mouth, but Stu got there first, and Cal just sat back and let him blow. We were alone in the break room, with no one to overhear the graphic varieties of gruesome death that Stu'd been contemplating for as fussy, egocentric, pigheaded and uncooperative a musician as he'd ever had to work with.

"...he's always been a flaming arsehole." Stu was winding down, finally, but he was red-faced, and I could see one vein thumping away, just above his left eye. It was a good thing his wife Cynthia wasn't there to see it; she's not as fierce as Bree is about my health, but she'd have been heading for Bergen with intent to damage, at the very least. "I know that, I didn't agree to do this eyes blind. But he's got worse. He's got much worse. You know what's really getting to me? He's using Suzanne as a shield, a way of getting what he wants. 'Do this my way or I'll take it out on Luke's kid. Look, watch, I can make her cry.' Fucking sod."

Cal and I shot each other a look. Stu emptied half of his beer at one gulp, and wiped his mouth with the back of his hand. "And she's letting him get away with it. I say no, something won't work the way he wants it and here's why not, and he gives me that fucking *look* of his. You know that look? He knows he's going to pull shit, I know it, and he starts in on Suzanne, picking at her, little barbs, little daggers. She's making kicked-puppy eyes and trying not to cry and trying to please him. She turns to me and there goes any way of actually producing this bullshit CD of his without making her bleed for it. I'm not getting anything done in there, it's giving me ulcers, and you know what, I almost want to ring Luke and tell him to get on the plane and come get his stepdaughter, never mind the fucking launch party. Bergen Sandoval is messing that girl up in ways I don't even want to think about."

Cal and I were dead silent. There was nothing to say—I'd no-

73

ticed it back in Seattle, what he was talking about. Stu was silent, as well; he'd said his piece. But the hand holding the rest of his beer was shaking.

"Cal?" Might as well get it all out on the table. "What's Elaine doing in there? Tell me it isn't as bad as what Stu's having to put up with."

Cal took a hit of his fruit juice—he went dry back around 1980. "Nowhere near, but no fun, either. Every step is two steps backwards first. It's not the band—they're fine. It's all Elaine Wilde. She wants to argue or discuss or dissect every damned thing I suggest. Part of it seems to be that she's never worked with an actual producer before, and part of it's just the way she is. But I think there's more going on. I'm getting...I don't know the word I want. Resentment, maybe? As if the label had forced some rockstar producer on her and she's narked about having to have me in there? Whatever it is, it's slowing things down to treacle in February mode. I feel like I'm negotiating a hostage crisis, not producing a record."

"Bloody hell." I looked from Stu, looking as tight as I'd ever seen him, back to Cal. "Okay. I get it. Not to be selfish, but I've got one big concern of my own. I'm damned if I want Bergen Sandoval to fuck with my piano player. Bergen suckered him into adding keyboard to the new CD—you know how Bergen does it."

"Yeah, I do." Stu sounded bitter. "What did he do, dredge up some obscure thing Tony played on that no one else has heard for forty years? Hand on the arm, flattery, bullshit and snake oil, not quite deferential, oh, how smashing, been wanting to meet you for years? God, he's a fucking reptile."

"He's all that and worse, but this is about Tony." I locked eyes with Stu. "Tony's set to do Bergen's keyboard overdubs the day after tomorrow. How likely is it that that's going to happen on time?"

74

The grin he gave me was sour enough to curdle milk. "You serious, JP? Likely? With Bergen being a pissy shit and the way he's slowing things down to a crawl? Right up there with me elbowing David Beckham aside and kicking the winning goal at the next FA Cup final. Don't hold your breath. Yeah, I know the Fluorescent party's set for the same night, and yeah, I know we're supposed to wrapping it up with Bergen's CD by then. WildeChild doesn't have the tight schedule, do they, Cal? But the Geezers CD is supposed to be done by Friday night, and Bergen's as well. And Bergen's deadline? Not going to happen."

I was about to answer that, but I didn't get the chance. The door to the break room banged open, so hard that it smacked into the wall. Suzanne stumbled in. She was blubbering like a baby. There was someone behind her, out in the corridor.

"He told me he doesn't want me anymore." She wasn't even trying to control her voice. "He said—he told me I don't sing, I moo like a mad cow. He gave me the sack. I hate him, I hate him, he's a right bastard!"

Cal caught her as she swayed, and held on. I wasn't thinking much beyond the desire to go find Bergen and kick him until my shoe wore out, but Stu looked murderous. He'd told me once that his Cockney mum used to tell people to mind out, young Stu's got his Irish up. His wife Cynthia, as celestially calm an English rose as you'll find, uses the phrase to this day. The look on his face as he glanced over Suzanne's shoulder out into the shadowy hallway was enough to clue me in what she'd meant.

The bloke in the hallway stepped forward, into the break room. Next to me, Stu muttered something and let his breath out. It wasn't Bergen Sandoval, it was a total stranger with his arms full, and he was stammering.

"Whoa. Sorry, but the receptionist sent me back here. I'm from Waiters on Wheels. Did someone order lunch...?"

My memory of the next two days is on the fuzzy side. There was so much going on, so many damned personal dramas, so much bloody pointless interpersonal noise, that nearly the only clear memories I've got from the ALS sessions are of burying myself in the Geezer mixdowns, and worrying about just how sick Bree was. Almost everything else that happened, between Bergen dumping Suzanne and us getting dressed at our hotel two nights later for the Fluorescent kick-off party at Silver Streak's hot new club, is distorted and unreliable. It's like trying to do a jigsaw puzzle with some of the pieces gone missing.

I'd left Stu and Cal consoling Suzanne, and headed back into studio one with our lunch. Yeah, I know, that sounds like me being passive-aggressive, but it wasn't; I have an iffy history with Suzanne, and an even iffier history with Bergen. Right then, my brain wanted to focus on what I was actually there to make happen: putting together the Fog City Geezers' first official release, and making damned sure it was the best work we could do.

I apparently got back into our studio just in time to miss Bergen coming out of his. He must have sussed that he'd gone too far this time, because at the end of the day, Stu had them back at work, and he'd actually got a better handle on the whole mess. Cal told me later that Stu'd sent Suzanne off to wash her face and told her to get back inside and get her headphones on when she was done. He was the producer and he decided who was playing and who wasn't, and there wasn't going to be any arguing about it, do what you're told. Apparently, once she'd trotted off, he'd let Bergen have it with both barrels. I was sorry I'd missed being a fly on the wall for that little dressing-down. Cal had left Stu to it, and gone back in to yet another round of what he called "but-why bullshit" from Elaine.

One thing I'm not likely to forget was Carla's visit. She came by the studios with a member of her staff, a young intern, and popped her head in just as we were finishing up the seventh song on the CD's set list, and getting ready to take a break.

I was cranky. We'd been working our arses off, and I was tired. Damon was being an absolute rock, but Tony was getting edgy, champing at the bit to get next door and record his keyboard sections for the great Bergen Sandoval. It was taking his attention from where it needed to be, which was on the Geezers, and I'd had to call him on it. I hadn't done it in front of Damon— Tony's his boss, and that would have been way the hell out of line, you know? But Tony doesn't like being called on his shit any more than anyone else does, and there was definitely some tension in there.

"Oi, Carla. What brings you down to the work zone?" I took a look at the kid behind her, and raised an eyebrow. "Sorry, didn't see you back there. Andy sick with the tour bug, then? He left the gig in a hurry the other night."

"Hi, JP. This is Marjorie, my new PA. Marjorie, this is JP Kinkaid—hi Tony, hi Damon. Guys, this is Marjorie Kamby. She'll be making the rounds with me for awhile. And yes, Andy's still out sick with the flu. How's Bree? She was looking pretty rocky herself, the other night."

I held out a hand. The girl looked about seventeen, and she was cute as a kitten. You could actually see her trying to look nonchalant: *wow, okay, be cool, don't blow it, don't go fangirl in front of Carla.* "Bree's in the same boat as Andy, I'm afraid. She seems to be on the mend, though. Hello, Marjorie, nice to meet you. Carla, you been down the hall yet?"

She rolled her eyes, very slight, but it was there. "Nope—on our way there now. JP, can I get a minute...?"

We stepped out into the corridor. It was just the three of us, the red light was on over both the other doors, but Carla kept her voice down anyway, and she got right down to it.

"I took Stu and Cal to dinner last night. They were pretty up-front about the way things were going. Stu tells me that Bergen

Sandoval's being the pig of the western world. He says Bergen's using Suzanne McElroy as a weapon to jerk everyone around, that she's a sobbing wreck. Plus, Cal is out of patience with Elaine Wilde—he says she's being a diva and a platinum-plated pain in the ass, and she won't stop bitching about how she doesn't see why she shouldn't produce the CD herself."

I blew out air. She wasn't wrong. That pretty much summed it up, so far as I could tell.

Carla shot a look over my shoulder, down the hall. "Talk to me, JP, please? I found out this morning that Mac and Luke are on their way—they're coming for the Fluorescent party tomorrow night. Mac and Domitra are probably clearing customs at LAX right about now, and Luke and Karen get in later tonight. To tell you the truth, from the way this sounds, Luke's going to walk in, take one look at his stepdaughter, and redecorate the Plus Minus with Bergen's intestines. It may turn into a family affair, because Solange and Curt are already here—they checked into the W this morning. Solange told me this is supposed to be their honeymoon. They didn't get one, did they?"

"No, they didn't. She was starting school, he was heading out on tour with Mad At Our Dads." I took a deep breath. There was something unsettling about talking about this stuff in front of the new kid. "Okay. I'm not much use, I'm afraid. I've stayed out of it. But from what I've seen, yeah, there are issues. No clue where they are with their stuff, but I've been up to my arse in mine, and it's nearly done. We've got two songs left to do—I'm saving 'Americaland' for last. But I was there for one of Suzanne's meltdowns, where Bergen sacked her. He likes having an audience when he pulls rubbish like this."

Carla stayed quiet, but there was trouble in her face. I met her eye. "Luke's not going to be happy, Carla. She's not just singing with Bergen, you know? It's—complicated."

"So I gathered." She sounded grim. "Jesus, what a toad. What

78

is she, fifty years younger than him or something? I know, I know, she's a grownup and she can say no, but still. Anyway. Cal seems to be handling Elaine, but this mess with Bergen is going to suck on every possible level. I just hope Andy's well enough to make the party tomorrow night. He knows the club scene like nobody's business, especially the way Streak works. He can keep an eye on things for me. That whole insider knowledge thing is what I pay him for. This is really not a good time for him to have the Official Road Crud."

"That's right, he used to work for Streak. I'd forgotten. Club manager, was he?"

"Money man. He handled all Streak's books. Streak himself told me he wouldn't have half the clout he has now, if Andy hadn't been there to keep it together for him." She looked at her watch. "I should let you get back to work—I'm going to check on our problem children, and see for myself. Send Bree my best, and tell her I hope she's well enough for the launch party tomorrow night."

I headed back in. Tony didn't ask me what was up with Carla; there was still that tension in the air. Right. Time to chill that out. We didn't need any more aggro right now.

"Checking on progress, and introducing her new assistant. Tony, I'll tell you what, let's push it a bit harder, all right? If we can get 'Americaland' sorted out and ready for prime time this afternoon, you'll be able to do a few hours for Bergen tomorrow..."

Of course, that backfired on me; Tony was so chuffed, we ended up staying until nearly midnight. The upside was, we got the rest of the CD done. I took the phone out into the corridor and rang Bree at the hotel midway through the evening, to let her know what was happening, and to check on her.

"I'm feeling much better—I slept all afternoon. And you're really almost done?" She really did sound better, and that lightened me up. "That's great! Does that mean Tony gets to go play with the DOM tomorrow?"

I blinked at the phone. "The DOM?"

"Dirty Old Man. Because he is. But Katia was telling me on the phone that Tony was being really cranky because —"

She stopped, and swore under her breath. I could practically hear her kicking herself.

"Not to worry, love." I managed a grin, even though there was no one there to see it. "I'd have to be completely dim to miss it, locked in the studio with him the past few days. I've already had to play the heavy with him on this one. But if we get this done tonight, he can go spend all day tomorrow being made to feel like the bottom of Bergen's shoe if he has a fancy to —"

I stopped. Doors were opening, down the corridor, and people were coming out of studios One and Two.

"I have to go." I'd just got a look at who'd slipped out of their sessions. "I'll ring you later."

I clicked the phone off in a hurry, and stayed where I was. Elaine saw me; she must have, since I was right in her line of vision. So far as I could tell, she didn't care who else was out there. She was too busy facing down Bergen Sandoval. He was standing with his back to me, arms folded, rocking back and forth, heel to toe.

"Oh look, it's the luscious Elaine." The tone of his voice was about as bored as it could get, with a good hard edge of contempt, or maybe just disinterest. "I'd heard you were about. Hard to believe you're still gigging. Does anyone show up? Who wants to see some fifty-year-old rocker chick? All sags and bags. Though I must say, you're not looking nearly as decrepit as I'd have expected. Hitting the botox, are we? Got a good source of it down here?"

"I wouldn't know. I don't live in LA. And it's not 'we', you miserable manipulative thieving sack of shit. That would be 'you', grandpa, and to tell you the truth, from the looks of it, it's going to take more than Botox to make you look human."

80

I backed up a step. If he'd sounded bored, she was concentrated hatred. The last time I'd heard that level of malice and viciousness in someone's voice, it had been coming out of a convicted murderer.

I started edging back towards Studio One. Above Bergen's head, the red light suddenly flashed green, and began blinking. Suzanne opened the door and stood there, her mouth half-open, with Stu at her shoulder.

Bergen ignored them. "Now now, dear, we don't want to give away our inner bitchiness, do we? It's as hideous as you are, all naked."

The boredom was transmuting, becoming something else entirely. I'd heard it before, coming from Bergen; this was the tone he used when he not only knew he'd pressed buttons, but was storing the info up for future use. He was digging it. "At least, not in front of the crumpet or my annoying arrogant little producer. And certainly not in front of JP. He gets shocked easily, and you know, he actually likes women. As people, I mean. Don't you, JP? Are we shocking you?"

"The only thing shocks me is that they let you out without a fucking keeper."

Oh, bloody hell. I'd let him startle that out of me; I honestly hadn't realised he'd known I was there. My own tone of voice was pretty nasty. *Right. Come on, Johnny, don't let him pull you into his shit.* "Sorry, Elaine. I toured with this mingy berk when I was still young enough to not know better and I haven't missed him. Not trying to listen in on your business. Unless you want witnesses? Happy to oblige."

She grinned. It was a genuine grin, pure pleasure, and it was nasty enough to make me wish I'd gone out the front door and halfway to Topanga Canyon to ring Bree. Anything that would have had me anywhere but here would have been all right with me.

81

"Actually, JP, I'm glad you're here. I don't really need a witness, but hey, the old bat likes showing off. So here you go, folks. Witness this, motherfucker!"

Suzanne said something, swallowing her words, smothering a yelp. Elaine's upper body tensed. Her right shoulder jerked, and she decked him.

I'm not joking, and neither was she. It wasn't a slap, or a backhand. She nailed him with what looked like a professional boxer's right cross. She was small, but the punch she threw, I'm surprised she didn't coldcock him entirely; she got almost completely off her feet to get to his jaw, but she got there, and got there hard. It took him completely off-balance and knocked him back and down on his arse, practically at my feet.

"Nice punch."

I jerked my head around so hard and fast, it hurt. Domitra Calley, Mac Sharpe's personal bodyguard, was standing in the doorway that led from the front desk to the studios. She was in full protect stance, and Mac was right behind her, looking amused and being protected. Out in the reception area, I could see a pile of luggage.

"Oi, Johnny." Mac's eyebrows were as high as they could go. He jerked his head over Dom's shoulder. "Oh, hello, Bergen. I take it you're Elaine Wilde? A pleasure to meet you. My bodyguard—oh, this is Domitra—speaks for both of us: that was a gorgeous punch, absolutely brilliant. Most of Bergen's mates would be queuing up to pay you to do that again. They've been wanting to punch him in the face for years. Haven't they, Bergen?"

"Sod off." Bergen was on his feet. He was swaying again, but this time the motion wasn't smooth—he was as rocky on his pins as I'd used to get in my drinking days. He had one hand to his jaw, and I could already see the beginnings of a spectacular bruise. Good thing he wasn't a singer, because opening his mouth too wide for a few days was going to be no fun at all. I just wished she'd decked him days ago, and saved us all some grief.

"I'm not done with you," he told Elaine. His voice was thick, whether with hate or because his face was already swelling up, I don't know. They'd locked stares, like a couple of dogs circling a fireplug, and Suzanne was saying something, just noise, but Bergen was ignoring her. "Not anywhere near done with you. This'll cost you, you cow. Trust me for it."

He stumbled down the corridor, not back into Studio 2, but into the washroom. I could hear water running.

Mac stepped around Dom. There was an odd look on his face.

"Interesting rest breaks you people take." He'd got hold of Elaine's hand. He wasn't letting go, and she wasn't showing any signs of trying to get it back from him. "And how very nice to be in Los Angeles again."

# Chapter Six

I don't generally do nightclubs. There's not enough time left in the world to do the stuff I actually want to do, and hanging out in loud rooms with music I can't control, and no security to keep the rest of the world out when I want breathing room, doesn't qualify as a good time for me. Besides, I'm not a party animal, really. I never have been.

Given a choice, I'd probably have passed on the Fluorescent launch party at Streak's club. All things considered, though, blowing it off wasn't an option.

"Wow. John, this whole velvet rope thing is—bizarre."

I looked up at Bree. We'd been moving up the queue, as people were checked in by a couple of Streak's enormous muscle blokes, but the whole thing was moving too slowly for my taste. I'd actually heard myself muttering under my breath: *come on, mates, hurry it along, will you please?* The MS doesn't do well with me standing about for more than a minute or two, and Bree was still shaky on her pins.

Flu, the kind we usually refer to as the Tour Crud or Tour Bug, is a common reality when you're touring by bus. You get run down when you're touring, even at the best of times, and your immune system lets you know all about it. You're more susceptible. And once it's there, there's no escaping it: if one person's got it, there's a good chance everyone else on the bus is going to wind up curled under blankets in their bunks, coughing and miserable, dragging themselves onstage every night because that's how the job works.

This particular flavour of Tour Crud had been selective, but really nasty; fewer people than usual had got nailed, but everyone who'd got it had got it quite badly. Bree'd been in bed for two days, alternately sleeping and coughing, and she wasn't the only one who'd got hit with it. Hank had been toughing it out, Kris and Billy were both still on the vitamin C and fluids regimen, and WildeChilde's drummer, Jake Somavilla, was still looking pale and shaky round the edges. Bree'd gone down the hardest, probably because her immune system was already trashed from exhaustion and diabetes. Of anyone on the Fluorescent tour, my wife had the least resistance to this stuff.

"Bizarre how?"

That was an idle question, really. I knew what she meant. There was a shitload of people, herded behind barricades. Streak had done a superb job of playing both sides of the PR coin for this party, or maybe it had been Carla. On the one hand, the event had been seeded in all the appropriate LA and Hollywood media outlets. Names had been dropped, coy *a little bird told me to expect Blacklight—that's right, the whole band!—for tonight's Fluorescent Records new release launch party at Derek Silver's hot new spot, the Plus Minus in NoHo!* hints to make sure people turned out in droves. Of course, once they got there, they never got close enough to do anything but gawk and shriek and wave and yell out names from the other side of wooden barricades, because security, private and official, was out in force. Streak knows his stuff, and he knows his town. The only person who knows how to do this better is Carla.

I'd made eye contact with a couple of fans, smiling and nodding, nice and vague, lifting one hand in the occasional wave. It seemed safe enough; after all, there was plenty of muscle between me and them, and even if any of them did happen to be nutters, they weren't getting close. Bree wasn't making eye contact or anything else, but then, she's still trying to shed her desire to be invisible in my world. She spent a lot of years hiding from the public eye, and you don't just shrug that off. Losing a habit that longstanding takes work, and time.

She glanced at me, making sure not to catch anyone else's eye. "The whole thing's bizarre. I understand why the press is out, it's their job. But why would people want to take an entire evening out of their lives to stand crammed in with a bunch of total strangers, watching someone walk into a club, if they weren't being paid to watch? People are freaky."

"No argument from me, love." I craned my neck, looking behind me. "No sign of Tony and Katia, not yet. Katia go buy a new rig for this do?"

"I don't know. I didn't see her today—I went and sat in the hotel sauna, trying to get the aches out while you were over at ALS. Wasn't Tony still in the studio, doing his thing for the DOM?" She shifted from foot to foot; even though she was wearing lower heels than usual, she was pretty shaky. "I wish they'd hurry the hell up. I swear, any minute someone's going to throw me a dead fish and clap when I catch it in my mouth. I feel like a performing seal."

That surprised a crack of laughter out of me, and a few heads whipsawed our way. "Yeah, well, you don't look like one. But you're right, celebrity's pretty strange. I never really stopped to think about it, honestly. Maybe this is as close as they get to doing something they think is exciting."

She shrugged, a tiny movement of her shoulders, and I realised how tense she was. I got hold of her hand, and laced fingers with her. "Of course, they may just be gawking at you," I told her. "The way you look tonight, it wouldn't surprise me. That's a killer dress. Hell, if I were one of those blokes, I wouldn't mind standing out there watching you, myself."

"Wonderful tonight?" She shot me a smile. She doesn't do that often—Bree's not a smiling type—but when she does, there's usually something attached, a deeper meaning. This one was only there a moment, but it was intimate and warm. I hadn't been blowing smoke, either; she really did look brilliant.

The queue moved up a couple of feet, and we waited. I had no idea if anyone had got here early enough to get in without this stop and start rubbish, but a sudden increase in the noise levels and the repeated yells of a familiar name made it obvious that Mac, at least, had only just arrived.

I turned around and waved. Mac was there, all right, along with Dom, and the entire Hedley contingent: Luke and his wife Karen, Curt and Solange. Suzanne was with them, as well, and that was a surprise; I'd have expected her to come with Bergen, but it looked as if she'd opted for family solidarity. They looked to have all come together in the stretch limo that was just pulling away from the curb.

Luke saw me and began manoeuvring his way up the queue. I didn't recognise most of the people behind me—local label suits, press, whatever, I didn't really care. I was watching Luke, and so was Bree. His face was completely unrevealing, but I know Luke. If his face isn't showing anything, it's because there's something he doesn't want to show.

"Oi, JP. Hey, Bree, great dress."

He gave her a fast kiss on the cheek. As he pulled back, Bree's face registered awareness, and I saw what she'd seen. The muscles around his mouth were as tight as a painted mask.

Luke's not a temperamental bloke. It takes a lot to get him to the head space he looked to be in now. The last time I'd seen it, he'd been at breaking point over what he'd felt was his own failure to integrate Suzanne into the Hedley family when he'd married her mum. Considering what was going on now with Bergen Sandoval, I'd have laid good money on this being about Suzanne, as well.

"Look, can we talk?" You couldn't have heard him more than a foot away, and his voice was as tight as his face. "Maybe after the party?"

I gave him a straight look. "You got it, mate. The sooner the better. Maybe we can find a quiet corner inside, assuming we ever actually get inside."

The queue was moving again, still crawling along. I craned sideways, outside the velvet rope, and saw Streak. Right; time to get the hell out of it, and get indoors. "Hang on, Luke, will you? I'm sick and tired of standing about like a lawn flamingo. We've been posing like a cage full of monkeys for a good half hour. Oi! Streak! Can we move this along, please?"

If I thought the crowds had risked whiplash looking at us, they had nothing on Streak. His head jerked so fast, his hair moved before he did. "JP? Holy shit, what are you guys doing in standing in line...?!"

After that, we got in quickly. Flashbulbs popped, the crowd *oohed* and *aahed*; Luke made his way back through the queue, and as Bree and I were waved inside, I saw him whispering to Karen. There was no sign of Bergen outdoors, and no sign of any of the WildeChild contingent either.

As I've said, I don't do clubs, so I've got no clue whether the Plus Minus is typical or different, or if there even is such a thing as a typical club. I see places like that as potential venues anyway, so my take is always going to be through that particular set of criteria: capacity, acoustics, front of house access. It was a decently sized room, rated for three hundred or so people, but of course, it wasn't set up for live bands. The purpose was right there in the layout: they'd designed the place for dollybirds in skimpy club gear to crush together on the dance floor, jiggling all their bits and pieces, while the blokes picked what they wanted from the raised sidelines.

Never mind the DJ, and the tinned turntable: this was a meat market, basically. Seriously fucking creepy, you know? I remembered what I'd heard about the clubs during our Book of Days tour, the stuff we'd got from Solange and Suzanne. Just one more reason for me to avoid rubbish like this.

"Hey, JP, glad you got here! Sorry about how long it took to get in. I can't believe no one told you to ignore the line and come right in." Streak was eyeing Bree. "Aren't you—Bree, isn't it? Did I remember your name right? We met a few years ago, when you came down with JP. You haven't changed at all."

She murmured something conventional, I didn't get what. We were being spared the DJ tonight; the PA was running, and I heard a familiar crunchy guitar riff, Les Paul with a touch of reverb, and Elaine Wilde's voice coming out of the overheads. *You can look, but you better not touch...*

"Nice! That's a damned good mix. Not too shabby."

This time her voice was right behind us, and we both turned. She nodded at us, but her attention was on the tune pouring out of the P.A.; she'd apparently shelved that whole "I don't need a producer" attitude she'd been driving Cal bonkers with. She'd opted for full-on rock star mode tonight, head to toe leather. I wondered if she was going to press Bree's buttons, but Bree didn't seem to care, or even notice, really.

"It's fantastic!" Streak was clearly pleased. "And isn't this cool?

Carla gave us mix copies of all three CDs, and I ripped a few mix combos of my own. You guys are going to be the entertainment at your own party—oh, hi, Andy. Hey, are you okay? You don't look so hot."

Streak was right. Even under the house lights, Andy looked pale and queasy. He was a skinny kid anyway, but right then, he looked to have more bone than skin, and he was shaking.

"I'm okay—getting better." He sounded the way he looked, which was as if he'd be better off in hospital than shmoozing at a launch party. His voice was a thread. "The damned tour crud really nailed me. There was no way I was missing this, though. Is that Patrick Ormand over there? What's he doing here? I haven't seen him since the whole 707 mess."

"He's here because I told him to come down." Carla had materialised behind Bree. Carla's usually in pure LA casual work mode, but she'd tarted up for the party, and both Bree and Elaine were giving her dress—very short and very red—a good going over. "Patrick works for Blacklight and the entire band is here tonight, with their families. When that happens, he drops what he's doing—that's what we pay him a retainer for. He's running security tonight. Andy, maybe you ought to think about heading out early. You look like death warmed over."

"So Patrick's the reason we stood outdoors for twenty minutes?" I made a mental note, to let Patrick know that keeping your employers queued up because you want to peer up body cavities on guests you don't recognise wasn't on, but that wasn't really fair—he probably hadn't known we were out there. "Look, there's Stu and Cyn. Anyone seen Bergen? Is he blowing off his own release party? Because if he's here, I'd like to know which part of the building to avoid."

"He's already here." Elaine's face tightened. "I'm sure he did his little 'look at me, I'm the Queen of England' bullshit routine for the crowd. But I saw him when I came in. Hey!"

Mac, with Dom in tow, had popped up behind Elaine, and slipped an arm around her waist. It was just a quick squeeze; he let go immediately. "How's his jaw? Or did he run screaming before you could check? Evening, Johnny—good God, would you look at all these gorgeous women? I'm going to need elastic bands in my neck to keep up. Elaine, don't even think of telling me I can look but I'd better not touch. I have every intention of touching, quite a lot."

At his shoulder, Dom snorted. Elaine didn't say anything. Instead, she shot him a look, and my eyebrows went up. It was an intimate look, amused and aware, a joke shared between two people who were sharing rather more than jokes. It reminded me of the look Bree gives me, when we're doing that marital mind-reading thing. I heard Bree make a noise, a tiny exhale, quickly smothered. I wondered just what was going on here; when in hell had they had time to hit that level? Crikey, he and Elaine had only met two days ago...

"John?" Bree was watching me. My legs had gone shaky, a hot little tremor of myokimia running up the right side. I felt it move up my side, and down my arm. *Shit.* "Can someone find us a place to sit, please? No, John, don't argue with me!"

"Not arguing." I wasn't about to say it, but she looked rather unsteady herself. "Streak, can we get a couple of chairs, please...?"

As it turned out, there was a cushy loveseat inside the velvet rope VIP area, and Patrick Ormand was providing the muscle. He lifted the rope and waved us in, and exchanged a quiet word with Streak. A few minutes later, one of Streak's staff came over with a tray: a selection of nosh, ice water for me, and a glass of bubbly for Bree, with fresh raspberries in it. Bree took a mouthful, and her eyes widened.

"Holy shit, is this Cristal? Okay, I'm officially no longer jonesing to go back to the hotel and climb into bed with some OJ and aspirin." She took another sip, and sighed. "At least, not for the moment. But would you mind if we didn't stay too late? I'm really not up for an all-nighter."

"Sounds like a plan, love. Look, there's Cal and Barb. Still haven't seen Tony and Katia. Is this enough nosh to do you, or do you need a proper meal...?"

Later on, when I was asked what I remembered about the party itself, I didn't have much to offer. The loveseat was comfy, with decent back support, and Bree—who might have been up and dancing on any other night—stayed there with me. I kept one ear tuned to the PA, idly listening: they'd put a three-CD mix together, so that our cover of "Sweet Virginia" was followed by WildeChild's "You Don't Forget," and that was followed by a very cool piece off Bergen's CD. I didn't know the name of it, but I realised I was grinning; Stu'd mixed Suzanne's vocal up nice and hot, so hot that you heard as much of it as you did of the instrumentation. I wondered if he'd done it just to nark Bergen. That track was a revelation: Suzanne had a brilliant voice, a genuine touch of 1940s chanteuse, smoke and depth in there. I hadn't realised how good she was.

The club was very warm, too warm really, and I found myself nodding off. Resting the eyes, loud music, and my old lady up against me, that all pushed me toward wanting to sleep. It had been a long week, worrying about Bree, worrying about Tony, worrying about what sort of shite Bergen Sandoval was about to dish out, worrying about the CD mix, just worrying. There's few things out there can knacker me the way worry does.

I let myself drift. Every once in a while, I'd force my eyes open and pretend to be awake. It was very weird, but with the club's lighting doing the strobe thing, everything I remember seeing that night had a freeze-frame effect, little individual movie moments. I saw Mac and Elaine out on the dance floor with a spotlight on them, and most of the club probably taking notes for the morning edition. I saw Curt and Solange at a table just outside the ropes, sitting with Luke and Karen. They were having what looked to be a serious conversation, and none of them looked happy; I kept getting them in the strobe, little flashes of tense faces. I saw Tony, finally, talking to Carla in a corner. There was no sign of Katia.

I let my lids back down. I hadn't got nearly enough sleep recently, and really, the place was much too warm...

"JP? JP!"

I opened my eyes. This time, I was awake. Andy Valdon's voice wasn't leaving room to do anything except pay attention.

"What –" I jerked myself upright. The party was going full swing; the mix CD was still cycling, and some genius had turned on the mirror ball, enough to cause total disorientation. Where Bree had been, warm up against me, there was empty space. "What is it? What time is it? What in hell's wrong?"

"In the bathroom." Andy's eyes were so stretched, they looked about to pop out of their sockets. He'd been pale before, but right now, he looked like fireplace ash, broken up by the movement of the mirror ball. "The men's room. Problem. *Big* problem. Can you help?"

Patrick lifted the rope for us. I jerked my head at him, and he leaned over.

"Andy says something's wrong in the men's toilet. Not sure what the deal is, he didn't tell me, but we may need you and we may need Streak. Keep an eye on the door, yeah? Keep people out—if I need you, I'll signal, all right?"

He nodded. I turned and caught up with Andy, pushing open the door to the men's loo.

Bergen Sandoval was there, bent over the fancy sink. There was the remnant of a line of white powder on the chichi black granite. For a moment I thought he was having a sick-up, but I was wrong about that: he wasn't retching, he was babbling, a

93

steady stream of words that weren't really steady at all, because something had gone all the way wrong with his breathing.

"...did this no can't breathe pay you pay you back even it up with you no who did this you did this..."

He sagged at the knees, arching his back, going down backwards. I saw his hands scrabble against the granite and then the hands were doing what the rest of him was doing, flailing and spasming out of control. His jaw was clenched hard, but he was trying to talk, to say something, or at least I thought he was. What was coming out wasn't language anymore, it was more of a thin whistling scream.

I don't remember moving, but I must have done, because I was suddenly looking up at Andy from the floor, where I'd got the lower half of my own body under Bergen's, trying to keep his head from slamming into the floor tiles as he spasmed.

"Get an ambulance." Bergen was thrashing, his muscles locked and rock-hard, his feet kicking everywhere, connecting with Andy's shin. Andy didn't seem to notice; he looked to be in shock. "Find Streak. And get Patrick in here, fast. Tell him keep people out of here. Andy, mate, will you bleedin' move!"

"An ambulance. Okay." Andy was nodding like a bobblehead, but the rest of him wasn't moving. Definitely in shock, and shock wasn't what I needed just then. I watched him trying to shake himself back to reality—the effort was visible. "You want me to call an ambulance? He's still alive?"

The body I was hanging onto wasn't spasming anymore. The words that weren't words had become a tortured raspy attempt at breath that wasn't coming, through the locked jaw that was still blue at the edge from Elaine's punch. The muscles slackened, all together, and the room was suddenly full of the smell of ammonia as his bowels, bladder, all those things, loosened and went.

I sat there on the floor, Bergen Sandoval's head cradled in my lap and his bodily fluids pooling under the backs of my own legs.

Outside, in the Plus Minus, the PA was pumping out "America-land." I'd been right. That was one hell of a version we'd recorded.

I looked up, into Andy's face. Bergen was limp; I thought I saw one finger twitch, but I probably imagined that. "Get Patrick in here. And tell Streak to ring for an ambulance, but I doubt they'll be of any use. He's gone."

The hour that followed that last tortured little jerk Bergen gave before he died in my lap might just be the most surreal sixty or so minutes I've ever spent. It was straight out of what you might expect from eating a particular variety of mushroom, or maybe dissolving a tab of very bad acid under your tongue: looking back later, I couldn't be sure what was real and what wasn't.

I remember that I tried shifting. Sitting in a puddle of bodily fluids let go by a dying man is about as miserable as it gets—you feel you're being embalmed. But Bergen was already a dead weight in my lap, and somehow, I didn't know why, I had a very strong feeling that I shouldn't be moving him.

I also remember being seriously pissed off at Andy. He's not the sort I'd have expected to turn to stone in an emergency, but that's just what he did. Or, rather, maybe it was custard, not stone; hard to tell. Whichever it was, it wasn't helpful.

I sat on the floor, not able to move or anything else, and instead of heading out and getting Patrick and Streak, Andy doubled over the sink and started in with a noisy case of the dry heaves. Maybe the heaves weren't all that dry, because he turned on the water and I heard him rinsing out his mouth behind me, so he must have actually managed to bring something up.

"Andy...?" I was right at the edge of frantic. I'm damned if I know why, either. No one was going to be able to help Bergen Sandoval, not now, not ever. He was dead, limp, gone like a mystery train heading down the track and nothing was bringing him back, so why I was pushing Andy to move it, I had no clue. "Would you get the fuck out there and get me some help!"

"Sorry." He muttered it; his voice was way down. "I'll get someone. I'm really sorry."

He slipped round me, finally, and headed for the door. As he got there, he stopped and looked back at me, and down. I thought about just saying *ah, sod it*, putting Bergen into his own drips and stinks, and getting the others myself, but the look on Andy's face stopped me. He wasn't looking at me, he was looking at Bergen, and the look on his face—Christ. Stunned doesn't cover it. He looked like a schoolboy who'd been bashed in the skull with a rock for no reason at all, and who simply couldn't wrap his head around it. He raised his eyes, finally, and looked at me.

"He's really dead? You're sure?"

I took a good long breath. The room smelled terrible and the tickybox was beginning to feel as if it had some major work to do. "Yeah. Yeah, he's gone. Go get Streak. And get Patrick in here first—oh shit! Bad time, mate, use the ladies!"

I'd forgotten that this wasn't a VIP bathroom, it was just the men's toilet, and it serviced the entire club. The toilet might be as luxe as the rest of the club, but anyone could walk in and right then, with the door swinging in and missing smacking Bergen's shoes by about two inches, someone apparently had. When I saw who it was, I let my breath out.

"JP? What's happening in here?"

"Patrick, thank Christ! Serious shit, mate. We've got a dead bloke: Bergen Sandoval. Looks like an OD, or maybe a bad batch of whatever he was using for blow. We need people kept the hell away from here, and we need an ambulance. Andy, for fuck's sake, get out there and get Streak, will you? Third time I've asked—don't make me ask you again."

Andy went. Patrick's eyes had gone narrow, and sharp. *Right*, I thought. *We're off.*

96

Patrick used to be a homicide cop, and a damned good one. It hadn't taken me long to suss out why he'd been so good at his gig: he's a born predator. He likes the smell of blood. You can see it in his face, when he gets that smell, when it hits him that there's something wounded upwind from him, something he can get his teeth into and bring down, something he thinks needs to be brought down. He's got a brilliant poker face, as well, but I learned early on how to read him. His eyes are the colour of ice on a New York sidewalk in January, and just about the same temperature. They give him away every time. Just then, he'd got a good strong whiff of something nasty, something he thought need catching, and he was digging the hell out of it.

"What happened, JP?" He had the door closed, and his back against it. "Was he dead when you got here?"

"No. Still alive, but not for long; he went about two minutes after Andy got me in here, maybe less."

"Alive?" There it was, the copper's voice. *Something bleeding further on up the road...* "Did he say anything?"

"Yeah, alive. Hunched over the sink. He was seriously fucked up, though—babbling, shaking. He was having some sort of spasms, or seizures or something. His muscles kept locking up. He'd been doing blow, or that's what it looked like. Don't think I ever saw anyone react to blow like that, though."

"How could you tell?" He'd forgotten I wasn't a suspect, but hell, he'd apparently forgotten he wasn't a cop anymore, either. Right then, I didn't actually mind; I was far too freaked to want to cope with it. "Just the way he was acting?"

I opened my mouth to answer, and just then, the body in my lap moved.

For a moment, I thought the tickybox was going to explode: *oh shit I was wrong he's not dead.* Then I realised it wasn't Bergen shaking, it was me: reaction, MS, something. I didn't know and didn't care, not beyond the sudden need to get the hell out from

97

under the dead weight in my lap and get up on my feet.

"There's a line of blow on the sink," I told Patrick. "Pretty obvious. Look, I have to get up. I've got the shakes and it's not as if he's going anywhere, all right?"

I slid the body in my lap off me as carefully as I could and got upright, leaning against the wall for support. The backs of my legs were ice cold and clammy, where Bergen's leavings had soaked through my trousers. The smell was making me want to gag, but I managed to keep it down where it belonged. Puking my guts out wouldn't have helped matters.

I was sick at my stomach, shaky as hell, and not coping. All I really wanted at that point was for the ambulance to come. I wanted to find Bree and slip out the back, get to the hotel and toss the damned trousers in the hotel rubbish. After I did that, I was going to take a long hot shower, with as much soap as I could lay my hands on. I couldn't remember ever feeling as dirty as I did just then.

"Did you say there was the remnant of a line of cocaine up here?"

I twisted round. Patrick was staring at the granite sink, and his voice had gone from medium cop, all the way into seriously scary cop.

"Yeah," I told him. "I saw it when I came in. Just a thin line, but it's there. You can't miss it, especially against that black granite or marble or whatever it is. It's on the left side of the washbasin."

"There's nothing here."

He moved aside, and gave me a clear look. Chilly eyes, chilly voice, the lot. My brain had gone where his already was, and considering the implications, I got the reason for the chill. "The counter's wet. Has anyone been in here besides the three of us, since you came in and saw that stuff on the sink?"

*Shit.*

I locked eyes with him, and shook my head. I wasn't being dramatic, I just didn't have anything to say. Didn't need saying, anyway; both of us knew that things weren't looking too good for Andy just then.

"JP? Oh shit, oh shit, what the hell happened in here!"

My nerves must have been even more shredded than I knew, because I actually jumped, bumping into the edge of the sink. Streak had somehow managed to get himself into the loo without either of us noticing. He stopped just inside, staring at Bergen on the floor, and then from Patrick to me. He looked as if losing his dinner was next up on his agenda: sick and horrified. He was shaking as badly as I was.

"Oh shit. Oh, holy shit. I thought Andy was drunk or fucked up or something. I called an ambulance anyway, but I didn't believe him. This is nuts, it's crazy! What happened? It's true, Bergen's really dead? What the hell is that godawful stink? Smells like a sewer in here."

"Yeah, he's dead." I reached behind me, trying to pull the fabric of my trousers away from my skin. "Looks like he got some bad blow. Look, I need someone to get me some clean trousers if I'm going to be stuck here, because the backs of my legs are soaked with Bergen's piss and whatnot and I really can't cope much longer. I want my wife. Patrick, can you find Bree, please? Ask her to ring the hotel and have someone send something over. And let her know what's happening—she'll be flipping her shit, not knowing where I am."

"She knows. She's right outside. Andy told her." Streak was a really bad colour. "Look, I'm sorry, I can't—I have to –"

He almost made it to the sink, but Patrick turned him around. "If you have to throw up, use one of the toilets. This may be a crime scene, and the sink's off limits until LAPD homicide and the forensics team get here and tell us otherwise."

It was right there in his voice, and there was no arguing with

99

it. I'd heard that tone before. So far as I knew, there was only one crime that could get that look in Patrick's eye and that voice in place. He was still a homicide cop at bottom, was Patrick Ormand.

I hadn't thought Streak could have got any paler than he was, but I was wrong about that. He'd gone pretty much the colour of his own hair. He had one hand over his mouth, obviously wanting to ask Patrick what he thought he was on about. Problem was, if he opened his mouth right then, it wasn't words that were likely to come out, and he knew it.

"Crime scene?" I was locked up with Patrick, eye to eye. I wanted to hear him say it: *not talking about drugs, are you, mate?* "What crime are we talking about here, Patrick? Why would you want forensics for a line of bad blow?"

"You said he was having seizures." Dirty icy eyes, barely blinking. "Babbling, talking, muscles locked up, spasms. Is that what you saw? I'm not a cop and you're not under oath, but unless I'm mistaken, you will be at some point soon, JP, so you need to get it right. This is vital. He was having trouble with his muscles, you said. You were holding on to him. And he seemed to be locking up?"

"Yeah." The words were out before I even considered. "Hard as rock. It felt like hanging on to a block of stone, but he was still jerking about, or trying to. And...?"

"I can't say for certain. I'm not an ME. But what you described, his colour and that muscular reaction, sounds as if he ingested a toxin, not just a narcotic."

"What?" Streak had managed to get it out, but he was right at the edge. You couldn't miss it. "Toxin? Poison, you mean? What toxin?"

Patrick had turned to stare at Bergen, stiffening on the bathroom floor. Pumping away on the club's PA on the other side of the doors, I could hear "Sweet Virginia," with its driving beat and the hardcore punch of Tony's piano. "I told you, I'm not a doctor or an ME. But if had to put money it, I'd say he snorted a lethal dose of strychnine."

# Chapter Seven

Right around that point in the evening, something inside clicked into overdrive. There I was, standing in a posh toilet with a dead bassist and a puking club owner and a former homicide cop who looked as if he might seriously be regretting his career change, and out of nowhere, I lost it, just flipped my shit completely. I heard my own voice, yelling for my wife.

Of course, she came; with me yelling for her, it would have taken a lot more than Patrick Ormand to keep her out. I could kick myself for that one, because she really didn't need to see what had gone down in there. She didn't need to see me soaked in shit and she definitely didn't need to see Bergen dead on the floor, blue and stiff, one more visual of sudden death to have nightmares about. The problem is, I wasn't thinking; I just suddenly needed her there, and yelled her name, good and loud. I didn't even know I was going to do it. I probably wasn't nearly as calm as I thought I was, you know?

Bree came through the door so hard and so fast, she knocked Patrick over. I'm not exaggerating. He wasn't expecting it and the side of the door clipped his shoulder and sent him staggering halfway across the room, and he had to reach for the nearest surface just to stay upright. He made a noise and grabbed at his shoulder with his free hand, but Bree didn't even glance his way. She didn't glance down at Bergen, either, not that I could see. She was focused on me. Her face was pinched, and she reached out for me.

"John? What happened in here? Are you okay?"

"Yeah, I'm good, now you're here. Stay back a bit though, will you? Look, I've got to get out of these trousers or I'm going to go off my nut. I'm soaked in Bergen's drips. We're not going anywhere for awhile—we've got a situation here, or at least Patrick thinks we do. Can you ring the hotel, please? Tell them to send someone over with a clean pair of trousers for me. If I don't get a change soon, I'm not going to be able to cope."

She swallowed hard, but she nodded. She tends to stay calm in a crisis, does Bree, and I'm damned glad of it; that's what kept me alive a few years back, when I had a heart attack after a Blacklight show in Boston. "I'll tell Carla right now. She probably knows the hotel number and the concierge's name."

She glanced down at Bergen, finally. So did I.

It was a peculiar moment. There was a world outside the bathroom, a little self-contained party universe called the Plus Minus. People were out there, doing their thing. They were drinking pricey booze, the dollybirds were ripping up the dance floor, music was playing. Elaine Wilde was probably out there doing the bump with Mac, and Luke was probably laying down the law to Suzanne on the subject of Bergen Sandoval, not knowing Bergen had just stopped being that particular flavour of problem. A few hundred guests who had no clue what had happened in here were out there, rocking it and doing their thing.

Here inside, we had the bloke who owned the place, puking his guts out. We had a bloke who'd pissed off half the known universe, dead and emptied out, stiffening up on the floor. We had a bloke who'd spent most of his adult life hunting down murderers and drug dealers. There was nothing between us and them but the bathroom door, but we could have been on another planet. That's how remote it felt.

"Bree...?"

"I'll tell Carla. I'll do it now. I'll be right back." With one hand on the door, she turned round and looked at Patrick. "Has anyone called LAPD? Paramedics? Is there any chance –"

"No chance at all."

Patrick sounded kind. Bree seems to have that effect on him. She's one of the few people I can say that about; he's not the warmest human being on the planet. "I'm sorry, Bree. This is a dead man. Homicide should be on their way already. They'll be here any minute."

She understood. He'd put it as kindly as he was able, but there was that word, *homicide*, and that said it all. I saw it sink in, good and hard, saw her shoulders bunch as she inhaled.

"Okay." Her voice was quiet. "Thank you, Patrick. I need to go find Carla—she'll know who to call at the hotel. We'll get some clean clothes over here."

She turned and was gone, out through the thin divider between the bathroom and the rest of the universe. Right that moment, the one thing in the world I wanted to do was follow her out, call us a taxi, and go home, but of course that wasn't happening. I was stuck right where I was.

Streak followed her out about a minute later. From the sounds coming out of the stall, he'd been busy bringing up everything he'd eaten for the past couple of days. He'd had to flush the loo three times, but he finally made it up to his feet and came out, looking a bit less green.

"Jesus. Sorry." He wiped his mouth with the back of one hand. "I'd better get out there. The cops'll be here any minute and there are about forty media heads out there in the club. This is going to suck like a Hoover on hyperspeed."

Patrick nodded, and Streak went. The moment the door clicked shut behind him, Patrick turned back to me, hard and fast.

"Listen to me, JP." His voice was as driving and urgent as one of Billy Dumont's drumbeats. "We've got maybe five minutes, and that's a big maybe, so let's get this together. You said there was a line of coke on the sink, what looked like coke, when you came in. Are you ready to stand up in court and put your hand on a bible and swear that's the truth? Because there was nothing but a puddle up there when I came in, and I'm probably going to have to stand up in court and put my hand on a bible and do some swearing of my own. This could be Andy Valdon's life we're talking about."

"The bible thing is irrelevant. I don't do bibles." We'd locked up stares. "But yeah, I'd swear. And yeah, I know where you're going with this. I'm not completely dim. You're saying no one else could have got rid of the evidence on the sink, and okay, right, he has to have done that. But him killing Bergen, no. Andy came and got me. If he'd given Bergen Sandoval poison, if he murdered him, why would he have even left the loo? Can you come up with one reason? All he'd have to have done was stayed in here until Bergen was dead. He could have washed away anything and taken his time. Him coming out and getting me, asking for help while Bergen was still alive and talking? Sorry, mate. It won't fly."

There was something going on out in the club, sounds and commotion that hadn't been happening before, first a kind of silence and then a difference in the quality of the noise. Patrick's head jerked, listening.

"We're out of time. I'm not postulating Andy Valdon as a murderer, I just want to make damned sure that you understand all the ramifications. Because I can't tell them there was anything there for Andy to have washed away—all I can give them is a negative, what wasn't there. My testimony's basically useless, because technically, it's hearsay. This is going to be on you and you need to know what happens either way—shit! Yes, hello officers. He's in here…"

That bathroom was a decent size, about six stalls and with plenty of elbow room, but it filled to capacity in a hurry. There were cops and forensics experts and a raft of other people, responsible for who knows what. I managed to pick the copper in charge out from the lot of them. I didn't much fancy it—the bloke was another Patrick, just larger and older and meaner-looking—but I was damned if I wanted my wife to have to fight her way through half a mile of red tape, or yellow crime scene tape, either. I lifted an eyebrow at Patrick, and we stepped off to one side for a quiet word.

"Patrick, look. Not sure about these LA coppers, but we need to make sure they let Bree in without a fuss. They try keeping her out, she's capable of taking them apart strip by strip. I'm damned if I want to have to bail her out of the local lockup. Can you fix it? Talk to the bloke in charge? You speak the language, and I don't."

"Homicide patois?" He grinned at me, a genuine grin, but it was gone a moment later. "Sure. I want a word with the Lieutenant anyway. Just give me a minute."

I swear, homicide cops, even the retired ones, must have a secret thumb signal, or something. Patrick headed over, said something to the bloke in question, and the next thing I knew, they were both back over next to me and the LA lieutenant was offering me a hand to shake.

106

"Mr. Kinkaid? I'm Lieutenant Cunningham. I understand your wife will be coming back with clean clothes for you? No problem, I'll give our people the word to send her right in."

As I've said before, I notice handshakes. I'm a guitar player, and I'm always cautious of big blokes who squeeze your hand as if they're trying to show you how macho they are. Cunningham didn't go there; he had a nice light grip, despite being a good forty pounds overweight. A point in his favour, definitely. Either that, or he didn't fancy having to shake my hand.

"Thanks," I told him. "My wife's very protective, and she'd raise five kinds of hell if she thought you were trying to keep her away from me. Glad to know there's no problem there."

"None at all. In fact, I was going to set up a change of clothes for you, if hadn't already arranged it. We're going to have to impound the clothes you're wearing, as evidence."

He smiled at me, and with that smile, the entire facade cracked and fell away. Another damned predator, another damned barracuda getting the taste of fresh meat in the water, another pair of nostrils flaring at the smell of blood on the wind. Shit, if I'd thought Patrick's eyes were cold, I hadn't known what cold was. Cunningham's eyes looked as if they'd been made from the same stuff as that two-way glass in cop shops. He could see out, but you couldn't see in...

"Yeah, that's fine." I heard my own voice, nice and even. "It's not as if I was ever planning on wearing them again, you know? There's just something about being soaked in a dead bloke's piss and shite that puts you off wearing what you've got on. I'm curious, though. Why do you want them? I mean, you've got Bergen there to run tests on. He's all yours now, right? I mean, any tests you need to run, you can run on Bergen."

He smiled at me again, and I felt my insides tighten up and batten down. Just over his shoulder, I caught a tiny movement: Patrick, shaking his head. The movement was so small, I nearly missed it. But it was a clear signal: *be careful with this one.*

"Just a precaution, Mr. Kinkaid. Nothing you need to worry about right now. Excuse me, please."

He turned away, saying something to the medical examiner; they seemed to be having a good look at the bruise on Bergen's jaw. It was off-putting, me knowing just by looking at this grizzled old geezer and seeing what he was doing with Bergen that he was the ME. I'm not sure how I've found myself around enough dead people to have developed an eye for who does what around a corpse, but I could do without it.

I stayed in that bathroom for the next hour. Bree came back with a change of clothes after not too long, and they let her in without a blink. Just as well, because she had a militant look in her eye, which meant she was ready to give the first official of any flavour who tried giving us any trouble more grief than anyone in their right mind would want to cope with. Someone was wheeling a collapsible gurney, and a body bag, into the bathroom; behind him, I caught sight of Streak, waving his arms at someone on the other side of the bathroom door. He looked like a scarecrow having a fit out there.

"Here." Bree handed me a plastic sack with the hotel's name on it. If she cared about being the only woman in the gents toilet, she wasn't showing it. "I brought a full change, socks and shoes too."

"Ta, love. Just as well, because the lieutenant, here, says he wants all the gear I've got on. Half a mo, yeah? Let me get changed."

I ended up stripping down to my skin in one of the stalls. Bree told Cunningham and Patrick, in no uncertain terms, that I was going to need something to wash off with, and a towel or two to pat myself dry with. She still had that look in her eye, and neither man argued with her. I was given a handful of soggy paper towels, and someone found a pile of dishcloths in the club's bar for me to dry myself with.

I don't think I've ever been happier in my life to be rid of what I was wearing, though I'll admit I was cross about the shoes. They were brand new, and pricey as hell, and I didn't much fancy handing them over to the cops to run tests on, but sod it, that's life, yeah? I got into clean gear, and Patrick told me from outside to leave everything where it was, the Forensics people had special bags they'd put everything in.

"Right." I came out and went straight for Bree. "Thank you, love. If I had to keep that lot on much longer, I'd have gone off my head. Oh, Lieutenant, this is my wife, Bree Kinkaid. Bree, this is Lieutenant Cunningham."

"Nice to meet you." She wasn't even glancing his way; she was busy staring at me. "John, you're shaking. What in hell time is it? Where are your meds?"

She was right. I hadn't even noticed, but both hands were twitchy and my legs were wobbling. *Shit.* Bree turned and fixed Cunningham with a good hard stare.

"Lieutenant, my husband has multiple sclerosis. Stress makes it worse. And standing in one place is worst of all." She turned to Patrick. "We need a chair. *Now*, please."

There'd been plenty of low-voiced conversation going on in there, but her tone of voice—*you'll do exactly what I tell you and don't even think about arguing*—shut it down fast. I saw the look Cunningham shot Bree, and stepped forward, between them. I didn't even realise I was doing it, but I must have done, because there I was, locking stares with Cunningham and giving him a nice fake smile.

"Yeah, Patrick, would you get me a chair, please? Bree's right, the damned MS is kicking in. I'm your star witness—that's right, isn't it, Lieutenant? So you're not done with me yet? If I'm going to be useful, I'll need to keep the disease under control, and I won't do it by standing about. Patrick? Something to sit on, mate, if we're hanging about in here?"

The club outside had gone very quiet; two of the ME's staff had done what they do, and had zipped Bergen into a body bag. Next to me, Bree was as tense as an overwound guitar string. Cunningham and I were still locked up.

"Sorry about that." The scary tight little smile wasn't doing much to cover up that he wanted to smack my wife, or worse. I couldn't sort him out; he had to know by now that I'd been yanked in after the fact, to help. I wasn't a suspect for anything, so what in hell was all this attitude? "I didn't know about the MS. I don't really know much about it, period. But there's no need for Mr. Ormand to find you a chair—we're not going to be staying in here. You're right about one thing: I've got a few questions for you."

He turned and said something to one of the uniforms. I saw the bloke nod at him, and saw the look he shot me, before he smoothed out his face and his eyes turned the other way. He recognised me, that copper did. It was like some sick echo of the conversation I'd had with Bree before we ever got in, about celebrity. Cops aren't immune to it, either, even in Hollywood. I lifted one eyebrow at Cunningham, and damned if he didn't lift one right back at me.

"I'm told the club has been mostly cleared," he told me. "It looks like it's going to be a long night. Let's go find a couple of chairs outside, and get started."

Back at the beginning of Blacklight's 2005 North American tour, a sleaze named Perry Dillon got himself killed backstage at Madison Square Garden, and everything had pointed straight at Bree. Patrick had been the homicide cop in charge, and I'd honed some macho skills I hadn't even known I possessed into a fine art, dealing with him.

One thing I'd got damned good at was sussing out how coppers think, why the questions they ask get asked. It's not just the obvious reasons, either; I'm talking about the stuff behind, and beneath. The first thing I'd learned about homicide cops is that they're tricky buggers. They never ask you a straight question— they've always got an agenda. The second thing is that, if you can, you jump in first and get control of the situation. It's all about home court advantage.

Cunningham ended up having us sit just where Bree and I had spent most of the evening before Andy came and got me. It made sense, really, since it was behind the velvet rope. Not that a skinny strip of velvet-covered hemp is much use keeping people off, but I don't think the physical barrier was what Cunningham wanted, he was after the psychological barrier. It worked, too. Of course, the two uniforms stationed to keep people back until Cunningham felt like letting them in didn't hurt.

Bree came with me. She still had that *if you fuck with me I'll rip you into Happy Meal-sized chunks, and if you fuck with my old man you'll be begging me to rip faster and put you out of your misery* look in her eye, pure piss and vinegar. I was quite ready to back her up, if Cunningham was dim enough to try telling her to back off. I doubted he would, though. I got the impression there was nothing dim about the bloke.

"Have a seat." He smiled at us, and I saw Bree's shoulders tense all the way up. He didn't have quite as many teeth as Patrick did, but even without that, you couldn't miss the resemblance to a barracuda. "Did you say something about taking some kind of medicine? Do you need some water?"

The houselights were up now, and I looked out past the velvet rope. There were still plenty of people in the club, mostly looking horrified or bewildered. There seemed to be a double handful of uniformed coppers taking names and talking to guests.

I smiled right back at Cunningham. "Yeah, I do, but we've got bottled water right here. This is actually where we were sitting when the shit hit the fan. If you're planning on asking me questions, I think I'd like some backup. Haven't got a lawyer here, obviously, but Carla Fanucci, our record label's ops manager, is here. She needs to sit in on this. Oh, and Patrick Ormand—you met him in the loo—is our head of security. Let's have them in."

He opened his mouth, but I got in first. I'd seen the refusal in his face, and I was damned if I was having it. What the hell, I had the right to a lawyer if I fancied one, and truth to tell, I preferred Carla and Patrick to any lawyer I'd be able to get in Los Angeles in the middle of the night. I lifted my voice, pitching it to carry.

"Oi! Patrick! Can you get Carla, and come over here, please?"

Patrick, on the other side of the velvet rope, shot me an appreciative look. It was pretty clear he knew just what I was doing, and just as clear that he approved of it. It was scary, how well I could read him; if anyone had told me, back when he'd been sitting in the New York City edition of Lieutenant Cunningham's chair and sniffing around after my old lady, that we'd become as familiar with each other as a pair of socks in a drawer, I'd have thought you were mental.

Bree had dug out two of my antispasmodic capsules and a bottle of Volvic. She didn't seem to be paying much attention to Cunningham, or to anything else beyond me and my meds. "Here," she told me. "Unopened water. All things considered, I don't want anything that someone could spike or dose or add something to. Besides, it's still cold."

The look on Cunningham's face made me think of someone who'd bitten into an apple and discovered it was actually a persimmon instead. I couldn't really sort out why, though, unless he'd hoped Bree was dim as well as fierce, in which case I'd read him wrong. If he believed that, he'd have to be so stupid that he not only couldn't read people, he probably couldn't read an eye chart.

I swallowed the pills, taking my time and keeping one eye on

Patrick. He'd found Carla, and they were both heading towards us at a hard trot. Good. I was damned if I was handling this without some backup. They hit the velvet rope, said something to the copper playing dragon, and were waved on through.

Right. Showtime.

"Lieutenant Cunningham." It wasn't a question; Carla knew exactly who she was talking to, and probably his favourite colour, choice of vodka, and whether he liked boxers or briefs. She held out a hand, and he took it. "I'm Carla Fanucci, of Fanucci Productions. I handle the daily operations for JP's bands, and all the record label stuff."

Good, she was right on top of that "grab it first" thing. I shot a glance at Patrick; it was one of those moments when I wished I could do the same sort of mutual mind reading trick Bree and I have going with other people: *come on, mate, give me a cue, I really want to let Cunningham know you're a former homicide copper.* The problem was, I wasn't sure if doing it would be brilliant or a disaster.

Ah, sod it. If Cunningham didn't know it yet, he'd get it when he checked everyone out. Him knowing that Patrick was up on every trick in the playbook before he started in at us might save time and grief. Christ, it might even get us out of there before breakfast tomorrow.

"Carla, glad you're still here. Not sure if we've actually got a crime on our hands, or if Bergen's bad karma just caught him up, or what, but either way, this looks to be a Fluorescent Records family affair."

I was watching Patrick from the corner of my eye, and I would have sworn he gave me a tiny nod. Maybe he'd got some of Bree's ESP going on, after all. I gave Cunningham another smile, showing a few teeth of my own. "Of course the real luck is having a retired homicide copper right here when it happened. *Deja vu* on the Perry Dillon murder, Patrick, yeah?"

113

I'd thought Cunningham had looked sour over me insisting on having Carla there, but that bit of gen had him taking the concept of looking sour to a whole new level. Realising what he was dealing with in Patrick Ormand left him looking as if he'd bitten into a chocolate éclair and found it full of battery acid. My estimation of Patrick as a cop went up a notch; I hadn't thought about just how much being able to control your face plays into getting that job done, but it really does, you know? Being able read the bloke's face made him that much easier to deal with.

"Definite *deja vu*. Seeing Sandoval on the floor in that bathroom reminded me of the crime scene at the Garden." Patrick sounded as easy as he looked. "That was a long time ago, now. And a very messy case it was, too. Here's hoping this one's a lot more straightforward. Lieutenant? How can we help?"

"Let's see if we can get Mr. Kinkaid's information down first. That way, you can get back to your hotel that much sooner. I bet a hot shower sounds good right around now." Cunningham nodded at me, but it was clear he was talking mostly to Bree. Not so thick after all, our new copper.

He took me through the sequence of events. Five or six questions in, I began wondering exactly what he was after; he seemed to be interested mostly in who I'd seen doing what, and where, much earlier in the evening. I let one eyebrow go up, and shot a quick look at Patrick: *not sure what he's on about, is this safe?* Patrick had both of his up, not all the way, but high enough so that I could read him: *I'm not really sure where he's going with this, but it's okay for now.*

Then he turned away, and I realised what he was doing: scanning the crowd, looking for someone. Whoever it was, he wasn't finding them. Even though he kept the rest of his face smooth, his eyebrows kept wanting to furrow up.

We went through the earlier part of the evening, a flow of questions that didn't seem to have much to do with Bergen

Sandoval or anything else: Who'd been in the queue ahead of us? Who'd been behind? Who had I seen when I'd first got inside the Plus Minus? Who had I spoken to? Had anyone approached me...?

I answered Cunningham, open and honest. I couldn't imagine why he needed all that, unless he was trying to set the scene in his head, but I gave him everything I could remember.

"Did you encounter Mr. Sandoval at any point during the evening?"

Definitely not Patrick Ormand. Cunningham's voice was still casual, but not casual enough—he didn't have the control over it that Patrick had. I saw Carla's eyes narrow, as she heard the same subtle difference I'd heard. This was the meat of what he'd been after: sorting out where Bergen had been until Andy came and dragged me into the men's loo. No clue why he'd asked all those convoluted questions, why he hadn't just said *look, right, I'm trying to place the dead bloke, did you see him at all before he died in your lap,* instead of wanting to know about Elaine and Mac and everyone else, but it was his show, not mine. I'd make a piss-poor cop, anyway, because my head doesn't work that way. I'm just not twisty enough. All these great homicide types, they all seem to have minds like corkscrews. Whatever he was hoping for from me, though, he was doomed to disappointment.

"What, you mean alive? No, I didn't. All that standing about outside left me pretty rocky on my pins. Standing in one place is just about the worst thing for the MS—kicks it in every time. I'd had all I could take of standing, and we got a place to sit pretty much right after we came inside. Sorry, Lieutenant. Not much help, I'm afraid."

"You didn't see him at all?"

Patrick and Carla were both watching me. I shook my head. "Not until I found him dying in the toilet. He was already here when we got in, but I wasn't looking for him or anyone, really—I

115

just wanted to sit down while the legs were still doing what they were designed to do. Soon as we got indoors, we told Streak— that's Derek Silver, the club owner—that we needed a quiet place to sit, and he got what was wanted and led us straight here. Nice warm club, maybe a bit too warm, because Bree and I both sort of propped each other up and dozed off. We're both still getting over a nasty strain of tour flu, as well. We basically took a nap."

Out of nowhere, the barracuda was front and centre, and he was showing his teeth. "How do you know he was already here? If you didn't see him?

"Elaine Wilde told us." The words were out before I could stop to think whether dishing this much to those shiny teeth was the brightest move. "Right after we first got in. Remember, Bree? She said something about having seen him when she got here, that he was already here. Lieutenant, no offence, I'm not trying to tell you or anyone else how to do their own gig. But Patrick was doing security and Streak was right inside the doors, probably well before they even opened. That's part of what security does. If you need to know what Bergen was up to, why not just ask the people who'd know? Patrick?"

"Bergen Sandoval got here just before seven." Patrick wasn't having any trouble keeping his face from showing his feelings. Good job, too, because he couldn't have been thinking too highly of the LA homicide lieutenant for missing something so obvious. "He was one of the first guests in; we weren't really opening doors until seven. I'd been here since a quarter past six, and before Bergen and a couple of press people showed up, there was no one here except club employees, Mr. Silver, and the club's own in-house security people." He thought for a moment. "Oh, and Andy. He was here early too, around a quarter to seven."

"Andy was here that early? Did he say why?"

I jerked my head round, and so did Bree. Cunningham didn't

know Carla, and he didn't know how her voice sounded when she'd had a surprise. I do, though. Carla's so rarely knocked off balance by anything, we haven't had much opportunity to learn the cues. But the difference is audible, if you know who you're listening to.

"Not a word, other than hello." Patrick's face was about as revealing as a refrigerator door. "I waved him in, and the girl Streak had handling the access passes stamped his left wrist. It began getting busy after that, and we had a logjam in the line. That's why JP got stuck out there."

"This is Andrew—Valdon, wasn't it?" Nothing wrong with Cunningham's memory; he had the name right there at the front of his mind. "He's your assistant, isn't he, Ms. Fanucci? You seem surprised that he was here so early. Is there any reason he wouldn't be?"

"Just that he'd been hit harder than nearly anyone by the tour flu. He's been away from the office, out sick, for a couple of days, and he wasn't looking forward to tonight—he said he still felt like crap and hadn't been able to keep food down for a few days." She shrugged. "I'd have expected him to wait until as late as possible, be here for maybe half an hour, and head back home to bed. So I guess I am a little surprised."

"Thank you." There was something moving in Cunningham's face now, a kind of twitchiness. The bastard was smelling blood, all right. "I think it's time we had Mr. Valdon in here."

He lifted a hand, waving it toward one of the uniforms at the gate. Patrick reached over and laid a hand on his arm.

"Don't waste your time." Calm flat voice, pure Patrick. "I've checked over what's left of the crowd at least twice while you and JP were talking. Andy's not here. He's gone."

117

# Chapter Eight

We actually did get out of there in time to catch a few hours decent kip before breakfast. Most of the rest of the immediate band and label family weren't so lucky.

Looking back, Cunningham was probably just as happy to be shot of us. He'd messed up, letting Andy slip out, and he knew it. What was worse for him was that we knew it, as well. That little cock-up was about as amateurish as it could get.

Yeah, he worked Hollywood and yeah, he worked the celebrity circuit, but it was probably just as well he wasn't trying out for a starring role in anything, because he was crap as an actor. You don't want your suspect pool or witness herd or whatever the hell we all qualified as to know you're mortified half out of your socks. You need to be able to control how visibly you react, and Cunningham couldn't do it. It was all right there for us to see.

I looked out past Patrick and into the Plus Minus, trying to spot Andy. After all, it was possible Patrick had just missed him, or something. No sign of him, not that I could see.

Most of the extended family was still there. It was obvious that Elaine and the Hedley clan had been told to hang out; they'd been seated at tables not far from the velvet rope, with uniforms in attendance. Even at that distance, Suzanne looked to be either in shock or doped up to the eyeballs. Everyone around her was talking or slumping, but she was completely still, back straight, not moving. I had the feeling she probably wasn't blinking at anything like a normal rate, either—she had that whole glazed carved-from-stone thing going on. For some reason, it made me think of a rabbit, knowing something with teeth had just picked up her scent, and was snuffling outside the bushes.

Mac was still there as well, with Dom at his back. I suspect he wanted to keep Elaine company. He caught my eye across the room; I waved, and he was unbothered enough to blow a kiss at us, the cheeky sod.

"What do you mean, he's gone!"

That jerked my head around, and Carla's too. Cunningham's voice was furious, in a peculiar way: sullen, almost petulant, like a hugely overgrown kid about to throw a tantrum and start breaking things. His face had gone a nasty mottled red, and I saw a vein ticking away over his left eye. *Might want to see the quack about blood pressure meds*, I thought, *going to pop an artery, and believe me, the heart stuff's no fun at all...*

"Exactly what I said." Patrick was calm enough to be his polar opposite. "He's not on the premises. I've been looking around for the past ten minutes, and he isn't anywhere that I can see. He's not in the men's room—you left a uniform there. No, he's gone."

Cunningham was on his feet. He was quite a big bloke—burly's the word I want—and right that moment, he looked like a dancing bear in a Russian fairy tale, fists clenched up like enormous paws, heavy breathing, the lot. He waved one arm out toward the small clutch of uniforms standing about nearest the rope, and opened his mouth, probably to bark or howl or possibly bellow. He was good and furious, and I had the feeling the shit was about to hit not only the fan, but the walls and ceiling as well. I was getting ready to settle in for a long night of dealing with a pissed-off detective with a short fuse, when Bree spoke up, calm and clear and loud enough to get not only his attention, but half the crowd's, as well.

"Excuse me, Lieutenant. I'd like a word with you, please."

He stopped, his mouth half-open, and glared at her. She got up, caught his stare, and held it, good and hard.

"I'm sorry to interrupt you, but as I pointed out earlier, we're both still getting over a bad flu, and John's been through enough tonight. It's been a very long evening and I really don't feel like dragging it out until the sun comes up. Do you need anything else from either of us? Because if not, I'd like to go back to our hotel now."

Gordon bleedin' *Bennett*. The tone of her voice was about as close to tossing a jug of melted ice cubes over someone as I'd ever heard her get. Off to my left, I thought I heard Patrick swallow a noise that might have been a whistle. Carla's face was carefully blank, but she shot Bree one seriously appreciative look. Thinking back, I realised Carla had probably never seen Bree go parky; they've butted heads before, but that usually seems to lead to heat, not ice.

I still have no idea what Cunningham might have had on the tip of his tongue, because whatever it was, Bree didn't give him a chance to drop it. She walked past him, over to the velvet rope, and looked around. Streak was standing off to one side with a couple of guests—I was guessing the local entertainment telly types—and a uniform. Bree lifted one hand, and her voice as well.

120

"Streak! Could you make sure we have a car waiting outside, please? We're all done here."

She turned back and looked at Cunningham. He was breathing through both nostrils, and the mottled red had gone more of a purple. "You know where to reach us, Lieutenant. Feel free to call us if we can help, but not too early, please. The desk staff's already been told not to put any calls through before nine. John, could you grab my bag? I left it on the chair."

We left the Plus Minus in absolute silence. Patrick lifted the velvet rope and we walked out with Cunningham behind us, looking as if he didn't know whether to chase us down or have an apoplexy or both, and in what order.

Word must have got out about what had happened, because the street outside was a fucking zoo. There were people jammed in five deep, uniforms trying their hand at crowd control, and media vultures all over the place. The car Streak had got for us was also there, and a damned good thing, because it turned out Bree wasn't nearly as calm as she'd seemed indoors, coping with Cunningham. The chauffeur had barely got the door closed behind her before she started to shake.

I didn't say anything, just got both arms wrapped round her, and left them there. After awhile she got some control over it, and the shaking calmed down, but I wasn't letting go of her. That turned out to be a good move, because she finally just relaxed against me, and stayed there until we'd got back to the Beverly Wilshire. If the chauffeur was hoping for some insider gen, he was out of luck. Neither of us said a word the entire ride back to the hotel.

There wasn't much conversation after we'd run the gamut of press people outside the hotel, either. I probably should have expected it—news travels fast in Hollywood, especially when it's news about entertainment industry types. Besides, there'd been a shitload of media on the spot for the entire evening. It's not as if I didn't know that every last one of them had a Blackberry or an iPhone or some flavour of high-tech instant communications thing permanently attached to their left hand.

So I shouldn't have been surprised to find a small horde of media types in front of the hotel on Wilshire Boulevard, with a handful of city uniforms trying to shut them up and shut them down. I was, though—completely boggled by it. Bree, who hates anything smelling of intrusion on her privacy zones, was stone-faced and silent. That was just as well, because the people yelling at us—*hey that's JP Kinkaid, hey JP, can we get a statement about what happened, is it true he died in your arms, is it true you and Sandoval used to play together but he cheated you out of money, hey JP, over here!*—were making enough noise for feeding time at the circus.

I'd got hold of Bree's hand. She was holding on tight, not making eye contact with anyone. I looked beyond her, picked out the copper in charge, and gave him a small nod. The bloke nodded back; clearly, he'd got it, because he made damned sure everyone stayed back far enough to let us into the courtyard, through the lobby, and up to our suite. We could still hear them clamouring and ravening and yelling after us as the lift doors whisked shut.

That shower felt brilliant, but it may have been one of the shortest I've ever taken. I'd planned on a nice long sluicing down with hot water and soap, but that wasn't happening. For one thing, the MS had gone from a background tingling to something a lot noisier and more ominous. I hadn't been lying when I'd told Cunningham that standing in one place is the worst thing I can do to deal with the disease. Doesn't matter whether it's a sweaty dance floor or a shower at the Beverly Wilshire, standing about leaves me swaying and in pain.

For another thing, I was worried about Bree. She'd had a few shocks, the evening had been a pretty rough ride, and I didn't much like how quiet she'd gone. The way her conscience works, there was a chance she was feeling guilty about not minding that

Bergen was dead. Yeah, I know, but that's Bree for you. If that was what was happening, I wasn't having it.

So I stood under water as hot as I could bear it for just long enough to scrub away any remnant of Bergen Sandoval that might have even thought about sticking to my skin. Then I was out and drying off, heading towards bed as fast as I could go.

Bree'd put the light out, but she was still awake. "John? Did you remember to take your meds?"

"Yeah, I did."

I climbed in next to her. There was just enough light through the curtains to make out her profile. I was listening to her breathing, trying to suss out if she was upset or crying, but it was light, even, regular.

"Bree? You all right, love?"

She was quiet for a few moments, as if she were really thinking about her answer. Finally, I heard a tiny sigh.

"Yes. I think I was just..."

Her voice trailed off. She wasn't done, though; I could tell. I stayed quiet, waiting.

"John, are we bad luck?"

Yeah, well, I hadn't been expecting *that*. She sounded so normal, she might have been asking if I wanted a cup of tea. I sat up, blinking down at her.

"Are we what, now...?"

"I know it sounds insane, but, well, I can't help it. It just seems as if anytime we go somewhere and do something, someone dies. I feel like—like a lightning rod or something."

I snorted and settled back down, wrapping both arms round her. "Right, that's it. Come here, lady. You need a good cuddle. Seriously, Bree, you don't believe that rubbish, do you? I mean yeah, we've had a few people pop off around us the past few years, but crikey, love, you might want to think about the circs. Some of it's inevitable, really."

123

"What do you mean?" She was warm in my arms. She wasn't tense, either. "What circs? Why is it inevitable?"

"Well, for one thing, we've got some pretty high-risk sidelines in this job. Lighting rig people, heavy lifters, stuff that's hard on the body and low on safety." I was sorting it out in my head. "Money, for another thing. Fact is, where there's a lot of dosh, you get groupies and suck-ups. You also get some proper assholes, people like Perry Dillon, or Bergen. Money brings it out in people, Bree, you know? Even basically cool people get twisted up over money. Look at Paul Morgenstern. Nice bloke at heart, and look how he fetched up."

She spooned up against me; she was beginning to sound drowsy. "So you think money's the lightning rod? Not us?"

"Not just money. There's the celebrity bullshit, as well. That might bring it even worse than having all that dosh. People go nuts for celebrity. But either way, love, it's not us." I planted a light kiss on the nape of her neck. She was nice and warm. "And it's certainly not you, Miss Invisible. Now let's see about some kip, okay? Wake me up if you can't sleep."

I don't know what time it was when we actually closed our eyes, but whatever time it was, there wasn't nearly enough sleep between that and my damned cell phone going off the next morning. Yeah, so we'd told the desk staff not to put anyone through before nine, but I'd left the cell on.

"Shit!"

Bree was already out of bed, trying to find it and get it before it could wake me. She was out of luck; I'd left it in my trousers, across the room. By the time she got there and fumbled it loose, I was sitting up, rubbing my eyes, flinching at the number of places that hurt like hell. The MS was on, full throttle. Today was going to be miserable.

"Hello—Luke? What time is—what?" She was very still, her shoulders hunching hard. Even from across the room, I could hear the urgency in the tinny rattle coming out of the phone. Luke doesn't flip out easily. *"What did you just say...?"*

I was flexing my ankles, trying to get some mobility back into my feet; at the moment, they were basically disconnected from the rest of me. I flexed one, flexed the other, and the whole time, I had a silent commentary running in my head: *right, you do what you're supposed to do, no arguments, you're supposed to hold me up and that's what you're going to do...*

I took a quick look at the nightstand clock; it was twenty minutes of eight. Then I had both feet on the floor, finally, and Bree had turned round, waiting for me to get it together. She had control of her voice again, but there was a very strange look on her face.

"No, it's okay. He's up. Here, I think you should tell him." She handed me the phone. "It's Luke. I'll go get your meds together. You—might want to sit back down, John."

She headed into the bathroom. I stared after her a moment.

"Oi! JP? You there?"

He sounded half off his nut, and grim with it. "Yeah, here and awake. What in hell's going on, Luke?"

"We've got a problem. Suzanne just confessed something to us. I've got a call in to Patrick, and Carla's heading into her office. We need to confab on how to handle this, and we need to do it before that oversized lump of a homicide lieutenant finds out about it. I know it's early, I know it's a lot to ask, but can you and Bree get over to Carla's office?"

For a moment, I stood there like a garden ornament, stark naked and blinking. My heart was doing a two-step at warp speed.

"Suzanne—Luke, what are you on about? Confessed to what, for fuck's sake? Are you telling me she says she killed Bergen? Because I don't believe that. That's rubbish."

"She didn't kill him." I hadn't thought Luke's voice could get any grimmer. "She married him."

125

It's a good thing Carla's as organised and together as she is. In all the years she's run Blacklight's American operations, this was the first time she'd had to cram the entire band family into her office on the third floor of the small pink building on North La Cienega, as least as far as I knew.

Bree and I got there at half past eight, before nearly anyone else, and Carla already had a pot of good strong coffee ready. She'd got a tray of breakfast foods set up on the side table in the conference room, as well. The girl's good.

"Hey guys—sorry to get you moving so early, JP. Did you get anything to eat before you left? No? Bree, there's some whole wheat bagels over there, and some fresh gravlax, if you're counting carbs. There's some yogurt, too."

We followed her into the conference room. Carla's intern was there, the kid she'd brought along to the mixdown sessions— Marjorie something or other. Patrick was there as well, stirring his usual half-pound or so of sugar into a coffee mug. He nodded at us over the steam.

"Morning. Any problems getting back to the hotel last night? Was there a lot of media?"

"God yes." Bree was pouring coffee and I saw her shoulders move and settle. As far as she's concerned, any media is too much media. "Out in force. They were lined up on Wilshire. Horrible. John, here, take this one. Are there more clean cups – oh, thanks."

"Luke's on his way." Carla was refilling her own cup. "They should be here any minute – they were swinging by the W to pick up Curtis and Solange. Um – can I assume Luke told you...?"

I'd got myself seated. I don't like piling on the MS stuff, I try not to wallow in it, but the truth is that, most days, the disease defines what I can or can't do, and some days more than others.

As chronic illness goes, this one is pretty damned relentless, and today was shaping up to be one of those days when it called all the shots. I took a mouthful of coffee. At least my jaw wasn't playing me up, not yet.

"What, that Suzanne had gone completely off her head and married a sadistic miser three times her age? Yeah, he told us. I've been trying to remember whether Bergen was wearing a wedding band since I got off the phone with Luke, and I don't think he was. Of course, I wasn't really concentrating on his hands, you know?"

There was a moment of uncomfortable silence. Patrick broke it.

"Well, at least you won't have to take the stand and swear to that. I got a good look at both his hands while they were loading him onto the gurney. Nothing, no jewellery at all."

Bree opened her mouth, and closed it again. Patrick met my eye for a moment. "The ME was looking at his fingernails, I'd imagine checking for the blue tinge. I watched, and no, it isn't about me being morbid. It's just that old habits die hard, or maybe not at all. The blue tinge was there, which makes it pretty sure we're looking at a toxin, not just a narcotic, but there were no rings on either hand. Is that the elevator?"

I probably shouldn't have been shocked to see Elaine Wilde. After all, she'd got some heavy history of her own with Bergen Sandoval, heavy enough to have fuelled that nasty little back and forth with him at ALS, not to mention that gorgeous punch. Besides, she was Fluorescent family, and keeping her in the dark wasn't likely to appeal to Carla, however Carla might personally feel about our newly acquired diva.

Still, she wasn't Blacklight family, and this was all about Luke's stepdaughter having apparently lost her mind and done something monumentally stupid, and possibly unforgivable. And yeah, Suzanne was still a newcomer to the family, but we'd all been

127

protecting Solange from the time she was born. For me, at least, the instinct seemed to be to want to keep the strangers out of the family business, and in my head, Elaine Wilde was a stranger. As Patrick put it, old habits dying hard, or not at all. We were still waiting for the Hedley contingent a few minutes later, when Mac and Domitra rolled in.

Mac doesn't ruffle up or get frazzled easily. He's an even-tempered bloke, and it takes a lot to knock him off his balance. But he had a look on his face that morning I hadn't seen there in a long time, not since Patrick had been mulish over something and nearly got Mac killed. I couldn't quite suss the look – it might have been anger, or disgust, or something else entirely. Whatever it was, it didn't sit easily on Mac.

"Too early." Domitra wasn't smiling either. "Way too early. Cops call you yet?"

"No. Not on our cells, anyway." Bree had made short work of a bagel with fish, and seemed to be inhaling the steam off her coffee. She'd fixed Elaine with a steady stare, and it occurred to me: this was the first time the two women would be talking about something that wasn't trivia. Bree might be able to deal with Elaine, but that didn't mean they were off to be best friends forever. "But Cunningham obviously called you. Why?"

"Because someone, probably the front desk at ALS, told him about my little punch-up with Bergen. It's not as if they could miss the black and blue mark I tattooed on his jaw." Elaine was returning my wife's stare, and neither of them seemed to be blinking much. There was tension in the room, suddenly, and I wasn't sure why. "That uniformed sack of belly fat seemed to think that meant I'd somehow snuck into the men's john and fed Bergen poisoned cocaine. Just in case anyone's wondering, I didn't."

Bree shrugged. "John told me about the punch. I can't really imagine Bergen accepting coke or anything else from you, not

128

after that. But I'm not Cunningham, and who knows how his mind works? I wonder if he's talked to Luke yet?"

"Not yet."

I hadn't heard the lift – too busy concentrating on Bree and Elaine. Luke was just walking through the conference room door, with the extended family behind him, including the Bunker Brothers. There was no sign of Cyn Corrigan or Barb Wilson; they'd let their wives off the hook for this one, apparently.

And I hadn't seen Bree get up, either, but she was up, moving past me and heading straight for Karen. They'd become quite good friends these past few years, at least as much as living on different continents allowed for. Karen had been a huge help when Bree was diagnosed with diabetes, and something about Karen seems to bring out my wife's nurturing streak. Just then, going by the look on Karen's face, she needed a good cuddle or maybe just a few weeks somewhere, where her daughter wasn't fucking up or causing trouble or driving her mum and stepdad round the twist. Suzanne has a talent for getting into shit and needing other people to pull her out of it. Karen's a type one diabetic, so she gets pretty fragile. Solange just looked exasperated, and a bit worried, and Curt was busy looking at Solange. Definitely still on honeymoon, those two were.

Checking out Bree taking charge with Karen, I nearly missed Mac, leaning over and planting a kiss on Elaine. It was a hell of a kiss for half eight in the morning, but Elaine wasn't pushing him away and telling him to stop; she stretched her neck to hang on to it for a moment longer. I thought I saw Dom rolling her eyes, but she didn't look worried. She's probably used to Mac smooching birds at eight in the morning. He's just not much for doing it in public, usually.

Luke waved the family off to various chairs round the big oval table. There was a weird little tableau going on: Suzanne was trying to catch her stepdad's eye, and Luke wasn't letting himself do that. It took me a moment, but I suddenly got it: *crikey, he's so furious right now, he's afraid he'll flip his shit and lose it if he meets her eye.* That said something about the situation, because Luke is as dedicated a family man as you're like to find. It really does take a lot to piss him off to where he's letting steam out in public, or even letting it be visible. But he was now.

He jerked his head toward the outer office, where Marjorie the intern was sitting. "Can someone shut that door? I want this conversation private."

Carla clicked the door shut and sat down. This was her turf, her home court, but she was letting Luke handle it. Smart move, that was; she might be the one to have to pick up all the pieces afterwards, but this was Luke's family, and his issue. She had the sense to sit back and let him get on with it.

The moment the door was shut, Luke dropped the mask.

Gordon *Bennett*, it was fucking mind-boggling. The control went, just washed off his face and out of his voice. It went out of his muscles, as well; I hadn't got how rigidly he'd been holding himself until he let go of it.

He rounded on his stepdaughter. If she'd been wanting to lock stares with him, she was probably thinking better of it right then. Her face had gone a really odd colour.

"What in hell were you thinking?"

He didn't sound like himself at all. He was braced against the table, and everything looked stretched out, as if he'd somehow got longer.

Bree had an arm around Karen, but neither woman was saying anything. A few years back, when Luke had got fierce with Suzanne, Bree had gone to her defence, but she wasn't doing that now. And the look on Solange's face made me feel like a voyeur. It was clear she'd never seen her dad in that state before. I hoped for her sake she'd never have to see it again.

As for Suzanne, she looked half-dead, someone who'd lost

everything they valued. I didn't know whether it was Bergen she was grieving over, or losing Luke's respect. Either way, the girl was fucked, and she knew it.

"I'm really sorry," she told us. "But I didn't kill him. I don't know who killed him."

"I'm not talking about him dying." Luke was right at the edge of lunging across the table at her. "I'm talking about you marrying him. The man was older than I am. He was a mean, miserable, unpleasant little tosser who got his rocks off bullying people and jerking them around. What in hell was going on in your mind, Suzanne!"

"I loved him."

Something had happened to the planes of Suzanne's face. They'd gone soft, shifted somehow. Out of nowhere, you could see grief, raw pain. It was right there, as visible as a neon sign across her face. She'd spoken the plain truth: for whatever reason, she'd loved Bergen Sandoval.

Solange reached out suddenly, and touched her sister's arm. Her own face had twisted up, hiding tears; Curt got a hand behind his wife, stroking her back. Suzanne was still locked up with her stepfather. The room was absolutely silent.

"Yeah, but why marry him? I don't get it."

We all turned toward the window. Domitra was prowling the room; she was the only one of us who hadn't parked herself in a chair. Her eyes were narrowed and she was looking at Suzanne as if she might be some rare species of bug.

"Isn't love enough?" Suzanne had turned away from Luke, finally. He wasn't relaxing. "Why else do people get married?"

"Money, for one thing." Elaine sounded as dry as the Sahara in August. "Bertie-boy had a thing for money, especially if he could take it away from other people."

"Bertie?" Stu Corrigan looked about as wasted-tired as I could remember ever seeing him, and that included mid-tour. Christ, if

131

we were already this ragged round the edges, we were in for a very long haul while Cunningham and his minions sorted this one out. "What's that, some sort of pet name?"

"It was Bergen's real name." Carla was up at the coffee pot, re-filling her own cup. She had her back to us and I couldn't see her face. "He was born Albert Gordon Pinkleton. Didn't you know that?"

"I did." Elaine blew out air. Next to her, Mac was grimacing. Whatever was coming, he already knew about it. "I got his real name from the marriage certificate. He really, really didn't want me to know that, but who would be enough of a moron to believe that Bergen Sandoval was anyone's real name? I mean, 'Bergen Sandoval'? Please. The name was as fake as that stupid dye job of his."

"Marriage certificate?" Suzanne's mouth had gone slack. "What are you talking about? What marriage certificate?"

"My marriage certificate. Our marriage certificate." Elaine leaned around Mac. "Bergen and I were married, for seven delightful weeks. Once I figured out what a vicious little money-grubber he was, once I figured out why he'd married me in the first place, I dumped his sorry ass. Hey!"

Suzanne was up on her feet, moving so fast that the table rocked. "You're a damned liar! He wasn't married, he was single! I was his first wife! He told me, when he proposed!"

Elaine Wilde's face wasn't ideally designed for showing things like compassion, but I got the feeling it was there, under the annoyance and contempt. "Yeah, well, he lied to you, kid. Sorry, but that's the way it is. We got married in Las Vegas back in 2007. The asshole thought he was going to get his hands on my daughter's trust fund. He thought wrong. And you know, I didn't stay married to him long enough to check into his finances and I don't have a clue what they look like these days, but I hope to hell you haven't just been saddled with a metric fuckload of debt.

Considering what a cheap little – oh shit, whose phone is that?"

"Mine." Carla had her Blackberry out and open. "Fanucci Productions. This is Carla."

A voice rattled, swarming in Carla's phone like a plague of insects caught off guard in a trap. Outside, the haze was lifting over Beverly Hills; it was going to be a gorgeous day. With any luck, we'd get this over soon, and sort out whatever Luke wanted to do about Suzanne's latest cock-up. Then I could go back to the hotel, and back to bed. Even sitting, my legs were spasming, the ataxia kicking in hard. I was glad Bree was sitting with Karen, and not next to me; there's nothing she can do about the disease, and all it does it make her fret. She doesn't like helplessness.

"What?" There was something odd in Carla's voice, an edge of disbelief. "I'm sorry, Lieutenant Cunningham, could you say that again? Hold on, I have some people with me, and I'm going to put this on the speaker."

She clicked something, and set the phone on the table. Cunningham hadn't stopped to take a breath, and his voice flooded the room.

"…went to his apartment this morning, to get answers to a few questions. His neighbour told us they'd seen him heading out around six this morning, with a couple of suitcases. And I want to know where Andy Valdon is."

# Chapter Nine

Not being in Cunningham's confidence, I wasn't clear on just how completely Andy Valdon's disappearing act had got LAPD's homicide honcho focussed on him. Right then, with Cunningham flipping his shit at Carla over the phone, I didn't care. I wasn't feeling well enough to cope with him losing it.

When I say he was losing it, I'm not joking. He was screaming at her. It was such a bizarre little meltdown, it took us all a minute to realise he was actually accusing her of knowing where Andy'd got himself off to. He'd interrupted her twice before we caught what he was on about, but when that came clear, he got cut off midstream.

"Now wait just a damned minute!" Stu was glaring at the phone as if he thought Cunningham could see him. "Carla just told you she doesn't know where Andy is. If you don't believe it, that's your problem. The fact that he's gone, that's your problem as well. But you'd best watch who you're calling a liar, mate, unless you fancy a nice go-round with our lawyer. You asked Carla, and she told you she doesn't know. What part of no don't you get? This is your cock-up, not ours. You're the one screwed up, and let Andy scarper. So where the fuck you get off, calling Carla a liar, is beyond me. You watch your step!"

Silence. I could imagine that vein in Cunningham's forehead pounding away—I swear, if the bloke wasn't on blood pressure meds, he damned well ought to have been. Across the table, Patrick was openly grinning, no mask at all. Of course, since Cunningham couldn't see him, there wasn't much risk in letting it show. Still unusual for Patrick, though. He's a poker-face by nature and training.

"I'm sorry." Cunningham couldn't have sounded stiffer or less convincing. "But this is a murder investigation. If Andy Valdon gets in touch with you, please let me know immediately."

You could almost hear the snap as he hung up. Stu looked to still be narked. "Bloody dim-bulb copper!"

Cal shook his head. "I don't think he's dim, Stu. I think he's out of his depth, maybe, but I don't think he's stupid. Either way, he looks to be a royal pain in the arse and he's going to be a complete menace to cope with. Carla? You all right?"

"I'm fine, Cal. And thanks for calling him out, Stu. I'm starting to wonder if ever trusting Andy was the right move. But he had the skill set we wanted: he knows everything there is to know about the club scene, the way the clubs work, the players, the money stuff. And damn it, he's good at his gig. I wasn't wrong about that. I just…"

Her voice trailed off. Everyone looked to have forgotten about Suzanne's little bombshell, not to mention Elaine's. Mac got up, and stretched.

"So, Andy's gone walkabout? And he was the only person in the

135

loo with Bergen when Bergen snorted paint thinner or rat poison or whatever it was? Not looking pretty for him, I must say. But you know, if I get a vote, I say we let Cunningham deal with that. We got pulled out of bed to deal with an entirely different problem."

He turned to Suzanne. I've known Mac for longer than Suzanne's been alive, but right then I couldn't have told you whether he was amused, or narked, or what.

"Here's the thing, Suzanne. It doesn't matter whether you believe Elaine or not. We all knew Bergen, and we all knew him too damned well. Keeping that in mind, let me offer you some advice: If you've got even half a brain in that pretty head of yours, you'll get a very good lawyer and an even better auditor, and find out what in hell was going on with Bergen's money. And did I say very good lawyer? Depending on what you find out, you might want to make it two very good lawyers."

She gawked at him. He not quite rolled his eyes at her.

"An independent auditor, Suzanne. And then a lawyer. Your late not particularly lamented husband has been famous for being one of the mingiest, cheapest men alive for the past forty years. Elaine thinks he went through his dosh as fast as he made it, and maybe faster. But you know, the other extreme is entirely possible. He may have millions stashed away somewhere. And that's going to be a problem for you, isn't it?"

"I don't see—why –" She seemed to be having trouble getting words out. "What do you mean?"

"Motive." Solange had already got there. "That homicide cop will say it's a motive. Shit! Suzanne –"

"I wouldn't worry too much about that part of it, because it's not a motive. She's already rich—she can always point out to Cunningham who her stepdad is. But Mac's right about you needing to find out for certain. That needs to be high up on the priorities chart. I'm betting Carla's got a list." Bree patted Karen's arm, and got up. There was something going on in her face, but I was too tired myself, and feeling too rocky, to work out what it was. "Guys, can we finish this? I really want to get back to the hotel. Carla, can I get a word with you…?"

There wasn't much to finish, after all, just a few minutes of discussion about the ways and means of damage control when the rest of the world found out about Suzanne being Bergen's widow. Carla let everyone know she'd be getting auditors in to get Bergen's estate sorted out and lawyers in place to cope when Cunningham found out and landed on Suzanne like a SCUD missile. Everyone agreed that one was a when, not an if.

Luke hadn't said a word since Cunningham's call, and he wasn't saying anything now, either. He was still tight-lipped and silent. He didn't look to be any happier than he'd been when he'd stalked through the office door, and no less narked.

He still wasn't looking at his stepdaughter, either. But when Karen reached for his hand, he not only took it, he kissed it and tucked it under his arm. However furious he might be with Suzanne, he wasn't taking it out on her mum.

Carla came downstairs with us. We'd cabbed over from the hotel, but Marjorie had a town car waiting for us. The driver had opened the door for Bree, and was waiting for us to get in; the MS was kicking hard, and Bree was just standing about, looking as if she had something to say but not sure about whether she ought to say it, or how. I was about to say *sod being the little gentleman* and get in ahead of her, when she spoke up.

"Carla, look. I'm a little worried. Did you call Tony and ask him to come down for this? Or Katia?"

*Shit.*

Between the MS and the series of interpersonal earthquakes shaking up Carla's conference room, I hadn't missed Tony being gone from the headcount. Unbelievable, yeah? My best friend, and I'd been so fucking out of it, I hadn't even noticed he wasn't there. Bree'd noticed, not me.

"I did call. I left a message on Tony's cell, and one at the hotel desk for Katia. I couldn't call Katia directly, because she hasn't given me her cell number." Carla looked from Bree to me. "I was pretty surprised he wasn't here. After all, he's family. Hell, he's way more family than Elaine Wilde is. Is he okay?"

"No. No, he's not." Bree's voice was soft, tired, about as sad as I'd heard her in a long time. "I think he's in trouble. And I think it's about to get a lot worse than he realises."

I stood there like a department store mannequin, not saying a word. I've got no clue what my face was showing, but inside, I was calling myself the worst names I could think of. I was also crawling with shame.

Carla had already got that I hadn't noticed. She was asking Bree, not me, and Bree had the answer I couldn't have provided. Tony was my closest friend in the world outside my wife, and I couldn't have answered Carla's question. The accusing noise in my head, in my heart, was so damned loud, I missed the rest of the back and forth between the two women.

"...back to the hotel. John, you should sit." Bree was turning towards the car. "Let us get some sleep, Carla, okay? John's in full relapse mode right now and I'm wiped out. I just want to climb into bed for a few hours. We'll call you later."

This time, it was my turn to not say anything on the ride back. Everything hurt, every joint, my jaw, the balls of my feet. The myokimia, the burn moving up and down the destroyed nerves in both legs, was bad enough to make me wish for something that would numb me from head to toe, like those epidural things they give women in labour. But even if I'd felt fine, I wouldn't have been talking, not just then.

Fortunately, Bree didn't seem to expect me to talk. We got back to the hotel, got round the buzzards—the media was still there, a smaller crowd than the mob scene last night, but still there—and got upstairs. I hung the *Do Not Disturb* sign on the door, managed to get down a serious dose of pain meds, and got carefully out of my clothes and between the covers. Pyjamas weren't happening; at that point, even the sheets against my skin hurt.

Bree let me get settled in. Soon as I'd done that, she reached for her cell.

"I'm calling Katia."

That was all she said, but that was all she needed to say; there are times that marital mind-reading thing we do comes in useful. I nodded at her—do it, yeah, you're not the only one worried here— and closed my eyes. I was moving as little as possible, feeling the sweating and shivering kicking in. She stayed where she was; she'd got that, even though I was fucked up and hurting and not much use to her or Tony or anyone else at the moment, I needed to hear whatever she said to Katia.

Turned out there was nothing to hear. Keeping myself awake, waiting for Bree's end of the conversation, I was lost in that weird space the MS drops me into when it hits hard enough to take my legs out from under me. I never really know what time's doing when I'm that far out of it; things stop being linear, you know? It could have been an hour since she'd punched in Katia's number, or it could have been seconds.

The myokimia seemed to have gone redline on me. The pain was pegging the meter, and I lay there, waiting for the painkillers to kick in, knowing there wasn't a damned thing I could do about anything until it let up. And until Bree talked to Katia, I couldn't even let myself try to sleep.

Nothing. Silence. All I heard was Bree, breathing even and deep, being patient, waiting for Katia to pick up at the other end. I hadn't forgotten about Bergen dying in my lap, or about Suzanne and her latest spectacular cock-up, or any of that. I just didn't have it in me to care right then. It was taking everything I could do to not get lost in the disease.

139

"Katia? It's Bree. Listen, could you call me as soon as you get this? Please? I know it's early, I'm hoping you guys are just still asleep, but we're very worried about both of you. I can't leave John right now, he's not doing well, but I really need to talk to you. Call me, okay?"

I heard the click of her Blackberry, and opened my eyes. The lids seemed to weigh about ten pounds each, but I managed to keep them open long enough to catch Bree's attention. She kicked her shoes off, put the phone down on the nightstand and curled up next to me.

There was all sorts of shit circling round in my head, and the only good thing about that relapse was that it was bad enough to keep me from dealing with any of it. I actually did manage to doze for a couple of hours. I think Bree got a nap in, as well.

When I did wake up, it was because I felt the bed move: someone had knocked on our door. I knew, right off, that it wasn't Katia, or Tony; Bree was murmuring, and I heard the chink of trays being set down. She'd rung room service and got them to send up some food. Good. I might not have any appetite myself, but with her diabetes, she can't not eat, and I was in no state to have to nag her about it.

"Here." She'd climbed back on the bed, balancing the tray. "I had them poach you a couple of eggs, and there's some orange juice. Can you sit up? Do you need help?"

"I'm good." I pulled myself up, being careful not to upset the tray. I sounded like a stroke victim. "Jaw's stiff. Katia call? Tony?"

She shook her head. I reached out and got one hand around her wrist. If the pain pills had done any good, they'd already worn off; the pain was ridiculous, blocking almost every signal between my hands and my brain. But I steered my hand to hers, and even managed a faint squeeze.

"Go check." I felt myself wince with the pain, and hoped she hadn't felt me flinch. "Please."

140

She stared at me. I held on to her hand a moment longer, and let go. "Worried. Me too. I'm okay. Go check."

She swung her legs over the side of the bed. If I hadn't already known just how worried she was, that would have done it; she doesn't like leaving me when the MS is being half as bad as it was that morning. But she was worried enough about Katia, and probably about Tony as well, that she hit the floor running. She wasn't bothering about her shoes, either. She stopped just long enough to grab her Blackberry and her room key.

"I'll be right back." She was halfway to the door before she turned back. "Five minutes. I promise. I have my phone. Hang on, John. Five minutes."

"Go."

I don't know how long she was gone, five minutes or five hours. However long it was, I spent the entire time carefully eating one of the poached eggs. Not a lot of effort needed for that, fortunately; I barely had to move my jaw. The food seemed to help; I started on the other egg, taking slow small bites, basically letting the food break itself down and dissolve into something I could swallow, not using the jaw for anything unless it was really needed.

MS is a genuinely weird disease. You end up acting as a sort of interpreter between your brain and your nervous system, because the disease interrupts all that. It slows things down, having to tell your brain to hold a running one-sided dialogue with your fingers: *it's a fork, nothing dangerous there, right, okay now, fingers bend and pick it up, no that's not part of the fork you clot, it's your bleedin' breakfast, now get some of the egg on the fork and mind you don't drop it...*

I'd managed to get most of the second poached egg down when the door clicked, and Bree was back. I got a look at her face, and let the fork fall back to the tray.

"Bree...?"

"I knocked on their door. Nobody answered." Her face was bleached, pinched around the mouth. "So I went downstairs to the front desk and asked to be put through to their room."

I waited. Bree swallowed, loud enough for me to hear from halfway across the room. At least those neural pathways weren't clogging on me.

"She's not registered as a guest at the hotel anymore. Tony's still checked in, but Katia's not. She checked out this morning. She's gone."

That whole telescoping thing time does when the MS nails me went into serious overdrive that day. There had to be major shit going down in the world that afternoon, and most of it was probably close enough to us to mean I was going to have to sort it out eventually, but that day, time had no beginning, no middle, and no end in sight, either. There might just as well have not been a world outside the hotel.

Bree was still fighting off a post-flu headache. She kept the curtains drawn most of the day, so I couldn't even have told you when afternoon started moving into evening. I remember that I dozed, woke up, and dozed off again; even if the body had been up for letting me catch any serious kip, the mind wasn't going along with it. Between Bergen, Suzanne and the rest of the mess, it was much too busy trying to untangle things. Very surreal day, that was, because the brain seemed to want to sort things out in some bizarre dimension where the body was someplace else altogether. The whole thing felt like a flashback to a mescaline moment.

I'd had no trouble at all believing that Suzanne had indulged her ageing-rocker fixation by marrying Bergen Sandoval. I'd sussed that particular need of hers a long time ago; Christ, she'd hit on me while she was still at school. Having her on the road with us for Book of Days had pretty much shown me what she was all about. I could smell the need for some older bloke, preferably famous and hopefully some flavour of genius, coming off her in waves. I'm not a shrink, so I don't know what the proper term for that rubbish is, father figure or something, but whatever it is, Suzanne's got a bad case of it.

That was quite enough about Suzanne, and, still half dozing and seriously uncomfortable, I tried pushing her out of my head. I don't give a toss about what she gets up to, not beyond the fact that Luke does care about her, and considers himself responsible for her. Instead, I tried to imagine what in hell could have led Katia Mancuso to pack her bags and walk out of the hotel, out of town, and out of the middle of a murder investigation. None of the answers I came up with were acceptable, and none of them were pretty.

My first thought, that she knew something about Bergen dying and wanted out before Cunningham sussed it, was completely nuts, and I let it die away. I'd been worried about the Mancusos for quite awhile now, going back months before we ever climbed into Magic for the West Coast Geezers tour. Bergen's name hadn't even been on the table at that point, much less his piss-soaked shit-stained corpse in my lap, and I remembered reacting to Bree being closed-mouthed about whatever was going on, because she wasn't willing to betray Katia's confidence, even to me. So, no. Whatever was going on with them had nothing to do with Bergen Sandoval, alive or dead.

But it had to be major. One small titbit had stuck in my head from the scene in Carla's conference room that morning: Cunningham had called it a homicide investigation, when he'd been shouting at Carla on the phone. I didn't know what information he'd got, forensics or testimony or whatever, but he was in charge and he'd called it murder. And yeah, okay, Katia hadn't been there when he'd said that. But she had to know there was a good chance of Bergen's death being iffy. And you don't leave town, not when the cops have made it clear they'd rather you stayed awhile…

143

Doze, wake, doze, wake. It was a long, miserable, monotonous day, waiting for things to stop hurting and start letting me function again. Bree got up at one point, and ran herself a hot bath. I kept my eyes closed; a nice hot soak would do her a world of good just then, and I knew damned well she'd do without the bubbles and hot water if she thought I was awake and might need her. I noticed she took her cell into the bathroom with her.

But no one rang, not the band, not the cops, no one at all. It was obvious we weren't going out to eat, not even downstairs to the hotel restaurant; things were taking much longer than usual to ease up, and my feet were still stabbing, myokimia just waiting under the balls of my feet before it went straight up both legs and nailed me. That meant an early dinner from room service. Bree ate most of hers, which was a relief; she takes the diabetes seriously enough to mind what she eats, even when she's lost her appetite. So that was one thing I didn't have to worry about. Just as well, since I was already worried enough about what was going on with Tony.

While Bree was sliding the dinner tray outside for the hotel staff to pick up, I fumbled my phone open, realised I'd left it off since that morning, and got it turned on. *Shit.* If Tony had rung while the damned thing was off, I was going to kick myself, just as soon as I could get my feet to talk to the rest of me. But there were no messages.

"Nothing? Damn." Bree was reaching for her own phone. "I'm going to try Katia at home and—is that the door? Hang on, wait, damn! Coming! Oh man—Tony…?"

I've known Tony Mancuso thirty years and more. I've played with him, hung with him, toured with him. I've seen him stoned, I've seen him tripping, I've seen him wiped out wasted fucking exhausted, to the point where putting three words together to make a simple sentence was beyond him.

144

Maybe I was seeing things through the haze of separation I get courtesy of the MS. It was possible—things do seem really clear when that happens. All I can tell you is, that afternoon, he walked into our hotel room behind my wife, and for one really scary blink of time, I didn't recognise him.

"Hey." His voice was as strange as the rest of him: slurry, low, as if his brain and throat weren't communicating properly. I had a sudden bad moment: *bloody hell, he's had a stroke!* "I just got Bree's message. I was asleep, sorry. JP, how you doing? You look like shit."

I sat there in my nice pricey hotel bed, memory-foam pillows cushioning my back from the wooden headboard and dinner settling in my stomach, and gawked at him. He wasn't meeting my eyes, or Bree's, or looking up at all; I couldn't really see his face, but he didn't look to have shaved.

"Sit down."

I jerked my head away from Tony, so hard and fast I had to bite back a yelp of pain. Bree didn't sound worried, or sympathetic either. Her voice was black ice—that *sit down* had been a command. There was a tone in it I recognised, one I'd heard before, but the MS was messing with my perceptions and my memory as well, and I couldn't seem to pin down when or...

"I said, *sit down*." Her shoulders were hunched hard as tomb markers. She took a step toward him. "Do it, Tony."

Smell is supposed to be the most evocative of all senses, the strongest, the one that brings back memories and triggers other stuff. It is, too. Out of nowhere, something came across the room at me, a faint hint of scent. The pain mists rolled back just enough to let some light in, and the picture was there suddenly, complete as my memory could get it: Bree, not quite out of her teens, standing in the kitchen of 2828 Clay Street, balancing an empty bottle of Jack Daniel's in one hand, same look in her eye, same note in her voice: *You wanted me to handle it? Cool. We're doing it my way. Listen up: if I find another one of these in the house, ever, I'm going to christen your skull like you were the fucking QE2.*

Tony was swaying on his feet. The pit of my stomach had gone cold, knotting up as I got what was happening: He wasn't meeting our eyes because he couldn't.

Bree got one hand out. I heard Tony say something, not words, just noise, as she got hold of his upper arm. Before he could adjust to it or do anything about it, she'd sat him down, good and hard, in one of the fancy low-backed faux French chairs the hotel puts in its suites. She was standing over him on the balls of her feet, and her hands were balled up into the kind of fists that meant business. It was surreal. *Oh Christ she's going to hit him, deck him, black his eye, something...*

He sat there, rubbing his arm where Bree'd grabbed him. He still wasn't meeting either of our eyes; whatever was down there on the floor, it had all of his attention.

I took a breath, gritted my teeth, and got up.

It took more coordination than I had to spare, but I had no choice. Bree had her back to me, standing over Tony, ready to deck him or shove him back down or God only knew what if he even looked like arguing with her, so she wasn't watching me. Just as well, because I was talking to myself, literally mumbling under my breath, trying to get the signals to the legs so that they'd hold me up. Halfway out of bed, I remembered I was stark—when I'd climbed into bed, my skin had been too sensitive to cope with pyjamas or anything else—damaged nerve endings don't do fabric very well. I managed to get the hotel's plush robe over my shoulders, and took a few steps across the room.

The sick-drunk stench hit me from ten feet away. There was nothing faint about that smell, now that I was closer to it. It's been a very long time since I've had any myself, I've been dry for upwards of thirty years, but the sharp-sweet edgy reek of the tequila damned near knocked me over. It was enough to have

146

nailed me with an immediate headache, if I hadn't had one already.

Christ. My best friend, same horror movie I'd gone through myself, and I hadn't caught it. How long had this been going on? And how the fuck had I missed it?

"Tony?" I heard myself, and there it was, that feeling of being totally outside my own body. I hadn't planned on saying anything, better to let Bree talk for now since she'd already had some idea about what was going on, but words were coming out of my mouth and what the hell, might as well just let them come, yeah? "Talk to us, mate."

He looked up at me, finally, and I felt something move behind my ribcage. *Shit.* Bloodshot, dog-sick, defeated: he looked broken, somehow. Yeah, I remembered the look, a bit too well. I'd seen it in the mirror too many times before Bree pulled me away from it.

"Talk about what, man?" He had his stare fixed somewhere just over my left shoulder. His voice was a thread. "What do you want me to say?"

I saw Bree's shoulders slump, as she let her breath out. I hadn't realised I was as tense as she was, but when she eased up so did I, and I nearly fell over. I was about as unsteady as I'd been in a long time, but I stood, trying to get Tony to meet my eye. It wasn't working particularly well.

"Why didn't you tell us?" I couldn't get a read on Bree's feelings, not from her voice, and the marital mind-reading link seemed to be off. "Tony, please talk to us. We're not going to dump on you. Katia's gone—they told me she checked out. Is this why?"

"How should I know? You probably know better than I do. Hasn't Katia been telling you all our dirty little secrets?" His hands were shaking, sharp little jerks. He must have realised it, because he knotted them up in his lap. "Shit, that sounds nasty. I just meant, we haven't been talking to each other much for awhile. So I don't know why she left. But I guess this is probably why."

It was a peculiar moment. I was standing there in a bathrobe, barefoot, shaking and twitching from hip to ankle, not knowing what to say. I was keeping my eyes on Tony's face—it was as if I thought that, if I could just get him to meet my eye, everything would be okay. Tony was sitting there, God knows how many days the wrong end of a long drunk, and he was looking anywhere but at me or Bree. No one was talking; the room stank of tequila. I had no clue what to do. I just knew I had to do something, because if I didn't, he was fucked.

Bree went down on her knees, on the floor next to Tony's chair. She reached out got both his hands between her own, and he let her.

"Listen to me. Just listen to me. Please, Tony? Okay?"

She sounded soft and calm. I had a weird moment of something that might have been envy; she hadn't shown any softness when she was dealing with my drinking, back in the day. It had been more like a sledgehammer, tough love all the way.

"I want to be upfront about this. I knew something was going on, of course I did. Yes, Katia told me some of it. But she wasn't putting you down or badmouthing you, Tony. It wasn't about gossipy bullshit. She told me because she had no one else to tell and she was breaking apart over it."

He turned, finally, and made eye contact. They stared at each other, and I saw Bree's mouth working, trying not to break down and cry in front of Tony. Or maybe she didn't want to cry in front of me, not about this. I don't know.

"You have no idea what that's like, carrying all that stuff around for someone else, not having anyone to talk to about it or anyone to turn to. You just don't." She was still covering his hands, and she'd lost the whole no-tears battle; her face was wet.

"But I do know. That's why she felt it was safe to tell me. Please talk to us, Tony. It's not fair to John to just sit there and stay quiet."

He turned away from her then, and looked up at me. I've got no idea what my own face was showing, but I nodded.

It all came out, then. Standing there listening to him, I couldn't put it together in my head, or in my heart, either. I kept quiet and just let him unload.

He started out slow and halting. It was as if he wasn't sure, himself, how the hell a nice mellow piano player with a steady gig, a good band and a solid marriage had fetched up stashing bottles of Patron under sheet music in his piano bench, slipping downstairs when his wife was asleep to scratch that itch, lying about it in the morning, lying to himself, to Katia, letting it red-line...

"...when they started calling me shit like Bankcuso." He had hold of Bree's hands, but he'd gone back to not looking at either of us. Christ, I'd been there, you know? I'd been there too many years and I hadn't caught even a hint of it with Tony. "I was like, guys, what the fuck is that about, so I toured with Blacklight, who knew *Book of Days* was going to explode like that, I didn't know I was coming back with a bazillion dollars, give me a fucking break. But they just kept doing that shit. Bankcuso this, Moneybags that, always getting on me..."

"We get it, mate." My heart was stuttering, or trying to. "Believe me, we get it."

"Do you? Maybe, yeah, I guess." He sounded tired suddenly, too tired to argue or maybe even care. "If you get it, good for you. You're smarter than me, because I don't fucking get it. So you tell me, JP. How come, all of a sudden, people started calling me up? *Wow, you're fantastic Tony, come play on my CD. Hey, Tony, been a fan of yours for years, come party with us. Shit hot piano, Tony, come sit in with us.* I've been out there gigging my ass off since what,

1970? When did I hook up with Anton and start the Bombardiers, like, forty years ago?"

"Tony –"

"No, JP, I want to know. It's not like I wasn't here the whole time, but I do one tour with Blacklight and everyone wants me to come hang. What the fuck? Wasn't I any good before? Wasn't the work good enough to respect before?"

He got up suddenly, pulling his hands free of Bree's, lurching a little. She sat down with a thump; he'd caught her off balance.

"I don't need to party with anyone." His face was closed off. This was what I'd seen when he'd walked in, and for that one moment I hadn't recognised him. "I don't need my ass kissed either. And Katia can do whatever she wants. I don't give a shit. Maybe we can get it back, maybe not. How should I know? All I know is, I don't know who the hell I am anymore, or what I'm worth."

I opened my mouth, and closed it again. I had no clue what to say, and the lump at the back of my throat was big enough and hard enough to choke me. I don't think—honestly—that I've ever felt quite so useless in my life.

With one hand on the door, he turned round. Just for a moment, the Tony I know and love looked out of his eyes at us, tormented and miserable, trying to pull it together, failing, shrugging it off.

"Tell me where you want me to be, and I'll be there. I don't miss gigs and I don't fuck up. I'm a pro, with or without money. But right now, just leave me the fuck alone, okay?"

He was gone, leaving Bree and me staring at each other as the door clicked shut behind him.

# Chapter Ten

If anyone had told me I'd ever find myself thankful to be talking to Patrick Ormand—or anyone else—about a homicide investigation, I'd have thought they were mad as a brush. But
when Patrick rang up and asked if he could come round to discuss things, I jumped at it. Yeah, I still felt like an Aunt Sally left
out in the rain too long, but anything that could take my brain
off what was happening to Tony was good with me.

Besides, the silence was getting too heavy for comfort. Tony
had been gone a good half-hour, and neither Bree nor I had said
a damned thing. She had a lost, bleached look, something she
used to get back in the bad old days, when my first wife was still
alive. It doesn't sit well on her face; it's all about bleakness and
desolation, and I just fucking hate seeing it there. I didn't know
if it was Tony she was primarily worrying about, or Katia, or

even me, but whatever it was, she wasn't talking. She just climbed back into bed next to me and curled up with her back to me, about as close as a grown woman gets to a foetal position.

If Bree doesn't want to talk, you know it; there's no mistake possible. She doesn't just go quiet, she goes silent, and yeah, there's a difference. You can practically see the *No Trespassing* signs and barbed wire warning you off. I've got no real problem with her going quiet on me, but her silence is quite a lot weightier, and somehow, I never want to be the first one to break it.

That evening, that silence of hers was dense enough to have its own weather system, or maybe even its own gravitational field. No trespassing, you know? Since I was still feeling pretty rocky and hadn't got much to say myself, I just held on to her.

As I say, time telescopes during an MS relapse. It felt like hours going by, lying there with one arm draped lightly over my wife and the only noise anywhere the hum of the suite's air conditioning, but actually my cell went off not long after Tony'd gone. If Bree thinks I'm sleeping, she generally tries to get the phone before it disturbs me, but that time, she stayed where she was. So, yeah, she was seriously not into talking, or making eye contact, or anything else.

I rolled over carefully, got it off the nightstand, and took a quick look at the caller ID. I don't know, even now, whether I was hoping it would be Tony or not.

"Patrick? What's going on?"

"Hey, JP. Listen, I was just wondering if I could drop by, and share a little information. Are you and Bree feeling up for company? I just want a few minutes—I've got some ground left to cover tonight."

"Hang on a minute, and let me check with Bree." She'd rolled over, finally, and was watching me. I covered the phone with one hand. "Patrick. He wants to come round and talk, no clue about what. Probably got some gen from his copper mates at LAPD, or something. You all right with that, love?"

She nodded—still no words. "Patrick? Bree says yeah, no problem. We're in for the evening, I think."

"Great. See you in a few."

He rang off. Bree was still watching me, still in that foetal curl, still not saying anything. I sat down at the foot of the bed, rubbing my jaw.

"Bree, look. Stupid question, I know that, but I need to ask it. Are you okay? I know you're worrying. So am I. But beyond that, I want to know. Are you okay?"

"I don't know."

She sounded completely wretched. I hadn't heard her sound this way in longer than I wanted to think about; there it was, that note of desolation, and out of nowhere, I got what was worrying her. Saint Bree of Arc, always carrying a load of guilt for someone, whether it's hers or not...

"I don't what to do, John. I'm scared to death for both of them. I don't know how to help them. I love them both, and I don't know if there's anything we can do. I don't know how this happened." Her voice cracked. "It's not as if I didn't know. Katia told me. Why didn't I do something!"

"*Stop it.*"

Her mouth was trembling, trying to bite back whatever that weird little spur of hers is. I lay back down next to her, and pulled her up close. She was warm, and real, and there. She wasn't going anywhere. But Tony and Katia had been together thirty five years, maybe a bit more, and now Katia was gone. I couldn't wrap my own head round it, but right then, that wasn't number one on my priorities chart. I held on just tight enough to let her feel me there. It seemed important, somehow.

"So you knew it was happening." I kept my voice quiet. "Okay, I get that you're feeling you should have done something. But for

153

fuck's sake, Bree, what do you think you could have done? You want to tell me that? Christ, I've been riding the bus with Tony for weeks, recording with him, hitting the stage with him three nights out of seven. I didn't even notice. I knew there was something, but this? Never crossed my mind. I've been down the bottom of that same bloody hole, you know? Different reason, same damned bottle. You think I'm not feeling guilty for not sussing out what was going on?"

She'd begun to shudder. I held on, and kept talking.

"You can't blame yourself for this one. And I'll tell you what, neither can I. You pulled me out of it when it was my turn down the hole, but this isn't me, and Katia isn't you. And something you don't get, Bree: the only reason you could pull me out of it was because I wanted to go. That's the other thing—I wanted out of that mess. I didn't want to let you down, and I didn't want to let Blacklight down, and I didn't much fancy dying, either. But that's the way it works. If Tony wants to stay where he is, there's fuck-all you or Katia or anyone else can do for him. This is on him, Bree. You can't play god, and I can't wave some sort of magic guitar wand thing over his head and tell him he's all cured of it. Right now, pretty much the only thing either of us can do is just be there for both of them, in case we're wanted. So stop blaming yourself and feeling responsible, because it's rubbish and I'm not having it. Okay?"

"No. It's not okay."

She turned over and looked into my face. Bree's easier to read than I am—everything shows with her. I looked back at her, eye to eye, and got a shock. The penny that dropped somewhere in my stomach might as well have come off the top of a damned building.

"Your turn to listen to me." She wasn't pushing me away, but she wasn't holding on to me, either. Her voice was very steady. "You've been telling me to not feel responsible for things since I was seventeen. It's as if you actually believe that telling me not to feel the way I feel will make me stop feeling that way. Not going to happen, John."

Shit, shit, *shit*. I swallowed hard. "Bree –"

"People just don't work that way. At least, I don't. I'm not saying you're wrong about Tony needing to handle his own issues, or about why you wanted to kick drinking. I know you're right about that stuff, and I know you aren't trying to be insulting or patronising or condescending or whatever, by telling me to stop being who I am. But that's what you're doing. So stop telling me not to feel the way I feel, because you've been doing it for way too long and I've really had enough of it. Just—stop. Please?"

If she'd wanted to make me squirm, she'd made a damned good job of it; I was reading her now, loud and clear, and I was cringing inside. It was one of those moments, where you look back and think, *oh bloody hell, how long have I been doing that?* Incidents, moments, a good long line of them, moved straight into my memory as if they'd been hanging out, just waiting for a reason to make me want to kick myself.

I had a bad moment, of wanting to lash out at her: *Why the fuck did you wait thirty years to tell me?* That one faded fast, and left me feeling an absolute pillock. Christ, me telling Bree not to be who she was, telling her all her feelings were wrong, and then wanting to blame her for not calling me on it sooner? *Brilliant, Johnny. Could you get more arrogant, you berk?*

She had an apology coming from me, and we both knew it. But I had to find the words, and it wasn't going to be easy. No one likes being called on their shit, you know? And somehow, it's even worse when you're getting it from the one person you don't want to ever hear it from. But she was right, and it was time I copped to it.

I took a good long breath—*right, Johnny, don't overthink it, just say it*. And of course, Sod's Law being the tricky bugger that it is, someone knocked on the suite door.

155

Patrick Ormand rarely looks the worse for wear. It's something that's always narked me about him: three days with no sleep, phones ringing off the hook, dead bodies and forensic pathologists and whatever else, and he always looks pretty much the same. I'm not sure I've ever seen so much as a five-o'clock shadow on the bloke's chin. Don't know how he manages it, but it's always got on my nerves.

"Hey, JP, Bree. Thanks for letting me come by." He was smart enough to keep his gob shut about me being wrapped in a hotel robe. Maybe he genuinely hadn't noticed, or maybe he just didn't give a toss. "Were you able to catch some sleep?"

"On and off, yes. I think John got more than I did, though." Bree'd pulled herself upright and off the bed, and was heading for the fridge. "Do you want some Perrier, or some juice? Or should I call downstairs for coffee? And have you eaten?"

"Thanks—I've eaten. In fact, I had dinner with an old friend of mine. She works LAPD forensics, these days. But I wouldn't say no to a bottle of Perrier. I've been running around and it's warm out there."

He was talking to Bree, but oddly enough, he was watching me. I headed for the bathroom, where I'd left my clothes from the morning visit to Carla's. That whole scene felt so far away, it might just as well have gone down weeks ago.

They were both sitting at the table when I came back out. The sun had gone down over Rodeo Drive, finally, and LA looked to be getting its glitter on, people getting home, changing clothes, heading out into the clubs and restaurants, doing what Angelinos do. Out of nowhere, a sudden picture popped into my head: Andy Valdon, white and shaken, staring down at me while I sat there on the tiled floor with Bergen's body cooling in my lap: *He's really dead? You're sure...?*

"John?" Bree must have seen something in my face; she sounded anxious. "Are you okay?"

156

I shook off the memory. I could still hear Andy's voice in my head, still almost feel the dead weight of Bergen in my lap, holding me down. I could still smell him, the picture had been that strong. That was funky, nasty stuff—ghosts, and the wrong damned kind. I managed a smile for Bree.

"Yeah, I'm good. Just remembering a few things I'd rather not remember, that's all. Patrick, you sure water will do you? Okay. What did you want to talk about?"

"Just wanted to share some information." Leaning back in his chair with a bottle of pricey water in one hand, he didn't seem in any hurry to get started. "Carla wants me gathering as much info as I can. When I asked her if she had something specific in mind, she told me to follow my instincts, or at least follow my inner homicide cop's instincts. So that's what I've been doing."

"Right." I didn't say what came into my head—*yeah, right, go sniff something wounded out and kill it, is what she meant.* That last casual comment of his, about the old friend who worked forensics, had got all my red flags flying. "So what's the gen?"

"They've got the cause of death nailed down. It wasn't a cocaine overdose. There was virtually no coke in his system." He took a mouthful of water. "Good stuff, Perrier. Really got hot out there today."

We both watched him, neither of us saying anything. I don't know what Bree's reasoning was, but I was damned if I was going to feed his sense of dramatic timing, or whatever the hell that is. I'd learned a long time ago that the best way to get information from Patrick Ormand is to wait him out. You do that, he dishes. It's one of the few weaknesses he's got: other people not talking makes him twitchy. It's probably a leftover from his days as a cop.

"They did the full autopsy. From the description of Sandoval's death throes and certain post-mortem markers, they agreed they were probably looking at a toxin, rather than a simple narcotic OD." He was tapping his fingers against the table, a sure sign his

157

brain was working. Those mannerisms of his, those were things I'd sussed out about him back when he was a homicide cop. "Pam, that's my friend, ran the full tox screen."

Bree and I both stayed quiet. If Patrick was thinking what I was thinking—about that line of white powder on the counter, that line no one but Andy could possibly have washed away—he wasn't saying so. And of course, Bree hadn't been in the loo until after it was over…

"They got it within minutes." Patrick emptied the bottle. "Apparently, they found only traces of cocaine in the screen. What Bergen Sandoval ingested was close to pure strychnine, with maybe just enough coke in the mix to hide the effect on his taste buds. Pam said he must have snorted or swallowed close to five times the lethal dose."

I opened my mouth, and closed it again. No point asking questions, not yet; Patrick wasn't done. I could tell.

"That stuff used to be used as medicine, and you can still get it to kill gophers with. Lethal dose, for people, is half a grain, right around 32 mg. The official estimate for what was in Bergen was close to 160 mg."

His eyes were narrowed. Yeah, still a cop at heart, still smelling blood in the water. In some weird way, all this gen about someone getting painfully and messily dead got his rocks off.

"That's not for sharing, by the way—it hasn't been officially released yet and I don't want to pay Pam back for slipping me some behind-the-door info by getting her in trouble. But there you go. This wasn't bad coke, and it wasn't someone cutting coke with a cheap filler and accidentally using too much, either. The ratio of strychnine to the cocaine ingested makes that statistically impossible. Whoever handed over that stuff and passed it as cocaine knew exactly what they were doing. We're talking about a homicide here, I'd call it first degree. Bergen Sandoval was murdered."

158

"Yeah, well, I'm pretty sure we knew that, Patrick." Big dramatic line, all that, but it was rubbish. He wasn't done yet; there was more. "What's the catch?"

He shot me a look, hard to read; might have been irritation or appreciation. "The catch is in the timing of his reaction. I want to make sure I have this right. JP, you said it was just a couple of minutes between you and Andy walking into the bathroom and Bergen dying. Is that right?"

"Yeah, it is. Two minutes, max. Why?"

"Because strychnine doesn't work immediately, even in those concentrations. The lag between initial ingestion of the poison and the final convulsions averages out at between two and three hours. I was already at the Plus Minus when Bergen got there, just before seven. I checked my watch when Andy came out of the bathroom to get me. It was ten past eleven."

"What?" Bree's jaw had gone slack. "But—does that mean –"

"It means that, wherever and whenever he ingested a lethal dose of strychnine, it wasn't in the line of cocaine JP saw on the sink. And Andy Valdon apparently didn't know that." He got up and headed for the door. "I'm off to Carla's. Thanks for the time and the Perrier."

Considering everything going down just then, it's probably not surprising that the Geezers' debut CD release had got pushed to the back of my mind. Fortunately for me, Carla was on top of it; a shortlist of handpicked radio outlets had been given the pre-release pressing, and Carla and the new kid were fielding interview and in-studio gig requests.

Once that happened, I had to put everything else to one side, and deal with it. Making decisions about the PR for the Geezers are entirely on me—I don't get to shove it off on anyone else. And there was really no wiggle room in the timing, because we hadn't named the bloody thing yet. Until that happened, we couldn't finish the artwork and get it run and ready. So yeah, there was a gun to my head.

One of the trickiest things about getting a CD out is figuring out what to call it. It may not sound like an issue, but getting just the right name is a lot of work. The thing is, once you've named it, that's it, game over. It's not as if you can say right, sorry, title's not working for me after all, let's recall half a million copies and change it. It's branded, and everything that goes along with it is branded, as well. I remember an endless miserable week back in the eighties, sitting in Blacklight's London office with the band and the braintrust, trying to get just the right title for the CD we were putting out. It took days of shouting at each other before we finally agreed on the title, and I still don't like it. Not liking it's a stone drag, since the CD in question was *Every Minute Counts*, and it's Blacklight's fifth best-selling CD ever. Brilliant CD, bloody stupid title.

The morning after Patrick came by, I was feeling well enough to consider heading back over to Carla's offices for a confab on the CD schedule. Once Patrick had gone, I'd turned the phone off, and left it off. There was a bit of business needed doing, just between me and my wife, and I didn't want any interruptions.

Letting Bree know that she was right about me telling her how to feel or not feel, copping to my own shit, was no fun at all. I did it, though, and I meant it. If you want to know what I said, you're out of luck; I'm not sharing that apology with anyone. The important thing was that she accepted it, because she knew I meant it. She even promised to call me on it if I ended up doing it again. Funny thing, this growing up business, especially when you're coming up on sixty.

The problem with killing the phones was that, next morning, I had a shitload of messages. There'd been a couple of calls with no messages left; Tony'd rung from his cell phone, and there was one from someone who came up as No Number. I hesitated over

160

whether to ignore the fact that Tony'd rung off without leaving a message, and just ring him back; truth is, I was worried as hell about him. But he'd been upfront about him wanting us, me and Bree both, to just let him be. I didn't have a single good reason to not respect that.

Besides, there were quite a few messages after his hang-up, and it made sense to check them before I decided what to do, especially since I'd actually rolled out of bed too early to be ringing him. I did an experimental shake of both legs, and nothing hurt beyond the usual jabs and tingles; the exacerbation was finally moving off. Good. God knows what had been piling up while I'd been curled up, waiting for the MS to cut me some slack and let me get on with things.

There was a message from Henry, a basic thank-you for letting him drive us up and down the Coast in Magic, and letting us know the bus had been returned. I made a mental note to myself, to make sure Henry got properly thanked in the final liner notes for the CD, and moved on to Carla's message.

"(beep)...JP? Hope you're feeling better today. Listen, I have a list of six different media outlets who'd like to do spots or full appearances with you. Guitar Wizard also checked in—they've got their reviewer on the ground in West Hollywood and want to review the CD. Also, would you and the guys be up for a live set at Amoeba? It's a fantastic place to play and if that's a yes, should we get set up to record it? And we're going to need a name pretty damned quick, because the cover art's done and we need to get it together. I've got a short list of suggestions. Let's go over those, unless you've already got something in mind, because it's getting critical...(beep)"

"Shit!"

"What is it? What's wrong?"

Bree, just coming out of the bathroom, sounded as drawn and tired as she looked. I'd actually caught up on some sleep, but from the looks of it, she'd been awake half the night. Right—sod

161

the CD, Carla, and the rest of the world. Everything in her voice made it clear: she was expecting more bad news from the cosmos. I tossed the phone on the bed, and dropped both arms round my wife.

"Nothing earth-shattering, love, don't worry. Carla left a message, and I've just realised, the CD artwork is supposed to be sent off tomorrow. It's already together—live shot from the Seattle show, fog creeping in around the corners. We've got everything but the title and I haven't got a clue what the damned thing ought to be called. If it comes down to it, we can just have it be called the Fog City Geezers, but I'd rather it got a decent name, you know? Anyway, Carla wants me to come down there and confab over a list of possible titles, but –"

"Fogbound."

I blinked at her. She'd sounded pretty decisive. "Come again? What did you say, love?"

"Call it *Fogbound*." She smiled, but it didn't last; she literally looked as if the muscles of her face were too limp to sustain it. "That just sounds right, to me, anyway. Bound as in caught up in it, but also bound as in bound for somewhere. And it would work with the cover, right? Does that make sense?"

"Damn, Bree, that's brilliant!" The more I looked at it, the better it sounded. She was right, it caught more than one meaning: caught in the fog, but it also seemed to echo back quite nicely to the whole road trip aspect, Magic and the tour. "*Fogbound* it is. Well done, love. Cheers!"

So we had a title, and that was one thing to cross off my personal list of shit to worry about, at least. I rang Carla, and ran it past her; she loved it, and told me she'd get it moving. There was still one problem we hadn't talked about, and I was praying she wouldn't bring it up, but of course she did.

"...so about those radio spots, and Amoeba—did you get my message on that? Do you need a list to choose from, or do you

162

want to leave it up to me?"

"Right. Well…" *Shit.* I took a long breath. "Look, Carla, I can do all the guest spots you want, but live gigging might be iffy right now. You can book me anywhere in LA you fancy for PR stuff, but I can't commit the rest of the band. There's an issue."

"Tony?" She'd already guessed. Of course she had—I'd nearly forgot about that conversation between her and Bree, yesterday morning. You can't sneak anything past Carla, but it was worrying, how gentle she sounded. She doesn't do gentle, usually, especially if it's over something that's going to fuck with her professionally. "Anything I can do to help, JP?"

"Don't think so, but I'll let you know. He just wants to be left alone right now. In the meantime, let me know where you need me and when."

"Will do. I need to go, I've got a call holding for me on the other line. I'll call you when I've set things up."

We had a nice quiet breakfast, sent from downstairs. Bree poked at her toast, and made a face at her coffee. I lifted an eyebrow at her.

"Breakfast not right?"

She sighed. "No, it's fine. I'm just…"

She let it die away, and I grinned at her. "Rather be home, cooking your own? Yeah, I'd rather be eating yours as well. Soon, Bree. Do you want shore leave? Maybe take a couple of days, head north? I can tell Carla to schedule me for a couple of things tomorrow and then tell her nothing for a few days."

She bit her lip. There were purple shadows under both eyes; she looked as if she hadn't got a full night's sleep worth a damn since we'd got on Magic back in that South of Market parking lot all those weeks ago. Out of nowhere, I had a picture in my head, vivid and clear: my wife, in her own kitchen cooking, hanging out, shooing cats off the table, the kitchen smelling brilliant, pushing my breakfast across the table at me and the fog rolling in

163

under the Golden Gate instead of all this endless sun, and no fucking palm trees, either…

"Could we?" She sounded about as stressed as she looked. "Oh God, John, that sounds so good to me right now, you just can't imagine—okay, maybe you can. But what about Bergen? And what about Tony?"

"Tony was pretty damned clear, Bree. He wants to be left alone right now. And he's a big boy, you know? Don't know what you think we can do for him, but unless he's up for having it done, it's not happening. I don't like it any more than you do, but we're stuck." I reached across and got hold of her hand. "Besides, if Katia's gone north, you can maybe get together with her, and see if there's anything you can do. Okay?"

"Okay." She'd ducked her head, an old habit she'd got out of a long time ago. Things had to be really stressy, to be dragging that one back out. "And Bergen?"

"What about him? He's dead, nothing to be done for him, and sod Bergen, he's not our problem—oh, right, you talking about Cunningham? I'll ring him personally if I have to, but you know what, Bree, unless he's planning on slapping us in cuffs or something, I don't think he can order us about and tell us to stay here if we don't want to. I want a break from hotel suites and press conferences and all the rest of it. I want a break from bleedin' Los Angeles. What good's all that money we've got, if we can't wave it at lawyers, and make them handle the cops for us? Fuck it. Let's go home."

Getting out of LA—the logistics of it—turned out to be quite a lot simpler than I think either of us expected. I rang Carla back, and explained what was wanted; I hadn't got more than halfway through before she interrupted me.

"JP, you're on a roll for great ideas today. First the title, now this? Let the lawyers worry about Cunningham. That's why we pay them all that money. What's the earliest you want me to book you for media stuff? And when do you want to head out?

164

I'll get you a flight and a town car, and see if we can't have you guys home in time for dinner."

It was amazing, how much of a load got taken off, just knowing we were on our way home to our own house for a few days. Bree was as energised by it as I was; she got us packed at light speed. While she was folding gear and getting it stowed in our luggage, I rang down to the desk and asked for Tony's room. It was a balancing thing, the best move I could think of at the moment: if he answered, I could tell him up front what we were doing, and if he didn't, he'd have it in voicemail and I wouldn't have to deal with it. And yeah, I know just how weak that sounds, but you try having to let your best friend know you're leaving town while he's sitting in a hole he's dug for himself, basically flinging dirt to keep you or anyone else from helping him climb out of it.

I had a bet on with myself, that he wasn't going to answer. One ring, two rings...

"(beep) The guest in this room is not answering. Please leave a message at the tone."

"Tony? JP. Look, just wanted to let you know, Bree and I are going home for a few days. We're both still pretty out of it, and Clay Street's calling our names. We need a couple of days away from LA. Carla's setting me up for some PR stuff for the CD, but I've told her not until next week, and she knows not to commit the band. Oh, and by the way, we've got a name for the CD— Bree came up with *Fogbound* and Carla thinks that works. Ring my cell if you want to talk, or need anything, or whatever. Cheers, mate."

There have been quite a few times I've got off a plane after a Blacklight tour or a gig of some kind, and found myself cursing the San Francisco fog under my breath. That evening, pulling out of the SFO parking garage in the back of the town car Carla had waiting for us, I looked at a clear sky just going golden red as the sun went down, with a dusting of fog moving along the City, and thought it had to be the most beautiful I've ever seen Bay Area weather get. Just gorgeous.

We were back at 2828 Clay Street in time for supper. Bree had rung our housekeeper and cat sitter, Sammy, to let him know we were en route, but it had been rather late in the day to ask him to get something out of the freezer. Bree'd weighed the pros and cons of having the driver stop at the local market, so that she could shop and cook us a proper meal, but I had a fancy for Mediterranean food, and we opted for takeout from our usual place on Fillmore Street.

Sammy had got Bree's message, and left lights on for us. All three cats emerged from wherever they'd been hanging out, and came down the front hall to meet us; even Wolfing, who was sixteen now and mostly slept in a basket near Bree's computer these days, came and rubbed against my ankles. I bent down and scratched behind his ears, while Bree headed off towards the kitchen. I could hear the click and hum of the big Sub-Zero fridge, and a muted beep as Bree checked the house phone for messages. The house was cool, and clean, and it smelled right. Home, you know? Nothing really smells like where you live, except where you live...

"John?"

I jerked my head up. There was something odd about her voice. "Bree? Something wrong?"

"Can you come back here, please? I—need you."

I went down the hall at not quite a run. The cats, looking bewildered and annoyed, came along as well.

She was standing in the kitchen, with one hand on the pause button to our answering machine and a really peculiar look on her face. I felt the tickybox ramp up.

"Bree? What...?"

"We have a phone message." She took a deep breath, and lifted her finger off the pause button. "Or, actually, you do. Listen."

166

*"(beep) Mr. Kinkaid? Hi, this is Jeff Kintera, from the Seven Oh Seven Club up in San Rafael. I'm really sorry to disturb you, but I have a question, and I didn't want to bother Carla Fanucci with it. It's just a small thing and I gather she's on vacation. No big deal, but we're getting close to a booked run of shows, and I kind of need to be able to get to my own paperwork. So I was just wondering how long Andy Valdon's going to need to use my office? Oh! I almost forgot, congratulations on the Geezers tour—hope it went well. Thanks. (beep)"*

# Chapter Eleven

After listening to Jeff Kintera's message, my own instinct—to ring him back and tell him to put Andy on the phone and no damned arguments, either—lasted just long enough for Bree to suss out what I was planning. The minute she got it, she clued me in to something I hadn't considered.

"Cor stone the bloody crows!" I must have been gawking at the phone. "What the fuck is Jeff on about? What's Andy Valdon doing up here? He's, what, hiding out in the Seven Oh Seven management office? Did I hear that properly?"

"You must have, because I heard it too." Bree still had that look on her face. "John, what are you doing?"

"What do you think I'm doing? Ringing Jeff back and getting that git Andy the phone so I can wring his—what?"

She was shaking her head. I stopped punching numbers.

"We can't call Jeff back, not yet anyway. John, don't you get just how tricky it is? Andy's got to know he's wanted in LA. He has to know Cunningham has him at the top of the list of suspects, or persons of interest, or whatever the hell they're called these days. But he must have come straight here from LA. From the sound of it, he told Jeff that Carla was on vacation or something. I can't think of any reason he'd do that unless he wanted to make sure Jeff wouldn't call her."

"Yeah, I get all that, ta." I still had the phone in one hand. "What's your point, Bree?"

"My point is that he's a fugitive." She's not usually quite so blunt, not with me, but just then, she sounded like the business end of a jackhammer. "John, you're not thinking this through. At the moment, we haven't confirmed anything yet. It's all hearsay—Jeff's call might be a practical joke. We don't know for sure that Andy's here. But the minute you call back and get confirmation that Andy's really where Jeff says he is, we've got information. We know the whereabouts of someone wanted for questioning in a murder investigation. And that would get us into more trouble than I want to deal with right now."

"Shit!" I'd caught up now, and seen where this was headed. "Yeah, you're right. If we don't tell Cunningham, we're helping a fugitive, aiding or comforting or whatever. That miserable divvy would have us both for lunch and pick his teeth with our bones afterwards. Now what, Bree? We can't just sit back and pretend we didn't get that damned message."

She met my eye. I knew what she was going to say before she said it.

"Call Patrick," she told me. She was right, it really was the only way. "He's supposed to be protecting our interests, and not just ours—the whole band family's interests. But first take your afternoon meds. And then I want to order some kebabs before Houri stops taking phone orders for the night."

169

Patrick answered on the first ring. Used to be a time I'd have thought he did that because he'd seen Bree's name in the caller ID. It had taken me quite a while to add him to my own address book, but these days, I ring from my own phone, even if he's not exactly in my speed dial list. After all, he works for Black-light.

"Hey, JP. Carla told me you and Bree went north. Did you get home all right? Any problems?"

"We got home just fine, ta, but if we're talking about problems, yeah, one huge sodding problem waiting for us when we got here. Hang on, let me put this on the speaker—Bree wants to hear it." I took a good long breath. "Patrick, I'll cop to it, straight up: We're shoving this off into your lap, because neither of us has a clue how to handle it, and Bree's betting you do. We got home and Bree found a message for me our house phone. Jeff Kintera rang, from up at the Seven Oh Seven. He's got a run of shows booked and he wants to know how long Andy Valdon's going to need to use his office."

Silence. That doesn't happen often, Patrick Ormand not having a comeback right there and ready.

"Patrick...?"

"I'm here. Just thinking."

There it was, that change in his voice. He was thinking all right, but he wasn't thinking as a security bloke or a private detective. He was thinking the way he'd thought when he was Lieutenant Patrick Ormand, Homicide, pick a city because he'd worked in at least three. He was thinking the way he thought because someone out there was acting like a criminal and getting all his juices on the move.

"Patrick?" Bree wasn't settling down—there was food en route, and half her attention was on the doorbell. "Look, I'm sorry if we shouldn't have called you about this, but I really didn't know what else to do. I mean, we can't just call Jeff back, can we? Because wouldn't that make us accessories or something like that? I seem to remember…"

Her voice wavered and died off, and I reached out and got hold of her hand. I knew just what she was remembering: she'd helped my first wife, Cilla, slip in backstage at Madison Square Garden to talk to the bloke Cilla'd ended up killing with one of my guitar stands. The only reason Bree hadn't fetched up in some grim penitentiary somewhere in upstate New York was because Patrick, who'd been the NYPD homicide copper in charge of the case, had let her off the hook. He drives me round the fucking twist most days, but I owe him for that one, and always will.

"No, don't return that call." Patrick had gone crisp suddenly. I wondered if he'd heard that movement in her voice, and sussed where it had come from. Probably; he's got a major soft spot for my wife. "Don't even acknowledge you got it. Don't erase it, just don't respond or take any action of any kind. The last thing you guys need right now is to get on the wrong side of LAPD Homicide. Cunningham's already in a bad mood about having to deal with this much power and prestige, not to mention money. My feeling is that he'd be a tricky guy to work with anyway, but right now, that particular ice is especially thin. He's pretty resentful, and the fact that he let Andy slip away is bubbling just under the local headlines. Leave this one alone, guys, okay? I'll handle it from down here, and keep you posted on a need-to-know basis. Meanwhile, I was about to check my own messages. Glad you got home okay, talk to you later."

He rang off. Bree opened her mouth, and closed it again. She looked completely confounded, but relieved, as well. I could feel one of my eyebrows go up. We looked at each other.

"John?" She sounded very unsure of herself. "Okay, good, I wanted him to say he'd handle it, but—well—did he sound strange to you? Mad, or something? Because I didn't think either of us said anything to piss him off."

171

"He's not narked at us, Bree." I grinned at her, suddenly. "Yeah, he sounded peculiar, but that's because he was trying for a bit of professional courtesy. Cop manners, you know? I got the feeling he was biting down hard on a few choice comments about Cunningham, that's all. Didn't you?"

She looked relieved. "As in, that guy has a chip on his shoulder the size of a giant sequoia? Man, I hope that's all it is. I mean, I know this is Patrick's gig and his problem and anyway, it's his area of expertise. And I know I suggested it in the first place, but..."

"But you can't help feeling guilty for dumping it on him? No, don't look at me like that, Bree. What, you're not thinking I'm going to tell you not to feel guilty, after I just turned myself inside out apologising? I'm not that dim. I'm just asking you to remember that Patrick actually enjoys coping with this stuff, that's all. Was that the doorbell? Good, I could eat."

She headed off down the hall, and I hunted out a couple of plates. I was rummaging around in the fridge for juice when I heard the front door shut, and murmuring, more than one voice. I straightened up, and turned round, fast.

I've noticed this before: when shit happens out of nowhere, people seem to get old in a hurry. I'd had that bad few seconds of not recognising Tony, when he'd walked into our suite in LA. But if I'd thought he'd looked sick and wasted, he had nothing on his wife.

"Here. Sit."

It blew my mind, how normal Bree sounded, because she sure as fuck didn't look normal. Katia was behind her and couldn't see Bree's face; besides, it was quite possible Katia was past noticing that her best friend was in shock, anyway. But I could see my wife just fine, and for a moment or two, the tickybox went into overdrive, because it had to. Without it, I probably would have had a heart attack. I can't describe the look on her face, because I've

172

got no reference point. I've never seen anything quite like it there before and I hope to God I never do again.

Katia sat. She's tough, Katia is; she shows her Russian peasant ancestry. Occasionally, if she has too much wine at one of Bree's parties, she'll flex her muscles and tell people in a bad fake Russian accent that she's "strong! like bull!" She is, too—quite muscled and sturdy. Being on the short side myself, I've never really ever seen Katia as small before.

But she'd shrunk. There's just no other word for it; whatever had happened between her and Tony had somehow brought her down in stature, and made her small. She looked tiny. Next to Bree, she looked fragile. Worse than that, she suddenly looked old, scoured out. She looked every bit as broken as Tony had looked. She wasn't talking, either, and that was a dead giveaway, because Katia's a chatterbox.

It was hard to look at her, and in fact, I couldn't. The picture was there in my head suddenly, Tony reeking of tequila and looking as broken as his old lady suddenly looked, wondering out loud if anything he'd ever done had been good enough…

So I wasn't looking in Katia's direction when Bree went down on her knees in front of her best friend, the person she was closest to in the world that wasn't me. She'd done that for Tony, but this was different, somehow; she wasn't holding anything of herself back. It wasn't until I heard her voice that I was able to turn round, and bring them both into focus.

"How can we help?" No tough love, not this time; Bree sounded strong and warm as sunlight, as if she'd found enough strength for both of them, for all three of us and maybe for Tony as well. I pushed away the thought that wanted in: *yeah, if he'd fucking let us.* "Katia, please tell us. Is there anything we can do?"

"Like what?" Thin, husky, tired-out little thread of a voice. Out of nowhere, I suddenly wanted to find Tony and just bash him, shake him, shout at him: *what in the name of sweet bleeding*

173

*fuck do you think you're on about!* It was the wrong voice to be coming out of Katia. "Can you get my husband to stop thinking he's worthless? Can you get him to stop lying to me? Can you get him to come home?"

"No." I hadn't known I was going to say anything, but there it was, out in the open air. "The only person who can do that is Tony. And trust me, I ought to know."

Katia turned and met my eye. The misery and bitterness and exhaustion in that look was like a physical kick in the pit of the stomach. The thought came into my head, fully formed, absolutely paralysing: Had Bree looked like this, when I was down and wasted and falling apart and lying about it? Had I just not noticed? I took a good long breath.

"Katia, look. I don't know how much you know about me and Bree, back in the day. Thing is, we've been here, you know? We've been where you are now. My first wife liked her bourbon and she liked it too much, same way she liked a lot of things too much. That did her in, in the end. Don't get me wrong, I'm not putting any blame on her for my shit—I liked the booze as much as she did. Difference was, I got a wake-up call and answered the bell. Cilla didn't."

They were both watching me. Something was moving in Bree's face, Christ only knew what; that marital mind-reading thing wasn't happening, and maybe that was just as well. I've said it before: I do best telling the truth and getting at the root of things when I don't think too much about what I want to say first, or how I want to say it.

Still, it would have been nice if my old lady's given me some kind of cue. Yeah, I knew what wanted out, but the thing was, I had no way of knowing whether telling anyone, even Katia, was going to get notched up as a kind of betrayal. I couldn't speak for Bree, but speaking just for myself, I'd never told anyone about this part of our history.

I glanced at Bree. And there it was, a tiny nod, invisible to anyone who didn't know the signals, encouragement, approval: *it's ok, go ahead, tell her.* Marital mind reading, back on track.

"You may not know this, but back when Bree and I first got together, when I first moved here, I was a thorough soak." I had Katia's attention, all right. "Drunk six days out of seven, Katia. Classic drunk, pissed all the time, bottles stashed in odd corners. Bree didn't know at the time, but I woke up in a tube station in North London, when I was over there recording with Blacklight. No memory of how I got there. That was the wakeup call I was talking about, you know? I went home and I dumped the entire pile of shit in Bree's lap."

I stopped. Katia looked up at me. She's pretty blunt, generally, but just then, she wasn't talking. Just as well, really, because I wasn't done talking yet. And Christ, talking about this stuff was tricky; I could feel my own voice wanting to shake. I wasn't letting it go there.

"Bree got me dry. She made me show her where every bottle in the place was. She dumped them all down the sink and told me she'd bash my skull in if she ever found another one. Tough love, yeah? And it worked. I stopped drinking, never went back. Hardest thing I ever did, and the killer is, I was so fucked up I never stopped to think that however hard it was for me, it was harder for her. Because I'd asked her."

Bree's face twisted up, and then smoothed out. I stopped, and took another long breath. Weird thing: I was sweating and lightheaded, body temperature up, the same way I used to get back when I was drinking, or getting stoned off the harder stuff. You'd have thought I was drunk, or doing snowball, rather than just talking about it.

"That's what made it happen, Katia. I asked Bree to help me." Both women were watching me now, and this time, I picked my words more carefully. "She didn't suggest it, or dive into it. She didn't even know, not until I'd copped to it. That's what you're going to need, if you're going to get Tony back to himself: him asking you for help. And no, I have no clue how to get him to do that. Not sure there's any way it can be done from outside himself, you know? Maybe he just needs—what do you call that, Bree? A cluesticking? A moment, anyway. Something to bring him back, slap him back to reality, something to make him ask for help. Damned if I know what, though."

Katia's face was doing some odd things. I didn't know whether tears would help, or just make things worse; that wasn't my call and anyway, I didn't get a vote. But she wasn't crying, she was shivering, maybe with the effort to not lose it in front of me, or in front of Bree. Like I said, she's quite tough.

*Bree's tough as well, you pillock. You think she never had to push the tears down so that you wouldn't see, when it was her handling your issues?*

"John?" Oh Christ, Bree'd seen it in my face—I must have looked like death. There was no way to deal with it just then, no time and no space, not with Katia sitting there trying not to flip her shit and melt down entirely. But Bree'd seen it hit me, the realisation. Shit, shit, *shit.* "Can you get the door? The bell just rang. Katia, look, you need to eat. We sent out for some stuff from Houri—no, don't even think about arguing with me. You've lost weight and you can't really afford to. Strong like bull, remember...?"

She was settling Katia at the table as I headed off down the hall. Bree was right about wanting Katia to eat, and as far as I was concerned, Katia could have my chicken kebab and pita bread, and welcome to it. That moment of understanding just how much I'd dumped on Bree, how much I'd given her to handle without ever thinking about what giving me what I needed was costing her, had taken my appetite. I felt sick at my stomach.

The bell rang again, just as I got to the front door. I was scrabbling in my wallet, and muttering under my breath; I find I do that quite a lot these days. "Yeah, right, hold your horses, coming!"

I pulled the door open, and stood there like an idiot, holding out the credit card, like a department store mannequin in a MasterCard ad, or something.

It wasn't the delivery boy from Houri with our food. It was Andy Valdon.

It's probably just as well I don't think much about doing something before I actually do it, sometimes. That was a moment when thinking about what I was getting myself into would have fucked the situation up even worse than it already was. And from where I was standing—staring like a fish at Lieutenant Cunningham's prime suspect for feeding rat poison to Bergen Sandoval—it was already more than I wanted to cope with.

"I'm sorry to bother you." His voice was barely above a murmur. He sounded a lot more normal than he looked; he actually looked like someone who'd been dragged backward over a country road somewhere, as if he hadn't slept since he'd watched Bergen Sandoval jack-knife into my lap and die. There'd been quite a lot of that recently, what with the Mancusos, and watching Bree trying to hold her own shit together, and cope with it. "I'm really sorry. But I didn't have a choice."

As I say, I wasn't thinking. All I was really aware of was the need to get him the hell off the front stairs and out of sight before anyone else saw him. There was also a driving little voice at the back of my skull, saying the same thing over and over: *do something and for fuck's sake don't let Bree or Katia know he's here.* I wasn't looking at that particular thought, not just then, because there wasn't time. I opened my mouth to get rid of him—*look, mate, whatever you think you're up to it's not my problem, go deal with your own shit and stop dragging me and my old lady into it—*

177

when a small grey car pulled up, the blinkers went, and the delivery bloke from Houri climbed out. Our dinner had arrived.

I moved so fast, I spooked myself. I had Andy by the arm, indoors and into our front room before I knew I was going to do anything at all.

"Stay there." I doubt you could have heard me more than six inches away. "Stay there and shut up, for fuck's sake. My wife and Katia Mancuso are in the kitchen and I'm not having either of them put up on accessory charges. They find out you're here, I call the cops. We clear?"

He nodded. I pulled the door shut just as the delivery bloke hit the bottom of the stairs. My heart was thumping as hard as I could remember it going since the day they'd put the tickybox in. *Right, Johnny, keep it normal, yeah? Pay for the food, get him out of here, sort out what to do next...*

I closed the front door and slipped into the parlour. Andy was just sitting there at the edge of my favourite rocking chair, staring at the floor, hands between his knees. He looked like an overcooked veggie: thoroughly limp.

"Stay here." There was no way Bree or Katia could have heard a word, I was keeping my voice so far down. "Stay here and keep that door closed. I'll do my best to get things sorted out in the kitchen and when I do I'll be back. It may take a bit, but I'll be back. We're having a talk, you and me."

"John?" *Shit.* Bree was out in the hall; I could tell from her voice. "Do you need help?"

"No, it's cool, be right there. Just checking to make sure they got the whole order in."

I slipped out into the hall myself. Behind me, very quietly, Andy got up and closed the door.

I had no clue what I was going to do, none at all. Even if I got Katia fed and calmed down and out the door, I couldn't think of any way to keep Bree from finding out Andy Valdon had shown

178

up, never mind that I'd parked him in the front room without letting her know. Best I could hope for was that she wouldn't find out about it until enough time had passed to keep her from wanting to kill me. The truth is, I couldn't help feeling shabby, as if I was doing something dodgy. Didn't matter that I was doing it to protect her. I don't fancy lying to Bree, you know?

I don't know how I got through that meal without Bree sussing me out, but it probably had to do with her being really concentrated on getting something down Katia. There was plenty of nosh for everyone—I find most good Mediterranean places are really generous with their portions—but Katia's appetite had gone and Bree basically spent that meal cajoling her into taking a few bites of everything. I've never seen Bree doing the whole nurturing thing with an actual child, but if the work she put into getting Katia fed that night was anything to go by, any kid my wife had been given charge of would have weighed twenty stone. Katia ended up finishing an entire plate of food, and she didn't want so much as a mouthful of it.

We'd barely finished up when Katia got up and headed for the half-loo in the hall. I had a bad moment there, hoping Andy would have the sense to stay put. The kitchen doors were still swinging behind Katia when Bree turned to me, very fast. She had a taut, pinched look.

"John, listen. Katia stayed in a motel on Lombard Street last night. She doesn't want to go home—she doesn't want to sleep in their bed, and she really doesn't want to be there alone. I think if I offer to spend the night there, she'd be willing to go home. But I don't want to leave you alone, not when the MS has been so miserable. I just..."

Her voice died away. I got hold of her hands.

"Do it." Yeah, still feeling as if I were lying to her, but there was no denying her heading off with Katia would solve my biggest issue right then. Besides, she was right; Katia feeling she couldn't go home, that was rubbish and unacceptable and one more thing I wanted to shout at Tony about, if I could only get near him. "I'll be fine. Yeah, the bed's too big without you, but Katia's a mess and she needs help. Not a problem."

She was biting her lip. I could hear the faint gurgle of the plumbing, as Katia flushed the loo. "John, are you sure?"

"Yeah, totally. I'll ring you if I need you, but right now, go with Katia. She needs her best friend."

I'd worried Katia might argue, but it didn't happen. Bree told her in a nice flat tone that they were both going to the Mancuso's house on Portero Hill, and Katia nodded. That was it, bang, sod-all, no problem mate, Bob's your uncle. Bree didn't even have to pack an overnight bag, since we'd just parked our suitcases right there in the kitchen, when we'd got back from the airport.

I walked them downstairs to the garage, and got both women and Bree's luggage into our Jag. Katia had taken a cab in from the airport to her motel, and cabbed from the motel over to our place. Not a sound from the front room—Andy must have taken my warning to heart. Good. I wasn't actually feeling quite as well as I'd told Bree I was, and I wasn't really feeling spry enough to deal with very much more.

Turned out I'd been worrying about having to deal for nothing. The front room was empty. At some point during the past half hour, while Bree was bullying Katia into eating and I was pushing food around on my own plate and not knowing whether I was narked at Bree not noticing or glad about it, Andy'd gone.

"Right." I sat in the rocker, waiting for the tickybox to do its thing, talking to myself. Pure stress, that was, and lucky I knew it; otherwise, I'd have thought I was losing it. "Brilliant. Think, Johnny. Now what the fuck am I supposed to do…?"

The answer was just as obvious as it had been when we'd first listened to Jeff's voicemail, and Patrick must have had the phone

180

handy, because he picked up on the second ring. This time, though, the connection seemed noisy.

"JP?"

"Yeah, it's me. Question for you, mate: how safe is this line? Any chance the bloke in charge in LA has got an ear in on this? Because that problem from a couple of hours ago? It's just gone redline on me, and I don't much fancy anyone listening in."

"Well, it's my cell phone." He sounded less amused than I would have expected. There was quite a lot of noise in the background at his end, and I wondered where he was. "I can't imagine that it's any more or less secure than anyone else's. What happened? You didn't call Jeff Kintera back, did you?"

I gave him the full story—not the emotional stuff, that was none of his damned business, but the nuts and bolts. When it came to talking about the thing with Katia, I did have to give him the basic reason she'd walked out of LA, but I kept it to a bare minimum. To do him credit, he wasn't poking and prying after more.

"...so Bree's spending the night keeping an eye on Katia, and I'm sitting here wondering what the hell I'm supposed to do next." I was rubbing first one thigh, then the other, with my free hand. There were hot little wires of pain doing a twitchy dance down both legs. *Shit.* "Any advice or suggestions? I'm open to damned near anything right now, so long as it doesn't need me going anywhere. The two people who usually drive me are both unavailable at the moment. I'm not really up for dealing with much anyway. I'm not feeling all that well."

"For now, do what you were doing: nothing." I thought I heard a door slam in the background, but I couldn't be sure. Probably still at Carla's. "And no need to drag Bree into it, not at this juncture. I'll be at your place as soon as I can after I've finished what I need to do in the morning."

"Sorry?" I blinked at the phone. "Wait a minute, Patrick.

Where are you?"

"I just got to LAX and paid off my cabbie. I'm heading north on the next flight. I've already got a call in to Jeff Kintera. We're getting together nice and early tomorrow morning, in the club office at the 707." There it was, that hunter's voice, that tone of his. "And if no one's tipped off Andy Valdon, that conversation will hopefully be a three-way. Jesus, the security checkpoint line is nuts—anyway, I need to board. Try to get some sleep, and I'll call you from San Rafael."

# Chapter Twelve

I'd been right about the MS gearing up to nail me again. By the time I'd finished loading the dishwasher, I was heading for what felt like a monster of a relapse, to the point where it wasn't likely I'd be able to do anything at all until it passed. I've lived with this disease long enough to know when arguing with it is a waste of energy. Relapses this bad, the best I can hope for is that medicating it to the limit will take enough of the edge off to let me sleep until the damned thing's done with.

Even when the meds are doing what they're supposed to do, though, sleep's not always possible. The brain does something very annoying during the bad hits, or at least mine does: it turns all the way on, and does this sort of laser beam thing. And that really isn't the way my brain usually works, not at all. I told my neuro about it once, and she said it was probably a survival defence mechanism, that focussing on anything and everything that isn't the pure physical misery of the disease itself was my brain's way of giving my body some breathing room. She's probably right—it makes good sense, that theory—but the physical misery is still there. It makes doing small stuff, things like opening a tin of cat food or punching the numbers of our security code into the alarm keypad, tricky enough to have sent Hercules into a panic. And the truth is, I'm not used to being on my own anyway, especially not when the MS hits.

Tonight, though, it was all on me. The one thing that looked to be remotely sensible was getting myself down for the night as early as possible, with anything I might need to ride it out close enough to hand to not have to move to get at it. So it was nowhere near full dark when I fed the cats, set the alarm, and headed upstairs for what was looking to be a long bad night ahead. Normally, I'd have left my cell turned off and charging downstairs—I hate having it go off in my ear—but tonight wasn't normal. I plugged the cell into its charger right next to my side of the bed. There was no way I was putting myself out of reach, if Bree needed me. I just hoped she wouldn't, because if this one got as bad as I thought it would, I'd be able to do fuck-all for her, or anyone else.

Downstairs, Farrowen was being noisy and cranky and indignant. No surprise, really; cats have a lot of respect for order and ritual, and things were different tonight, all the way round. I took a serious dose of painkillers. Getting the twist-cap off the bottle left my hands sweaty and shaking. Getting the damned pills out of the bottle took far too long for something that simple, and I nearly dropped the bottle twice while I was doing it.

It wasn't until I'd got under the duvet, and was lying there shivering, that I realised something: this was the first time I'd ever spent a night alone in this bed. Yeah, there'd been plenty of tours and whatnot where Bree'd been here and I hadn't been, but this was the first night since we'd bought the house over thirty years ago that I'd ever slept in this bed without Bree. Christ, no wonder everything felt so off. I had a moment of sympathy with Farrowen, wailing away downstairs.

I shifted under the covers, trying to find a spot, anywhere at all, I could get a bit of physical comfort. It wasn't looking promising, and I was already psyched to expect a bumpy night.

And of course, right on cue, the laser-beam focus thing kicked in. Weirdly, though, it seemed to want to focus on something that should have seemed trivial: why in hell had Andy Valdon chosen the site manager's office at the 707 to do whatever he was trying to do? Was there something up there none of us knew about but Andy?

It was possible, that was the thing. The 707 had seen a shit-load of dirty dealings these past couple of years: the original owner, Paul Morgenstern, had gone to prison for second degree manslaughter, and had been so determined not to lose control of his club that he'd financed a minority ownership share, secretly, through a third party. The club itself had burned down, taking the third party with it as a casualty, and had been rebuilt. There'd been a ridiculous amount of backroom doings centred round the 707. Anything was possible.

A hot, miserable jag of pain moved up my left side, going heel to ankle, twitching and stabbing; as soon as the pain was up, the lower end started spasming. *Shit.* Yeah, this was going to be the pits, this particular little relapse. Anytime you get myokimia and ataxia coming together in waves, you're basically fucked. There's sod-all you can do, except hold your breath or mutter profanities or do whatever happens to take the edge off for you personally. I haven't really found anything that takes the edge off, not yet. It would be nice to think they'll have cured this damned disease before I do find something that works, but it's not happening. They don't even know what causes it, never mind how to get rid of it.

185

The wave rippled over, and I felt myself jerk. That one had been spectacular, bad enough to leave me with my teeth clenched.

All right. So there was the question: why the office at the 707? Whatever it was, it was clear Jeff Kintera didn't know anything about it. That phone message hadn't come from someone who knew there was any kind of problem. I'm not saying Jeff can't be subtle—some of the past dealings we've had with him made it clear that he can be straight out of the court of fucking Lorenzo de Medici—but this hadn't sounded or felt that way. He'd just wanted to know.

So why the 707? Bergen Sandoval hadn't had a damned thing to do with the club; Blacklight owns the majority share, Tony and a couple of other people have much smaller shares. What sort of information could Andy possibly have needed access to, up there in San Rafael?

Both feet were jerking now, not controllable, and the duvet was jerking as well. I didn't seem to be in control of anything my body was doing just then, and I couldn't remember a relapse nearly this bad anytime over the past couple of years. It wasn't passing, it was getting worse. And the prospect of dealing with it alone, upstairs in a locked-down house with my wife elsewhere for the night, was beginning to freak me.

I curled up into as tight and hard a tuck as I could get myself into, trying to push the pain back down, bracing myself against the next wave of it. *Right. Breathe in, Johnny. Breathe out. Try for some Zen. Let the brain do its thing. Remember what the quack said, about it buying you time to cope…?*

Right. So, Andy was the big question mark—he clearly knew something, or thought he did, because why else why would he have scarpered? The obvious answer was that he'd provided Bergen with the coke he'd been snorting when the strychnine kicked in. Yeah, not a pretty picture, but a lot of that goes on in the industry, people supplementing their income and adding to their speed-dials by providing the old Doctor Feelgood concierge service bullshit. When you're a rocker, especially a famous one, people want to hang out with you, get you what you want, have what they think is your glamour rub off on them. And coke's been one of the industry's drugs of choice going back to the Harlem clubs in the 1930s. I used to do a lot of blow myself.

But that reasoning didn't hold up. That coke hadn't killed Bergen; clean or not, it hadn't had the dose of strychnine in it that had taken Bergen out. And Andy, who'd obviously been panicked enough to wash the remnants of Bergen's last line of blow off the sink, hadn't known. He hadn't poisoned Bergen.

*Johnny? Breathe. Breathe now. You're going to black out if you don't get air into your lungs. Breathe, mate!*

I hadn't realised I was holding my breath, but the pain that had hit me mid-thought had smashed into my lower back, and I was making noise. I was also about to pass out or have a sick-up, or both, and that scared the hell out of me. There's not enough words out there to describe just how much that scared me, because the picture was there in my head: Jimi, Janis, Jim Morrison, Keith Moon, pick a rocker who'd gone out that way, plenty to choose from.

I sucked down air, trying to get some equilibrium back, trying to steady things enough to kick the tickybox into full-on "prevent the heart attack" mode. Right. *It's okay, Johnny, not going to happen. You're not dying, and you're not going out choking on your own vomit, either.*

I held on, waiting for everything to lower the pitch. I was damned if I was having Bree come home in the morning from playing Good Samaritan for her best friend, and finding me dead in bed in a pool of my own puke.

The spasm had passed, but it had left me too limp to even summon up the energy to care that I needed a piss. Getting my legs out of bed and under me was going to be a lot of work. Even if I was able to get that sorted out, getting the legs to carry me to the loo was going to be just as iffy. I took my time, getting over onto one side, sliding one leg out, then the other. It was tricky, all right. I couldn't feel the soles of my feet, not beyond a distant tingle.

It took awhile, but I got it done. I'd had the sense to leave my bedside light on; turned out that had been a good move, because right then the bedroom looked the size of Madison Square Garden, and it was full dark outside. I myself got across the room, taking it very slow, gritting my teeth, until I got to a wall I could lean against for support. My head had a serious wrestling bout going on: one part wanted desperately to get back to bed, get the phone, ring Bree and tell her how bad it was. The other part was telling me to shut the fuck up, stop whingeing, and be glad my wife wasn't here to see me shuffling about like an old man on a cruise.

I took another small dose of painkiller—the first lot had done sod-all, and I really couldn't cope with much more of this. The pain seemed to have settled in for the night, but unless I was imagining it, things were a bit less intense; I got back across the room and back into bed in less time, and with less trouble, than getting out had been. Good. Maybe there was some hope this particular misery would move on sooner than later.

Back into bed, glad the pillows had cooled off, glad I didn't have to try and move around trying to find a cool spot. I closed my eyes, and waited for things to relax. Of course, the brain kicked straight back into laser-beam mode instead.

Okay. Andy knew something, or at least thought he did, but he hadn't taken out Bergen. What about the rest of the field?

My head obligingly spread them all out for me, in a sort of bizarre mental visual that felt like a bad parody of a police line-up. Granted that Luke might have enjoyed decking the bloke who'd bullied and seduced his stepdaughter into a bullshit marriage, there was no way Luke had killed him. That idea was ludicrous, a joke. And while I could see Stu Corrigan committing an act of very satisfying violence against Bergen, that's just what it would have been had Stu done it, and that was just what this murder hadn't been. Stu might have battered Bergen with rocks, but poison? Not a bloody chance.

Right. Who else was there? Elaine? Suzanne? Streak?

Something moved down my back, and this time, it wasn't pain. I'd much rather it had been; I'd have coped better than I did with the cold feeling.

If Streak had killed Bergen, it was going to take Patrick or Cunningham or someone who wasn't me to sort it out. I couldn't imagine why he would, and I wasn't involved enough with the bloke to know if he had reasons for thinking the world would do better without Bergen Sandoval in it. Granted, I hadn't seen them interacting much, but he'd seemed just the same towards Bergen as he had towards the rest of us. I had a moment of hoping Streak actually had done it; if he had, things were going to be less wretched than either of the other possibilities.

If Suzanne had offed her brand-new husband, we were all fucked. The damage to Luke, to Karen, to the entire Blacklight family, was going to be catastrophic, beyond mending.

As for Elaine, that opened a whole new set of issues. Elaine wasn't a core member of our family, but I'm not completely dim. Mac looked to have got to a point in that particular relationship that he might not have got to with any woman before Elaine. He'd been hurt a little too recently to lose the new woman in his life, especially to something as grim as a murder charge.

Besides, if Elaine had somehow bunged her ex full of rat poison, Mac wouldn't be the only one affected. There was that kid to be considered, the guitar prodigy with the peculiar name. You can't be there for your daughter if you're rotting in prison, and a

189

girl needs her mum, you know? Christ, I was living proof of that: If Miranda hadn't been there at Wembley, Bree would be a widow right now. Miranda had been there, saving our lives and quietly covering Bree's back, from the first day I'd known her. How old was Elaine's kid? Twelve, or something like that? Too young to lose her mum.

The second dose of painkiller was kicking in, finally; one leg relaxed, then the other. Everything still hurt, but the body was dulling down, settling, letting me know I could try to sleep soon. The brain was relaxing as well, that laser-beam focus thing easing into something softer, duller, blurrier.

I got a hand up, and turned out the light. The phone had stayed quiet. Hopefully, over at the Mancuso house, Bree and Katia were talking things out, or crying things out, or doing whatever needed doing to turn a bad situation into something that Katia, strong like a bull and Tony's better half for so many years, could handle.

As I was drifting off, the brain turned back on, just for a moment. *Over at the Mancuso house...*

I was too close to the edge of sleep to follow where it wanted me to go. But there it was, the last thought of the day before sleep finally let me in.

*Not three possibilities, you pillock. Four. What if it's Tony?*

By the time I got my eyelids unglued next morning, the MS had backed so far down that I not only got out of bed without any more difficulty than I usually have, I even managed a long hot shower. I was well into my second cup of coffee before my phone rang.

"Hey babe—did I wake you?" Bree'd obviously waited until she thought I'd be up. "Are you okay?"

"Morning, love. Yeah, I'm good. Having some coffee—it's not half as good as yours. I've just done the cats."

There was something in her voice that made me wonder what time she'd got up herself, how many times she'd picked up the cell, thought about it, let her fingers rest on the keypad, checked the time, set the phone down so as not to risk waking me, and started the whole damned process again. Weird, how vivid that picture was in my head. No need to worry her by letting her know about that miserable meltdown last night.

"I'm fine, but I missed you. First time I've ever spent the night alone in that bed, and it's a lot bigger than I knew. Never mind about me, Bree. How are you doing? And how's Katia? You both all right, then?"

"I'm okay. Katia..." She sounded tired. "I don't know, John. She's in the shower. She keeps going back and forth on whether she wants to call Tony, or just get back on a plane and go down there and make him talk to her, and I'm sitting here feeling useless, just listening, trying to be here for her and keep my mouth shut but fuck, John, keeping my mouth shut right now is *hard*. He hasn't called, he's doing the whole masculine passive-aggressive denial thing, and meanwhile she's –"

She stopped, biting back on the words. I stayed quiet, waiting. If she wanted to vent, the best thing I could do was stay quiet, but apparently, she didn't. "Never mind," she told me. "I was thinking I'd come home in a couple of hours, unless you need me for something sooner?"

"No, not to worry, love. I'll do the washing-up and maybe get some playing in, downstairs, and you do what you need to do. Tell you what, ring me when you're on your way, all right...?"

I'd barely got my cup into the dishwasher when the phone went again. When I saw the name and number on the caller ID screen, I took a good long breath before I answered.

"Tony...?"

"Hey, JP. Yeah, it's me. So what's going on?"

I sat there like a department store mannequin, holding the

phone away from me, staring at it as if it had dropped out of the sky or something. He sounded completely normal, completely sober, completely unworried about anything at all. He sounded as if he'd just eaten a good breakfast, as if was heading into the shower in the next room...

"JP? You there?"

"Yeah, I'm here." I got hold of myself. "What do you mean, what's going on? You tell me, mate."

"Didn't you say Carla was going to book us in for some live PR? For the CD? So where do I need to be, and when?"

*Shit.*

Unbelievable. You'd have thought he was talking to a thick ten-year-old, or something. What had Bree called it, the passive-aggressive denial thing? Bloody hell, she'd nailed that one. Out of nowhere, I heard Katia's voice in my head: *Can you get my husband to stop thinking he's worthless? Can you get him to stop lying to me? Can you get him to come home?* I remembered the note in Bree's voice, when she'd said Tony hadn't rung Katia, and suddenly, wham bam thank you ma'am, just like that, my temper went south.

"No." I nearly jumped at the way I sounded. I wasn't shouting; this was quite a lot nastier than shouting would have been. "Carla's booking me in, not the band. I told her to do it that way because I had no clue whether you'd be able to walk away from the bottle or the coke or whatever you're fucking yourself over with long enough to show up for a gig. I'd ask Katia whether you were really up for handling it, but Bree spent the night at your place, trying to hold it together for your wife, and she tells me you couldn't be arsed to ring home. Why you'd think I'd tell Carla to book us all in is beyond me. Not that stupid, mate. I've got a lot invested in the Geezers, and a lot invested in this CD. I'll handle the PR on my own. If the rest of the band wants to know why, I'll tell them and be done with it. It's not fair to them,

192

letting them think they're not valued, and not fair to any of us, making us look bad. And I'm buggered if I see why I should suck it up and let them think I'm being a diva. I'm damned if I'm having you balls it up by showing up sozzled, or not showing up at all."

I stopped, breathing hard. Christ, I hadn't sounded that furious with anyone in a good long time. A thought went through my head, hard and clear: *Johnny, my lad, is that you talking to your best friend? You're getting too old for this rubbish.*

"I'm sorry." He wasn't sounding normal, not anymore. "Look, I get it, JP. Okay? I get that you don't want me or anyone else to fuck it up. I know how much you put into the Geezers. But I need to put it out there: you've got no right to talk to me like that. I've been working just as long as you have, even if I'm not a goddamned rock star. You think I'd say okay, book me, I'll be there, and then not show? Fuck that. I'm a pro."

"Yeah, right." Fuck it. I'd spilled my guts out to his wife about it, might as well let him in on it as well, yeah? "You're a pro? So was I, Tony. Right up to the point when I wasn't. You think I had a clue how close to the bottom of the damned bottle I was? You think I haven't wondered a hundred times how many thousands I cost the band, doing the same takes over and over again, thinking I was doing it right and they were the ones that were off?"

"What? I don't—what?" He was right at the edge of stammering. "What thousands? What the hell are you talking about, JP?"

The tickybox was ramping up now, so damned hard I could almost hear it my own ears, like a metallic pulse. "Blacklight, Tony. Back in the early eighties. The recording sessions for *Partly Possible*. Forgetting a chord progression here, dropping a phrasing there. Same takes, over and over. That was before I had a little blackout after a late night session and woke up on the floor of a tube station in North London. Right at the edge of shit-faced, session after session, not telling anyone, letting myself believe I was fine, telling myself I was getting it done. Yeah, I was a fucking *pro*. I was blind nine hours out of every ten and that blackout, that's what it took to get me to cop to it. Shit, I'd already done the junkie thing and got clean, and it still took another two years after that before I finally figured out the boozing had me. I rang Bree and asked for help. You can't be arsed to ring Katia, or anyone else. So you don't get to sit there alone in a hotel room in Los Angeles because your old lady's walked out thanks to your boozing, and tell me you're a *pro*. I'll handle the PR on my own, unless and until you get your shit together. We clear?"

Silence. I shifted the phone from hand to the other. Both my palms were sweating.

"Yeah, that's pretty clear." He sounded very far away, suddenly. "I guess I don't blame you. You firing me?"

"Fuck no." I swallowed something at the back of my throat. *Christ.* "Not at this point. You think I want to lose you? Not a chance. And if you're stupid enough to think I'm enjoying this, Tony, think again. I'd much rather you sorted this out and did whatever needs doing to get you through it. Best piano player I've ever worked with and anyway, I've learned a few things about loyalty, these past few years. Never really thought about it much back in the old days, but I'm getting old and loyalty's worth a lot to me these days."

"I know." There was something in his voice suddenly, a kind of colour, but I couldn't have said what colour it was. "It doesn't come cheap, does it? Not at our age."

"Fix it, Tony. Bree's there for Katia. I'm here if I can do anything, and trust me, there's not much I won't do if it'll be of use, but I'm not doing a bloody thing unless you're okay with it. Not having a go at reading your mind, either. Ball's in your court, mate. You want help, you're going to need to ask."

"I know. Thanks, JP." He'd got his voice under control, but it was knife-edge thin; I heard something that might have been

194

tears, or anger. I couldn't quite parse it. "I need to go. I'll call you over the next couple of days, let you know what's happening."

He clicked off.

I set the phone down and sat back down myself. My hands were slick with sweat, and shaking, and I didn't think it was all the MS, either.

That had been as miserable a back and forth as I'd ever had, and I hoped to hell I'd never have another. No matter what happened, it was going to be a very long time before I lost the bad taste of his voice, exhausted and defeated and as far away as the back end of the galaxy, my best friend, asking me that question: *Are you firing me…?*

My stomach was churning and sour. I had a sudden itch, to get my head back into a decent space by playing some music. I glanced at the clock; it had just gone eleven. Patrick had said he'd ring as soon as he'd sorted out his business up at the 707, but I suspected that wasn't going to happen for a few hours yet. Club managers aren't notorious for being morning people. Bree'd said she'd ring when she was on her way home, but that wasn't going to be for a while yet, either. I dropped my phone into my shirt pocket and headed downstairs.

For some reason, what I really fancied doing was plugging in my Zemiates, Big Mama Pearl. I wanted to play with the toggle switches and settings until I got her sounding as dirty as she gets, crank the volume to ear-bleed levels, and blister the paint off the walls. The whole mess with Tony, with what might be waiting in the wings depending on who'd taken out Bergen, had left me wanting to smash something. I've always found that loud music, the kind that shatters glass, is a damned good way to get some of that rubbish out of my system when it hits.

I hadn't quite got to the bottom of the basement stairs when I stopped, one foot in the air and my skin moving on my bones.

The door to my studio was open.

*Shit.*

I held very still. There was sunlight coming in through the upper half of the basement door, the one that opens out into the back garden. In the pale patch along the wall opposite the studio door, I saw movement, a shadow, something that might have been a head turning...

I backed up, good and quiet. Four steps, five...safe, back upstairs in the hall, quietly closing the door and latching it shut. The tickybox was handling things in my chest, but the rest of me wasn't too happy. I was sweating, and breathing hard.

Maybe it sounds a bit soft, me not grabbing an axe and charging down to cope with it. But we'd got an intruder in the house, and a house full of valuable stuff, and people who break into pricey homes don't generally let themselves in armed with watercress sandwiches and strong language...

*Right. How the fuck did someone get in, then? You alarmed the place, just before you went upstairs, yeah? Or did you?*

I headed down the hall. Truth is, I couldn't remember whether I'd done it or not. Under normal circs, I'd have said right, no-brainer, reflex action; after all, we've had a home security system for over twenty years. After that much time, dealing with it's automatic, really—just as much habit as brushing your teeth. But last night hadn't been normal circs, the MS had been on a rampage worthy of a gang of South London yobs in the seventies, and I couldn't remember.

The light was on, solid green. Whoever had broken in, however they'd got in, they hadn't tripped the alarm system.

I stood there, staring back toward the kitchen, trying to wrap my head around the fact that we'd got a burglar in the house, or maybe some sort of axe-wielding mental case. And apparently, he or she had superhuman powers or something, because they'd apparently managed to beam themselves in like something off *Star Trek*. And I hadn't got the first clue what to do next; I just knew I

196

had to sort it out and get it taken care of one way or another before Bree got home...

The phone in my shirt pocket buzzed. I jumped a mile, but there was a small voice at the back of my head: *Good, if the thug in the basement hears the phone up here he won't worry about me interfering with him oh shit shit SHIT the guitars...!*

I went straight for the kitchen, where Bree keeps her racks of chef's knives, and I was moving fast. You find courage in the oddest places, sometimes. If it had just been me, I'd have stayed upstairs and called the coppers, or let the bloke make off with things. But Little Queenie was down there on a stand, Bree's wedding gift to me. Big Mama Pearl, all irreplaceable hundred thousand dollars worth of her, was down there.

The funny thing was, while I was mentally nerving myself for some kind of bizarre knife fight with someone who probably looked like one of those Nazi blokes in old movies about the Second World War, I was answering my phone. No time to glance at the caller ID, not this time, and no attention to spare, either.

"Hello?" I reached the kitchen, went through the swinging doors and past the cats, heading for the knives. All three of the felines looked up at me as if I were some sort of nutter: *right, what's his little issue, then?* I had an ear cocked for any noise from downstairs. Nothing, so far as I could tell. "Oi! Hello?"

"JP? It's Andy."

I dropped the phone. It went skittering out of my hand and bounced across the kitchen floor. I scrambled after it; my legs were shaking and I was swearing like a navvy under my breath.

I edged back towards the hall. *Okay. Get rid of him fast. Then ring the cops, and get the hell down there before the Texas Chainsaw bloke makes off with your guitars, you nit.*

"Andy, look, believe it or not, this isn't a good time. I've got someone in the house and I need to cope with it and ring the

197

police. I probably don't really want to know where you are, either, because –"

"That's just it." He sounded quite a lot calmer than he'd been last time I'd spoken to him. Crikey, was that really less than a day ago? "Could you come down to your basement, and let me in? Because I just went outside to call you and I didn't prop the door open and it swung shut, and now I'm locked outside in your backyard."

# Chapter Thirteen

I've thought about that morning quite a lot since it happened. It's one of those *what should I have done* deals, the kind you play over and over in your head instead of counting sheep when you're having trouble nodding off for the night. After the fact, it's easy to play with a no-win scenario, and wonder what might have gone down had you done it differently.

What I actually did do, first thing, was wonder if he was having me on. I walked over to the bay window in Bree's little office alcove. It overlooks the garden.

Andy was standing on the little brick-paved path that winds out to the cafe tables and benches near the roses and fruit trees. He saw me in the window, and waved. I lifted a hand and waved back.

"Hang on," I told the phone. "I'll come down. Might take a

few minutes—I had a bad night with the MS and I'm not moving very quickly this morning."

I clicked off.

At least the question of how he'd got in past the armed security alarm was answered: he hadn't. He hadn't needed to, because he'd never left. The bugger'd been down the basement, in the garage or my studio, since yesterday. Somehow, the idea that he'd been wandering loose in my house while I was upstairs in bed, helpless with an exacerbation, made my skin crawl. I hadn't locked any of the interior doors last night, because I'd been too ill to cope and besides, why would I? No one there but me and the cats, so far as I'd been aware. Except, of course, Andy Valdon had been there the entire time.

I made sure I was well out of sight of the window, flipped the phone back open, and punched in Patrick's number.

That was pure instinct, but even now, looking at it, I don't see how I could have done better. I couldn't refuse to deal with Andy, not under the circs, and I wanted him the hell out of my house before Bree got back. We paid Patrick a fortune every year. He could damned well cope with this rubbish.

He answered on the second ring. "Ormand. JP?"

"Yeah, it's me, and don't talk, just listen. Andy Valdon's in my back garden, waiting for me to come down and let him in." I explained what had happened, nice and fast. Patrick being Patrick, he did his usual phenomenal job of listening without interrupting.

"…and the problem's the same as it was when he showed up the first time. If he's here when Bree gets home, that makes her an accessory to something, God knows what but whatever it is, I'm not having it. What the hell should I do about it? And tell me quick, mate, because I don't want him spooked into climbing the fence. That only leads to our neighbours' back gardens and he doesn't need to add a trespassing charge to being wanted for questioning in a homicide."

"Are you worried about a confrontation?" Patrick sounded very crisp. "Did you get the feeling he's armed or dangerous?"

"Not any more than he was yesterday. How could he be, if he hasn't left? It's much more likely he's chilly and damp. There's ground fog everywhere. The poor sod's probably freezing his bollocks off out there, wondering if he's going to fetch up in hospital with pneumonia or something. Not sure where you are, Patrick, but this is your nice basic San Francisco summer morning. The weather's fucking miserable." A thought occurred to me. "Actually, where are you? You up at the 707?"

"No, I'm in my office. We're not quite as foggy south of Market as you seem to be. I'm on my way over. Can you disarm the alarm system? About Andy, your safest move is probably stall him if you can, but it could take me fifteen minutes to get there, and stalling him for fifteen minutes might not be possible. He's not an idiot."

"I did tell him I'm moving slow—I had a really bad MS night and by the way, Patrick, I'd rather you didn't mention that to Bree, yeah? She spent the night taking care of Katia Mancuso and I don't want her made to feel guilty about not being here. She couldn't have fixed it and she doesn't need to know about it, all right?"

"I won't say anything." There was a flicker of warmth in his voice, or maybe it was approval. "On my way—I'm just starting the car. Stall if you can, but if you're feeling safe about going out and confronting him, go for it. Either way, make sure you turn the alarm off so that I can get in without having to ring your bell."

He hung up. I took a good long breath, headed for the hall closet to grab a jacket and disarm the security system, and headed for the garden.

"JP?" I hadn't been wrong about Andy being damp and miserable—the bloke was drooping like someone's scarecrow. Now I thought about it, there really wasn't anything soft for him to have crashed out on down in the basement, or in the studio either. He couldn't have got much kip, what with one thing and another. "Thanks for coming down and letting me in."

I held up a hand. "Half a mo, mate. I haven't let you in yet and I'm not sure I'm going to, either. Bottom line is, the homicide people down in LA want a word with you. I don't know if you took Bergen out and I don't care, actually. But standing about talking to you, I've got knowledge of the whereabouts of someone wanted in a murder investigation."

"I didn't —"

"I said, I don't care. Point is, I'll risk it for myself. But I'm not having you within half a light year of my wife. She's already been through a police wringer once before, and I'm damned if I'm letting you or anyone else put her through it again. We clear about that?"

"Of course. I'm sorry." He had his arms wrapped around himself, good and tight. "Can we go inside? I understand if you'd rather stay out here—you don't have any reason to trust me, I know that. It's just kind of cold."

"Yeah, it's chilly." He looked like six sorts of hell, ragged round the edges, gaunt and tired, dark patches under both eyes that looked as if someone had bashed him, but probably just came from not having slept. "We can go indoors, yeah, but I want to make damned sure you get it: I don't owe you anything and I'm not promising you anything, either. I'm not your doctor or your priest or your dad. No promises, Andy. If that's an issue, you can climb over one of the fences and find your own way out. Just don't let the neighbours catch you and you might want to avoid the yard with the big fir trees. They've got a dog."

"No, I get it." He wasn't pushing it, just standing there, looking pathetic and cold. "I just want to talk to you about something."

"'Something'? Understatement of the decade, mate. Shit!" A wet splash of cold water had hit the back of my neck; the fog had collected on the eaves of the house, and it was dripping like a leaky tap. "Right, that's it. Let's go in."

I turned back towards the house, Andy right behind me. If I needed proof that I didn't think Andy had killed Bergen, it was right there: I wasn't bothered by turning my back on him. "Make sure that door's shut properly," I told him over one shoulder, and headed upstairs.

It really was pretty surreal, you know? I got him settled in the breakfast nook and got a pot of coffee going. I rummaged around in the fridge and got a few leftovers together. Christ, at this rate, I was going to run him a warm bath or offer him a nice neck rub, or something.

"Nice cat."

I pulled my head out of the fridge. Simon had jumped onto the table, something he knew better than to do when Bree was home. He had his tail curled round his feet, just sitting and staring at Andy. He was also purring like a small generator, because Andy was tickling him under the chin, in precisely the right spot to turn most cats into a puddle of drool. Right. That was going to make it harder to distrust him. He knew his way around a cat, did Andy Valdon.

"JP—did I say thanks yet?"

I slid in across the table, managing a fast look at the clock. Patrick should be here by now, or at least any minute. Andy was wolfing down everything on his plate, hardly even slow enough to chew any of it. "Don't know. I wasn't listening and it doesn't matter, not really. Look, Andy. Now that you've got me involved, you might as well dish, yeah? What in hell were you doing, scarpering like that? And why the 707?"

"How –" His face had gone slack. "How did you know…?"

"Jeff Kintera left a message on the house phone." *Shit.* Where in sweet hell was Patrick? "We got home from LA and found it. He wanted to know how long you were going to need his office, because he's got gigs booked and he needs to be able to get to his stuff. It sounded as if you told him Carla was on holiday. I have that right?"

He didn't say anything. "Look," I told him. "You're the one asked for this conversation. You said you wanted to talk to me about something, then bleedin' talk, all right? Why did you need to hit the 707, Andy?"

"I didn't. I mean, not specifically."

He got another mouthful of coffee. Having something to sip is a brilliant way to give yourself time. I've done that myself plenty of times, when I wasn't ready to talk about something or wanted a minute to find the right words. Smokers light their cigs or their pipes, the rest of us use coffee or tea.

In its own way, the situation was bizarre. I was waiting for Patrick to walk in. At the same time, I was hoping Bree wouldn't call or walk in herself, until this was sorted out. And in the meantime, I was using the same technique to get Andy to dish that I use on Patrick: waiting him out. And damned if it didn't work; something about me staying silent made him nervous.

"I didn't need the 707. I just needed a computer with internet access, and a private room to use it in. The 707 office was the first place I thought of. And besides, it was away from LA. I –" His voice died off, and he tried again. "I really don't want to be near LA right now."

"Motel on Lombard Street not up to snuff?" If my ears weren't playing tricks, there was a car pulling up out front on Clay Street. Good. With any luck, it was Patrick about to show, and he could do the whole Father Confessor thing and let me off the hook. "No free WiFi? Laptop lost its battery?"

Andy flushed. "I couldn't get a motel room. I used all my cash in hand getting the flight up here. I'm pretty broke. I mean, I have money in the bank, but how the hell am I supposed to get at it? I'd have to use my debit card, and anyone with access to those records could track me up here. So I couldn't pull cash and I'm not dumb enough to use a credit card for a motel room. I didn't know just how hard Cunningham was looking for me. I still don't. And I don't have my laptop, either. The goddamned thing is at Fanucci Pros, in my office. The minute that call from Carla came in, telling me there was going to be a meeting, I got my ass out of town. I slept on a couch in the band room at the 707 the first night, and then last night I slept down in your basement. This is the first food I've eaten since yesterday. If you're wondering what I'm thanking you for, you can—hello?"

A few years back, I finally sussed what I should have done twenty years ago: telling when something's got Bree tensed up by looking at her shoulders. Turns out she had nothing on Andy Valdon. The click of the front door, light footsteps heading down the hall, had an effect on him that made Bree's boulder-shoulder thing look subtle. There was one major difference, though. He didn't just hunch up, he went very still. With Bree, you get the feeling she's holding her breath, waiting for disaster to hit, waiting for the axe to fall.

Andy went feral. He looked like a wild animal, a fox or something, hearing the hounds baying in the distance, gathering himself and tensing to jump and run. And that was nuts, because he'd come here willingly, you know? Hell, he'd wanted to talk to me so badly, he'd camped out in our fucking basement...

Patrick Ormand turned the corner and came through the swinging kitchen half-doors. For a moment, he and Andy stared at each other, not saying anything. I wasn't saying a damned thing, either. I did wonder if my own shoulders were like rocks, I was that tense.

"Excuse me." Andy was up, on his feet. His face was tight, and his voice was tighter. "I have to go."

"Whoa, hang on." Patrick sounded easy, nice and normal. On the other hand, he wasn't moving away from the door. "Don't let me drive you away."

"Please move away from the door." Not so tight anymore; there were cracks showing in his voice now. "Unless you're arresting me. But you're not a cop anymore, are you? You can't do that."

"No, I can't do that." They were staring at each other, eye to eye. I could have been back in LA for all the attention they were showing me. "But it's not about that, Andy. I work for Carla. So do you. Yes, Cunningham put the word out. He wants to talk to you. You're a person of interest, and frankly, he's pissed off. You made him look bad, and I don't think he's the forgiving type. But you've put JP in a jam right along with you, and that's one thing I'm supposed to prevent. You can't run indefinitely. You're in serious trouble, and you're not getting out of it on your own. You need help."

"I need –" Andy swallowed whatever he'd been about to say. "Look, Patrick. You can't keep me. And I wasn't running forever. I just—I need to get some time and space to get done what I have to get done."

Patrick was silent, watching him, waiting. I had a mad thought: I use this technique on Patrick, and it always works. I'd used it on Andy, and it had worked as well. And now here was Patrick using it on Andy. All we needed was for Andy to shut up and try waiting us out, and we'd be sitting about like the three monkeys…

"There's stuff I have to do." Andy's voice was ragged suddenly, and urgent with it. "There's some information I need to track down, that's all. I swear that's all. I didn't murder Bergen and I'm not going to jail for something I didn't do. Fuck that. And I'm not going back to LA until I find out what I need to find out. I need to find a computer and a way to get online that doesn't involve me using a credit card or my name or anything anyone can

206

find yet. I don't want to get JP in trouble, Carla's already going to kill me once this is all over with, but I know what I have to do. So would you please step away from the door now?"

Patrick didn't budge. "You need a computer? And online access in privacy? That's it?"

"That's it." They were locked up. "Can I borrow some money?"

"Hell no." Patrick moved finally, standing aside. "But I've got an office with a computer in it. I've got high speed internet access. There's a perfectly good sofa in there, too. If you need a roof and internet access and privacy, you've got it. There's only one condition, and that's that you don't mention to anyone, ever, that you came within half a mile of 2828 Clay Street, no matter what happens. Deal? Good. Let's go."

After they'd gone, alone in the house with just the cats for company, I shelved the idea of locking myself in the basement and making some music. I didn't realise how rattled I was until I found myself heading down the hall towards the front room, and straight for my rocking chair.

We've got two of those chairs, a matched set. They were one of the first purchases Bree and I made together when we bought 2828 Clay, back when she was still a teenager; our bed, those chairs, and our first set of dishes. We still have all three.

Over the years, they've come to mean continuity for both of us, normalcy, safety. Bree's lives upstairs, in the master bedroom; that chair's been her safe place, her bolt-hole when the universe has got all the way up in her face and shit starts piling on too fast for her to cope with, since the day the chairs were delivered. It's her *time-out, take a breath, get the inner resources together* sanctuary, is that chair. It's where she'd sat trying to cope with too many moments of bad news, going back too many years: me leaving to take care of my first wife, her own cancer diagnosis, and quite a few more.

207

Mine lives in the front room, next to my guitar stands. If I'm in the front room and I've got myself parked in that chair, I've generally got a guitar in my lap and my wife on the sofa, listening to me play and maybe having a sing-along. My own bolt-hole's down in the basement, in the studio. I don't fancy hanging about in the front room alone, not usually.

So it was a surprise, to find myself settling into the rocker, getting into the nice easy motion of it under my weight. No guitar, not today. I just leaned back, rocking and wondering what in hell was going on. So far as I could tell, our pet detective had gone completely off his nut.

I couldn't sort out what Patrick was doing. He knew damned well Cunningham wanted Andy; shit, Cunningham was so narked, he probably wanted Andy's intestines on a salad plate, with chips on the side. Patrick wasn't just an ex-cop, he was an ex-homicide cop, and he knew the drill. He knew the consequences, as well. So what in hell had got him to—what was the phrase? Comfort, was it? Aid and abet?

Because that was just what he'd done, hiding knowledge of a murder suspect's whereabouts from the cop in charge. And that was nuts. If Cunningham found out about it—*when* Cunningham found out—he was going to have Patrick for lunch. I was pretty sure that, at the very least, hiding Andy from Cunningham could cost Patrick his detective's license. And Patrick had to know it. So what had he been thinking?

I closed my eyes, rocking, nice and easy. The MS seemed to have backed down entirely; that was good, but my chest felt tight. This getting old rubbish, it's not easy, you know? I'd already decided I wasn't telling Bree about last night, not without a gun to my head. The tightness in the chest was worrying, though.

*Yeah, well, maybe you ought to try breathing, you nit.*

Apparently the little voice in my head was on to something, because I was doing it again, holding my breath. I couldn't sort out why I was doing it, nerves or worry or whatever, but I decided I'd had more than enough of it.

During the bad days after Wembley, Miranda had taught me a technique, while I was recovering from the heart attack and the infection: Long deep breaths, hold and exhale, count to five, repeat, lower the count to four, repeat, and keep on with it until it was steady at a ratio two beats of inhale to exhale. Bree'd sat with me, holding on to both my hands and talking me through it. All I'd really wanted to do was sleep until things felt normal again, but neither woman was having that. I'd hated the whole thing at the time, but looking back, thank God for bossy women in my life, yeah?

The technique had worked for me then and it seemed to be working now. The tightness eased up, and the breaths got easy and normal again. I made a mental note to tell my cardio bloke about it next time I went in, and filed the whole thing at the back of my mind. There was other stuff had a better claim on my attention just then.

When my phone went off, there was no need to look at the caller ID, because Bree's got her own music on my phone. It's my song, "Remember Me"; I love that tune beyond sense or reason, but the thing is, it was what had been playing on the PA at Wembley when I'd gone into V-fib and been shocked back to life by Miranda and her magic paddles. And Bree can't hear the song, which is all about her in every way that counts, without wanting to scream and throw things. That's rotten for both of us, because for me, the song is about my wife and my life, and getting to keep both. It's my song of triumph, you know?

I'd had it as my basic ringtone for a few months, but watching Bree stiffen up every time my phone went off had finally clued me in to the fact that I was being thoughtless and possibly even cruel, and I'd taken it off. The solution was obvious: have it be her ringtone, since she wouldn't be there to hear it, and I'd al-

209

ways know it was her. *Now I lay me down to sleep, you're everything I want to keep, if you should wake and find me gone, feel free to live, to carry on...*

"Bree? Hey baby."

"Hey, John." She sounded much more like herself than she had when she'd rung earlier. "I'm just leaving Katia's—I'll be home in a few minutes. Do you need anything? Should I stop and pick something up? I could hit Houri, or I could just come home and put together a scratch lunch."

"Scratch lunch'll do me, but we're low on milk. You sound much happier. Katia all right, then?"

"I think so. I'll be home in awhile. Is that your phone beeping, or mine?"

"Mine—that was my call waiting. Someone's ringing on the second line. See you in a bit." I clicked off, and glanced down. Local number. "Hello?"

"Mr. Kinkaid? This is Jeff Kintera. I'm really sorry to bother you, but would you happen to know where Patrick Ormand is? I really need to get hold of him."

I opened my mouth, and closed it again. *Choose the words carefully, Johnny. You don't want to step in anything nasty...*

"Mr. Kinkaid?"

"Yeah, still here." I shifted the phone. "I don't, not really. Sorry. He not answering his cell?"

Over the past few of years of dealing with him, I've discovered that the 707's manager is a hard bloke to worry, or even to catch off guard. He's quite even-tempered, and generally not one to get his knickers in a twist. Of course, that's a quality you want in a job where you deal with pampered divas, neurotic newcomers, pissy promoters and a shitload of details on a daily basis. Just now, though, he was sounding pretty rattled.

"I just left him a message on his cell, but it went straight to voicemail. He may be travelling. God, I hope not. I left one on

210

his office phone too. I really need to talk to him."

Yeah, he was definitely in a flap. I felt one eyebrow lift, even though there was no one there to see it. "What's the problem, Jeff? Anything I can help you sort out?"

"Not unless you can tell me what happened to my user account."

"Sorry? Your what…?"

"My user account to the 707's computer network." He took a breath, a good long one. "Patrick downloaded some stuff off the club's hard drive, and something must have gone wrong somewhere, because the computer won't let me in. I'm going to have to rebuild my user account before I can get any real work done. And we have gigs coming up."

"Sorry about that. I'm not really handy with computers, but can't you use the history function deal to find where you've been? I know that's what my wife does."

"That's the browser function, not the files." He sounded glum. "It's a whole other problem, but yes, it's a problem: the entire browser history cache for the past week's gone. Temp files, the cache, the whole nine yards. Patrick must have erased everything and I don't know whether it was accidental or not, but I'm hoping he can –"

"Hang on." A light bulb in my head had suddenly gone off. "When was this? When was Patrick up there, I mean?"

"This morning. He was actually waiting for me when I got here—he'd let himself in."

Jeff was sounding restive, and edgy. Not a surprise; I suppose having to confront a bloke who you can't tell to sod off because he works as muscle for your majority shareholders might make anyone twitchy. And considering the bloke in question used to lock people up for several years at a time, never mind the occasional one getting strapped to a table for lethal injection, I couldn't blame Jeff for getting his knickers in a twist over it. "He

211

didn't tell me what was up and I didn't ask him, but of course I assumed it had to do with what happened in LA, with Bergen Sandoval. And with Carla on vacation, I really didn't have anyone else I can ask about it."

"You said he downloaded things." Things were coming clearer in my head, now. I'd been sitting longer than I should, and my feet had begun tingling; I got up, shaking both legs. "You sure about that, Jeff?"

"Well, he was sitting at my computer when I walked in today, and his thumb drive was sticking out of the USB port. If he wasn't downloading, I can't imagine what else he was doing. I guess he could have been uploading, but since I can't access anything, I can't really tell."

"Right." My own head was ticking away suddenly. All of a sudden, Patrick taking Andy off with him and sitting him down at the Ormand Investigations desktop, without anyone watching over their shoulders to see what they were on about, didn't sound quite so barmy. "Not to worry, Jeff, at least not about Patrick getting back to you. Patrick's quite reliable about checking his messages. Do you want me to point him in your direction if he rings me? Not to worry, shall do. Cheers."

I rang off.

*Right.* Straight back down the hall to the front room, and back to the chair. My mind was doing a series of cartwheels that left me dizzy.

That idea I'd had, about Patrick not wanting to get to San Rafael too early, had been rubbish, all wrong. He'd not only got there before Jeff did, he'd apparently made a point of doing it. It made an oddly clear picture in my head: Patrick, setting his alarm for what Domitra calls "the asscrack of dawn," showering and shaving, heading north over the Golden Gate before the sun had got near the horizon yet, punching in the security code for the club, letting himself in, powering up the computers...

212

He'd had a set of keys to the club in his back pocket, not to mention the security codes for the alarm system, ready to go when he'd got there. He certainly hadn't got either thing from Jeff Kintera. There was only one other way I could think for him to have got his hands on either thing, never mind both, and that was from Carla.

So Patrick had known what he was going to do before he ever got to the airport in LA. And that meant he'd known exactly what he was looking for on the 707's computer system before he'd come north. He hadn't flown back looking for Andy Valdon. He'd flown back because he wanted a clean uninterrupted shot at the 707 computer files.

I know Patrick Ormand. I've got quite a good handle on the way he works. I'd have to be a complete clot not to be able to read him, at least on certain things. We've got enough history together, both as antagonists and as conspirators, for me to know when his rat terrier brain gets hold of something and starts ripping away at its insides.

He'd got hold of something now. Whatever it was, it hadn't quite kicked the switch that jumps him over to full scale predator, but he had something. It was obviously something to do with Andy, but beyond that, I couldn't even guess.

I'd actually closed my eyes and dozed off when I felt the floor vibrate as the garage door opened under me, and heard the hum of the Jaguar's engine being shut down. A minute later, Bree let herself in through the basement door.

"John? Damn! Were you taking a nap? Did I wake you?"

"Just resting my eyes." I followed her down the hall to the kitchen. "Oh good, you got milk. How's Katia holding up?"

She'd put a pan on the range, and was setting things out on the island: ceramic mixing bowl, eggs and cheese out of the big Sub-Zero, milk. "Tony called, just before I called you. I took my coffee out on the deck, so I have no idea how that went, but

213

Katia's definitely breathing a little easier. She told me she'd be fine but that she needed to hit the supermarket and restock the fridge. I've got the feeling Tony must have said he was coming home. God, I hope so." Butter sizzled in the pan behind her, and she turned the flame down. "Is a basic cheese omelette okay? Or did you have eggs for breakfast?"

"Omelette's lovely."

I settled in, watching her. The kitchen had the usual brilliant smell it gets when Bree's cooking. Just then, though, I couldn't relax and enjoy it; that careful little voice at the back of my head kept looping, reminding me to keep my gob shut and not let one word about Andy and Patrick...

"So, what's the word from Patrick?" She flicked her right wrist and the omelette turned over. "Did he ever track down Andy? Has he checked in?"

"No clue, love." It wasn't the truth, but I wasn't actually lying, either: I really hadn't sussed out what Patrick was up to. "I'm betting someone will let us know if anything happens, or if we're wanted for anything. At the moment, I'm not going to worry about—damn, there's my cell again. Carla? That you...?"

I'd gone tense myself, worrying that she might have something to say that would put me or Bree back in the middle of whatever Patrick was doing, but no. She was ringing to let me know she'd scheduled me for three guest spots, two tentative on radio and one confirmed on television, doing PR for *Fogbound*.

"...I set the TV spot for next Tuesday, early afternoon. You're the A-list guest—it's that hot new music show, *Ears on LA*." Carla sounded preoccupied. Not surprising, since she was probably rushed half off her rollerblades. Yeah, she had the intern helping out, but the kid couldn't have enough experience under her belt to really be of use. Plus, if any coping was being done with LAPD, or with the media wanting to know more about Bergen's death, Carla'd be the one dealing with it. "You could do the radio spots by phone, but since you've got to be down here for the TV thing anyway, I'd suggest that we schedule at least one of the radio spots for Wednesday, and maybe the Amoeba in-store thing too. That way, you'd only have to spend one night away from home—I could book you a flight Tuesday morning. You could do the TV thing that afternoon, spend Tuesday night down here, do the two radio spots, and we'd have you back in San Francisco on the first flight out of LAX after that on Wednesday. Does that work?"

"Yeah, it does. Thanks, Carla. Send me and Bree the info, and we'll plug it into the calendar. Might want to have a go at some media stuff up here, as well—I could do a few in-studio things with Elaine Wilde. Anything else...?"

"Well..."

She stopped, and went silent. *Shit*. Why in hell had I asked her? Pure habit, that was, but I'd forgot for the moment that, if there was anything else, I really couldn't afford to hear it.

Bree was watching me. She'd slid my omelette onto a plate, and the bread had popped out of the toaster slots, but she wasn't moving, not pouring coffee or hunting out a fork or buttering the toast. She was just watching me.

I was rescued by the double *beep* on my cell that means a call waiting. "Carla, look, if there's anything, tell me later, yeah? Luke's just ringing in on the other line. Don't forget to send that info, right, cheers..."

Bree stopped staring at me, finally, and reached for my coffee mug. I clicked the second line on.

"Luke? Oi, mate, what's going on, then?"

"JP?" His voice was off the scale, all over the place, barely recognisable. "Shit! Look, I can't get hold of Carla, that kid in her office says she's on the phone –"

"Luke! Bloody hell, mate, what is it? What's wrong?"

"They've detained Suzanne. Cunningham's got my daughter at

215

the station and he says he wants to talk with her attorneys. Something about information they've got their hands on, about Bergen's finances. JP—I think he's going to charge her."

# Chapter Fourteen

So much for our nice little break from Los Angeles. That call from Luke was the end of that.

I hadn't wasted my time or my breath trying to cool Luke down. No point, not really; I had nothing to cool him down with. I couldn't say *don't worry, Cunningham isn't stupid enough to honestly think Suzanne could have done Bergen in*, at least not with any conviction. From what I'd seen of Cunningham, he was just that stupid and maybe worse, and Luke knew it as well as I did. At best, the bloke in charge was completely unpredictable.

So Luke had every reason to flip his shit, and that was just what he was doing. I had a moment of wishing he'd never laid eyes on Suzanne. However much we all liked her mum, the girl had caused him, and us, nothing but aggro.

Meanwhile, I was hoping to at least get him coherent. "Luke, right, listen. Hang in, and tell Karen to hang in, as well. Bree and I will be down on the first flight Carla can get us. Did Cunningham tell you anything solid?"

"No. Just what I've told you, that he's found something to do with Bergen's estate that points up a motive." He was making an obvious effort to keep his voice steady, and I wondered if Karen was in the room with him. If she was, she had to be in shock, because I couldn't hear anything besides Luke, no noise, no conversation, no crying, nothing. "Carla's got a lawyer for her, and this bloke had best have her out of there on bail by tonight. I'm not having my daughter sitting in a fucking cell."

"Damned right." Christ. The media would be going off its collective nut down there. There was no way we were heading back to the Beverly Wilshire. The place would be arse-deep in reporters; if I'd thought the feeding frenzy after Bergen's murder had been bad, this was likely to ratchet the misery to a whole new level. "Luke, I've got to ring Carla and get a flight down. I'll let you know as soon as we're there. Hang in."

I clicked the phone off. Bree was staring at me, white-faced.

"John? What…?"

"Cunningham's arrested Suzanne. He looks to be charging her with killing Bergen." I was punching Carla's number on my speed dial. "New evidence, something about Bergen's finances or his estate or something. We need to get back down there, Bree. Luke's in total meltdown and if he's losing it, Karen's got to be in much worse shape. Carla? It's JP. I just got off the phone with Luke…"

Of course she was already on top of it. She'd left us enough time to eat, do the washing up, pack and get our house sitter, Sammy, lined up, but not much beyond that; the towncar would be picking us up in an hour.

"…and I don't think the Beverly Wilshire's a good idea. I sent Marjorie out for a look, and she says the place is crawling with media." Carla sounded crisp, and terrifyingly competent, which meant she was horrified and probably furious about the entire mess. "I'm thinking that, on the one hand, a small boutique hotel would be good, because we've got a lot of very good ones down here. The downside is that if they do figure out you're staying in one of those, it'll be a lot harder to keep them away from you. Big hotels have the extra layer of security, at least. What's your preference, JP?"

"Jesus, Carla, do you really need to ask? Put us wherever the Hedleys are. We need to be near Luke, because Bree's going to want to be there if Karen needs her." I glanced up at Bree, who'd caught her lower lip between her teeth. Christ, there it was again, a look I hated, that desolation thing on her face. It used to be she only ever looked that way because of something I'd done, or hadn't done. Now it was there for Tony and Katia, for Luke and Karen, and I was finding I didn't care for it any more than I ever had.

"Okay. I'll make sure the driver at LAX knows where to take you." She hesitated. "I'm really sorry about this, JP. I know you and Bree are pretty damned sick of LA right now, and I know you're both recovering from the Tour Crud. I've got a fantastic lawyer lined up, from your neck of the woods actually, someone Patrick recommended. She's landing at LAX in about two hours, so hopefully this will get cleared up fast. I'm going to put out a call for a general meeting at my office in the morning. We need to get our ducks in a row. I'll see you tomorrow. Call me if you need anything else." She rang off.

"I should go upstairs and pack." Bree wasn't moving, not quite yet. She wasn't even glancing at her lunch, either. "John, should I call Karen? I don't know if she's up for talking to people on the phone right now. Would it be better to wait until we're there?"

"Don't know, but if I have to guess, I'd say to wait. We're being picked up in about an hour, so we'll be back down soon enough,

I'd say. Right now, what I'd really like is for you to sit and get some food down you, Bree, please."

"I can't. I'm not hungry."

I put the phone down and got both arms round my wife. She was looking bleak, and uncertain, and it was making me want to kiss her until she felt better. "Come on, love, let's finish off this food and get the dishes done, yeah? Then you can pack a couple of bags and I'll let Sammy know—oh bloody hell, now what? Can we just get a little peace around here, please?"

Bree's phone had gone this time. I was a split second too late to get it away from her and tell her to let the voicemail kick in while she got on with her lunch. From the way her face brightened up when she answered it, it was just as well.

"Katia? Hey, I was going to call you. Listen, John and I have to go back down to LA, Luke called and all hell is breaking loose, he says that asshead Cunningham is arresting Suzanne, can you believe that fucking moron—what? Oh, honey, thank God! Yes, of course, just remind him that we'll be on a plane for an hour later this afternoon, so John might not answer. I'm so relieved, and so happy for you. Talk later—bye."

She tossed the phone aside, and sat down, reaching for her plate. She still looked tense, but she'd stopped chewing at her lip, and the desolate look was gone. She also seemed to have got her appetite back. I lifted one eyebrow at her.

"Tony back home, then?"

"Not yet, but he's apparently just getting on a plane." She was wolfing down her eggs. "Katia asked me to tell you that Tony said he was going to call you later. Crap, my toast is cold. Have we got time for me to make some more? And why aren't you eating? I thought you said you were hungry. Don't you want your lunch? What are you grinning at…?"

Fortunately for both my nerves and my temper, the phone stayed quiet all the way through until the "please turn off all electronic devices" announcement on the plane. They stayed off until we'd climbed into the town car Carla'd sent. No limo this time, just a basic black Mercedes, with a bloke in a black suit waiting for us.

"Mr. and Mrs. Kinkaid? I'm your driver—I hope you had a pleasant flight. Ms. Fanucci asked me to remind you that she has a meeting planned for tomorrow morning. Will there be additional luggage to be picked up...?"

Just like that, off to the car, off to the hotel with no attention attracted and no fuss at all. There'd been no sign with our name on it, either; he'd clearly been shown a photo beforehand, because he knew who we were. It's moments like these I realise just how much *nous* Carla's really got: there was nothing, not a damned thing, to attract the attention of any journalists or local reporters or photographers or whatever who might have been lurking about, covering the airports. It's the little things she does, knowing how it works, knowing what to do and what's going to make everyone's life easier, including her own, that make her the best in the business.

She'd taken my thing about Bree wanting to be available to Karen seriously, as well, because the car pulled up in front of the W, in West Hollywood. We'd never stayed there before—it's very trendy, ultra-modern, and both Bree and I tend to prefer a more traditional kind of thing. The W in San Francisco's nice and understated, but not this one.

"This is the W?" Bree was peering around me. "Boy, this place looks—pointy. Or maybe just shiny. Or something. Huh."

That got a grin from me. "You don't sound too sure about it, love. I should have remembered about the Hedleys being here. Didn't Luke say something the night Bergen got killed, about Solange and Curt doing their honeymoon at the W? Probably the whole family in residence."

"Here's hoping the place is more comfortable than it looks

from out here." She sounded glum, and I suddenly got just how much she'd wanted that break from Los Angeles, how hard it was to have to turn round and come straight back again. "The outside looks as if the beds are going to be made of stainless steel and all the walls will be black Lucite, and the restaurant will probably have anorexic androgynous waiters in black turtlenecks swanning around with their noses in the air, and I bet their idea of dinner is tiny portions of raw fish and seaweed, and –"

"Oi! Bree!" She was working herself into an even worse mood than the one she'd started out in. That habit of hers, it drives me round the fucking twist. Time to nip this one in the bud if I could—the last thing either of us needed were more reasons to be cranky. "Let's get inside before you go up on Yelp and tear long strips off the place, all right? For all we know, the food's the roast beef of Old England. After all, Solange takes her food as seriously as you do, and she opted to stay here. Give it a chance, yeah?"

She was quiet. The car had stopped in front of the main doors, and the driver had got out. I reached for her hand.

"I'm sorry, love." I was keeping my voice low; no need for the driver to hear me. "As soon as we can get this mess sorted out, you can get back on a plane and head home, I promise. Luke says Carla's got some hot-shit lawyer lined up for Suzanne, so it could be as early as tomorrow. Ah, here we go—ready?"

Bree'd been wrong about one thing, anyway: from the look of the restaurant just off the main lobby, it wasn't serving anaemic sushi. We didn't really have time to hang about and read the menu, though, because there were reporters after all, at least half a dozen of them.

*Shit.* That was the downside of having to stay in the same hotel as the girl who'd married the dead bassist: the jackals were already there and waiting. They were being herded away from the welcome desks, but they were there, and what's more, they'd already seen us.

222

"Fuck!" Bree'd ducked her head, and she was keeping her voice down. Just as well, because there was hate in it. "I recognise that blonde bimbo with the hair mousse and the teeth. She's the Queen Bee off that damned gossip channel."

"Queen Hag's more like it, I'd say. Bloody bint." We'd got to the desk behind the driver. The place was actually quite impressive, in a glass-and-trendy sort of way. "Crikey, check out that staircase thing! Bloody huge. Let's just get checked in and get the hell upstairs. We'll send out for food, all right? These wankers can sit down here and rot, for all of me. Sod them, they can starve to death, and welcome. Hotel management can bury them under that spiral staircase thing."

I'll give the staff points for having it together: we got upstairs into something called a Wow Suite without being bothered by anyone. I've had other occasions to bless hotels for being smart enough to provide key access-only lifts to their private suite floors before, and I was thankful for it now. This mess with Suzanne looked to be ratcheting Bergen's murder up and beyond even the annoyance and stress levels of Perry Dillon's murder. Any control over our own privacy was going to be useful, and possibly even sanity-saving.

The Wow Suite—I have to agree with Bree, it was a stupid name for anyone who isn't easily distracted by bright shiny things—actually turned out to be brilliantly comfy. Bree'd already taken a scunner on the W, and she was right at the edge of a good solid sulk, so it took her a few minutes of sitting on things and moving about the place before she was willing to admit it was well above decent. I left her glaring at the rooftop steakhouse's menu to see what she considered edible for dinner, and sat down with my cell phone.

I rang Luke first, and got dumped straight into voicemail. I wasn't sure if that was a bad sign or not; it could have meant anything from a dead battery or Luke having left the phone off to

223

him being locked up in a cell somewhere because he'd beaten Cunningham into an unrecognisable lump. Luke's one of the most even-tempered blokes I've ever met. It takes a lot to get him off on an edge, but if anything's going to do the trick, it would be a threat to his family. I left a message: *(beep) Luke, it's JP, we're here at the W, just wanted to let you know and see if there was any news, ring me back, cheers (beep).*

Next call was to Patrick Ormand. Yeah, I know, Patrick was probably the last person on earth I ought to have been ringing, all things considered. I'll admit it, I was curious. Besides, I'd told Jeff Kintera I'd nudge Patrick about locking Jeff out of the club's computer system. And yeah, I know, curiosity killed the cat, but I'm not a cat, am I, and might as well.

No joy there, either; two rings, and into voicemail. And with Bree sitting within earshot, I had to be careful with what I said, and how I said it. *(beep) Oi, Patrick, look, we've had to go back down to LA. You probably already know this, but Cunningham looks to be charging Suzanne Hedley with Bergen's murder, and Jeff Kintera rang because you did something that destroyed his access to the 707 computers and can you ring him back as soon as you get this so that he can do his job, use my cell or Bree's cell if you need us for anything, we're at the W in West Hollywood, cheers (beep).*

"John?" Bree was sounding less grumpy. "How hungry are you? Could you eat a small filet mignon, or would you rather have seafood?"

"No preference, love. Whatever you're having, get me that as well." I was running the question round in my head, whether or not to ring Tony. He'd gone to the trouble of telling Katia he was going to ring me, but there was nothing.

"...and some bread with that, please. No, no wine, thank you. Yes, just charge it to our suite. Thanks, bye." She put the phone down. "Dinner in about forty minutes. Anything from Tony? Whoa, what was that look for? What did I say?"

"Nothing earthshaking. It's just that, sometimes, I still get a huge kick out of the whole marital mind-reading thing. No, nothing from Tony. Part of me wants to ring him, reach out, you know? But he said he'd be in touch, and the other part of me wants to give him the space. What do you think, Bree?"

She must have been thinking about it herself, because she had the answer ready. "I wouldn't call him, John. You said it yourself, remember? About how fixing things doesn't happen unless the person who's responsible for dealing with it actually, well, deals? You said that to Tony, too, and if you go back on it, he gets the right to not take it seriously. He said he'd call, and it's up to him. Okay, now what did I say? Why the whole new look?"

"Nothing, really. Just mentally agreeing with you."

It wasn't nothing, but considering what was moving round in my head, I wasn't up for sharing with Bree. I wasn't about to ask her if that answer she'd given had actually been so close to the surface because of what we'd been going through with Tony and Katia. I had a nasty suspicion that who this was really about was me. I wasn't about to ask her if she was remembering our early days, bad times, me asking for help and her having to shake up her entire life to get it done. Had I pulled shit like this, promising things and not doing them, asking for help and not cooperating, ballsing things up, making them worse?

The thing is, I couldn't remember. I'd been in bad enough shape then to make anything I think I remember about that time about as trustworthy as a hired assassin. So maybe I'd done my own version of this rubbish, not ringing, flaking out, expecting things to happen without me lifting a finger.

I could ask Bree. I could say *right, be upfront and truthful with me, did I fuck up this badly back then?* But I wasn't asking. I didn't really want to know. I pulled myself away from that line of thought and gave my wife a smile, a real one.

"Let me just ring Carla. I want to get the schedule for the

225

morning. After that, I'm done until someone gets back to me."

We ended up having a nice quiet evening, eating steaks almost as good as Bree's, sending down for in-suite massages, curling up side by side on the huge bed, glasses perched on our noses, reading. Not what most people would consider a glamorous night, but it was mellow, and very comfortable. The only fly in that particular ointment was the background hope that Tony would ring, and get it done. But there was no call from Tony, and nothing back from Patrick.

I didn't hear back from Luke, either, but Carla got rid of that particular worry for me. She rang around ten that night to let us know a hired car would be waiting for us at nine, and that the front desk would let us know it was there.

"...that way, you won't have to risk a head-on with the media. But it's an all-hands meeting in my office at nine-thirty. The Hedleys have an earlier meeting with Suzanne's lawyer, so they'll be coming separately. Dom and Mac aren't staying at the W, so they get their own ride. Elaine says she'll get here by herself, and I know Tony and Katia are back up north." I could practically hear her take a long breath. "I ought to give you the heads-up now, JP. Cunningham is going to be there."

"Oh, bloody hell, is he? That'll make for a nice restful little do, won't it?"

Bree jerked her head away from her book. My voice had been disgusted enough to not only get her attention, but get her shoulders bunched hard. I rolled my eyes at her, and grinned, and she eased up slightly.

"Sorry about that, Carla. No big deal and not to worry, but Cunningham's not exactly on any of my holiday card lists, you know? And I suspect neither of us will have had enough coffee to make him doable that early in the day. Still, we'll cope. Why do you want him anywhere near the place, though?"

"I'm not thrilled either, JP, believe me." Crikey, was that defen-

226

siveness I was hearing? No, not possible. "But Luke says Cunningham's being cagey about why he thinks he has grounds for charging Suzanne. He won't tell Luke, and Luke can't really push it, because Suzanne's not a minor. And this hotshot lawyer I hired says that's bullshit, that she can make him spill it."

"Got it. You want to use your conference room for a little home-court advantage."

"That's it. Thanks for getting it, JP. And about that coffee, I'm sending Marjorie out for enough of the best damned Italian roast she can find to make everyone happy. Nine o'clock pickup. I'll see you in the morning."

I know I've said this before, but as a lifelong touring musician, I've never done mornings very well. One of the realities of doing my job is a requirement for late nights. Over the years, I've got my body clock synched nicely to staying up as late as it takes to get it done, waking up at ten in the morning and taking my time for however long it takes.

So mornings have always been miserable, but with the MS to cope with, they're a stone drag. If you want me to do more than grunt and snap and say rude things under my breath, trust me, you'll want to wait until it's gone at least ten.

It turned out I didn't actually have to do much more than grunt, because Carla, clever girl, had got us the same driver who'd fetched us at the airport the day before. The desk rang to let us know he was downstairs, we finished the mouthful of toast and coffee Bree'd had the sense to have sent up just before she'd hit the shower, and we headed off to cope.

"Jesus."

Bree had oversized dark glasses on, very forties *noir*. She looked like she'd stepped out of a Veronica Lake or Rita Hayworth flick, right in tune with the hotel and its little Hollywood glam themes, but of course that wasn't why she'd put them on;

she was glaring through them at the media crush. "What's wrong with this hotel? Why don't they just get their security to kick these assholes out? They can't possibly all be staying here, can they?"

"No clue, but it's probably some sort of unwritten Hollywood rule, that not wanting to nark the press thing. Must be a fine line they've got to walk, between protecting their guests and losing their posh status, or whatever."

I let Bree get in first. I wasn't giving the vultures the satisfaction of turning round and giving them back stare for stare, but then, I didn't really have to. Between the shiny black car and the shiny white hotel and all that glass, I was getting a nice clear reflection of the whole sodding horde of them, pressing closer to the doors. For a nasty moment, I saw them as all mouths, open and hungry, showing teeth.

They weren't coming out past the lobby, though, or making any move to get near us or give us shit. As I was settling in and the driver was closing the door behind me, I realised why: the hotel's security staff actually was doing its collective job. They might be invisible, basically, but there were definitely bodies between us and the media. Two points to the W, then. They weren't as hands-off and unconcerned as Bree'd thought they were.

We weren't the first to arrive. There were a few cars outside when we pulled up, a couple of black Mercedes towncars just like the one we'd come in. Their drivers were still in them, doing whatever hired drivers do while the people they're ferrying about are off doing their thing. There was also a black car with no one in it, definitely not a Mercedes. It wasn't marked, nothing to distinguish it in any way, but for some reason, it just said "cop" to me.

"Oh, joy, Cunningham must be here." Bree'd got out behind me, and was giving the empty car a dirty look. "Ugly-assed car. Who in hell drives a Crown Vic if they don't have to…?"

Carla'd made good on her promise to keep the coffee flowing.

228

Just as well, because the way things turned out, we needed it. Her conference room is a good size, but it was pretty full. Bree stopped to say something to Marjorie at the front desk; meanwhile, I was taking a visual roll call on the other side of the glass.

Luke and Karen were at the far end of the table, with an empty chair between them. Karen looked wasted, wrung out and dried, past caring. Suzanne was at her mother's left side, white-faced and staring at Cunningham as if he was a man-eating tiger. He was staring right back at her across the table; he had both beefy fists resting on a big brown envelope. Solange and Curt were shoulder to shoulder—young Curt may have been on the road since his wedding, but he'd already had time to pick up on the family solidarity thing the Hedleys do.

I kept scanning. Mac and Dom were there, Mac looking just the way he always does. Dom was chugging from what was probably a cup of drinking chocolate; that's much more her thing than coffee. The Bunker Brothers were there as well, Stu looking to be right at the wrong edge of pissed off, but there was no sign of either Cyn Corrigan or Barb Wilson. It looked as if, once again, both their wives had given this do a miss. Now I considered it, Barb and Cyn had managed to sidestep the worst of this particular mess. Wise women, both of them. I just wished I could have done the same, and Bree right along with me.

There was obviously no Patrick and no Andy, no Tony or Katia. Still, I had the feeling I was leaving someone out, but I didn't have time to think about it just then, because someone else had got all my attention.

There was one more person, halfway down the table, sitting next to Suzanne. She had most of her back to me. I couldn't see her face, but there was something familiar about those shoulders and that back: the hair was familiar as well, grey wisps coming loose of an outsized bun.

For some reason, every warning button my nervous system's

got left to it was twanging away like a Stratocaster with one string gone. She was waving her hands about, making some kind of point. Must be Suzanne's lawyer…

Oh, bloody *hell.* Lenore Tannenbaum.

I don't think I'm particularly dim most days, but just then, I felt a complete nit. How in hell had I not sussed it out before now? A hot-shit lawyer from the Bay Area. What had Carla said, that Patrick had recommended her? Yeah, hot-shit lawyer, all right. It must help you along in your profession, not having any heart or scruples or sensitivity.

Lenore Tannenbaum was a barracuda. Last time I'd seen her face to face, I'd been ripping her a new one for dumping my wife as her client with no reason given, leaving Bree dangling and upset, afraid Tannenbaum thought she was a murderess. I hadn't got one good reason to think I'd ever have to deal with the woman again, and I didn't have any reason to want to, either.

So yeah, it was a damned good thing Carla had coffee ready and waiting. Problem was, locking eyes with Lenore as she climbed out of her chair and trotted towards us, coffee wasn't what I wanted. What I was thinking just then was *fuck the coffee, what I want is a bottle of brandy and maybe a few lines of coke to sweeten it with.* Not pretty, but true.

She had that shark's grin on her face, as toned down as she could get it. Not toned down enough, though—she was in lawyer mode and there was no way to hide the fangs, not under those circs. She wasn't nearly dim enough to offer a hand for shaking, but she did get the first word in: setting the tone, grabbing the advantage, letting me know she was going for informality. I didn't mind, not really. It's what she was trained to do and anyway, it kept me from having to decide what to say.

"Well hello, JP." She spotted Bree over my shoulder. "Bree, so nice to see you. I haven't seen you for a while. How are you? Doing well?"

Bree walked straight past her. Not a word, nothing; Tannenbaum might as well have been made of air. She circled the table, heading for the empty chair next to Karen. She wasn't looking back, or acknowledging that the little lawyer had spoken or that she even existed. She murmured something to Karen, who was sitting at Suzanne's other side, and looked straight over Tannenbaum's head.

"John? Do you need a chair? There's one down here, next to Luke."

It was as complete and brutal a snub as I've seen my old lady dish out to anyone, ever. Even Lucien Santini, the racist cop who'd dragged her and Dom off to a French jail a few years back, hadn't merited this. And Santini had been one of the few people Bree refused to shake hands with under her own roof.

My stomach was doing a slow twist, and I was gawking like a department store mannequin. I wasn't alone, either. Every head in the room, no matter what else they'd been doing, swivelled round. Everyone was staring, either at Lenore or at my wife.

Lenore Tannenbaum just stood there. There were scarlet spots, spreading in a fast ugly flush, burning high up on her cheekbones. She's a tiny woman, in her sixties at least; physically, anyone in the room could have folded her in half and tucked her into a cupboard without breaking a sweat. But right then, she looked murderous.

Bree had made her look a fool in front of a room full of people, and she knew it. More than that, it had been deliberate, and she knew that, as well. Whether Bree realised it or not, she'd just thrown down a gauntlet to someone I couldn't help feeling would make a very bad enemy.

"Marjorie, hold all my calls, please." Carla was ignoring the whole thing, probably because she'd been busy doing her own internal headcount. "Nothing and no one for the next little while. Unless—no, never mind. Nothing and no one."

231

She pulled the door closed behind her, and I headed for the spare chair between Luke and Mac. I stopped to pour two cups of coffee on the way; Bree hadn't stopped to get herself anything on her way to Karen.

"Here you go, love. Coffee." I slid the cup across the table. I had one eye on Lenore, who was making her way back to her seat. Her lips were pressed so tight they looked like a wrinkle, not a mouth. "Luke, shove over a bit, will you? Right, that's done it. Thanks."

"If everyone's ready, let's get started."

I'd only been out of Cunningham's vicinity for few days, but I'd managed to push damned near everything about him to the back edge of my memory. I'd forgotten just how mean and self-important he could sound when he knew he was in charge. Yeah, I know that whole control thing is part of the deal about being a cop, and yeah, Patrick's attitude when he'd sat in that particular chair, that chilly smugness of his, had made me want to throttle him. But Cunningham wasn't Patrick; there were things about Patrick I could trust, even if I didn't much care for them. Cunningham was a different story. There was nothing about this bloke that didn't hit me wrong. And what he brought up in me wasn't trust, either.

"Yes, let's." Lenore had flipped into full lawyer mode. "A very good idea, Lieutenant. My client, Mrs. Sandoval, tells me you're claiming possession of new evidence, and that on the basis of that evidence, you're considering laying a capital charge against her. Is that correct?"

"So far as it goes, yes." He sounded grudging. Having to part with any information at all seemed to have the same effect on Cunningham that the need for a root canal might have on anyone else. Bloody stupid, that was—he'd agreed to this meeting, and he'd known, coming in, what it was in aid of. If he'd actually thought Suzanne was going to turn up without her lawyer and her family at her back, he was too dim to be let out of doors without a keeper.

"Are you prepared to ask for an arrest warrant for my client at this time?" They were locked up, good and hard. I'd seen Tannenbaum do that with Patrick, and she was damned good at it. "Because if so, I'm going to need to know the nature of the evidence in question."

He showed his own teeth suddenly, a tight, nasty little grin. Next to me, Luke suddenly stirred in his chair.

"All in good time, counsellor, all in good time. Before we go any further, though, we seem to be missing someone. I agreed to Mrs. Corrigan and Mrs. Wilson not being here for this—their presence wasn't necessary. And I'm aware that Mr. and Mrs. Mancuso are back in the Bay Area for health reasons. None of that explains why Ms. Wilde isn't here."

*Shit.* I'd been right—there'd been that niggling feeling, that we were missing headcount. In this crowd, and with Elaine being such a recent addition to the Fluorescent family, I'd spaced on her completely.

"She's in San Francisco—or, rather, she's on her way to San Francisco. She got the first plane out this morning."

We all turned to stare at Mac. He was leaning back in his Aeron chair, looking completely relaxed. That was bollocks, though. I've watched him moving about onstage for more than thirty years, and I know when those back and shoulder muscles mean business. Just then, they meant business, all right. He was ready for a solid go-round with Cunningham on the subject of Elaine Wilde, and that meant he'd come expecting to have one.

Still, expecting one and wanting one are two different things, and he was smart enough to want to head it off if he could. He went straight on, not giving Cunningham a chance to ask questions he couldn't or didn't want to answer.

"She's a single mother, Lieutenant. Her daughter Martina is being cared for by Elaine's sister Hilda—Hilda takes care of Maret when Elaine's on the road working, and has done since Maret was born. Hilda rang very early this morning, to say that Martina had spent the night in hospital, and that she needed her mum to be at home with her. Her mum agreed. So did I."

Cunningham opened his mouth, and shut it again. There was that purple flush again. The bloke was a cardiac event waiting for a moment to happen. I couldn't help wondering if there was anyone who'd actually mind when it did.

"We got her a flight and a taxi to the airport." Mac was looking steadily at Cunningham, practically daring him to get shirty over it. "She's got her cell with her, and you have the number if you need her. I'd really think twice about bothering her right now for anything that isn't completely necessary, though. She's worried as hell about her daughter."

We'd all been silent up to then, but of course that broke it. There was a sudden burble of questions: *Does she need any help, have they sorted out what's wrong with her daughter, is the kid going to be okay, is there anything we can do?*

"No, nothing. I'm sure she'll let us know, if there's anything." Mac was still eye-locked with Cunningham; there seemed to be some sort of thing going on, just between the two of them. I wasn't sure what it was, but if it had been anyone other than Mac, I'd have thought it was tree-pissing, big dog warning off the smaller one. "I just wanted to make sure the Lieutenant had all the pertinent information. Now that's done, did you say you wanted to get this moving? Because I was up much too early and I've got a radio interview scheduled in about three hours, and I'd like to get on with it."

"A very good suggestion." Lenore wasn't bothering to look at Mac. Next to me, Luke was rigid, not moving at all. "I believe I asked Lieutenant Cunningham a question, as to the nature of the evidence he's presenting."

"Certainly, Counsellor." There it was again, that mean little grin. I've had mixed feelings about Patrick Ormand from the

234

time I'd first come up against him; most days, I'm still not sure whether I like him or not. No question about Cunningham, though. The voice was as mean and as smug as the grin was. It wasn't about doing the right thing, not from Cunningham—it was about winning. He slid the envelope across the table. "I think nearly thirty million dollars would qualify as a pretty good motive for murder, for most people."

Next to me, Luke suddenly relaxed. So did I. I saw the same letting out of breath ripple round the table. The only three who weren't easing up were the cop, the lawyer, and Suzanne herself.

"Not necessarily. In fact, not at all." Mac sounded amused, almost bored. He was watching Lenore Tannenbaum open the envelope and slide the contents free. I wasn't wearing my readers, so I couldn't see what it was, not beyond the notary stamp and what looked to be a bunch of signatures. "Actually, in our case, money's probably the least plausible motive you'd want to look for. We're not most people, Lieutenant, not when it's a question of money. Sorry if that offends your proletariat sensibilities, but the simple fact is that if Suzanne wanted thirty million dollars, all she'd have to do is ask her dad for it. I'm not saying he wouldn't notice it, but he could write her a cheque without a blink. Luke?"

"Damned right I could." Luke wasn't grinning, and he didn't sound amused, but his breathing had gone back to normal. "And it would still leave me a few bob in the bank to be going on with."

Cunningham was purpling up. Maybe it was because he was being made to look a complete pillock in front of a room full of people again and he knew it, or maybe it was something in the way Mac and Luke had said what they'd just said. He opened his mouth to say something, but Lenore got in first.

"Hold on a moment, please." She turned to Suzanne, and I got a full-on look at her face. She could taste the blood in the water; Christ, she was damned near licking her lips. "What was the date of your wedding, Mrs. Sandoval?"

Suzanne was blinking hard, and her voice was shaky, all the way down. I wondered if she was about to start blubbering, or if it was just nerves. "The thirteenth of March."

"Of this year?"

"Well, of course. We only met for the first time last winter, when I laid down some backing vocals for his CD, at my dad's mobile." Suzanne looked bewildered. "Why do you want to know that? I don't understand."

Lenore tapped the thin pile with one finger. "This document is Bergen Sandoval's last will and testament. Barring any later will that may surface, it's binding. It's a very simple will: a few bequests to a few charities, and everything else—all property, money, assets, everything—I quote, *to my beloved wife*. The will is dated August 18, 2007."

Bree said something under her breath, and draped her arm around Karen. The rest of us were watching the back and forth across the table, everyone except Mac; for some reason, he'd suddenly gone as rigid as Luke had been.

"But—I hadn't even met him in 2007." Suzanne's voice was spiralling up. I had a moment of actually feeling sorry for her. Christ knows the girl brings most of this rubbish on herself, but she couldn't be enjoying this, especially since she seemed to have actually loved Bergen. "I don't understand. How could he leave me anything when he didn't even know I existed?"

"Dumb question, yo. He didn't." Domitra had finished her chocolate, finally. "Lawyer lady here just said he left all his shit to his beloved wife. She didn't say he left it to 'Suzanne.' So who was his beloved wife in 2007? Wasn't that Elaine Wilde...?"

# Chapter Fifteen

"Hey, everyone, this is Listen Up with Skip Terry, and you're listening to 99.1, KRNR, covering Greater Los Angeles and a few funky suburbs—you know who you are, Venice Beach and the PCH! Thanks for checking in, people, and believe me, you're going to be glad you did. We've got Blacklight ace guitarist JP Kinkaid in the studio today, talking about *Fogbound*, the brand-new debut release from JP's side band, the Fog City Geezers. There's all kinds of other cool stuff on the burner too, including a taste of some new tunes for you..."

After thirty years, I've done so many promo spots on radio, I can do them in my sleep. It's probably just as well, because that day, as preoccupied as I was, I'd have ballsed that interview up beyond fixing if I'd had to think my way through it.

"Hi, JP, and welcome to Listen Up. So, let's start out with the new CD. *Fogbound* is a live double CD, and it's the first release by your long-time side project, the Fog City Geezers—and for anyone listening, no, you can't get it yet, it comes out on Blacklight's Fluorescent label next week. Tell us a little about it. How is the Geezers music different from Blacklight's repertoire? Is there a certain amount of crossover?"

"Hey, Skip, pleasure to be here. Yeah, the CD's a live double, best of our recent West Coast tour. It's cherry-picked, the best version of each song. There's no Blacklight material on there— there's really not much crossover, usually. If Mac Sharpe happens to be in the same time zone when we're gigging, he's been known to sit in. And if Mad At Our Dads isn't touring, Curtis Lind comes and sings 'Americaland' with us, since he wrote the lyrics to that one. We've got a brilliant cover of that on the CD, from the Seattle show. But we're really more about classics and standards: Chuck Berry, Bo Diddley, Rufus Thomas, the Stones. And blues, of course, that's my main thing, you know? Bottom line is, Blacklight's a rock band. The Geezers play rock and roll, the older stuff. Not a lot of recent material in there, unless it's stuff we wrote ourselves..."

That bombshell back at Carla's office, yesterday morning— Gordon *Bennett*. I couldn't wrap my head around any of it. What in sweet hell had Bergen Sandoval been up to?

What had Elaine said, the morning after Bergen had died? That she'd married him in Vegas and dumped him when she sussed what he was up to, trying to get his hands on Martina Wilde's trust fund? But that wouldn't fly. If he was trying to get his fingers on Elaine's dosh, why had he left her everything? Thirty million dollars is quite a lot of money, especially since we were talking about a bloke who'd left his hired band stranded because he couldn't be arsed to pay a bed and breakfast proprietor two night's lodging...

"The Geezers are an interesting amalgam of Bay Area local

238

players. I know you've been gigging a long time, but you guys have only toured down this way a few times in the past. You've got a serious following up north. Is this tour a signal that you're looking at playing outside the Bay Area more often?"

"Well, a lot of that depends on availability, you know? If Black-light's touring or in the studio, they get first claim on my time. Same goes for the rest of the Geezers, with their own projects. But we really dig playing down here—very good audiences you've got—so yeah, time and health issues allowing, there's no reason we wouldn't be back down here soon enough…"

No matter how I looked at the issue of Bergen's will, I couldn't sort it out. The more I thought about it, the more it felt as if the entire thing was leading Cunningham down the garden path, all the way into the wrong territory. There was no way in hell I could see Elaine Wilde offing her ex to get her hands on any amount of money, period. She wasn't that sort. And besides, she might not make Blacklight's kind of dosh, but if her daughter had a trust fund set up, with enough money in it to catch Bergen Sandoval's attention, she wasn't exactly boosting tins of soup when the supermarket staff wasn't looking, either.

And if I was wrong, and the will was somehow connected to Bergen being bunged full of rat poison, then what in hell was Andy Valdon up to? What did one thing have to do with the other? If there was any connection between those two pieces of information, it was going to take someone who actually enjoyed sorting this rubbish out to parse it. I heard a small voice at the back of my head—*yeah, well, that would be Patrick Ormand, so why don't you let him deal with the bullshit, and get back to your own job, promoting the CD?*

"I'd like to let our listeners know that *Fogbound* isn't the only goodie on the table today. It's one of three CDs that mark the launch of Fluorescent Records USA. JP was kind enough to bring along advance copies of all three. We're going to play you a taste from each one—told you campers you'd be glad you tuned in! Let's start with this one from WildeChild's first CD on her new label. This is Elaine Wilde and the band, tearing it up on 'You Better Not Touch'..."

The music cranked up, and I closed my eyes for moment. If my host thought I was listening, he was dead wrong; I was trying for a moment of Zen, and I tell you what, I needed one just then. It had been a long morning. Any day that starts off with me and Bree having a row is pretty much fucked from the start.

It had been as stupid a reason for either of us getting pissy as you could imagine: she'd announced, last minute, that she'd changed her mind about heading home, that she wanted to hang out in LA for a few days longer. That was bollocks, and I knew it. The media swarm in the lobby downstairs hadn't eased up at all, especially not after some ass ran a coy "a little bird told me" bullshit piece about "new developments in the Sandoval murder, centering around his will." I could cheerfully have hunted the berk down and throttled him, and the rest of the staff of the shitty little rag as well.

So Bree was feeling completely trapped in the hotel, she'd only come down because I'd guilted her into feeling she had to provide support for Karen, and now, of course, I was the one feeling guilty about it. She was only saying she wanted to hang out because she didn't want to leave me on my own. Besides, Carla had already booked her a flight and a car to the airport.

So I'd put my foot down: I'm a big boy, I can look after myself, you know you didn't want to come down in the first place, I'm not having you made miserable, all that. And yeah, that was all true, but what I wasn't saying—that the two of us cooped up in a hotel suite while she was this cross and cranky and had no way of getting out was a drag for me, as well as her—coloured what I did say, and Bree being Bree, of course she sussed me. That led to a few terse nasty moments, with her calling me "little man," and, well, there you go. We'd made it up, and she was home by now, I'd redeemed myself by personally escorting her downstairs to her car and offering to bash anyone who hassled us, but my stomach was still knotted. I hate rowing with Bree.

"...and the second release from this particular trifecta of hot discs takes us onto some pretty tricky ground. This is 'Movement' from Bergen Sandoval's final effort, engineered by Blacklight's own Stu Corrigan. Sandoval's distinctive early jazz training on bass really stands out on this one. Check out the world-class vocals from Suzanne McElroy..."

I closed my eyes again. My host wasn't going to mention the investigation; he'd been told upfront by Carla that anything to do with Bergen Sandoval was off limits on the air, and that trying what she called an end run around that would make sure that no Fluorescent artist would ever guest on KRNR again. He didn't look to be the type to commit career suicide, and I doubted he was going to push it.

So I could relax a little and actually listen, and I realised, suddenly, that this was the first time I'd actually heard the thing. Stu really had done a brilliant job; hell, considering the fact that he and Bergen had nearly come to blows at Streak's excellent recording digs, the quality of Bergen's final album was remarkable. It was probably going to make his estate a nice dollop of dosh, even more than it would have done had he not got himself murdered. Quite a nice little bonus for Elaine and the junior guitar prodigy, assuming Cunningham didn't drag her off to prison before she could collect.

"...one of three tracks on this one featuring Tony Mancuso, stepping outside his usual boogie-woogie mojo into something a lot sleeker and more sophisticated..."

I had another motive for wanting Bree at home: I still hadn't got that promised call from Tony. Bree'd been right about me not ringing Tony first, unless I wanted to make a nonsense of what I'd told him about him needing to make the first move, and own his own bullshit. But waiting for him to ring, with everything else that was going on, was playing hell with my own mood and headspace. Bree wasn't the only cranky one in the family right now.

"We're talking with legendary guitarist JP Kinkaid about *Fogbound*, the double live debut CD from his band, the Fog City Geezers. I want to play a couple of cuts off this one, and I'll leave the choice up to our guest…"

Maybe it was because I'd just been thinking about Tony, but I picked the version of "Sweet Virginia" we'd used, from the Vegas show. Vicious piano, just killer stuff, with the rest of us hanging back and letting Tony's fingers take those ivories and tickle the starch out of them. I wondered suddenly, had he really been shit-faced, sitting there and playing so perfectly that he'd nearly melted the stage around us? And if he had been, why was I surprised? Christ, I'd spent a good three years doing the same, recording guitar parts, standing on stage at night in front of fifty thousand people, drunk off my arse and never showing it.

"Wow, that's some incredible keyboard work. That's Tony Mancuso, right? Just him, no backup? That's awesome stuff."

"Yeah." My stomach was trying to shake hands with itself. Long day, bad day. Stupid pissy row with Bree, alone in LA to go do the PR rubbish, the nonsense with Bergen's will. Why in hell hadn't Tony rung? He'd gone out of his way to have Katia let Bree know he was going to… "Yeah, that's Tony Mancuso. He's a monster piano player, one of the best in the business, and one of the most underrated. You don't hear a touch like his very often, you know? What? Oh, right, second track? Definitely 'America-land.' That's Curtis Lind of Mad At Our Dads on vocals and rhythm guitar. He wrote the lyrics…"

Eyes closed, trying to relax, and this time, I actually was listening. A minute, two minutes, the song building, the crowd chanting in the background. I'd given some thought to just how much of the audience I wanted in the final mixdown; too much audience and the music can get swamped, not enough and it sounds canned rather than live. But that primal chant the crowds had got into, "*Americaland! Americaland!,*" people holding their fists in the air like the old Black Power salute, was just too bloody strong a hook to not use.

"KRNR, can I help you? Excuse me—oh, wow, cool! Yes, he's here, hang on."

My eyes popped open. The DJ was holding the phone out.

"Nice timing! It's Tony Mancuso, calling for you. If he wants to say something to the audience, let me know, and I can hook him up on the air."

"Right." I reached for the phone. My hands were shaking, and I didn't think it was the MS, not this time. "Oi! Tony?"

"Hey man. Yeah, it's me." He sounded calm, straight, just the way he'd always sounded, thirty years and more. "I'm sorry I took so long to call you, but I needed a little time, to try and straighten some shit out in my own head, and with Katia, you know what I mean? I know you're in the middle of a spot, I don't want to keep you. Let's talk more later, if you're up for it—but I wanted to check in, and let you know I was okay. And I want to ask you something, really fast."

"You got it." I swallowed. "What?"

"That addiction recovery clinic you started in London—do they handle booze issues?"

"Yeah, they do." I wondered if Katia was listening, if Bree was there, where he was ringing from. This wasn't a conversation I wanted to have on live radio, with a complete stranger listening, even if all he could hear was my end of it. "Look, mate, the song's running down. Let me finish up and I'll get back to you from the hotel tonight, yeah?"

"Sounds good." He hesitated, just the barest pause, hardly a breath long. "JP? Thanks for what you said about me on the air, about me being underrated. Maybe I should stop underrating myself. That might take care of some shit. Talk to you later."

A click, and silence. I handed the phone back to the DJ, as "Americaland" spun itself down, fading with the crowd noise and the chanting, and my own voice, fronting my band, telling the crowd *goodnight, you've been a great audience, thanks for coming out, goodnight...*

"This is Skip Terry, and you've been listening to Listen Up on KRNR 99.1 FM. Our guest in the studio today was JP Kinkaid. JP, any plans for another gig in LA while you're here?"

"Nothing planned for the full band; we just finished a West Coast tour, and that was a lot of work. The rest of the blokes are getting a few weeks off. But if anyone's interested, I'm just heading off to do a live afternoon solo gig at Amoeba Records in Hollywood. Cheers, and thanks for having me in."

Carla had a car waiting for me outside the studio, to get me cross-town to Amoeba. Settling down in the back with my two guitar cases, I turned my phone back on. There was just one voicemail, a short impersonal one from Bree, letting me know she'd got home safely; from the sound of it, she hadn't quite got over being narked at me. Hopefully that wouldn't last.

There was also a text message from Carla: *JP am coming to in-store gig this afternoon.* Good. Radio or telly, that's no big deal: you're indoors for those, one on one mostly, with a solid layer of walls and distance between you and the public if you fancy it. A live in-store gig, though, that's a different story. People are there to see you, get up close; that's the whole point of doing the event. It can get overwhelming, depending on what else is happening, so it was nice to know Carla would be there to make sure I had some sort of buffer.

As it turned out, I needed one. I don't know why I was surprised at the size of the crowd at Amoeba. I hadn't thought much about it beforehand, but if anyone had asked, I'd have said I expected a smallish turnout. We weren't talking about Saturday night, you know? This was the middle of a weekday. And after all, this wasn't Blacklight or even the Geezers, it was just me with a couple of guitars.

But there were a couple of hundred people out in front. I'm not generally worried by crowds—normally, I'd have found the size of the crowd flattering—but for some reason, I had a moment of wishing I had some backup, someone to run interference for me: Bree, or the rest of the band, or Domitra.

Shop management must have offered their staff extra pay to act as security and crowd control, though, because I actually made it through the crush of people without too much bother. Once I'd got indoors, I smiled and made polite noises at a few people I didn't recognise, shook hands with the people in charge, and was just making sure they'd set out what I needed—a stool, a small table, bottled water—when I saw Carla heading for me, cutting her way through the crowd.

"JP? Got a second?"

She sounded very focussed. That got my attention, because Carla sounding that pinpointed usually means she's got something major on her mind. And yeah, Bergen dead, Andy in hiding, three CDs debuting one right after another, all of that was plenty to focus on. For some reason, though, all my nerve endings suddenly decided to tingle.

"Half a mo, Carla, all right? Be right with you."

I got both guitars out on their stands, and all the various bits that go along with them—cables and capos and assorted whatnots—set up. Someone had made sure there was a nice little Boogie waiting for me, just right for the size of the venue. The place isn't all that huge—it's a record shop, not a theatre—and it was filling up quickly. The staff seemed to be making damned sure people stayed a reasonable distance back.

245

"Right, okay. Here we go."

I turned back to Carla, and discovered she had someone with her—not the office intern, for a change. "Oi, Streak, nice to see you, mate. I didn't know you were coming along. How are things down at ALS, and the club? Press not driving you too nuts, I hope?"

"Hey, JP. Yeah, Carla invited me; she thinks it's a good plug for ALS, especially since Elaine Wilde's coming down next week with the band to do a gig here. I'll be introducing you to the crowd. The press? Hell, could be worse, I guess."

I lifted an eyebrow at him; that last bit hadn't sounded particularly sincere. "Really? If it's half as bad as what we've had to cope with at the W, I'd have thought they'd be driving you straight up a wall. The fucking vultures have been stacked three deep in the hotel lobby."

He shrugged. "Yeah, well, I guess we Angelenos get used to the talking head brigade, especially in Hollywood. It's against the law to carpet-bomb them, so we have to live with them. All part of the turf down here: you don't get anywhere without the press. Oh, sorry, Carla. I didn't mean to get in your way."

"No problem." She was looking rushed, but that laser thing was still there. "I needed to make sure Suzanne had a seat—she walked in about two minutes ago. I wish she'd called and let me know she was coming first, but she said it was a spur of the moment thing."

"Suzanne's here?" I glanced around the crowd, trying to spot her. You'd have thought a head full of natural red hair would have been an easy pick among all the blondes and brunettes, but no luck. "What, she just come down to have a listen? I hope she hasn't got her bloody lawyer with her. And spur of the moment? I'd love to know how she got past all the paparazzi, without them leeching on like remoras."

"Good question." Carla caught my eye. "That's not what I

246

wanted to ask you about, though. Mac said he was coming down. He wanted to know if you might be up for him sitting in: he said a little harmonica and some lead singing if he gets here in time, but he also said not to sweat it if you have a full set list planned already."

"Hell yeah, love it." I grinned at her. "Think this lot would fancy a nice little cover of 'Liplock'?"

"Great! I'll call him and let him know. He's probably sitting in cross-town traffic right about now. He said he'd bring his harps just in case you were up for it." She had her Blackberry in one hand, wincing against the noise. "Jesus, it's loud in here! Feeding the lions at the zoo, or something. Back in a minute. Did they bring your Volvic…?"

She was off again, presumably for a quiet corner where she could use the phone properly. Streak stayed put. He was watching me; I'd got settled, and was tuning up the Martin.

"Look, JP, can I ask you something?" Streak kept his voice lowered. "I wouldn't want to ask Carla, I don't know her well enough, and to tell you the truth, she kind of scares me. But maybe you can help me out? I'm really worried."

"Worried about what?" The D-string felt rough, a bit dead. *Shit.* I'd meant to change strings before we came back down, but things had been moving too fast, and I hadn't got round to it. "What's the problem?"

"Do you know if Andy's okay?" He sounded worried, and his face matched the voice. "I mean—I got this call from the cops, telling me to get in touch with them if Andy called. I told them he hadn't called, and that's the truth. I'm really worried about him. He hasn't called me for help, or anything. So, do you know if he's okay? Does he need anything?"

Around us, the record shop had got up to a steady level of noise, the hum of conversation and the scrape of chairs being moved into place as people settled in and got ready for some live music.

247

"Andy? No clue. He's gone walkabout." The lie was out before I suddenly remembered why he'd care, or why he'd think Andy would ask him for anything. "Shit, I'm sorry. I'd forgotten he used to work for you. He'll be all right, Streak—probably just keeping out of the picture until things get sorted out, and I tell you what, he's not stupid. Cunningham's actually looking into some stuff that hasn't got anything to do with Andy, so who knows? But really, not to worry. Andy's family, and we don't leave family having to cope without backup. Doesn't matter whether it's Blacklight or Fluorescent, doesn't even matter whether we like someone or not. The kid's one of our own. We'll make sure he's covered."

He opened his mouth to say something, but Carla was back. She had the store manager in tow.

"Mac says great, he'll be here in about ten minutes. Ready, JP? Streak, are you sure you don't want a small mic setup? No? Good, then we're ready to roll. Remember, this is being taped to air later, so watch the language, guys. None of the Seven Words, okay?"

"You got it." He grinned at me over one shoulder. "Have a seat, JP. Ready, steady, go!"

I'd been wondering why Carla'd thought Derek Silver was the appropriate person to talk me up to a crowd, but he was maybe fifteen seconds into his intro before I'd got it. He had a fantastic touch with a crowd, absolutely brilliant. Maybe it was years of introducing the DJs and whatnot at his clubs, or maybe he was just a born frontman. I didn't know. Either way, it was a pity he wasn't a singer, because he could have fronted a band easily, and made quite a good job of it.

"...thanks for being willing to blow off hitting the beaches on such a gorgeous day, but we're pretty sure you won't regret it. In fact, prepare to have your socks knocked off. Our guest is a legendary guitarist, one of the UK's original great session players.

248

He's been a member of Blacklight for over thirty years, and somehow manages to find the time to gig and record with his own group, the Fog City Geezers. Their first CD is a monster, a double-live called *Fogbound*, and it rocks like a Lamborghini on full throttle down a five-mile straightaway. I ought to know, it was mixed at my place, Another Line Studios, right here in LA..."

The Martin was balanced on my knee, I'd snapped the capo on at the third fret, and the slide was handy. The crowd was going to get a nice mix of material; I was planning on doing a couple of things from the CD but, without the band here, I wanted to keep it simple. That meant going back to the roots of where I live musically, Delta and Chicago blues, some early rock and roll, a lot of slide and finger picking, basic signature JP Kinkaid guitar work. Out in the middle of the house, I'd finally spotted Suzanne, in dark glasses and a tank top.

"...Elaine Wilde, with her band WildeChild, will be coming down from the Bay Area in a couple of weeks, to blister the paint off Amoeba's walls. I caught their last show and trust me, when Elaine handles that mic and sings that you can look but you'd better not touch, you're going to have a hard time following instructions..."

One final tweak at the Martin's D string, and one more look over the house. Nice mellow crowd I seemed to have pulled in for this one, and thank God for that. The day had started off badly enough to leave me wondering if everything that happened between that miserable little row with Bree until the last stroke of midnight was going to be fucked up. And yeah, you're probably rolling your eyes and thinking I'm a superstitious nutter, but the truth is, all musicians are superstitious as hell. Any musician who tells you otherwise is lying to both of you. Still, the radio show had gone off without a hitch, so maybe things would sort themselves out after all...

"…ladies and gentlemen, put 'em together and give it up for *JP Kinkaid!*"

Right. Showtime.

I started off with some traditional Delta goodness on the Martin, a classic Robert Johnson tune, "Stop Breakin' Down." I've got some nice slide tricks for that one; normally, I'd play it on my Byrdland, the axe Bulldog Moody left me when he died a few years back, but the Byrd was safe at home in the basement studio, and the Martin did quite nicely. Good strong midrange, that axe has. The song can be played crunchy and edgy, the way the Stones did it on *Exile on Main Street*, or it can be played sun-soaked, evoking the quiet street down in Mississippi or Tennessee, the men heading for the local bar with their wages and some old dice in the pockets of their sharp Saturday Night suits, eyes out for the pretty women. Knowing that Robert Johnson had died after one of those evenings in one of those bars hanging with the Saturday night women he'd been singing about, when a jealous rival poisoned him, that gave the song a few raspy dark edges, that cut their way into the vocal.

I went for sun-soaked and kept the vocals simple, since simple vocals are the only kind I'm halfway good at. Nice little four-minute grinder with some vicious slide work in the middle and there we were, the crowd standing up to clap, and some actual catcalls and cheers from the back of the shop. I love American audiences, you know? They're really gratifying to play for, enthusiastic, easy to please.

I'd got everyone settled down after a minute or two of natter, and was just about to start up again, when I heard a commotion, some noise at the back of the shop. I stopped, and grinned out at the crowd.

"Right," I told them. "I don't think Streak mentioned I might have some company up here, when he introduced me. Oi, Mac, glad you got here. Got your harps?"

Of course, the place went bonkers. Gasps, cheers, whispers, whistles, because he's Malcolm Sharpe and he's like Planet Charisma, with his own damned gravitational field. He headed up the side of the crowd, with Dom leading the way. She's about the most effective way to clear a path I've ever seen, because no one in their right mind argues with her. If anyone had any notions about hassling Mac, they had the sense to stow them.

"Oi, Johnny! Thanks for having me."

"What, stealing my spotlight?" I grinned at him. "Means I don't have to try singing again today, mate. Carla, can we get someone to find Mac something to perch on? Great, another stool, brilliant, ta. Okay, here we go. Ladies and gents, just this one time only, feel free to go nuts: here's Malcolm Sharpe, come to tart the show up. Give the man a hand, all right?"

It took a few minutes to get them to quiet down, but we managed it, finally. Mac had his harp case with him, and that made the choice of what to do next easy: we headed back to the Mississippi delta for 'Moody's Blues', the instrumental tribute I'd written for my mentor and inspiration, Bulldog Moody. Mac got into the harp, just wailing away, sounding as if he were channelling Sonny Boy Williamson; Domitra, never far from his shoulder, kept an eye on the crowd, not on her boss. She looked about as intent as Carla did, but of course, Dom's gig is to protect Mac, and that means looking scary. She does it quite well, too.

"Right." I set the Martin in its stand, and reached for Little Queenie, flicking the amp off standby mode. I was doing the talking—since this was my gig and Mac was guesting, he was laying back and letting me do my thing. "So, anyway, here's a question for you. I thought we might have a go at doing 'Liplock', just me and Mac. Anyone up for that...? Right, here we go."

It may have been just the two of us in a record shop in Los Angeles, but I remember that as one of the best covers of the song I've ever had a hand in. Mac's done it in front of over a hundred thousand people—we played it at every gig on Black-light's Book of Days tour, well over two hundred shows, and some of those gigs were at the huge soccer stadiums in South America. He's done it in clubs as well, places a lot more intimate, like the Seven Oh Seven. The song gets a different handling in the smaller venues, where he can jump offstage and grab some bird out of the first row and leave her damp and drooly by singing the song straight into her eyes with one hand on her hip.

But this was a shop, no stage at all, and the only barrier be-tween us and them was about eight feet of floor space and one scary-looking bodyguard. The crowd had to be feeling as though they'd somehow stumbled into a living room session, with the band deciding that, what the hell, they were here so might as well let them hang out and listen. They were fucking blissed, and the energy, that sense of them not quite believing their luck, got into the vocal and the guitar. I'm glad the gig, short as it was, was taped. It would have been a shame to not have it.

From "Liplock," we headed straight for Bo Diddley, hitting a hot bitchy little two-parter on "Mona." I let Mac handle the front work on that one, him trading off between the hot drawly vocal and a spine-punching line on the harp. I was playing al-most pure rhythm, the classic three-two Bo Diddley riff. There's not much thought goes into that, it's something I can do without any concentration at all.

So my eyes were wandering, checking to see if there were any late arrivals, when I suddenly realised I was staring at Patrick Ormand.

It was a damned good thing I was just playing rhythm, because I nearly stopped in sheer surprise. For a moment, I was completely disoriented. That couldn't be Patrick—Carla would have said he was coming. Besides, he was in San Francisco, doing whatever the hell he and Andy Valdon had needed to get done. Was that really Patrick? Bloody hell, yeah, it was. What was he doing here…?

Three-two, three-two. Mac was singing, eyes closed, swaying on his stool, moving his shoulders to the rhythm. The crowd was rocking, just digging the hell out of it.

I wasn't having some sort of bizarre acid flashback episode; it really was Patrick, and he was moving along the back edge of the crowd, skirting chairs and dancing people. He seemed to be heading toward the front, where we were.

*"Oooh, Mona..."*

Three-two, three-two, the Bo Diddley beat, the Afro-Cuban rhythms of *clave* and *son*. Mac had the harp up to his mouth, eyes closed, taking a long solo. Patrick was halfway up the rows of seats now, and something was happening at the back of the room: uniforms, four of them, fanning out. And in the doorway, coming in last and standing there as if he wanted to make damned certain no one left without his say-so, was their boss: Detective Cunningham, in the house.

The crowd was beginning to notice, finally, the people all the way at the back seeing the uniforms. I heard the first uneasy murmurs. I was suddenly back in 2005, onstage at Madison Square Garden, seeing the wings swarming with uniforms because a tabloid reporter had been bashed to death in my dressing room. That had been NYPD, but the memory as right there, clear and sharp and not anything I wanted to remember. And it didn't help that Patrick Ormand had been the man in charge at the Garden that night.

Domitra hadn't moved. At least, she was in the same spot, but she'd seen the uniforms, seen Cunningham, seen Patrick, and somehow she was closer to Mac than she'd been, and larger as well. The harp was wailing, a vicious hard cascade that managed to be sharp as well as mournful. Three-two, three-two...

"Mac." I said it as quietly as possible. I needed his attention but I was damned if I wanted to let one word travel past that eight feet of open floor and out into the audience. Whatever was happening, we didn't want a stampede, and I wasn't having anyone hurt. "Mac, keep playing, but we've got a police action. LA Homicide just showed up. Something's happening."

His eyes popped open. Now, there's a born frontman for you: he never missed a breath. I watched the muscles around his eyes tighten as he took in the uniforms, Cunningham, Patrick scanning the rows of seats, Domitra's change in stance and attitude— she's been with him a dozen years and more, and he knows just how to read her body language. I saw him nod, very slightly— whether it was at me or Dom, I couldn't tell you. And then he was back blowing the harp, kicking the intensity up a notch, standing up, using his whole body to draw every pair of eyes in the place back to him and away from whatever it was Cunningham's boys were up to.

Three-two, three-two. The last few bars, harmonica and guitar together, ending just in time for the sudden commotion at the back of the house. Cunningham and Patrick and two of the four uniforms had surrounded someone, and whoever it was scuffling hard.

"Let go of me!" It was a high-pitched whistling scream. "Let go! Let me out of here!"

That got everyone's attention. There's something about silence following music: it's more silent than normal silence. Denser, you know?

So we had no trouble hearing Cunningham's voice, nice and clear and calm, booming across the heads of about eighty people, sitting like they'd just been shipped in from Madame Tussaud's.

"Now, now, Mr. Silver, just calm down. We don't want to make this any worse than it already is, do we? I have a warrant. You'll be able to call your lawyer from the station."

# Chapter Sixteen

Back during Blacklight's Book of Days tour, I'd noticed an interesting phenomenon about the way the band family had got together in the hotels we'd stayed in. When Bree was with me, our suite always seemed to be where the rest of the band fetched up when group comfort was needed.

She'd missed some of those gigs, a few when our oldest cat Wolfling had got sick, and the entire Japanese leg to a bad bout with pneumonia. Those times, we'd ended up holding meetings or emergency conferences or international phone conversations in whatever suite Blacklight Corporate had rented.

I'd finally sorted it out: without Bree there, making sure people had food and coffee and a comfortable place to park themselves, that particular sense of welcome just wasn't on. And of course she wasn't there in LA, the day of the Amoeba gig, which was probably why we ended back at Carla's office, sitting round the big conference room table. I don't know that I'd felt Bree's absence quite so intensely since she'd gone missing on me, a few years back.

We actually finished the Amoeba gig, me and Mac, another five songs and a brilliant encore. We'd managed to get the crowd back into it by basically playing dumb, the pair of us—letting them see us scratching our heads, shrugging, looking bewildered: *right, what in hell was that about, then? No clue, sod it, might as well get back to some music, all right?* Yeah, I know, sounds the wrong side of cold-blooded and manipulative, but those people had come out to see and hear us. We owed them some music, the best we could do. And that's just what they got.

Hell, they not only got the music they'd come for, they got a nice little bonus at the end, when Mac got up and pulled Suzanne out of the audience. He introduced her, let them know it was her voice they'd be hearing on Bergen Sandoval's final record, and charmed her into singing lead on a nice bluesy cover of "Fever." She was gobsmacked at Mac doing that—you could tell—but she did the song, and if the way she torched it was anything to go by, she dug it. In a room that size, you got to hear just how killer her voice was, and yeah, it was killer.

So we sent them home happy. I wasn't worried about the thing with Cunningham—that could be edited out of the final mixdown. Once that was sorted out, the show was going up on the Geezers' website, a nice free download for the fans.

"Brilliant." The place had mostly emptied out, and Mac was up and stretching, some of his yoga moves; a backless stool isn't the most comfortable perch when you're our age. "A damned good gig we did, there. Suzanne, that was an absolute groin-crunch of a vocal. I'm starting to think you're wasted as a rock singer, you really ought to consider jazz—Carla, good, there you are. If you don't mind my asking, what the fuck was all that, and

256

what was Patrick doing here? Acting copper's nark for LAPD, or was he just having a moment of auld lang syne, getting to play homicide hound at a live gig again?"

"He was here because we arranged for him to be here." She met his eye. "I really don't think this is the ideal place for this conversation, Mac. Besides, Patrick told me that as soon as he's done at Homicide, he wants to talk to all of us, back at my office. There are two cars outside whenever you guys are ready. We can send Marjorie out for some food. Suzanne, I want you along for this. JP, are you about done packing up? Great, let's go."

So, instead of the nice comfy hotel suite and my old lady making sure everyone had whatever they needed to make it work, we got the conference room at Fanucci Pros. Seemed to me I'd spent too much time parked in a chair at that particular address recently. And yeah, I was missing Bree.

I got an inkling of just how much I didn't know about whatever had gone down, about how much planning had been going on in places I wasn't watching, when we walked into Carla's office. We weren't the last in—looking up through the big glass doors behind the reception desk, I saw Stu, and Cal, and Luke, already there. None of the women had come along

That got to me. Barb and Cyn, yeah, I could see them stopping away. They'd given the entire situation as wide a miss as they could; those marriages were long-lived enough for the women to not feel they had to be there for support every time something went down. But Karen Hedley wasn't there, either, and that marriage was a different story—nice and new, still almost in the honeymoon phase even after a couple of years. Even though Karen's not much for climbing into band business, it was obvious that Luke was much happier when she was there with him. Besides, Suzanne was right in the middle of the entire thing.

None of them were here. And that meant the band had been

asked to either leave their wives at home, or been quietly asked not to tell them about it at all.

Walking into the conference room, I knew both my eyebrows were up, about as high as they could go. It was probably just as well Bree was up north, and hopefully not narked at me anymore, because I was damned if I'd have left her home, at Carla's request or anyone else's.

"Oi, JP, Mac. Good, you're here safe and sound." Stu had a cold beer in one hand. "Amoeba gig go off all right?"

"Yeah, it was fine." I headed for the sideboard and grabbed a bottle of juice. I was feeling shaky, probably because I hadn't eaten anything since breakfast. That was one more thing that wouldn't have happened if Bree'd been here. "Unless you count Cunningham and his storm troopers dragging Derek Silver off in a police cruiser in the middle of the gig. That wasn't actually on my set list."

"Bloody hell." Luke looked to have been dozing when we walked in, but he opened his eyes and focussed on me. He had his feet up on the table. "You serious? They actually grabbed Streak in the middle of a song?"

"Just as we were climbing out the back end of the harp solo on 'Mona'." Mac grabbed a seat. "Carla, did you say something about food? Because I could do with some serious protein."

"Marjorie's already sent out for some Italian food—she called Medici, that great place over on Roxbury. Waiters on Wheels will be here in about half an hour. Think you can you hold out that long?"

"I suppose I can make it without actually going flat out on the carpet, yeah. I'll just live off my stored fat until someone passes me a plate of lasagne or something." He grinned at her, but the grin was gone a moment later. "Waiting about for Patrick to show up, though, that's something else entirely. I don't really think I'm willing to do that, Carla. As Johnny already pointed out, having five burly yobbos from LAPD Homicide drag the local club owner off in the middle of a live show is thoroughly disturbing. I want to know what just happened and I'm fairly sure I'm not alone."

"No waiting necessary, Mac. I'll answer any questions anyone has for me."

Patrick had come in without anyone noticing, letting the conference room door click shut behind him. He was alone. Out in reception, Marjorie was on the phone, not even glancing his way. Carla's new kid was learning the ropes rather quickly.

"Have a seat." Cal, surrounded by empty chairs, made room. "Oh, you might want to grab a water or something to keep your voice going properly, because trust me, mate, you've got some talking to do."

Patrick grinned, no teeth, just a grin. He looked tired, and that made him look more human than usual. "I know, Cal. I just want to make sure everyone's here who needs to be here, because I don't want to have to say things twice. I think we're ready to go."

"Everyone? I don't think so. Where's Elaine Wilde? Why is she being let off?"

We all turned to stare, everyone except Mac. Suzanne sounded as if she was having trouble even saying Elaine's name.

"Elaine's not here because she was bringing her daughter home from the hospital today, in San Francisco." Carla sounded good and crisp; I had the feeling she'd been expecting something of the sort from Suzanne. "What happened to Bergen Sandoval may be our first priority, but under the circumstances, I'd say parenthood trumps murder. This is all on the QT, unofficial. And you're being let off too, Suzanne. If you weren't, I'd have made damned sure Lenore Tannenbaum was here to cover your back."

Carla and Patrick had locked up, and there were clearly some signals being passed back and forth. Patrick cleared his throat. "Let me get you caught up, okay? The main point is that Derek

Silver has just been formally charged in the death of Bergen Sandoval. What the exact charge will eventually be, I can't tell you yet, because I don't know. It was homicide, first degree, but that may not stand, not under the circumstances."

Stu craned around Cal to stare. "What? What circumstances? If you're saying it wasn't a planned murder, seems to me you've got some fancy dancing to do. Dead bloke, registered poison. Either Streak did it or he didn't, right? This wasn't just bad coke, not from what we've been told. I don't get what you're on about, Patrick."

"It's not that simple, Stu." There it was, the old homicide cop, peering out of Patrick's dirty-ice eyes. I knew it was in there somewhere; nothing like getting into the details of who'd got dead and who was about to pay for it to set the predator off. "Yes, the strychnine-laced cocaine was supplied by Derek Silver. But there's clear evidence that the stuff wasn't intended for Bergen. There's also clear evidence who it actually was meant for, and why."

I don't know how or why, but suddenly there it was, nice and clear, a picture in my head: Andy in my kitchen and Patrick in the doorway, me trying to get the pair of them the hell out of my house before Bree got home and found herself legally aiding and abetting someone wanted for questioning in a murder. I could hear Andy's voice: *There's some information I need to track down, that's all. I didn't murder Bergen and I'm not going to jail for something I didn't do. Fuck that. And I'm not going back to LA until I find out what I need to find out...*

So that's what they'd been up to, Andy and Patrick. That's why Andy had needed a locked door and a computer and a lot of free access to hunt. *Not going back to LA until I find out...*

"Andy? That who Streak was after?" It took me a moment, everyone swivelling round to stare at me as if I had two heads, to realise it was me asking the question. "Why? Money, was it?"

260

"Yes, he meant it for Andy." Patrick was playing to the gallery. He does that a lot. Used to make me want to bash him, that habit of his, but he'd earned the right to do it this time. "And yes, of course it was money. It usually is. Cunningham has a CD sitting on his desk right now that's going to keep Derek Silver's legal team very busy for a very long time. Hell, they'll probably be able to build a new wing on the law firm's office, considering what was involved here. The CD in question has about fifteen years' worth of documented transactions, names, dates, amounts, you name it."

"That's right, Andy used to work for the guy." Domitra was focussing. "I'm guessing it's something to do with the finances of one or more of those clubs."

"You could put it that way." Patrick grinned again. This time, the grin was feral. "Derek Silver has been running a high traffic importing operation, bringing in rock cocaine from suppliers in Columbia and Thailand, for at least fifteen years. Running the numbers, he may be the most prolific importer on this coast. It's probably how he was able to open cutting edge nightclubs and keep them open, even in a dismal economy. It's probably longer than fifteen years, and probably from other geographic distribution points, but that's as far back as we could trace. As evidence goes, fifteen years is plenty."

There was a long silence, everyone taking that in and wrapping their heads round it. The weird thing is, I wasn't surprised. Shocked, a bit, yeah. But not surprised.

"So Andy knew about it." It wasn't a question; the only thing Mac was asking for was confirmation. "And that makes Derek Silver a complete idiot. He can't have only just decided, right, Andy knows all about my little White Powder Express thing, I really ought to take him out, now why didn't I think of that before? No, really, Patrick. If Andy knew, why didn't Streak arrange a quiet little accident or overdose ages ago? Delicacy of feelings? Tender-heartedness?"

Patrick shrugged. "I have no idea. Maybe just a matter of opportunity and availability coming together. Silver's a cautious guy, very savvy. He's certainly smart enough to know that his money man dying under suspicious circumstances right after he went to work for someone else would raise a few red flags. Or he may not have felt threatened enough to act right away. But the most recent line item shows a large shipment from a firm operating out of Costa Rica, and the firm in question has a legitimate business as a front: they sell registered toxins to labs around the world."

"So that's where that strychnine shit came from?" Dom shook her head. "What I don't get is why he thought Andy was using. Dude, Carla's not stupid. She wouldn't hire some cokehead. She wouldn't trust one around here, not with all our business and all our numbers. That's bullshit."

"Thanks for the compliment." Carla smiled, but it was gone a moment later. "As it happens, you're right. I know cokeheads and junkies when I see them, and Andy wasn't one. Patrick?"

"Well." He sounded careful suddenly, choosing every word. "From what I gather, Bergen told Andy he wanted a gram or so, good quality, please go find me some. Andy approached his former boss. Streak obliged, with coke laced with enough strychnine to take down anyone who used it, and maybe a few close friends too. I gather Andy didn't tell Streak it wasn't for him, but why Streak thought Andy was into that stuff, I honestly don't know. I also gather there was no secret about Bergen's fondness for coke?"

"Secret?" Cal snorted. "Christ, he wouldn't have been half the nasty little shit he was without the blow. But you're not thinking it all the way through, Patrick. Bergen wanted some blow, he told Andy to find him some, and Andy went straight to Streak to oblige? That what you're saying?"

"Crikey!" I'd got it, and for once before Patrick did—our pet detective was actually looking puzzled. "Yeah, if Streak didn't know Andy was onto his import business, and Andy made it very clear that he knew Streak would have coke on request? There's your motive, mate. 'Hi, I need some coke so I came straight to you because I knew you'd have it.' What was that you said, about opportunity and availability? Look at it that way, the motive's in there, as well."

"JP's in the right of it, I'd say." Stu popped another beer. "If I'm a big time coke importer, twenty to life if they nick me for it, and my former flunkey shows up and asks me to hand over some blow, I'd have felt threatened, myself. Nice little spur of the moment killing, there. But he got the wrong bloke—oh, shit, Suzanne, I'm sorry."

We all turned at that. Suzanne was crying.

She was completely silent. The tears were rolling down her cheeks, and she wasn't knuckling them away. For a change, she wasn't trying to hide—she was just sitting there. She's not an easy person to feel sorry for, but that did it.

"Christ." Luke scooted his chair over and dropped one arm around her, holding on. "It's okay, love. It's all right."

No one said anything for a moment—nice uncomfortable scene, that was. Of course, it was Domitra who broke the silence. She doesn't do delicacy very well.

"So where is Andy? The little ray of sunshine over at the cop shop, swearing out paperwork against his old boss?"

"Andy who?" Patrick got up and stretched. "As of today, there is no Andy Valdon. This case is a big one, and believe me, Bergen Sandoval dying accidentally is by no means the biggest part of it. Here's a tip: If you ever stop to pump gas somewhere in Nebraska or Mississippi, you may find someone who looks and sounds just like him sitting inside the glass booth. If that happens, one thing's for sure: his name tag will say Harvey Scheller or Phil Garfinkel or Louie O'Malley. But it won't say Andy

Valdon. If that ever happens, do yourself, and him, a big favour. Just smile, look blank, and keep on driving."

Any worries I had, that Bree might still be pissed off at me, disappeared when I got off the plane in San Francisco that night. Carla'd got me on the first available flight, and I'd asked her to ring Bree and let her know not to worry, I'd get a taxi home.

She was waiting for me, just outside the gate. Used to be you could wait in the lounge where the plane landed, park yourself in an actual chair and watch the plane taxi up to the gate, but not these days. That went west after 9/11, along with a lot of other small freedoms.

"Hey." She snaked an arm around my neck and kissed me, fast but tongue tip to tongue tip. Definitely not cross anymore. Good. "How was the flight? Are you hungry?"

"Oi! Let's have a proper kiss, all right?" I set the two guitar cases and my overnight bag down and got both arms round her. People moved out and around us, most of them smiling. All the world loves a lover. "No, I'm good for food. Nice easy flight, and I ate back at Carla's office. We ended up having a conference kind of thing, after the Amoeba gig. She sent out for some very good Italian food, from some place in Beverly Hills. Next time we're down in LA, we ought to try it."

"I heard." She rubbed her cheek against mine. "About what happened, I mean, not about the food. Carla told me a little, when she called to tell me you were heading home tonight. But what the hell, John, taking a taxi? Oh, please. The car's down-stairs. Taxi, my ass. Did she really think I wasn't going to come get you?"

"Don't blame Carla for that one, Bree, all right? It wasn't her doing, it was mine. I thought you might still be narked at me, and I wanted to give you the out, you know? No, I'll get the guitars. Can you grab the carry-on...?"

We got my stuff stowed away in the Jag and headed out of the airport carpark. We'd barely cleared the on-ramp to the highway when Bree spoke up.

"Okay. So how about telling me what actually happened today, John? Did Cunningham and a bunch of cops really interrupt your Amoeba gig and drag Streak away, kicking and screaming?"

I blinked at her. "What, Carla tell you that?"

She edged the Jag away from a black SUV that had got one wheel over the line. "No. All Carla said about that was that Streak had been arrested. The rest of it actually showed up as an AP news trailer on my Yahoo headlines page. It's really weird, seeing my husband's name crawl by on a computer news story. It's even weirder when there's a photo attached to it."

She was watching the road, not me, and all I got was her profile. I couldn't read what was going on in her head. I couldn't quite get a read on her voice, either. "I'll admit I was kind of hurt that you hadn't called home to tell me about it—I don't like getting news about you from the media first. But when Carla called, she told me things had been nuts, that Patrick had called an emergency get-together at Fanucci Pros and that you hadn't had ten seconds to yourself to spare. So I chilled out about you not calling. Of course, I was assuming she was telling me the truth, and not just pouring some PR snake oil for me to swallow."

She turned towards me then, just for a moment. *Shit.* She hadn't been joking, about feeling hurt; if anything, she'd understated it. "Was she telling me the truth, John?"

"Pretty much. But that's not an excuse, Bree. I should have rung. That's on me." I took a deep breath. "I mean, yeah, things were nuts, but the truth is, I didn't know how cross you were about that row this morning, and I just couldn't cope with another one. I'm sorry, love. That was me, being a pillock. You ought to thump me, once we're out of all this traffic."

"Bad husband, no biscuit? Apology accepted."

265

She meant it, I could tell. She shot me a sideways glance. "So what in hell really happened at Amoeba? I saw the news story and freaked for a few minutes, but you were obviously okay. Can you talk about it, or did Patrick swear you all to silence?"

I gave her the whole story, everything that had gone down from the time I'd got her to the airport that morning. After Patrick's little bombshell about Andy and the Witness Protection Program, a few things had come out.

The second bombshell had been the story behind Bergen's will. He'd actually signed it between Elaine's turfing him out and the divorce itself, and, at the time he'd signed it, he'd owed over seven millions dollars. Typical Bergen, really, a nasty little joke, leaving the woman who'd had the cheek to dump him with a pile of debt.

A few months ago, though, Fluorescent had acquired Bergen's entire back catalogue from his old record label, and that had restocked Bergen's piggy bank to the tune of a hundred million dollars. God knows what he'd done with about seventy million of that, but the thirty or so million dollars that was still his was going to Suzanne, because she was his wife and, so far as anyone could tell, the will was valid. No clue why he hadn't altered it later, and no way to know now. I'd have bet a few bob of my own that she was going to refuse every penny of it.

I also told Bree about the call from Tony, while I was doing the radio spot. It was her turn to let her breath out.

"Oh, God, John, I'm so glad he called you. I haven't talked to Katia since we left for LA, and I was really worried."

We were off the highway now, and into San Francisco proper. It was full dark, stars beginning to spark up behind Coit Tower, twinkling down on the bridges over the Bay. It was official: I was home, and what was even better, I got to be home for another ten days, not having to go anywhere or even leave the fucking house if I didn't fancy it. Just then, knowing I was almost there

266

and Bree was with me, I pretty much decided I wasn't getting out of bed for a day or two. Neither was my wife, whether she knew it or not.

"So he's thinking about checking into the London clinic?" We'd hit Pacific Heights, now. Almost there. "It seems weird that he'd go all the way to London for rehab. There are some damned good clinics in the US, and some of them are local. My mother could hook him up easily. Why go all the way to London?"

"I didn't ask him, Bree. If I had to guess, I'd say he wanted to get away from the Bombardiers, from all the close connections, and just be somewhere else while he concentrates on getting it done." I didn't add the rest of that thought—*that's how I felt when I did mine, right after I met you*—but I didn't have to. Nobody knows more about me than Bree does, and no one has ever known me better.

We were both quiet, the rest of the drive back to 2828 Clay. It wasn't until Bree'd pulled the Jag into our garage, and got the big door down and alarmed that she finally broke the silence, and it was quite clear, she didn't want to.

"I have to say this. I hate to say it, Billy and Kris are our friends and I like them, but—oh, shit. Do you remember what Tony told us, back in LA, when he came to our room? I did wonder, when we were on the tour bus. They kept teasing him, John, getting on him about having money. They kept doing it, even in the band room at shows. I could see he hated it, that it was making him really uncomfortable. I just don't get it. Why would they do that? Couldn't they see it was getting to him?"

"No. No, I don't think they got that. If they'd realised it was getting under his skin, they'd have stopped. They aren't monsters, Bree, just—I don't know. Envious, maybe?"

I slid the two guitar cases out of the Jag and headed for my studio. The guitars, the ones I play and use the most, live in there. Bree slipped ahead of me, and got the studio door

267

unlocked and open. I kept talking, thinking out loud really, talking it out to get it clear in my own head.

"I mean, yeah, they made out quite nicely after Book of Days got so big. 'Liplock' was credited to them. I don't know what the numbers are, but the royalty on that one made every member of the Bombardiers a millionaire. And every time some radio DJ plays it or the CD sells another copy, they get paid. They're not exactly starving artists themselves anymore."

Bree watched me get Little Queenie out of her case and onto her stand. "Then why would they be envious? And why would Tony let it bother him so much?"

"You're asking the wrong man, Bree. I don't get pissing and moaning over money, you know that. I never have. But again, just guessing, I'd say the envy wasn't about money anyway. More about visibility, the whole professional class system thing music's got going. And they probably didn't even know they were doing it. Bottom line is, we musicians are a self-absorbed lot. And yeah, we can get quite shirty when we think someone's getting a better break than we are. How many times have you seen one of the Bombardiers—the whole band, Tony as well—roll their eyes and get on me about Blacklight getting into the Hall of Fame? Good, all done down here. You've got the key..."

We headed upstairs. Bree was still watching me. I must have been more tired than I knew, because there we were again, me not being able to suss out what was going on in her head. I didn't fancy it, much. Reading Bree's not usually a problem for me, you know? I latched the hall door that leads to our basement stairs, headed for the kitchen, and lifted an eyebrow.

"Bree, just dish, will you? What's going on? There is something, yeah?"

"Damn." She was filling the kettle, her back to me. Simon and Farrowen were banging into her ankles. "Okay. I've never asked you about your rehab. We've never talked about it. And I just..."

Her voice died away. I waited, but she wasn't saying anything else. Right; this was on me, apparently. She'd never asked, and I'd been just as happy to not talk about it. But if she wanted to know now, it had to be because she thought it was going to maybe help her deal with what Katia was likely to have to go through. And if that's what was happening, she'd get the full story. I wasn't looking forward to this.

"Okay. Let's wait for tea, love, yeah? Not even going to try this without a cuppa. That kettle's on the boil. Any decaf Earl Grey in that tin...?"

I gave her all of it, at least as much as I could remember. Doing that, making myself look back and talk about it, that was one of the trickiest things I'd had to do in a good long while.

I don't look back at the month I'd spent in a London clinic thirty years ago with any kind of pleasure. I'd blocked quite a lot of it out, because no one who's not a nutter goes down those roads unless there's a gun to their head. But I looked as far and as deep into what I might have pushed away all those years as I could manage, and I told her about it. Not a pretty story. I just hoped she'd be able to get some use out of it.

She heard stuff I never thought I'd talk about in this life, or even willingly think about: how I'd felt under arrest in hospital here in the States, waiting to be deported back to the UK. That was after a teenaged Bree'd answered my stoned panicked phone call at her mum's drug clinic and stolen what could have been a lethal dose of heroin and coke for me. I told her about the way I'd dug my heels in and refused to touch the methadone they'd offered, because I was damned if I wanted to trade one addiction for another. How I'd felt when I'd got off the plane at Heathrow and found that Cilla, my wife, hadn't bothered about showing up. What it had been like being isolated, signing a promise to not have any visitors, not see anyone or have any contact at all except with the doctors who worked for the rehab centre just outside London, for a full month. Agreeing to random piss tests and blood tests at odd hours, lying awake in a cold sweat for three days, staring at the ceiling, knowing the mirror was one-way glass, that they could watch me sleep, watch me grind my teeth, watch me suffer, watch me heal.

And the kicker was, it had all been my choice. It needed to go down that way. I'd known it then, bone-deep, and I knew it now. If I could go back in time with a list of things to change, that stay in rehab wouldn't be on the list.

When I'd finished talking, my cup was empty and my mouth was dry as a bone. I'd gone shaky, and the palms of my hands were damp.

"Thank you, John." Her voice was warm, and quiet. She poured me another cup. "I know you didn't want to go there. I'm really sorry. Want some more decaf? Let's get some sleep tonight, okay?"

I managed a smile for her, and managed to keep a mouthful of tea down, as well. Good trick, that was; my stomach was moving unpleasantly. Not much chance of sleep tonight, not with the ghosts I'd brought up in my own memory, but I wasn't about to tell her that.

She'd said once, during a very bad time, that she'd never asked me to do anything and never asked me not to do anything. It was true, and we both knew it, so when she does ask now, I do it, no matter what it is. Hell, her asking me not to die after the heart attack at Wembley, that's why I'm alive at all.

By the time we'd finished our tea, both the cats and my stomach had settled down. I'd gone down the hall to set the alarm code, when I noticed something on the hall floor. Someone had managed to slide a sheet of paper under the front door.

"John...?" She had one hand on the door to upstairs, waiting for me. "What is it? What's the matter?"

"Half a mo, love." There was no envelope—just a sheet of pa-

270

per, folded in half. It had come off a printer; the only thing hand-written anywhere on it were my initials: *JP*. What the hell…? "Someone's slipped something under the door, and it's got my name on it."

I knelt, and picked it up.

# *Epilogue*

"I probably shouldn't be writing this down, but I wanted to. P said it would be okay, that as long as I didn't sign anything with my own name, it wouldn't really matter or get me in any trouble. He told me the cops can't match up printers the way they used to be able to match up old-fashioned typewriters, and he probably knows what he's talking about. He also said he was going to scrub me off his computer, get rid of all traces that I ever used it. That feels pretty strange to me, as if I was being erased from the whole world. I have to trust him, I guess. I don't have a lot of options left."

Bree was at my shoulder. Before I could fold it, put it away, get her away from it, she was peering at the note in my hand, reading along with me. Shit, shit, *shit*.

"...I'm not going to get too deep into anything, but I do want to let you know about why it happened, because I get the feeling from you that you'd lose a lot of sleep over it, if you couldn't figure it out yourself. And you were nice to me when you didn't have to be. You could have called the cops when I was locked outside in your back yard, or told Jeff Kintera what was really going on. I'd have been fucked seven ways to Sunday if you had, but you didn't. I'll always owe you for that. Besides, you already have enough junk to keep you awake at night."

"Locked in our yard?" Bree whispered it, under her breath. "Who was? When? What the hell is this?"

"...I've got plenty of stuff to keep me from wanting to sleep too. Who sleeps when they don't feel safe? Not me. Want to hear what's really sick? The whole time I was running the money on Streak's books, I knew what he was doing, and what's even sicker is, he knew that I knew. But I never actually said to him that I did, and I guess that meant he wasn't thinking about it. If I hadn't actually asked him for that crap for Bergen Sandoval, Streak probably would have left me alone. Even though I knew all about his shit, even though I had enough on him to put him away for a thousand years or something, he would have left me alone. How dumb is that? P says that maybe knowing that I never used drugs made me safe somehow. Who knows?"

Bree was chalky, breathing through her nostrils, her hands balled into fists. Right then, for a really bad moment or two, I hated Andy Valdon as much as I'd ever bothered hating anyone in my life. Even gone into hiding, even with a new name and a new identity being handed to him for turning state's evidence, the miserable little berk was managing to jerk me around and make my life complicated.

"...I'm not naming names or writing down numbers. Knowing that stuff could get you killed. But the cops have it, because P let me use his computer to get it. More dumb stuff, Streak didn't do anything at all to move the info or hide it or anything. Most of it was right where it was when I went to work for Carla. He hadn't even changed the passwords. Dumb, dumb, dumb.

"I'll tell you just a little bit, and you can probably figure out the rest of what you want to know. Bergen called me at home, the morning of the launch party, and asked me to get him a few grams. So of course I went to Streak, called him right away, and Streak just said to come over. He didn't ask me any questions and I didn't offer any information.

"P asked me a couple of times, am I sure I didn't tell Streak I wanted the blow for Bergen? Yes. I didn't say a word, just that I needed some and I knew Streak was the man to always have some. P also asked me a couple of times, whether anyone could have tampered with the coke after I picked it up from Streak. The answer is no. I got the stuff, got in my car, and went over to the hotel where Bergen was staying. He cut up a few lines and did them, just to make sure it was good quality stuff, I guess, before he paid me. He even offered me some, but I don't do that stuff, so I said no. That was about four o'clock, maybe three-thirty, something like that.

"You know the rest of it. I washed that line off the sink at the Plus Minus—I had to. I thought that was the line that killed him. I wasn't thinking too clearly, I was pretty freaked out. Otherwise I would have understood that the whole bag was bad, and that whatever it was, it took a few hours. I watched Bergen snort that stuff up back at his hotel and I didn't know I was killing him. I sure as hell didn't know Streak thought he'd be killing me.

"I don't think I want to say anything else, and anyway, I don't really have anything else to say. Just that I really appreciate you letting me hang out and not turning me over to the cops. And also that I'm really sorry I nearly got your wife involved. Thanks, and goodbye..."

"Oh, you motherfucking son of a bitch!"

Bree turned on her heel, and went.

I stood there like a garden ornament, drop-jawed and completely disoriented. She was heading for the door to the basement, and I suddenly got it: she was leaving. I dropped the note and went after her, fast as I could go.

I caught her up in the basement, just as she was trying to unlock the Jag. She dropped the key; her hands were shaking.

"Bree, listen…" I got the key off the floor, and kept one hand closed hard round it. "I was only trying to make sure you weren't dragged into it."

She turned on me, and I got the shock of a lifetime. Angry wasn't the word for whatever was going on there.

"You are such a fucking hypocrite." She was talking through her teeth, just spitting it out. This was something new, something I'd never seen from her, not in all our time together. "How many years did you resent me for trying to make sure you were the one who stayed protected from stuff? Aren't you the one who bitched me out for daring to not understand that I wasn't doing you any favours by keeping secrets from you? Aren't you the man who fucking walked out of a hotel in New York and left me alone in the middle of a murder investigation for doing exactly that? Hypocrite, hypocrite, fucking *hypocrite!*"

"It's not the same."

"Bullshit." She held a hand out. "Give me my goddamned car key, John. I'm out of here."

I was getting just as furious as she was, but I wasn't going to show it. Something new, this was, and I had no yardstick, no experience to use to react to it. I had just enough *nous* to know that losing my own temper right then probably meant losing my marriage as well.

"No, it's not bullshit. I wasn't hiding any knowledge, I was trying to keep him from dragging you in as an accessory—and fuck, Bree, not just you. It would have dragged Katia into it, as well. I didn't get a vote—he showed up at the front door when Katia

275

was crying in our kitchen and I thought he was the bloke bringing our dinner from Houri."

She stared at me, stony-faced. I held the stare. My own voice was very steady.

"Not the same. I wasn't hiding a damned thing. I wasn't being patronising. And I wasn't protecting the little woman, either. If you don't know that, you bloody well should. If it had it been just you in the kitchen, I'd probably have invited the fucker in for kebabs. But if you think I had any right to do that to Katia, then maybe you need to take out your definition of loyalty, and give it a good rub. It's gone rusty."

Something was happening to her face. It was going softer, but she looked to be trying to wrestle it back to stone. I held out the key.

"You still want this, Bree? I don't want you going anywhere, but I'm not dim enough to think you couldn't get it off me anytime you liked. Honestly, though, I'd much rather you just told me to hang it back on the hook where it belongs, and come back upstairs, where we both belong."

That did it. She went down, sitting down hard on the garage floor, her face in her hands, sobbing like a child. I went down right beside her, and gathered her in, just giving her the space to let it out. Thirty years and a bit's a long time to keep something inside, you know? When it does finally manage to work itself loose, it's going to make some noise.

"I'm sorry." I said it into her hair; nice thing about not standing up is, we're pretty much the same height then. "I was clumsy as hell about it, but I couldn't see letting him pull anyone into his shit if it was avoidable, especially Katia—she had enough on her plate. And once I handed him over to Patrick, I couldn't say anything to anyone at all. That was the condition. Otherwise, he'd have refused to go."

"Okay." She was as limp as a wet dishrag up against me. She

also had the hiccoughs, which made her seem about six. "Wow. I wonder where *that* came from? I didn't really mean any of that nasty stuff I said, John."

"Yeah, you did." I turned her face round, and got us eye to eye. "And I'm glad you got it out. I've had that coming for about thirty years, every word of it. What, you think I don't know that?"

"Oh, God. Best husband ever."

She kissed me, tongue tip to tongue tip. In the middle of that, she hiccoughed, got surprised, and tried to swallow a laugh. Of course, that sent the hiccoughs into overdrive...

We got upstairs after awhile. It was full dark now and we were home again, house alarms set, cats demanding we stop our arsing about and get them their supper. Bree was rummaging in the fridge, looking for things to throw into a pot that might make what she considered an edible meal.

"Bree."

"What?" She'd got a pile of veggies out and ready to chop on the butchers block, and her big wok on the Viking six-burner. Vegetarian stir-fry, from the looks of it; there was a bottle of sesame oil out there, as well.

"We good? That light still on?"

She paused, looking at me across the veggies, the table, the kitchen, more than thirty years. She was taking the question seriously. Good. I'd meant it seriously.

"Always on," she told me, and there was that smile, the one no one else ever sees. "Always burning. Do you want mushrooms in this...?"

*JP Kinkaid*

277

Deborah Grabien can claim a long personal acquaintance with the fleshpots—and quiet little towns—of Europe. She has lived and worked and hung out, from London to Geneva to Paris to Florence, with a few stops in between.

But home is where the heart is. Since her first look at the Bay Area, as a teenager during the peak of the City's Haight-Ashbury years, she's always come home to San Francisco, and in 1981, after spending some years in Europe, she came back to Northern California to stay.

Deborah was involved in the Bay Area music scene from the end of the Haight-Ashbury heyday until the mid-1970s. Her friends have been trying to get her to write about those years—fictionalised, of course!—and, now that she's comfortable with it, she's doing just that. After publishing four novels between 1989 and 1993, she took a decade away from writing, to really learn how to cook. That done, she picked up where she'd left off, seeing the publication of eleven novels between 2003 and 2010.

Deborah and her husband, San Francisco bassist Nicholas Grabien, share a passion for rescuing cats and finding them homes, and are both active members of local feral cat rescue organisations. Deborah has a grown daughter, Joanna, who lives in LA.

These days, in between cat rescues and cookery, Deborah can generally be found listening to music, playing music on one of eleven guitars, hanging out with her musician friends, or writing fiction that deals with music, insofar as multiple sclerosis—she was diagnosed in 2002—will allow.

Visit her website at www.deborahgrabien.com

CPSIA information can be obtained at www.ICGtesting.com
Printed in the USA
LVOW111509111012

302489LV00004B/3/P

9 780984 436293